CW01501551

Bad Blood by Lily Hayden is published by independent publishers Hayden Woods Creative.
For rights, books, news and contact details, follow us on Facebook, Twitter, Instagram and LinkedIn at Hayden Woods Creative or via www.haydenwoodscreative.com

We're excited to bring you news of upcoming titles and look forward to meeting you online. Your feedback and reviews mean everything to us. Thank you for reading!

The Wedding Day

Tim was the first to receive the call.

He had barely slept a wink the night before, and he had left the room quietly to avoid waking the children, taking a walk before heading to the restaurant to breakfast alone. Yesterday when they had checked into the Cedar Vale Hotel and Spa, he had glanced over the menu and had been looking forward to the luxury of an unhurried breakfast, but this morning he found that he had no appetite. He knew that he should go back to the room. He should have waited for Eleanor, and they should be breakfasting as a family, but he just couldn't bring himself to face her.

His phone, permanently glued to his side, trilled announcing an incoming call and he jumped in surprise, splashing black tea onto his hand and the white linen tablecloth. He squinted at the screen and seeing a local number that he didn't recognise instead of the name he had been expecting, he let it go to voicemail.

Rose was the second to receive the call, but the first to answer it. Her alarm had gone off half an hour before, but she was still a little groggy and hazy and had only just managed to prop herself into a sitting position. She could make out the outline of her sister fast asleep and snoring gently in the bed next to her, and she wished, not for the first time, that she could have afforded a room to herself as she took in the chaos of three people's belongings in such a small space. Belle had commandeered all the hanging space in the tiny wardrobe for her multiple outfit choices, and Rose's simple dress for the day was hanging over the door to the en-suite bathroom. There was no kettle in the room, and Rose was dying for a cup of tea.

She was just sat quietly in bed, thinking these quiet,

uncomplicated thoughts to herself when her phone rang, and she glanced at the unknown number curiously. She tried to press the touchscreen to answer, but between her wooziness and the phone's temperamental condition it took two attempts at pressing down hard to accept the call. She didn't know the person on the other end, and she listened in confusion to the unfamiliar, gentle voice. It was a short call, no longer than two minutes, but when the caller hung up, Rose stared blankly at the wall in front of her, momentarily struck speechless. She wasn't sure how long she sat there, but it was only when she heard Belle begin to stir that she finally snapped out of her daze.

At the same time that Belle was waking up in the very basic room of a Bed & Breakfast on the outskirts of the village she'd grown up in near Gloucester, Will Jones was showering down the corridor. He thought that he could hear Craig talking over the sound of the shower, but he didn't bother calling out to him.

He can bloody keep talking, Will thought irritably as he lathered his hair with shampoo.

The water pressure was pitifully weak and nothing like their power shower at home, but he stayed put, dragging out the time to himself. It was only when he started to shiver as the temperature began to dip from lukewarm to just cold that he turned the shower off to wrap himself in the slightly rough towel. He braced himself for a sarcastic comment from Craig about ignoring him or using all the water, but instead he was sat on the edge of the bed looking as pale as the towel draped around Will's waist.

Will felt a jolt of panic as he saw his own phone in Craig's hand and his mind frantically rewound trying to remember if he'd cleared his search history.

"What's the matter?" He asked, suddenly terrified of what might come next.

Not today of all days, Will pleaded silently.

"You might want to sit down," Craig said shakily. "Your phone rang while you were in the shower."

"Right," Will was careful to keep his tone level. The last thing he needed was to upset the apple cart today.

"It's your dad," Craig looked up at him, meeting his eyes for the first time. "Will, he's dead."

Three Months Before

They all received the invitation on the same day.

As it was, Tim Jones left his house every day at 6am and was rarely home before 7pm. He was practically unreachable to anyone but his colleagues during that time, immersed in the world of banking. He could be reached in dire emergency by contacting his PA, but this was a number only known to Tim's wife Eleanor and even this contingency had been forced upon Tim after he had almost missed the birth of his second child. He didn't look at his personal phone until he was back at the house, and so the missed call from his younger sister went unnoticed.

*****

Rose Connors passed the local postwoman as she was walking to the bus stop on her way to work. Rose had lived in the same little suburb outside Cardiff for almost all her adult life, and Jenny had been delivering her mail for years.

"Good morning," Rose smiled warmly as she passed her at the entrance to the cul-de-sac.

"Oh, I've got something nice for you today!" Jenny exclaimed.

Rose had approximately three minutes until the bus pulled up around the corner and she couldn't afford to miss it, but she couldn't bear to be rude so she waited politely trying to hide her growing anxiety while Jenny rummaged through her brimming bag. The worst part, Rose thought as she tried to not let her impatience show, was that it would no doubt be another overdue bill; that was all she ever got through the letterbox these days.

"Oh, here it is," Jenny declared triumphantly as she withdrew a thick, creamy envelope and handed it to Rose with a flourish.

Rose peered at the unfamiliar handwritten cursive on the front and turned the envelope over, looking for a clue to who this could be from. She didn't notice Jenny holding out another more basic envelope with the words "Final Demand" stamped across the front in bold red font.

"Looks like an invitation," Jenny said conversationally stuffing the envelope back in her satchel when it became clear Rose hadn't noticed her outstretched arm. *The woman always looked harassed*, Jenny decided quickly, *there was no point in spoiling her day with the remainder of the mail. It could all wait until she got home.* "I'll pop the rest through your door, lovely. Nothing else interesting."

"Thank you," Rose smiled gratefully as she turned back towards her path.

She slid the edge of her nail into the seal wiggling it around until the rigid flap started to give, and she could pry the stiff card envelope open. Rose caught a glimpse of a single square of ivory-coloured card, a pattern of scattered leaves across the top that gave way to a line of deeply embossed gold font below.

'Francis & Linda Request the Pleasure of Your Company to Celebrate Their Marriage...'

Francis?

Rose wrinkled her nose in confusion. Her father's full name was Francis, but everyone knew him as Frank, and besides, if he was getting married surely, he'd have told her that he'd met someone. She ripped the rest of the envelope in her haste to find out, drawing to a complete halt to take it all in.

'Francis & Linda Request the Pleasure of Your Company to Celebrate Their Marriage on Saturday 2nd June at St Michael's Church, Hampton Dale, Nr. Gloucester at 2pm.

Reception to follow at Bluebell Farm.

RSVP to Linda Lambe on.....'

Her heart jumped into her mouth in complete surprise as she recognised her father's address and home telephone number. She had to admit that she didn't see her father very often, or speak to him that regularly for that matter, but she'd never even heard of whoever this Linda Lambe was. Surely, he would have mentioned if he'd met someone when she spoke to him at Christmas. She stared at the invitation for a moment before another thought crossed her mind.

I wonder if the others have been invited, she pondered, but before she could even begin to speculate if they had and what that might mean, she heard the familiar rattle of the bus turning into the stop ahead of her and she had no choice but to stuff the fancy card into her bag, and break into a run for the last two-hundred metres.

*****

Will Jones was executing a near-perfect piece of parallel parking outside an empty warehouse in South West London, the location of today's shoot. Radio One had been playing some classic 90's pop on his drive to work and he'd had a little karaoke session to get himself in the mood for the day. He turned the volume down, but kept the car running as he spotted his best friend Raya, face barely visible beneath a bright red puffa-coat, darting towards him through the drizzle.

"Hey buddy," she wrenched the door open and flopped into the seat, slipping her hood back to reveal a honey-coloured cloud of hair around her pretty face. She reached into her coat to withdraw an ivory-coloured envelope. "This came for you. You need to change your address, Will."

He took it from her, barely glancing at the writing on the front, his mind already on the shoot ahead of them.

"Yeah, sorry. By the time I get around to telling everyone, I'll have probably moved again."

"I hope you're joking," Raya shot him a disapproving look. "Trouble in paradise already?"

Will looked away sharply and pretended to study the envelope in his hands. "No, of course not. I've changed all my bills and stuff; it looks like an invitation so..." He trailed off unsure where he was even going with it and opened the heavy card as a diversion.

Even without looking at her, he could sense that Raya could tell he was avoiding her question and was warming up for an inquisition, but before he could think of a deflection, his eyes fell on the wording of the invitation making his breath catch in his throat.

"What's the matter?" Just as he'd predicted, she'd been gearing up to interrogate him about Craig, but seeing his face pale beneath his year-round tan, she thought better of it.

"It's from my dad," Will said, and to his horror, his eyes welled up with tears.

*****

Belle Hudson's eyes were stinging with fatigue as she returned from the school run. She'd been working nights for the past few months, but her body clock was refusing to sync leaving her permanently exhausted. She stepped over the threshold to her flat, ignoring the clutter of post on the mat. She headed straight to the kitchen to flick the kettle on to boil. She frowned at the absence of the familiar sound of the kettle kicking into life, and her tired eyes followed the wire back to the plug to check it was switched on. It had been working fine when she'd arrived home this morning, and baffled she switched it off then on to try again.

Nothing.

She looked around the kitchen, still hazy and disorientated, before her gaze settled on the microwave display, the usual incorrect time missing.

Bloody Ben, she grimaced in frustration.

She pushed the clean mug away in irritation heading to the electricity meter to confirm her suspicions. She should have known he was too irresponsible to keep on top of it, she thought annoyed at herself for not reminding him. It wasn't the first time that he'd messed up, and she groaned aloud in exasperation at the thought of heading back out to the shop when all she wanted to do was fall asleep.

I should never have agreed to moving in with him, Belle scowled.

But now she was stuck with him. The rent was too high for her on her current wage, plus there was no way she could keep her job if she was on her own. She had no childcare other than Ben and she was acutely aware that it was impossible to get a job with hours that worked around Toby. It was this, or back on benefits and she was fiercely determined that that wasn't a route she was willing to go down. As she headed back out, she noticed the ivory envelope sticking out amongst the junk mail and flyers that the postman had shoved through the door. It stood out to her amongst the cheap, bold leaflets and intrigued, she scooped it up off the mat, turning the envelope over in her hands.

Belle Jones.

She frowned, puzzled at seeing her old name in swirly, fancy print on the front.

Who would write to me at this address that knows me as that?

The image of her brothers and sister popped into her head, and she felt a burst of excitement as she tore the envelope open. Her eyes frantically raced over the words and the excitement disappeared as her stomach filled with dread.

Rose

Rose's day started just like all her other days; her bladder woke up at 6am and pinged emergency signals to her brain. For a few hazy moments, it was a stand-off between the warm, cosy cocoon of her bed and the pressing urgency to pee. It crossed her mind that one day her wakeup-pee schedule would fall out of sync and she would have to resort to those massive incontinence pads that they sold alongside boxes of tampons in Asda. She was only forty, yet this seemed suddenly inevitable, just like death.

She pondered these cheerful thoughts as she attended to the call of nature, wishing her bladder could just wait until her alarm went off. Once out of bed, she was wide awake as always, so there was no point even trying to slip back between the sheets until the scheduled alarm. The house, icy-cold for nine-tenths of the year, took forever to warm up, so she wrapped herself in a scruffy, purple robe to wander down to the kitchen for a morning cup of tea. Since her youngest son had moved away to study in September, she'd been at a loss of how to fill her spare time and sleeping had become the only comfort from the loneliness of her empty-nest.

Well, almost my only comfort, she thought glancing at the half-empty Supermarket-Value Gin bottle on the side. Rose quickly stashed it back in the cupboard under the sink. *Out of sight, out of mind.*

She ignored the uncomfortable gnawing feeling in the pit of her stomach that was made up of half-guilt, half the contents of her liquid supper swishing around undigested and turned her mind to the day ahead as she pottered around, tidying utensils that weren't out of place just for something to do.

Three weeks ago, she had started a new, full-time job as a Sales Executive, which she had soon realised was just a fancy name for pushy Tele-Sales. Despite her very valid reservations about the role, it was actually a welcome distraction from the constant state of melancholy since Jack had jumped ship to join the big, bad world. He was the younger of her two sons; his older brother Tom was in his final year of a Psychology degree in Manchester with no signs of planning to return to Cardiff when he graduated. On one hand, she was almost ablaze with maternal pride that they were both in University and on the other, she was despondent that her role as a mother now seemed redundant. There was another ugly sliver of emotion that she tried to ignore recognising it as bitter envy. As proud as she was of her offspring, it was a stark reminder that she had given up on her own dreams in order to be their mother, dropping out of her teaching course at nineteen when she fell pregnant with Tom.

She'd launched herself fully into motherhood, shelving any aspirations in exchange for nappies, bottles, and Mummy groups. Her then-husband Phil had been more than happy for her to be a stay-at-home-mother for the best part of the boys' lives, content with her handling the housework and the school runs, the constant activities and the attitude while he climbed the ranks from newly-qualified teacher to Head of Department at Wakefield Comprehensive school and continued with his pre-children hobbies of bi-weekly football matches and nights down the pub. In fact, he had positively encouraged it, discouraging her from going back to finish her course. He certainly showed no signs of resentment when she was the one getting up at 6am on a Sunday morning to drive the boys to football tournaments up-and-down the country or stripping bedding and handing out sick bowls at 3am during bouts of childhood illness while he snored blissfully on the sofa after one too many beers with his mates. After Jack had started secondary school, Phil began to make little snide comments about Rose getting a job, but by then the only positions she was remotely qualified for were ones Phil considered beneath their socio-economic status.

"You can't work there!" She could remember him snarling at her applications to shops and factories. *"People will think we're having money troubles!"*

The memory brought a flush of shame to her cheeks at the way she'd let Phil dictate to her. The truth was they bloody well were having financial difficulties, thanks to Phil and his desperate need to keep up with the Joneses. She shook her head, chasing away the bitter memories of Phil and his controlling, manipulative ways.

To think, I'd been devastated when he left me. Arsehole.

She studied herself in the hallway mirror as she walked past, cup of tea in hand. There was no way she could stretch out another day without washing her hair. Unfortunately, dry shampoo was a luxury these days, just like keeping the heating on and running a car, so reluctantly she headed to the shower. Halfway through the tedious task of blow-drying it, she gave up trying to coerce the grey-streaked tangles into some semblance of a presentable 'do and clipped it all up into an unflattering bun at the back of her head. She regarded her sallow, puffy skin and the thin lines that were webbing out from the corners of her eyes and her mouth in the mirror.

Oh, what's the point in even trying?

She pulled on the first items of clothing from her wardrobe, passed the point of caring, and headed out to the bus stop for the twenty-minute trip, alighting at the business park just outside of the town centre. The journey was already growing familiar, and she usually spent the twenty minutes leafing through the notes she'd made from training and testing herself ready for the daily recap quiz, but today she couldn't think of anything other than her father's upcoming nuptials.

It was only when she reached the office and croaked a gruff "Good Morning" to the receptionist that she realised she hadn't spoken a word to anyone, other than the postwoman, since she'd left the building the previous evening. As she waited for the vending machine to dispense a lukewarm plastic cup of vile coffee, a shrill jingle emitted from the worn-out contraption. Rose glanced over her shoulder, quickly checking that there were no witnesses if she'd somehow broken it with her overzealous jabbing at the touchscreen before she realised that the sound was coming from her handbag. She jammed a hand into the depths of her battered tote and extracted the phone. Her first thoughts, as always, were that it was one of her sons and her chest tightened in anticipation.

"Rose? It's Will!"

She couldn't remember the last time she'd spoken with her younger brother, and she felt a flicker of happiness, despite the bizarre circumstances of the call. "Will, hello! It's so nice to hear your voice."

"Yours too," Will replied, but she could tell it was an auto-response. "Hey, did you get an invitation from Dad?"

"Yes," she could hear the stress in his voice and felt a rush of empathy for her brother. While Rose wouldn't describe her relationship with their father as close, she knew that Will and their father's past was fraught with bad-feeling. In fact, she was pretty sure that Will hadn't even seen their dad since he'd been back in the country. Rose tensed as she wondered if their dad had even bothered contacting Will, worried that he was calling her because he'd had the information second-hand. "Have you?"

"Yeah," the few times she had spoken with her brother over the past years, he was always so animated and cheerful, but he sounded pretty shaken. "Did you know he was getting married?"

"No," Rose lowered her voice as she watched some of her new colleagues begin to file into the training room. "I spoke to him at Christmas and he didn't mention anything, or anyone."

"I've not seen him for years, Rose," Will confided. "I didn't even know he had this address for me."

"I've got no idea about any of it," she glanced over at her new friend Lena waving frantically to her. "Look, Will, I'm at work so I really do have to go, but I'll give Tim a call on my lunch break and see if he knows anymore. Perhaps his wife gave Dad your address. Can I call you back?"

"Yeah, of course," Will agreed. "Thanks Rose. It's nice to speak to you anyway."

"You too," she said before hanging up and rushing over to the training room before she was marked down as late.

Belle

Belle had known that trying to sleep was futile, and once she'd been to the shop, cursing Ben in her head every step of the way, she headed on autopilot to her friend's flat around the corner. She held down the buzzer until she heard the familiar click of the lock release, pushed open the heavy door and kicked the pile of junk mail out of the way, taking the steps two at a time until she reached the door to Katie's home.

She wandered in, peeling off her jacket and tossing it carelessly onto the sofa. Katie looked up from her seat.

"Shouldn't you be in bed?"

"I had to go to the shop," Belle flung herself down next to her friend. "Ben hadn't topped up the meter."

Katie rolled her eyes. "He's useless."

"I know," she sighed. "It's been one thing after another with him and bills since we moved. I pay the rent and the council tax, he's meant to pay for the utilities and the shopping, but he's so flaky that I end up paying for everything."

"He couldn't afford to get the shopping last week," Katie reminded her. "Yet he's got a brand-new iPhone and all the sports on Sky."

Belle groaned and buried her face in her hands. "I know, I know. I need to have it out with him, but he's always got a million excuses, and he'll probably go off in a sulk for days leaving me with no childcare."

Katie gave her a sympathetic smile. "Well, you know I'll help you if you're ever desperate."

Belle smiled back gratefully. She knew that Katie meant well, but the logistics were impossible without disrupting Toby. "Thanks, it'll be fine though," she pulled the invitation from her coat pocket and unfolded the crumpled square. "Look what I got in the post this morning."

Katie took the proffered card to inspect it. "Is that from your dad?"

"Yeah," Belle nodded. "I'm shocked he's invited us. He's never even met Toby."

Katie saw the tell-tale shine of unshed tears spring to her friend's eyes and she leaned over to hug her. Belle leant into the embrace, feeling strangely comforted by the woman's soft chest against her.

"It's fine," she felt a lump form in her throat and pulled away sharply, uncomfortable with the sudden emotion. "Sorry to burst in on you."

"Don't be silly," Katie gave her hand a squeeze and gestured towards the kitchen. "C'mon, I'll make us a cuppa. How old is he to be getting married?"

Belle shrugged. "About seventy, I think."

"When's the wedding?"

"June."

"You are going, right?"

"I don't know," Belle shrugged. "I haven't seen him in years. We were never close, and you know I left home when I was sixteen. I send him Christmas cards and sometimes he sends them back."

"That's so sad," Katie was close to her family and couldn't imagine not having them in her life. "Are your brothers and your sister going?"

"I don't know," Belle accepted the cup of tea gratefully. "I'll text them and find out."

"Where do they all live?" Katie pushed open the kitchen window with both hands and lit a cigarette.

Belle eyed the plume of smoke enviously. She hadn't smoked for years, but the torrent of emotions had kickstarted a buried craving. "Any chance I can pinch one?"

Katie looked surprised but handed one over. Belle lit it, inhaling a deep lungful; the first rush of nicotine making her head spin.

"You should call your dad," Katie said decisively. "Belle, I know you're too proud to reach out, but everyone needs family. Plus, wouldn't it be great if Toby had a chance to get to know at least one grandparent?"

A flicker of hope sparked beneath the fatigued fug of her mind, but she pushed the feeling away. It was naïve to expect anything to change with her family, she reminded herself. Her and Toby were fine on their own.

Tim

The door opened before Tim had even had a chance to slide his key into the lock, and he stepped back at the sight of his wife looming ominously over him on the doorstep. Surprise made way for irritation and he stepped forwards, forcing her to move backwards into the hallway.

"You're not going straight out, are you?" He asked in annoyance, equating Eleanor standing in the hallway as a sign that she was waiting to pass him the childcare baton so she could dive off to some exercise class or slimming club with one or other of her tiresome friends.

He was freezing cold from the brisk, five-minute walk from the station and mentally exhausted from the office. He really wasn't in the mood to heat up a frozen shepherd's pie and respond to his son's never-ending demands that were hollered down the stairs at two-minute intervals every evening between his bedtime and theirs.

Eleanor shook her head, and placed a gentle hand on his arm, causing him to look up in surprise.

"You'll never guess what came today," she said passing him a square of ivory-coloured card.

He scanned the invitation and looked up at his wife in disbelief. "Is he bloody joking?"

"Evidently not," Eleanor replied. "Did you have any idea he was 'seeing' someone?"

"Seeing?" Tim barked a sharp, mirthless laugh. "He's bloody seventy! Has anyone spoke to him to find out who this gold-digging Linda is? I've never heard him mention a Linda before!"

Eleanor held back from retorting that he wouldn't have heard anything as he barely spoke to the man. "I'm sure she's not a gold-digger, Tim. Hampton Dale is hardly the

Playboy Mansion. She's probably just a little old lady from the village. It might be nice for him to have some company after all those years on his own."

Tim pressed his lips together in a tight line. Typical that Eleanor would have her head in the clouds as always. He brushed past her in annoyance, his head already going to what this would mean for him and his inheritance. He pottered about in the kitchen, eating his dinner alone on the new kitchen island in his shirt and suit trousers. He had always preferred to get changed straight from work, but these days he'd learned not to go upstairs until he could be completely sure that his children were definitely asleep. He breathed a sigh of relief when Eleanor gave him a thumbs-up from the bottom of the staircase to confirm both Hugo and Bea were finally out for the count, and he crept up the stairs as quietly as he could to change. He slipped his personal and work phones from his pocket and noticed for the first time that he had a missed call from his sister Rose. He fought the urge to groan at the thought of having to speak to her, but he knew that she was the one who would be most likely to know what was going on.

"Hello," after twenty years living in Cardiff, his sister had a hint of a Welsh accent and it annoyed Tim for some reason. "Have you heard the news?"

"We had an invitation in the post," he didn't bother with the usual social niceties. The last thing he needed was for his sister to start rabbiting on to him about her kids or the weather. "Did you know about this? Have you spoken to him?"

"No, I had no idea. It came in the post today." Rose sounded concerned. "Will had one too, and he said Belle did. I didn't have a clue that he'd met someone. I spoke with him at Christmas time, but he didn't say anything."

"Didn't you go down there?" There was a hint of

accusation in Tim's tone.

"No, I didn't have time," she replied defensively. "I worked all over Christmas and the boys were home. Did you go down?"

"No," Tim's response was curt, and he didn't feel the need to justify himself to his sister. She had no idea how busy his life was. "So, have you spoken to him now? Tried to talk some sense into him or at least, established that this woman isn't some gold-digger?"

"I'm sure she's not a gold-digger," he could hear the exasperation in his sister's voice. "I was going to give him a call, but we wanted to see if you'd spoken to him first and knew what was going on."

"Right," Tim replied. "Well, find out. I might have to pop down there and find out what's going on before it's too late."

"Too late?" Rose echoed incredulously. "What do you mean?"

"Yes, too late," Tim stiffened. "This is bound to have an impact on the will. I need to make sure he's not gone bloody soft in the head, and this woman isn't manipulating him."

"The farm belonged to Mum's family though," Rose sounded concerned. "It's not his to give away, surely."

"We should really check Mum's will to see if she's made provisions for this scenario," he replied. "Look, just give me a call when you know what's happening."

"Ok, no worries," she said. "It might be nice if we all go down and see him, meet this Linda. I can't remember the last time we were all together..."

"Yes, yes," Tim cut her off distractedly, his mind already moved on. "Thanks, Rose. Speak soon."

He ended the call with a curt jab of his thumb against the touchscreen and, forgetting his sleeping children, called down to Eleanor. "Can you remember which solicitors dealt with my mother's estate?"

His yell was immediately answered by a loud wail from the baby's room, followed by Eleanor's footsteps across the landing and a muted "for God's sake, Tim" before he heard her soothing their startled daughter.

He exhaled heavily and sank back against the pillows, thinking that it was just one more inconvenience in the never-ending list of things to do.

Will

Friday nights were usually a quiet affair for Will. He'd been working as a photographer since he'd been back in the country and Saturdays were usually his busiest day. He knew from experience that working with a hangover was just not worth it. Tonight, however, they were heading to Bristol for Craig's sister's engagement party.

Will checked his reflection once more in the full-length mirror. Raya, a woman of many talents, had given the back and sides of his hair a quick once-over with the clippers and tidied up the perfectly straight line of his designer stubble. He was wearing a navy shirt and chinos, and he was pleased with the overall look. He had to admit that he was feeling a little nervous about meeting Craig's family tonight. He couldn't remember the last time he'd been with someone long enough to get to the 'meet the family' stage.

The drive was brutal; Friday rush hour traffic combined with dark, wet roads, impatient commuters and the tightness of the chinos Will had squeezed himself into meant he was stressed out and uncomfortable by the time they actually arrived at a social club on the outskirts of the city. Will discreetly slipped a hand underneath his armpit, checking for any patches as Craig reached into the back of the car to grab the card and token champagne bottle for the happy couple. He grimaced at the clammy beginnings of a nervous sweat; the only saving grace was the fact that it wouldn't be too noticeable through the dark colour of his shirt and he'd slathered on enough deodorant and cologne to mask any odour.

"Did you just check your pits?"

He snapped around to face his boyfriend, who was grinning in amusement at Will's subtle self-assessment.

Will masked his mortification with a contemptuous glare. "No! Of course, not!"

"That's why I told you to wear the dark shirt," Craig laughed and slipped his free hand into Will's, squeezing his fingers playfully.

Despite Will's embarrassment he managed to smile back as they approached the door to the noisy little club. The party inside was in full swing; disco lights lit up the dancefloor, cheesy pop music blasted from the DJ's speakers and the tables were adorned with banners, balloons, and love heart confetti. Craig was immediately swept up in the arms of a plump, dark-haired woman dressed in head-to-toe leopard-print and Will felt a lurch of anxiety in the pit of his stomach as Craig's fingers slipped from his hand, leaving him feeling alone and self-conscious amongst the room full of strangers.

"Oooh, is this him?" The woman had passed Craig over to a slim, blonde woman and had turned her attention to Will.

Craig was locked in the fierce embrace of his new assailant, leaving Will to his own devices. He pasted a warm smile onto his face to mask how overwhelmed he felt.

"Hiya. I'm Will."

"Ooh, you're handsome," she looked him up and down appraisingly before pulling him into her arms with surprising strength. "I'm Kelly, your new sister-in-law!"

She released him quickly, swinging him in a semi-circle before gripping his shoulders tightly, forcing him to come to a stop face-to-face with the blonde woman. Will was too startled by the zealous greeting to know what to say, but the blonde beat him to it.

"Will!" Her eyes lit up and she pulled him against her chest. "We've been dying to meet you. We've heard so much about you."

"Will," Craig rolled his eyes dramatically, but Will could see how happy he was to be around his family. "This is my big sister Kelly, and my Auntie Ang."

Before Will had had time to catch his breath, he was dragged around the bar being introduced to countless aunts, uncles, cousins, and childhood friends. He felt a little out of his depth as he was passed from arm to arm of Craig's assorted relatives, and he found himself eyeing the queue at the bar with longing.

This was one huge family.

Finally, he was corralled into a seat next to Craig's Mum and a pint was pushed into his hand. He took a large gulp, needing the alcohol to soothe his jangled nerves.

"So, tell me a bit about yourself?" Craig's mother beamed over her Malibu and Coke. "I can't believe Craig hasn't brought you home to meet us all yet. You're a photographer, he says."

"Yes, that's right," Will replied feeling uncharacteristically shy. "That's pretty much all there is to me."

"Well, love, we've been very excited to meet you," she continued. "It's very strange for us to only be meeting you now; we're such a close family. We're still not used to him being all the way over in London and not being able to pop in for a cuppa."

"Craig said you're all very close," Will smiled. "It's lovely to finally meet you too. We'd have come down sooner, but work has been picking up and as I'm self-employed, I have to take it while it's there."

"Of course," she agreed. "Craig says that you've worked abroad a lot. That must have been exciting."

Will launched into a quick summary of all the countries he'd lived in since he'd finished college. All in all, he'd spent more time overseas than he had in England in the last fifteen years, living a nomadic life flitting from job-to-job to get by. Most of his friends in London had been people he'd met at different stops around the globe, and even Craig had been introduced to him by a mutual friend that Will had backpacked briefly with through Cambodia. He had been back in the UK for over a year with the intention of building up some cash before jetting back off on his next adventure, but somehow he'd ended up hitting it off with Craig and since then everything had happened so fast.

"But you've put down roots now," Craig's mum beamed. "There's no place like home. All I need now is to convince you and my son to move closer to us, and we can all live happily ever after."

Will chuckled politely, hoping that the horror he felt at her words wasn't emblazoned across his face. The truth was he liked the freedom of wandering the globe with little responsibility and few ties. It had crossed his mind that he was growing old now, and maybe he should be *thinking* about putting down roots somewhere, but he had barely had time to think about what he really wanted to do when Craig had come into his life. Next thing he knew, he was moving in with him, and Craig was talking about joint accounts, mortgages, and family parties. It all felt like it had happened so fast that Will was having trouble adjusting.

"It must be very hard for your family too," she continued. "I bet they miss you very much. Craig says you're from Gloucester way originally. You'd be closer to your family if you and Craig move to Bristol."

"Oh, it's only my dad out there now," Will said awkwardly. "Both my sisters and my brother have moved away."

"Oh, well your dad must be lonely without any of you," she lowered her voice and covered his large hand with her own small, bejewelled one. "Craig said you lost your mum quite a long time ago. I'm sorry to hear that."

He could feel the threat of tears spiking at the back of his eyes and he racked his brain to think of a way he could turn the conversation away from his family. Even coming here, which he'd been dreading in the run up, had been a welcome distraction from thinking about his family since he'd received the invitation. He knew that he needed to make a decision, one way or another, but he just wasn't sure if that was a door that he was ready to open. Before the same recurring worries came flooding back, he caught sight of Craig waving him over from the dancefloor, and Will gratefully got to his feet to accept the diversion.

Rose

Rose slid her key into the lock and pushed open the door to 31 Petunia Gardens. Outside, the evening was dark and bitterly cold, but inside the narrow hallway wasn't much warmer. She fumbled for the light switch bustling into the kitchen to deposit her handbag and switch the heating on. She would keep her coat on until the house had warmed up a little. She flicked on the kettle turning her attention to the depressingly bare fridge in search of something tempting.

Since Jack had gone off to university in September, she hadn't been eating well. It seemed pointless cooking for one and she'd become especially negligent of her own health since she'd started her new job. Her once-full lips, now chapped and sore from the weather, curled up in distaste at the paltry options available. The long hours were taking some getting used to and that, combined with the constant feeling of emptiness that hung over her once bustling house, had stripped her of any desire to eat. Instead, she found herself picking; a slice of toast here, a couple of biscuits to stave off any light-headedness, more toast, a bowl of pasta if she was feeling ambitious.

Rose Jones, technically still Connors as she hadn't gotten around to filling in all the paperwork required to revert to her maiden name, had been a mother for twenty-one of her forty years on Earth. She was something of an expert in whipping up nutritious dishes and well versed in the negative impact of an unhealthy, unbalanced diet. She was very much aware that she was trapped in a vicious circle: she felt too tired to cook but then she felt even more fatigued from not eating properly. She'd gone her whole life wondering in dismay at the ignorance of people who made no attempt to break negative habits like smoking, over-eating or laziness, yet it had taken until her fortieth year of life to realise that it was more than possible that perhaps these people knew full well the self-inflicted adverse effects. Maybe they, like her, had just stopped caring.

She acknowledged that her poor diet was having a negative impact on her health and she was aware that she had been feeling a little low for some time. Had she had this thought five years ago when the boys were still at home, she would have been horrified and sought professional help. She knew a lot of people who had suffered with depression; some short bouts, some long, ongoing struggles. She, herself, had taken a course of antidepressants for about twelve months after her marriage had broken down. In Rose's opinion, there was no shame in asking for help. She just didn't want help right now.

Uninspired by the offerings of her cupboards, she dug the gin bottle out from the back of the cupboard and sloshed a healthy measure into a glass. Melancholy followed her, as it often did nowadays, from room to room; the boiled kettle forgotten and left to grow cold again as she pottered around the house preparing herself for an empty evening in front of the television. She had declined her new team's invitation for after-work drinks to celebrate the end of the working week. The eight other new starters had a median age of twenty-two, and she knew they were only inviting her out of a sense of duty. It would be like going for a night out with one of her sons and as much as they both loved their mother, she knew that they would rather die than be seen out on the town with her. She had no interest in sitting in a darkened bar with music blasting feeling awkward and uncomfortable as the young ones had fun amongst themselves. It had been four days since she'd received the invitation from her father, but she still hadn't managed to get hold of him. His wife-to-be Linda, who seemed like a nice enough woman over the phone, had answered the farm's landline promising to pass the message on, but he hadn't called, and Rose didn't want to come across pushy. She was conscious that Frank or his fiancée would think they were sticking their nose in if they suddenly started bombarding him with calls now after years of barely seeing one another. Tim, or more accurately his wife Eleanor, and Rose still made perfunctory efforts to keep in contact with their father out of duty; a once-a-year visit usually for Rose and Eleanor always sent a card for his birthday and Christmas. Will and Belle on the other hand had both struggled to remember the last time they had even spoken to him, and neither of them had been back to Hampton Dale in years.

Rose had left the village at eighteen to go to university, but an accidental pregnancy had resulted in her dropping out before the second year. She and Phil had made a pleasant enough life in Cardiff for their family despite the unplanned circumstances until he had solemnly announced that he had met someone else and was leaving her. Their marriage had been dead for years, yet it had come as a devastating blow to her.

The following few years were a bit of a blur, and Rose's visits to her father grew less frequent as she focussed on just keeping her head above water. She'd had to get a job after Phil had left, and she had been happy enough working part-time doing admin at the local primary school, but the budget had been cut year-on-year resulting in her being made redundant last summer. She'd had a couple of months without a job, wanting to make the most of both boys being home over the summer, but rather than spending time with them, she'd just ended up draining her meagre savings on bills while they both flitted in and out of the house between nights out and trips with their friends. She'd been lucky enough to find a job in the supermarket, but working in retail had meant she'd had to forgo her usual Christmas time visit to see her dad, and now she wished she'd gone in the summer when she had the chance. She hadn't minded her last job, but they'd brought in zero-hour contracts and she hadn't had a choice but to look for something else. It was longer hours and shift work, but at least the salary was guaranteed.

As long as I can make it through probation, she chewed her sore lips anxiously at the thought.

She'd not worked in a Call Centre before, and the numerous systems and the rigid rules were taking some getting used to. The other new recruits were all young, confident and computer-literate, and Rose felt old and stupid next to the youngsters. There weren't many people her age there, and the closest she'd come to making a new friend was a lovely, kind woman named Lena who had taken Rose under her wing. Without her help, Rose didn't think she would have passed the roleplay sign-off today. She had tried to remain positive about the new job, but she couldn't help the uneasy niggle in her stomach about the whole set up. Something didn't feel right, but it was a case of beggars not being choosers and she had no choice but to suck it up and try her best.

Exhausted but restless, Rose reached for her phone and tried her father's home number again. It was past eight thirty now, and she frowned when nobody picked up, wondering where her seventy-year-old father could possibly be.

Although, she mused as she switched off the television and headed up to her bedroom to lie down, *he must have a better social life than me to have met someone.*

She avoided eye contact with the mirror as she moved

around, washing her face, brushing her teeth, and changing into pyjamas. She didn't need the physical reminder that she was now sagging in places she hadn't ever imagined *could* sag nor did she need the harsh lighting to highlight the streaks of greys bursting through the flat, medium brown of the supermarket box dye she applied every six weeks. She was very aware that time had not been kind and, with that thought, she flicked the switch plunging her bedroom into darkness, crawled into her bed and lay down to invite a deep, dreamless sleep to relieve her of her wretched emptiness, if only for a few hours.

Tim

"May I have your attention please on platform 3. We are sorry to announce that the 5:50 service to Liverpool Street has been cancelled due to disruption on the line. Apologies for the inconvenience this may cause you."

A collective groan went up from the suited early morning commuters. The woman next to Tim threw up her arms in frustration, jostling him.

"Fuck's sake," she mumbled aloud. "Fucking selfish jumpers."

Tim shot her a look of disapproval before glancing up at the board, trying to weigh up whether it was worth waiting out the next train or if it would be quicker to get a cab. If he got a taxi in, not only would it cost a fortune, but it would take forever to get into work. On the other hand, if he waited for the British Transport Police to get the line cleared and the network up-and-running, he could be waiting all morning. The rest of the trains would be chaos with the backlog. The woman grabbed her laptop bag from her feet and, seemingly making her own decision a little quicker than Tim, stormed off in the direction of the taxi rank. He watched her purposeful strides, impressive in the four-inch heels, and decided she was probably right in her decision-making. He followed suit, watching as her striking purple coat ducked into a waiting vehicle. The expensive delay set the tone for the day. The annual results were being published next week and everyone was a nervous wreck. By midday, Tim's head was pounding and as he made his way in the glass elevator up to the boardroom, he felt his mouth dry up at the thought of the earbashing he was about to receive.

"Every year," he mumbled to himself, watching the

elevator display tick away the floors.

This year had been diabolical; between constant talk of Brexit, the state of the economy and the regulators breathing down everyone's neck the numbers were abysmal. If profits didn't pick up heads would roll, centres would shut and then they'd all be screwed. The elevator pinged loudly, and Tim exhaled sharply, loosening the collar of his shirt before marching to meet to his fate. He took the ritual humiliation with the usual stony-faced acceptance. He'd been in this game long enough to know that it was expected to take the arse-kicking without stuttering excuses, no matter what level he'd climbed to.

God, if anything the abuse got worse the higher the spot on the ladder.

Another, albeit shorter, train delay meant it was gone 8pm by the time he arrived back at the house, exhausted and drained. Eleanor had permanently condensed her working hours to a four-day week at the dental surgery since Bea was born, spending every Friday with the baby and playing the dutiful mother by completing Hugo's school runs, yet somehow this meant the house was always a bombsite. Over the last few years he had started to dread returning to the once-peaceful childfree sanctuary, and he found himself tensing in anticipation before he entered the house. Tim rolled his shoulders as he exhaled through clenched teeth, wincing at the knots of tension in his rotator cuff as he pushed open the door.

As predicted, the hallway was littered with tiny shoes, garish character-emblazoned backpacks, and brightly coloured scooters. He stepped over the debris, feeling the familiar bubble of irritation that was never far from the surface.

"Daddy!"

A joyous screech pierced the white-noise of the Jones

household as a pink onesie-clad Bea hurtled on unsteady chubby legs from the kitchen towards him. Tim braced himself for the minor impact of the twenty-pound infant, letting her hug his legs before he reached down and disentangled the little arms to allow him to continue into his house in search of his wife.

"Hello, darling," Eleanor appeared in the doorway, a bottle of milk in one hand and a knotted bag containing a nappy in the other. "Come on then, Bea. Let's get you off to bed, sweetheart."

Eleanor's hair was damp and loose around her face, and she was dressed casually in jeans and a blue V-neck t-shirt, with Hugo at her side, his hand snaking around his mother's leg in a possessive fashion. Bea toddled back over to her, extending both hands to her nurturer in a demand to be lifted. Eleanor passed the child the bottle and scooped her up onto her hip. She switched the nappy bag to the hand of the arm that cradled Bea and with her free hand took hold of Hugo's, leading him into the lounge. Tim glanced into the room as he walked past, oblivious to the warmth of the family scene playing out before him; a loving mother preparing to read a bedtime story with quiet persistence to a lively, fidgeting five-year old, and the sweet-faced toddler, one finger swirling her soft baby hair in circles as she grew hypnotically heavy-eyed. Tim didn't look on at the scene and marvel at how fast these children were growing or at how Eleanor, despite the puffy bags under her eyes, had grown more beautiful with motherhood. Instead he scowled at the thought of having to microwave his dinner, thinking back to the pre-children days when they ate together every night like civilised adults.

"Tim?"

As the microwave beeped, he heard Eleanor call him and he set the plate down on the counter in exasperation.

He popped his head around the door. Bea was almost asleep now; her finger still working circles around a strand of hair, but her eyes were closed. Hugo was sprawled back against the cushions flicking through the pictures in the book now his mother had finished the story.

"I let the kids stay up to see you," she smiled up at him. "Do you want to read to Hugo before he goes up?"

"I'll see them all weekend," Tim replied diplomatically. He was starving and wanted nothing more than to eat his dinner, get changed out of his suit and finish the rest of the bottle of wine. "They both look exhausted."

"Take Bea up then," Eleanor said.

He suppressed his annoyance and hefted Bea into his arms, but when he looked down at the sweet rosy cheeks and the soft, coppery lashes of his sleeping daughter he felt a surge of love and affection. Her warm, sleeping body was simultaneously both weightless and solid in his arms and as he tucked her into the walnut cot bed, smoothing down her tufty red curls, his heart expanded with love for his child, strong and overwhelming. He kissed the tip of his finger, pressing it down gently on her tiny forehead and tiptoed from the room. The rush of emotion stayed with him as he pulled the door closed behind him and he was shocked to feel his eyes had grown misty. Eleanor kissed their sleeping children every night before she went to bed, but that was the first time he could remember making the heartfelt gesture. The sudden recognition of its origin brought a fresh burst of emotion and with it, hot tears that scalded the back of his eyes.

Bloody hell.

He leant against the sturdy door as the memory of his own mother, dark hair falling over her face as she leant over the twin beds in the room he'd shared with Will, gently pressing fingertip kisses to each of the boys' foreheads each night like clockwork. Another memory, hazy and out-of-focus in his mind's eye, tumbled to the front of his mind of her struggling up the stairs ahead of him with a pink bundle in her arms. The recollection was so vivid, he could feel Will's own small fist tucked firmly in his own hand as he dragged his wayward, lively younger brother up behind their mum.

"Sssh, Will!" He could almost hear himself hiss. "It's bedtime and you'll wake the baby."

His heart lurched as he saw his mother turn towards him, a soft, grateful smile lighting up her face.

"You're a great big brother, Tim," she whispered back. "Now, up to bed like a big boy, Will, before Dad gets home and you're all in trouble!"

A ten-year-old Rose, in a long-sleeved nightie, scampered past the boys, completing the family scene in Tim's mind's eye and he found himself smiling, despite the bitter-sweetness of the memory. He shook away the unusual wave of nostalgia and went back to his dinner. Eleanor had successfully dispatched Hugo to bed, and she joined him at the kitchen island, pulling out a stool.

"Any news on your dad?" She asked, pouring herself a small glass of wine.

"No," Tim shook his head. "My sister was meant to be trying to find out what all this is about, but I've not had time to speak to her since. I'll give them both a call tomorrow, and if I don't hear anything, I might have to take a trip down there."

"It's certainly unexpected," Eleanor agreed. "It might be best to check that he's not being duped or anything like that. I mean, the land alone has got to be worth a fair bit."

"It's a shame they sold so much of the land off back in the eighties when they stopped farming," Tim frowned. "But there's still a good seven acres attached and even if the house is in dire need of updating, I'd say it would still fetch upwards of a million." He sniffed and looked at his wife pointedly. "Enough for some dubious spinster to want to wheedle her way in."

"Well, hopefully it's all above board," Eleanor had an annoying habit of always looking on the bright side. "But it might be worthwhile checking in on him to make sure."

Belle

Rays of sunlight broke through the thin cotton curtains, illuminating the whorls of dust in the air and rousing Belle from her deep slumber. It was a rare cloudless morning, and the sky was blue instead of the usual miserable grey. She fumbled for the duvet, pulling it over her head to drown out the sunny assault on her unconsciousness, but creaking footsteps outside the door pulled her further from her hazy state. Frustrated and resigned to being awake, she threw back the duvet and sat up, waiting for whoever was behind the door to announce their presence. She didn't have to wait long before a tentative knock came, and her pyjama-clad son appeared in the doorway.

"Morning," she patted the bed next to her and Toby clambered in.

"Hi Mum," he slipped under her arm and snuggled close.

Her annoyance at the premature wake-up slipped away as she cuddled her son close to her. Toby was seven years old, and she knew he'd soon consider himself too grown-up to jump into bed for morning cuddles. It was already a rare enough occurrence that he was awake before her and even rarer that Ben wasn't sprawled, naked and snoring, in the bed next to her. She'd worked last night out of sheer necessity and stumbled in a little after 6am this morning. Ben had been passed out on the sofa, the TV still flickering, and a couple of empty cans discarded on the floor. She had been planning on catching a few hours on the sofa so not to wake him, so she had been delighted at the rare luxury of a few hours in an empty bed. Belle reached for her phone to check the time. It was almost 10am and she groaned, knowing she wouldn't be able to function tonight in work if she didn't at least get a few more hours.

"What are we doing today?" Toby asked, interrupting her thoughts.

Belle yawned and stretched, and Toby, now free from her motherly embrace, wriggled out of the bed.

"I'm working tonight so I need to sleep a little longer," she told him. "Ben's asleep in the room so I'll bring you breakfast in here. You can play games on my phone if you're quiet. What do you want to eat?"

She pulled on a hoodie and turned back to Toby for his breakfast request, already mentally searching the cupboards hoping there was some decent cereal left as she was pretty sure they were out of bread for his usual chocolate spread on toast. Instead of spouting off his breakfast order, Toby was staring at her with a beseeching look in his eyes.

"Please don't go to work!" He reached out and grabbed the sleeves of her hoodie, surprising her.

The imploring tone of his voice pulled at her heartstrings, but she shook her head firmly.

"Sorry babe," she told him. "Mummy has to work to pay the bills. If you want lots of birthday presents, then I have to go to work. I'll be able to put you to bed before I go."

"Please, Mum?" He was still holding onto her, his grip unexpectedly strong. "I don't even need any presents. I've got loads of toys."

"Well, I need to pay our bills," she said firmly, trying to ignore the swell of guilt in her stomach. "Ben will be up in a bit. He might take you for a kick-around up the park if you ask him nicely."

"Please don't go, Mum!" He wailed, throwing his arms around her. "Why can't you just go to work in the day? I hate being here by myself."

"You're not here by yourself," she frowned, confused by his sudden neediness. Her latest job meant she could be there for him before and after school, and he was already fast asleep when she left. "Come on now, Toby. You're being silly."

"I'm not, Mum!"

She could feel warm, wet tears on her neck, and she pulled back to look at his face in alarm. He turned his head away as if he couldn't bear to meet her eyes, and intuitively her heart dropped to the pit of her stomach.

"Toby," she started carefully, trying to keep her tone light even as fury began to work its way through her veins. "Are you worried about being on your own? Did Ben go out when I was in work?"

He said nothing, but she felt his skinny arms tighten around her neck confirming her fear.

"Why didn't you tell me?" She asked gently. "If I'd known…"

He sniffed noisily, but she could feel he was physically trembling with fear and it was enough to make anger inflate within her chest, intense and primal.

"Don't say anything," he begged, his voice muffled as he spoke into the tangle of her dark red curls. "Mum, please don't say anything."

His desperate plea almost shattered her heart. Sadness and guilt struggled within her, muting the anger temporarily, and she squeezed him close, murmuring assurances that she wouldn't say anything while her mind spun at his revelation.

Fucking Ben, she thought angrily.

It had crossed her mind that he had taken to the new arrangement with less resistance than she'd envisioned. They'd been together, on and off, for the last two years, but had finally moved in together a few months back. It had been the perfect solution to her lack of childcare. Rent and living costs were rising constantly, and she'd moved further and further out of the city at the end of every six-month contract. Her current job was rubbish, she was under no illusion that her once-fabulous career had taken a nose-dive, but the pay was good and having Ben here to watch Toby meant no more worrying about calling in or feeling like she was palming Toby off with whichever of her friends would watch him. Ben didn't have to do anything; she made his dinner, cleared up, put him to bed.

All Ben needed to do was stay in the house and even that was clearly too much for the selfish dickhead, Belle could feel the anger bubbling up into her chest, and she felt an overwhelming urge to storm into the living room and drag him off the sofa and out onto the street. *But then what?*

If she kicked Ben out, she'd have no choice but to quit. The jobs she was qualified to do wouldn't pay nearly as well as her current gig, and the thought of having to move Toby to yet another home and another school would break her heart. She knew more than anyone that jobs for people like her were hard to come by. Everything was zero-hours contracts and inflexible shifts that wouldn't allow for school runs. She knew that even raising the subject with Ben would result in a blazing row that would end with him storming out and going AWOL for days. The anger deflated a little as she pictured the meagre savings she had set aside being eaten up by the cost of food, gas, and electricity. There was no way she'd be able to save enough on benefits to get Toby the games console that he so badly wanted. She knew that she was trapped before she'd even began to fully fantasise about dragging Ben out into the courtyard. For a start, he was bigger and stronger than her, but more than that, she needed him.

It was probably just a one-off, she tried to convince herself. *It's my fault for expecting him to stay in and babysit my kid on a Friday night after he'd been working all week. He'd probably only been down the pub for a couple of pints. No harm done.*

She pushed these excuses around her head as she made Toby breakfast and got them both dressed, knowing she was too riled up to sleep now. Ben was still out for the count on the sofa snoring when they slipped out of the flat to catch the bus into town to have some fun bowling to lessen her guilty conscience. As they clambered aboard the bus, her phone rang and she fished it out, hoping it was Katie so she could broach the subject of Toby sleeping over tonight. She couldn't bear to think of Toby scared and upset, but she was conscious she had used up all her favours with Katie recently and she didn't want to exhaust her only real friend's patience. When she retrieved the phone though, it was her brother's name flashing up on the screen. Out of all her siblings, Will was the only one who didn't feel like a complete stranger. They had been in touch about the unexpected wedding invitation, but she still hadn't made up her mind whether she was going to go, stuffing it in the bottom of her underwear drawer.

Out of sight, out of mind.

"Hey," she swiped her finger across the screen to answer tucking the phone between her chin and her shoulder.

"Hey," Will greeted her. "Are you busy?"

"Just on the bus into town," she told him. "Me and Toby are going bowling."

She grinned at Toby and he beamed back excitedly as she said it.

"Cool," her brother replied. "Tell the little man I said hi."

"Uncle Will says hi," she passed the message on and Toby gave her a thumbs-up. "What's up anyway? I'm honoured to be speaking to you twice in one week. How long is it usually?"

"Too long," Will replied a little wistfully. "Listen, Rose has just called me..."

Belle felt a tug of resentment that the rest of her siblings all seemed to be communicating with each other. Will was the only one that made any effort with her and it stung.

"Both she and Tim have tried to get hold of Dad, and he hasn't got back to either of them," he continued, oblivious to her stony silence. "Tim has got a bee in his bonnet now that this Linda is some kind of gold-digger and he's planning on going down tomorrow. Rose thought it might be nice if we all went down."

"To Dad's?" Belle heard her own voice come out shrill and high-pitched. Toby shot her a curious look and she lowered her tone. "I can't go down tomorrow. I'm working tonight, and I've got Toby, and God only knows how much it would be and how long it would take to get to the back of beyond on a Sunday."

"I'll pick you up," Will volunteered cutting through her excuses. "Come on, Belle! Toby can come. I'm sure it's all fine and Dad's just a horny old goat, but it'll be a good chance for us all to clear the air before the wedding."

"I don't know," Belle knew that she had tons of her own daddy issues that she should really work through, but with everything else going on she was reluctant to open the Pandora's Box and send herself into a spiral.

"Please, Belle," Will pleaded. "I haven't seen Toby for so long and it's the only day off I've got in weeks."

She glanced at her precious son who had his face pressed up against the window staring out at the concrete jungle that they lived in, and it hit her how different his childhood was to her own. Even though the area they lived in was considered quite nice, they were only ever a few miles away from a news report of a stabbing or drug bust. She wouldn't dream of letting Toby even walk to the playground that was less than five minutes from their flat, yet she could remember running wild in the fields and surrounding woodland at his age. From nine or ten, she'd been entrusted to walk through the lane to the village to meet her friends, knowing to stay on the grass verge so she didn't get run over. She felt another pang of guilt that Toby would never experience the freedom that she'd had, nor the simple pleasures of country life. She reached out to ruffle his hair affectionately.

"What do you think, Tobe?" She asked him. "Want to come on a trip tomorrow with me and Uncle Will? I reckon some of the lambs might have been born already."

"Lambs?" His face lit up. "Yeah!"

"Fine," she responded to her brother, her tone cool and unphased even as her heart skipped a beat in panic. "We'll come."

Will

Will pulled his car to a stop eyeing the block of ropey-looking flats sceptically. The building stuck out like a sore thumb in an otherwise nice area, and he realised, without an ounce of satisfaction, that his assumption that he was the least successful out of the four of them might not be the case. He fired off a quick text to tell her he was outside, ignoring the message from Craig that had pinged through while he was driving.

Despite his reservations, he'd had a lovely time Friday at the engagement party, and he couldn't fault how lovely and welcoming the Milligan family had been. In fact, everything had been so perfect that Will had begun to think that his initial worry that he and Craig were moving too fast was just a case of cold feet. Craig had laughed off Will's reservations in the self-assured, no-nonsense way of his that was so convincing. For every doubt that he confessed, Craig had a structured, practical argument to counter it, but Will still couldn't shake the misgivings that he had.

But it wasn't just how fast they seemed to be moving. He frowned as he thought about the way Craig flipped every minor disagreement around, implying that Will had no idea how the real world and relationships worked. On more than one occasion, he had accused him of 'running away from his problems'.

Will grimaced at the thought. *There may be a bit of truth in that.*

That was the tricky thing about his funny feeling; most of what Craig pointed out was valid. He was so loving and attentive that it made Will feel guilty just having these thoughts, which is why he hadn't voiced them to anyone, not even Raya.

A prickle of remorse made Will reach for his phone to accept Craig's olive branch. They had ended up arguing last night about today's trip. It had been a difficult enough decision for Will, but he'd felt spurred on by nostalgia at the thought of his whole family together, especially after seeing how close Craig was to his sisters. Craig had been excited for him, but somehow, he had jumped to the conclusion that he was invited. As much as Will loved him, it was something that he needed to do alone, but Craig had taken it as a personal affront. He had tried to soften the blow when it became clear that Craig was upset, citing his tiny car and his passengers as the primary reason he couldn't come along for the ride.

"I'm sure we can all squeeze in," Craig had protested.

"Craig," Will had tried to be diplomatic. "You can barely fit a bag on my back seat. It'll be a tight enough squeeze for just my nephew and he's only seven."

"Does he have to go?" Craig pouted. "Your sister can sit in the back."

"She hasn't got anyone to have him."

"Well I'll drive," Craig had folded his arms across his chest as if that were the end of the matter.

"Craig, I need to do this alone," Will had felt his temper fraying. His nerves were jangled enough as it was without Craig adding to them.

In the end, Craig had recognised that he wasn't about to back down and had sulked all evening instead. The text he'd sent seemed to be a peace-offering and even though Will was still annoyed, he accepted it.

The car door opened pulling Will from his thoughts, and he beamed with genuine happiness to see his sister.

"Hey Toby!" Will ruffled his nephew's hair as he slid into the back of the car, before turning to his sister. "How's it going?"

"Good to see you," she grinned leaning in for a quick hug. She pulled a tablet and headphones from her bag and passed them to her son behind her.

"You too," he said meaning it. "How are you feeling about today? You look tired."

She pulled a face at her brother flipping down the sun-visor to check her reflection. Her curls were gathered in a messy plait hanging over one shoulder, but she hadn't had time to disguise the dull, greasy roots. Her green eyes, usually her best feature, were narrowed behind puffy, dark circles and her porcelain skin was marred with a break-out of angry pimples. She sighed and closed the mirror; too tired to care.

"I've had, like, three hours sleep," she said by way of explanation. "How are you feeling about everything?"

Will shrugged, his eyes fixed firmly on the road ahead. "Weird, to be honest. Weird and nervous," he paused and took one hand off the wheel to rub the stubble at his jaw. "It's been about ten years since I last saw Dad."

"Same," Belle admitted sheepishly. "I've not been to Hampton Dale since before Toby was born."

"I feel a bit guilty," Will admitted. "I've been back in England for over a year now and it hadn't even crossed my mind to go down and see the old man."

"It works both ways," Belle replied petulantly. "He doesn't make an effort with us."

They both fell quiet, lost in their own thoughts and regrets; the silence pierced by intermittent beeps from Toby's game in the back.

"It's sad though," Will said finally. "I can't remember the last time I saw the others."

"I wasn't going to come today," she admitted. "I still send a Christmas card every year with my address on it, and sometimes I get one back, sometimes I don't, but he doesn't even send a birthday card for Toby. He clearly doesn't think of us, so I don't see why I'd even want to go to his wedding."

Will winced at the resentment in his sister's tone. He knew that she had her own issues with their dad, but he'd genuinely believed that his siblings had some semblance of a relationship with their father, and that he was the family outcast. From what he'd heard over the past week though, it seems like they were all islands in the stream.

"It's a bit strange that Rose and Tim haven't been able to get hold of him," he said to change the subject. "You'd think sending us invitations was his way of reaching out."

"Maybe it was his wife-to-be's idea," Belle shrugged. "I can't think of anyone called Lambe though from the village, can you?"

"No," he replied. "I can't believe he's met someone at his age. Although I was always surprised that he didn't get remarried; it's been sixteen years."

"He was such a miserable git," Belle retorted. "I don't think anyone would have put up with him except Mum."

"That's true," Will chuckled. "He's got the farm though which would be a sweetener for any savvy spinsters."

"Hmmmm," Belle hadn't wanted to admit that she'd been thinking about the will in case her brother thought she was callous, but now he'd brought it up she pressed on trying to keep her voice casual. "This wedding will change the will then, I guess?"

"That had crossed my mind too," he admitted wrinkling his nose. "I remember Tim saying something about them having mirror wills, but it was so long ago."

"I didn't get told anything," Belle said, and Will felt a pang of sympathy for his sister.

He had already left home and was living in Manchester, studying photography, working in a bar, and living his best life, when their mother received her diagnosis. He'd been completely absorbed in his own pain when she had died, and had taken himself off on his first backpacking trip in the aftermath, no thought for his fourteen-year-old sister left alone at the farm with just their detached father to comfort her.

He took his eyes off the road ahead to glance at her. "I'm really sorry that I took off back then. I should have stuck around to be there for you."

Belle shook her head vehemently. "Don't be daft, Will. I wasn't your responsibility, and you were barely any older than me. It would have been stupid for us both to be trapped and miserable," she turned to him and smiled, but Will couldn't help feeling like it was bravado on her part. "Anyway, it was fine. I was used to looking after myself and I had my friends in the village. I wasn't far behind you anyway."

"Yeah, I suppose," he said not knowing what else to say. "Well, I guess Tim will know what's going on."

"Yeah, probably," Belle agreed before they both lapsed back into a heavy silence.

Tim

The Red Lion Inn was a white-washed detached building, with a large bay windows to the front that gave it the look of a traditional family home. At the front was a gravel car park and Tim reversed his car carefully, taking care to move slowly to avoid any stones flicking up and scratching the paintwork. He hadn't been here for years, but it looked exactly the same as he remembered.

That was the thing about village life, he thought as he checked his watch out of habit. *Nothing ever changed.*

They had agreed to meet up at the pub outside the village, but Tim had had plenty of time to spare so had taken a quick drive through the village to check it all out. The High Street looked exactly the same as it had when Tim was a boy, except the Newsagent's where he used to pinch penny sweets was now a Tesco Express, the wool shop was a Domino's Pizza and Mrs Burke's video shop was a tanning bed chain. Tim looked at his watch again. It was bang on the time that they'd agreed to meet, and it irritated him when he was kept waiting. He had suggested that Rose came, knowing she had more patience for social niceties than him, but she had invited the other two along resulting in the day turning into a family reunion much to his chagrin.

A boy racer car with a dented wing and a taped-up wing mirror crunched noisily onto the gravel next to Tim's immaculate BMW. He held his breath as the driver over-steered, swinging the rear-end dangerously close to his own vehicle. He was a split second from sounding the horn, palm raised and nostrils flaring, when he caught sight of his sister's face through the windscreen and stopped himself. The car door flew open and he watched as his sister extracted herself clumsily from the car. He was aware that it had been some years since he'd last seen her and they'd all aged, but he was surprised to see how much she had changed. She had always been a dead-ringer for their mother with her pretty heart-shaped face and a kind smile, but the woman who raised a hand to greet him had a tired, weary expression framed by unkempt grey-streaked curls. She moved around the car and stopped dead a couple of feet in front of him. Tim, usually well-versed in etiquette for any occasion, found himself uncomfortably uncertain whether he should hug her or shake her hand. He could tell from her forced smile that she was also feeling awkward, but she bridged the gap to hug him fleetingly. It lasted only a split-second and they both stepped backwards, grateful for the immediate distance.

"New car?" Tim raised an eyebrow intending to make a joke to break the ice, but it came out haughty and mocking.

"It's Jack's," Rose flushed. "He didn't take it up to university with him, so I thought I'd give it a run out."

"Shall we go in?" Tim dropped his eyes to his watch in embarrassment. "Or should we wait for the others?"

"Shall we give them another couple of minutes?" She suggested.

Tim nodded. "Have you been up to the house yet?"

Rose shook her head. "I tried to call again, but there was no answer. I thought we could all go together."

Before Tim could convey his irritation at the whole scenario, a white hatchback spun into the car park screeching to a stop in front of them. Will and Belle emerged from the car followed by a small dark-haired child wearing over-ear headphones and clutching a tablet. Tim watched on as Rose folded Belle then the child and finally Will into her arms.

"Wow, look at you!" She addressed the boy. "Toby, you've grown so much!"

Will and Belle smiled awkwardly, unsure whether to attempt to hug Tim and settling on half-hearted waves.

"This is your Auntie Rose. You've met her once when you were little," Belle ducked her head, glad of the distraction of her son. "And this is your Uncle Tim. I don't think you've seen him before."

"Hello Toby," Tim found himself replicating the half-wave of his younger siblings. "How are you?"

Toby looked up at Tim, as if surprised by his formal greeting before looking to his mother for guidance. Belle shrugged, hoisting her bag onto her shoulder, and turned towards the pub.

"Are we going in then, or shall we go straight to the house?"

"Shall we just go straight there and get this over with?" Tim suggested glancing back at his watch like he had somewhere to be. "Find out what's going on."

He caught Will and Rose exchanging glances with each other from the corner of his eye, and he felt his irritation return.

They're clearly hoping to turn this into a long and leisurely family reunion, he thought in annoyance.

"Sure," Rose agreed diplomatically. "Maybe we can come back here and get some lunch after?"

"Are we going together?" Will loitered awkwardly by the side of his car. "Or…"

Tim felt all their eyes on him and even though he knew he'd have been equally annoyed if they didn't defer to him, he felt irritated that they couldn't make a decision without him. It all felt needlessly over-the-top for them to be feeling awkward about turning up at their own father's house, and Tim felt a flicker of sadness through his exasperation at the sorry state of it all.

"Why doesn't Rose come with me?" He suggested

softening a little. "And you bring your car, Will."

As Tim drove the short distance to their childhood home, Rose peered through the tinted window and began pointing out landmarks of their childhood. When he didn't respond, she seemed to sense his impatience at her chatter and fell into an uneasy silence. He pulled to a stop at the top of the access lane, feeling an unexpected lump in his throat at the sight of their childhood home. The emotion snuck up on him from nowhere and, for the first time, he felt something stronger than just concern for his rightful inheritance. The land had been in his mother's family for over a century, and while they had stopped farming back in the eighties and sold off large parcels of their land to neighbouring farms, the fields and a crescent of woodland remained in their name. He felt a pang of nostalgia for long summer days tearing around with his friends in the long grass and building dens in the trees, heading back to a warm and noisy kitchen to fill a rucksack with snacks and drinks. Bluebell Farm was more than just a portfolio or an investment; it was his home, and it was all they had left of their mother.

Tim had been twenty-six when Kathleen Jones had died. He'd been heartbroken, of course, but he was already living in London in a house share with some other young bankers and had just started dating Eleanor, a pretty, newly qualified dentist from a well-to-do family. He was sad that he'd lost his mother so young, but he had a whole new life and after the funeral, he hadn't thought twice about how the rest of the family were coping. In hindsight, he thought that maybe it had been easier for him than the others. Without the anchor of their mother, his visits home became less frequent and he couldn't remember the last time they'd all been together.

"Makes me feel a little bit tearful," Rose's voice pierced

his thoughts.

He cleared his throat to mask his discomfort and got out of the car to open the gate, before proceeding down the long driveway. As a boy, Bluebell Farm had felt like it stretched for miles as he ran the length of the fields on skinny, grazed legs, playing tag and hide-and-seek, but it seemed smaller now. The main house stood at the end of the lane; the roof now weathered and moss-covered, the hedges around the house were overgrown and tangled.

Tim pulled up next to a saloon car parked haphazardly in front of the drystone wall that he was surprised to see still standing. The house looked run down and dilapidated with two of the first-floor windows hastily boarded up, and the nets that hung in the sitting-room window looked ancient and grubby. Tim heard Will utter a low exclamation beneath his breath, and they hung back cautiously allowing him to approach the front door alone.

He caught a glimpse of a silhouette behind the swarms of frothy fabric, but when he tapped sharply on the heavy wood door, it remained unanswered.

"There's definitely someone in." Rose told him in a hushed tone as they waited. "Shall we go around the back? We never used the front door, did we?"

He paced towards the side of the house, taking in the once-pristine yard. Once upon a time, it had been a testament to their mother's love of gardening filled with planters bursting with colour bordering an immaculate patio and a neat lawn with a slide and swing-set. Now, the patio was grim with dirt, weeds sprouting between the slabs and where terracotta pots had once been, recycling boxes overflowed with rain and household waste. Tim turned the corner expecting to come face to face with the back door and flinched in surprise at the woman he presumed was Linda stood on the doorstep. It was almost midday, but she was wrapped in a plum-coloured terry-towelling bathrobe. Her hair was bleached a brassy yellow, cut short around a tanned face that was lined, but still attractive for a woman that Tim guessed was in her fifties.

"We knocked," Rose tilted her head towards the front of the house. "You didn't answer."

Her face was stern and unwelcoming, but recognition flickered across her eyes. "You must be Frank's children."

"We've been trying to get hold of you," Rose smiled apologetically. "I'm Rose."

The woman hesitated before stepping down from the threshold to wave them inside. They shuffled past her in an awkward assembly line introducing themselves in turn.

"We've had some trouble with the house phone after I spoke to you. I was just saying to Frank that I was going to pop to Argos and try to get a new handset." Linda addressed Rose once they were inside. "He's through here."

They followed the stranger, their step-mother-to-be, through what had once been the hub of their busy home. The flagstone tiles of the large kitchen were the same, Tim noticed, and the original exposed beams hadn't been covered up by an Artex ceiling or some such similar horror. The old Aga was gone, and there was no dog basket in the corner which made him even sadder somehow. He glanced around at the faces of his siblings, and from their expressions he imagined that they too were hunting for familiar, comforting memories amidst the strangeness of the situation.

She led them through to the back room that had once been Tim's bedroom, calling out as she walked. "Frank! You'll never guess who's here!"

There were four bedrooms upstairs in the main farmhouse, but two of the rooms were barely bigger than a box. Once Tim had hit the obnoxious teenage years, he'd objected to sharing a room with his little brother and their mother had dragged the antique pine dresser and overstuffed sofa into the kitchen so that he could have his own room. Even after they'd all drifted off one-by-one, the room had remained a bedroom and towards the end, when Kathleen was too tired and weak to use the stairs, she'd slept there. Their father had never cared for interior design and the few times that Tim had visited the house had remained unchanged. Rather than seeing his father, looking smaller and wizened in an armchair facing a bulky television set, the first thing Tim noticed was the gaudy floral wallpaper and the trinkets and knickknacks littering every possible surface including the pine dresser. He winced, partly at the awful aesthetic and partly with the surprise at how deeply and quickly this stranger had marked her territory on their home. The force of the emotion made him uncomfortable, and he quickly turned his attention to the grey-haired man in carpet slippers staring up at them.

"What's going on?"

Tim had had no naïve notions that their father would scoop them all up into his arms, laughing with joy to see all his offspring so unexpectedly, but he hadn't predicted the unsmiling confusion on his face. Frank looked at each face in turn, eventually settling on Belle who looked away uncomfortably.

"We've been trying to get hold of you," Tim stepped forward taking charge. "There's been no answer on the landline, so we decided to come down and make sure everything was alright."

"Oh," Frank pushed the blanket from his knees to rise stiffly to his feet. He had once been a large, imposing man, but now he looked old and vulnerable. "Well, everything is fine."

He stared at his children unblinking, and it struck Tim

that he seemed a little groggy and disorientated. Rose crossed the room placing a hand on his shoulder in concern.

"Is everything ok, Dad?" Rose was the shortest of the siblings but where once Frank had towered over her, his body was stooped and she was almost eye-level with him. "We were a little bit worried, that's all. We're here now though, so shall we have a catch up?"

Tim could hear Rose's real question beneath the high-pitched cheeriness in her voice. He glanced around at the others and knew they were all thinking the same.

Does he even know who we are?

Frank blinked slowly, and then in front of their eyes he seemed to come to life. His thin lips moved slowly into some semblance of a smile below a grey moustache, sweeping his eyes back over them one-by-one as if seeing them properly for the first time. His eyes settled on Toby and he looked back to his youngest daughter quizzically. "Is this your boy, Belle?"

Belle nodded, slipping a possessive arm around her son, before coolly introducing them. "Yes. Toby, this is Frank, your grandfather. Dad, this is Toby."

They all stiffened at the frost in Belle's voice, but if Frank noticed it, he didn't react.

"Shall we go into the kitchen?" Linda suggested her tone rivalling Belle's for iciness.

They had all been huddled together in the doorway and they sprang apart to let Frank past, trailing behind him awkwardly back into the main hub of the house. Tim hung back and watched as his siblings took in the decorative changes.

"I like what you've done with the place," his youngest sister smirked as she pushed a cast-iron poodle doorstop out of her way with the toe of her shoe, and Tim watched Linda throw her a look of contempt in return.

Nobody said anymore until they were seated around the pine dining table; Frank taking his traditional seat at the head and Linda swiftly squeezing between him and Will to slip into the spot next to him.

Frank glanced at her in confusion. "Are you not going to put the kettle on, Linda?"

She frowned in response. "Oh, are they all staying?"

"Well, they can stay for a cup of tea," Frank looked exasperated. "They've come a long way."

Linda got to her feet curtly, but the scowl on her face barely registered with Tim as he studied his father's reaction. He felt a flicker of relief that the disorientated and wizened old man sat in an armchair, looking ten years older than his age, had faded and the irritable father they knew had returned.

"Tea would be lovely, thank you if it's not too much trouble," Rose, always the peacemaker, could never bear an atmosphere and she overcompensated with a bright, sunny smile. "We were all very intrigued to receive the wedding invitations! How exciting for you both!"

Belle pulled a face at Rose behind Linda's back and Will swiftly dispatched a sharp elbow to her ribs.

"How did you meet?" Will asked when neither Linda nor Frank responded to Rose's gushing congratulations.

Frank looked up at Linda expectantly, but she finished filling the kettle placing it on the hob before she replied. "Oh, we've known each other a few years, haven't we, Frank?"

"Do you live in the village then?" Will inquired politely. "We've all been away for years, but it's a such a small place. We thought we knew everyone."

"Linda used to work at the Howells' dairy," Frank answered for her. "Can we count you all in for the wedding?"

"Of course," Will and Rose answered in unison.

Tim nodded his head, but Belle remained stonily silent. Tim watched as Frank looked at her for her response, but Toby sensing his mother's reluctance tugged on her arm.

"Can I go outside, Mum?"

Belle pushed her chair back roughly, scraping across the tiles. "I'll come with you."

Frank barely glanced at their retreating backs. "Why don't you go and show them the new lambs in the field, Linda?"

"I'm sure they can figure it out themselves," Linda retorted, before she seemed to catch herself and added. "But why don't I finish making this tea and then I'll come and join you?"

Will rose to his feet feeling hemmed in around the table. "I'll give you a hand with the tea."

Linda tried to shrug off his offer, but Will and Rose were both on their feet so she had no choice but to let them help before following after Belle and Toby with a regretful glance over her shoulder.

"Well, I didn't expect to see you all," Frank said once she was gone. "You couldn't get through, did you say?"

"I spoke with Linda earlier in the week," Rose volunteered. "And she said you'd call back, but we couldn't get an answer when we tried again."

"Oh," Frank took a sip of his tea thoughtfully. "She must have forgotten to mention it. I haven't heard the phone ring though."

"Linda said she thought there was a problem with it," Will said diplomatically as Rose and Tim exchanged concerned glances.

Frank made a noncommittal noise. "How have you all been?"

"Fine," Tim replied brusquely. "We were a little

concerned that we hadn't heard of Linda before we received the invitations. How long exactly have you been living together?"

"Oh, since Christmas," Frank replied easily. "You didn't come down this year, Rose."

"I was working all over Christmas," she said apologetically, before looking around the room. "The house looks different. What happened to the windows upstairs?"

"Hailstorm." Frank said by way of explanation.

"Have you got someone coming out to fix them?" Rose asked with concern.

"Linda's nephew does windows," Frank nodded. "He'll be out next week. The whole house needs replacing with double glazing. We'll get that done first, and then the bathroom and the kitchen after the wedding."

"All very costly," Tim raised an eyebrow. "I imagine that will come to a fair whack."

"I'm probably going to sell off the lower fields," he responded matter-of-factly. "I rent them out to the Howells', but it makes more sense to sell them off and get a cash injection for updating the house."

"Woah, hang on!" Tim interjected. "You can't sell the land off!"

Frank flushed. "Well, I can't be expected to do it up on my pension."

"If you go selling off the land, you'll devalue the whole property," Tim cited haughtily.

"Is that what you've all hightailed it down here for? To check on the will?" Frank looked incensed.

"No!" Rose gasped. "Of course, not."

"We came down here," Tim said with deliberate control. "Because we were looking out for you. How well do you even know that woman? She's a good deal younger than you and could well be taking advantage."

"I'm more than capable of looking after myself," Frank replied stonily. "And don't patronise me that this visit is out of anything other than concern for yourselves."

"Oh, Dad," Rose reached for his hand, visibly distressed. "Don't say things like that. I'm sorry I've not been in contact as much as usual. I've had a lot going on with work."

Frank let her take his hand, softening a little. "You've always made more effort, Rose, but I've not seen hide nor hair of the rest of them for years."

"I've been out of the country for years, Dad," Will sounded uncharacteristically irritated at the accusation. "Contact works both ways. I've been working six days a week since I've been back, so sorry that I've not been to see you. You're retired, Dad; you could come to see us or call us anytime."

Tim nodded his head in agreement, but Frank flinched.

"Well," he said finally. "We could go around in circles forever, couldn't we? You're here now though, and you can see that Linda's not some money-hungry widow-hunter."

Tim made a noncommittal noise in response. "If you are looking to do up the house and you want any advice, you can give Eleanor and I a call. We've just had a lot of work done at ours, plus I work in banking so I can give you advice on the best ways to finance any refurb."

"So, does Linda have any children?" Rose changed the subject when she saw neither her father nor her older brother would back down. "Have you got everything ready for the wedding?"

"She's got a daughter, but she lives in Spain," Frank turned away from Tim coolly to address her. "She'll be back for the wedding. It won't be a big do, just family and a few close friends from the village. We've got a marquee from the Howells' and someone from the village is catering."

Rose smiled pleasantly. "Oh, that sounds lovely. We're looking forward to it."

Tim didn't mention the will again, not wanting to antagonise his father further but made a note to contact his solicitor to see where he stood legally. He looked at his watch and then to the door, wondering when his sister and nephew would return. Will and Rose would be happy to sit and chat to their dad for hours now they were here, but even though he hadn't seen Belle for years and couldn't claim to really know her at all, he could already sense that she was as loath to be there as he was.

Rose

Rose could sense that Tim was eager to leave and there was a part of her that wanted to retreat too. Seeing so many changes to her childhood home had revived unexpected emotions, leaving her with a pressing urge to be alone to process it all. She could be back at her house in less than two hours, curtains closed and tucked up under a cosy throw in front of the television, but as tense as the atmosphere was she couldn't deny how comforting it felt to be around her siblings for the first time in years.

In the end, they stayed at their father's house for about an hour before Linda made noises about the shops' closing times. The four siblings debriefed over a quick drink back at The Red Lion, but Tim vetoed Rose's suggestion of lunch and Belle was quick to agree that she had to get going too. Rose's heart ached with nostalgia at the sight of Will and Belle stood side-by-side next to Tim's car as they said their goodbyes. She could picture them clearly as small children stood in front of the front door in their back-to-school uniforms, shiny Clark's shoes on their feet. She could see their Mum cajoling them into smiling for a picture, the click and the whir of the camera winding on. The photograph would have been printed off down at the chemist's in town and displayed proudly on the mantelpiece of the huge fireplace; one of her and Tim, unsmiling teenagers in their grey blazers, and one of the little ones in their maroon pullovers. Every September, the photographs would be swapped, and the old ones pasted into a heavy red leather album that charted their lives together. It hit her that the proud chronicling of their lives had died with their mother.

Imagine if that was Tom and Jack, Rose thought

suddenly devastated by the thought. Imagine her two little boys growing further and further apart until they were practically strangers. It would break her heart and she realised that it would have broken her mother's. She'd see her siblings again at the wedding, but then when next? At Will or Belle's wedding if either of them ever got married, maybe.

"Come on then, Will," Belle was growing impatient, and Will shot Rose an apologetic look.

She could tell that he, like her, had wanted to come today, not just because of their concern for their father, but to try to build a bridge between their disconnected lives. Despite the five-year age gap, she'd always felt that she and Will were the most similar. Tim and Belle had both always been boisterous and quick-tempered compared with their gentler, more sensitive siblings. There was no question that Rose and Will were their mother's children when it came to their kind nature. It was crazy that they could look and act so similar, yet they were little more than strangers now.

Will folded Rose into a tight embrace. "It's been lovely to see you. Let's try to stay in touch."

Rose nodded her agreement. "Definitely."

She hugged Belle and little Toby too, before retreating to her car where she sat for a few minutes blinking to clear her misty vision. She berated herself for being so foolishly sentimental, but her siblings darting off back to their lives and partners had emphasised to her how utterly alone she was. She hadn't had any expectations for today other than to check in on her father but seeing her brothers and sister had made her realise how much she missed that anchor to the past. Blood was meant to be thicker than water, yet their links felt flimsy and uncertain.

Rose turned the key of Jack's car to start it and it gave a pitiful chug before cutting out to nothing. Used to the temperamental vehicle, she tried again. This time, it didn't even chug.

Oh, for God's sake, she banged the palm of her hand against the steering wheel in frustration.

It had started fine this morning, despite sitting unused in front of the house for sometimes months between Jack's visits home. She crossed her fingers hoping it was just the battery; chances were that someone would have jump leads in the pub, whereas she definitely couldn't afford breakdown recovery or an expensive garage bill. The last thing she needed was a lengthy Sunday service trip home on public transport. She hurried back up to the pub, her stomach grumbling at the smell of the roast dinners wafting through the air. Despite her lack of appetite that was one thing she could happily devour, but she hadn't been able to tempt any of her siblings to stay and was too self-conscious to eat alone.

"Hi," she smiled apologetically at the young woman behind the bar. "I'm really sorry to trouble you, but my car won't start. I was wondering if anyone here had any jump leads?"

"Rose Jones?"

She turned quickly towards the sound.

"Gareth Edwards?" A genuine smile of pleasure spread across her face at the sight of her old school friend. He was just as handsome as he had been in their school days, and it came back to her in a flash that all the girls had gone through a phase of having a crush on him to the point where it was almost a rite of passage. He had aged exceptionally well, the touch of grey at the temples of his thick, brown hair and the little crinkles in the corners of his deep, brown eyes only adding to his good looks. "What a lovely surprise!"

"It really is!" He drew her to him in a warm, familiar

hug making her flush with pleasure. "Home for a visit?"

"Yes," Rose remembered the woman still waiting to answer her question and turned back apologetically. "I was just heading home, but my car won't start."

"Is it the battery?"

"I hope so," Rose grimaced. "It's my son's car and he's away at university, so it doesn't get used very often."

"I've got leads back at the house," he said. "I walked here today, but I can go back if you need them."

"Oh," she could see the menu in his hand, and didn't want to inconvenience him. "I don't want to tear you away from your family and your lunch." She glanced back at the barwoman hopefully. "I'm sure someone here will have some."

The young woman came around the bar to peer through the bay window at the car park and grimaced. "There's not that many cars outside- I'll go and ask Tony in the kitchen." She glanced back at Gareth. "I'll be back with you now."

"Sorry to hold you up," Rose said embarrassedly. "I'll be out of your way soon. Hopefully."

The woman reappeared with an apologetic smile. "No luck, sorry. I can ask around in the restaurant if you like."

Rose hesitated. She hated disturbing people, but she really needed to get the car started.

"I'll stick my head in and ask," Gareth volunteered before she could say anything more, but he returned empty-handed. "Nobody has got any leads to hand. I'll go back to mine and get my car."

"Do you want to order first?" The barwoman interjected. "We're only serving until three."

Gareth glanced up at the clock and grimaced. "It'll take me a good twenty minutes to get home."

"Please have your lunch first!" Rose objected. "I don't

want to put you and your family out. I can wait."

"It's fine," Gareth waved a hand dismissively before admitting. "I'm on my own anyway."

"You are?" She tried to hide her surprise.

"Sad, I know," he grinned self-consciously. "I tell you what, Rose, Sunday lunch is my guilty pleasure, so why don't you join me and then I'll try and get your car up-and-running?"

She paused, not wanting to trespass upon his weekend treat with her presence, but the smell of roast beef wafting in from the kitchen was enticing and it did mean he wouldn't feel obliged to rush. "Sure, that's really kind of you to help me out."

She had to admit that as embarrassed as she felt to be infringing upon his time, it was lovely to have friendly, uncomplicated company and Gareth was certainly that. He was just as affable and down-to-earth as she remembered, and it was refreshing just to have company outside of working hours. She was surprised that he was going through a divorce, but he seemed to be taking it admirably in his stride. The afternoon passed in the blink of an eye, and Rose was surprised to see that almost two hours had gone by in his company as she sat beside him in his car heading back to The Red Lion car park armed with jump leads.

"So, you'll be back for the wedding then?" Gareth asked.

"Yes," she nodded. "It's funny to think of my dad meeting someone now at his age."

"Maybe there's hope for us all," Gareth joked. "Hopefully, I won't be waiting until I'm retired though."

Rose laughed. "I'm sure you won't have any problems meeting anyone."

She blushed as she heard her own words aloud.

"Same to you," he smiled cheerfully, not noticing her

embarrassment. "It's difficult with the hours I work to date anyone. Everyone our age has either got loads of emotional baggage or is too busy with their kids and their jobs."

Rose could honestly say she wouldn't know as it hadn't even crossed her mind to start dating. She didn't even know where she'd start; times had moved on from pulling someone on the dancefloor of a smoky bar to all these apps and websites. It felt too scary and potentially humiliating; she definitely didn't have the confidence to put herself out there to be rejected by balding, beer-bellied blokes. She couldn't say this to Gareth though, so she changed the subject. "I bet it's so interesting being a police officer though. It sounds so much more exciting than my new job."

"I love it," Gareth admitted. "It's hardly the wild, wild west out here though."

He mimicked picking up a radio from the dashboard. "Ten Four copy that, Sarge, we've got a flock of sheep loose on Walker's Lane. Suspect is a white male from out-of-town wearing hiking boots who doesn't understand the importance of shutting gates. Possibly armed with a flask and National Trust map." Rose giggled, and Gareth grinned at her. "If only it were that exciting."

He started her car with relatively little fuss, and she realised she'd been enjoying his company so much that she was almost sorry when the engine roared to life.

"Thank you so much for your help," she beamed as they parted ways. "I'm sorry I've stolen so much of your day off."

"Honestly," he grinned back. "It's been lovely to see you and to have some company. You know where I live now, so if you're ever back visiting your dad feel free to pop in."

Even though she knew it was an empty gesture, she felt warm and fuzzy from the offer and his kindness, and for the first time in weeks, she found she was still smiling when she climbed into bed exhausted and happy that night.

Belle

Belle turned the key in the door and pushed it open, feeling the resistance of the junk piled behind it. The one lone screw holding the coat rack on the wall had finally given way sending jackets, coats and bags stuffed with miscellaneous items tumbling to the ground when she had left for work last night. She should have known that it was too much to hope for that Ben would have put it back up without being asked. Belle held back a growl of anger slamming the door shut behind her. She could feel her blood simmering already and knew that she should go through to the bedroom to give herself some time to calm down. She'd been in a constant state of aggravation since Toby's revelation, and as much as she'd been trying to keep a lid on her anger, she knew she was just one insensitive comment away from completely losing it. A fug of smoke hung thick in the air and Belle stormed past his snoring body on the sofa to yank the heavy curtains back to open the window. He opened his eyes and groaned at the rude awakening.

"It stinks in here," she said in as level tone as she could muster. "Can you open the windows if you really have to smoke."

"What's the matter with you?"

"Nothing," she tried not to snap, conscious that things were already strained between them. "I'm just tired from work and you know Toby's had a bad cough again. Just have some thought."

Belle snatched up the empty can that he'd been using as an ashtray carrying it out to the kitchen bin. The kitchen worktop was littered with empty bottles and plates, and she fought the urge to scream. It was five in the morning, and the only thing she wanted to do was crawl into bed, curl up in a ball and fall asleep. She'd have to get Toby up in a couple of hours for school, but she knew that once she was asleep, she would struggle to get back up. She didn't like Toby seeing the flat in disarray, but today it felt too overwhelming and she gave up, crawling into bed still fully dressed.

"How was work?" Her head had barely touched the pillow when Ben appeared, slipping between the sheets.

"Fine," she stiffened as she felt his hands reach for her beneath the covers. "I'm really tired, Ben."
He ignored her, wriggling closer and she grimaced. If she were honest with herself, she had gone off Ben a long time ago, but she had been lonely and broke, and at times he could be good company. They'd only moved in together because it had been convenient. She had been looking for a new place as her rent had increased again for the third time in less than two years and he'd just so happened to be between places. It made sense to have someone to share the bills with, he'd reasoned, and it also meant on-tap childcare which allowed her to finally take the job that Katie's sister had been trying to talk her into for months. With two incomes, she had dared to imagine that she might be able to start making inroads with her mountain of debt. She was barely surviving as it was; if she kicked him out, she had no idea how she would keep her head above water.

"Ben, don't," she warned him as she felt his hot breath on the back of her neck. "You've got to get up in an hour for work. Just go to sleep."

"I'm not going," he said not taking the hint and pulling her back to him. "Two jobs got cancelled."

Despite her exhaustion, she spun around to face him. "Are you joking? You didn't say anything yesterday?"

"I forgot," he shrugged reaching for her again.

"Get off, Ben," any diplomacy was out the window as thoughts of their bills filled her mind. "How is Darren paying you then?"

"I'll have to sign on," he looked completely nonplussed. "He said he'll give me a call when he's got work for me."

Any chance of sleeping had disappeared with his revelation and Belle pushed his hands away, wriggling to sit up. She looked at him with undisguised contempt. "Ben, you need to be able to pay half the bills. That was the agreement when you moved in. It's your turn to get the food shop this week. How are you going to afford that with no pay?"

He turned his back to her in annoyance. "You're working. I don't see the problem."

"We need to eat, Ben," she could hear her voice rising hysterically, but was helpless to stop it. "That's the problem! You must have had some notice from Darren."

"You've got money," he hit back. "Don't be so dramatic."

"Oh, yeah," she shook her head slowly in sarcastic disbelief. "I'm rolling in it, Ben. Have you got any money saved at all?"

"No, you know I haven't," he huffed. "And anyway, it's hardly fair that I've been paying half the bills when there's two of you to pay for."

She'd been struggling to keep her temper up until that point, but his pettiness lit the fuse on the fury that had been bubbling away beneath the surface. She ripped the bed cover from him jumping to her feet. He barely flinched at her sudden movement, catching the duvet in his hand, and pulling it back over himself.

"Don't start," he warned in a low tone. "You're tired and emotional, Belle. Go to sleep and we'll talk about this in the morning."

"I'm not emotional," she shot back. "I'm furious with you, you selfish bastard!"

"Don't take this out on me," he sounded completely calm in the face of her anger. "You've been in a mood since you came back from your dad's. Just go to sleep before you wake Toby up and upset him."

Her blood was still racing furiously through her veins, but the mention of Toby forced her to temper her reaction. Toby had been flat out exhausted after their trip to Hampton Dale, and she had warned Ben as she left for work not to leave the flat for even a minute. He had claimed that he'd only nipped down to borrow some tobacco from a neighbour when she had confronted him, but as much as she wanted to believe him, she wasn't convinced.

Still, she thought to herself as her heartrate began to return to normal. *The last thing I want to do is get into a screaming match with him and upset Toby before school.*

She figured that she'd have all day to argue in private with Ben, and in the time that she'd been debating what to do for the best, his breathing had grown heavy. Realising he'd fallen asleep, she begrudgingly slipped back into bed.

Belle shut her eyes, willing her mind to go still and sleep, but she was wide awake from the burst of adrenaline, and she found her thoughts wandering back to yesterday's trip back home. She rolled onto her back as Ben began to snore and stared up at the ceiling.

The trip home had opened up old wounds as well as new ones, leaving her feeling angry and sad, confused and homesick. She'd shunned her father's attempts to talk to her, wanting him to try harder, but they'd been there barely an hour before his fiancée had started making a fuss about having to go out. Linda had been acting nice as pie in front of her father, but Belle could see right through the brassy woman. She'd followed her and Toby outside at Frank's insistence, but instead of making a fuss of Toby and showing him the best gap in the hedge to see the lambs, she'd gruffly pointed up the lane and then hovered in the garden, fussing about with her washing on the line. Toby had found a tennis ball in the hedge to play with, and the evil old cow had had the audacity to shout at him for hitting the rickety old security camera on the side of the house.

Well, Belle chewed her lip. *She didn't quite shout, but there was definitely an edge to her tone.*

She didn't like the woman, and the tiny scrap of possibility that she and Frank could build a bridge had been well and truly scuppered by the woman's presence. Seeing her dad looking so old and vulnerable had lowered her defences, but they had shot back up when he did nothing to stop his heartless harpy shooing them all away like cold callers who'd overstayed their welcome.

She felt the tell-tale sting of tears prickle at the back of her eyes and she squeezed them shut defiantly. She knew she hadn't been the easiest teenager when her mum had passed away, but her father had been the adult. He should have been there for her. Since having Toby, she had firmly placed the blame at Frank's feet knowing that she would walk through fire to be there for her son. Instead of seeing her behaviour as a symptom of her teenaged grief and heartache, he'd pushed her further away with his harsh temper until she had packed up and left home at the first opportunity, thinking she was an adult when she was still just a child. The first few years were tough, and if at any time he had begged her to come home, she would have in a heartbeat. Anything would have been better than the dingy bedsits that she had found herself living in through a combination of bad luck and poor choices. But then at nineteen, her luck had changed. By some twist of fate, she had landed work as a model, moving to London and for a few years, everything was charmed and golden. She'd made plenty of friends and dated fancy men, she'd been earning good money and had spent it, and then some, like there was no tomorrow. But then she'd fallen pregnant with Toby. Her work had to be put on hold and her friends from that world disappeared with it. She'd foolishly married Toby's father in a grim registry office wedding, probably out of fear of loneliness, but then he'd taken off when their son was barely three months old, leaving her in a flat she couldn't afford with a ton of debt that he'd taken out in her name. She'd spent a year on benefits, which was hard enough with a new baby in London but excruciating for someone used to living a champagne, designer lifestyle, no matter how fleeting it had been. Before she'd struck lucky with modelling, she'd only worked in retail and catering, and the hours were so antisocial that she struggled to get a job that worked around Toby, and when she did have one she struggled to keep it, having to take time off for childcare and sickness, or having her hours cut forcing her to look elsewhere. It was a vicious circle, and a constant battle to keep herself afloat. If she kicked Ben out now, and she really wanted to, it would mean she'd have to give up this job and look for something else. She didn't love the job, but it paid a hell of a lot more than she'd get in retail or some factory, and the hours were perfect. She got to pick Toby up and spend time with him, rather than running around like a headless chicken trying to figure out who could watch him when she got saddled with a weekend shift.

Her mind flickered to her brother Will. He had been back in the country for a while now, and it had briefly crossed her mind that he might be able to help her out, but as quickly as the thought came to her, she shook it away. She loved Will, but he had his own busy life; she couldn't expect him to help. She knew that there was no magic solution to her problems, and no amount of pining for her family would make them any closer. That ship had sailed long ago. The only person she could rely on was herself.

Will

Sheets of rain belted down almost horizontal as Will dashed from the entrance to his apartment to the waiting cab. The car idled just metres away, but he was soaked through by the time he slid into the backseat slamming the door behind him. The driver gave him a sympathetic grin in the rear-view mirror as Will pulled at the sodden fabric in a bid to stop it clinging to his chest. The damage was already done, and he resigned himself to the fact he was stuck in a soaking wet shirt for the night. He turned his attention to the streets of London as the taxi whisked him through the dark, miserable night and marvelled that out of all the places he had lived in he had chosen a rainy, British city to finally settle down in. As he gazed out at the bright lights of the traffic, blurry beneath the torrential rain, he felt a familiar yearning for sunnier climes and new faces.

"What's the matter with you?" Craig asked him hours later as he set down another round of drinks on the table.

They were out on the town with Craig's friends. The abysmal weather had dampened their big plans to bar-hop and instead they were crammed into a booth at a cheap-and-cheerful bar for the evening.

"I'm just a bit tired." Will replied honestly. "It's been chaos in work. It'll be worth it if the magazine is happy with the shoot."

He had been enjoying being his own boss, but it was starting to feel monotonous. He opened his mouth to voice his thoughts aloud as Craig dropped into the space next to Will, but something stopped him. Instead Will rested his head against his broad shoulder, waiting for the feeling of contentment to settle over his frazzled mind. His eyes were itching with fatigue and his clothes, now dry from the heat of the packed bar, felt constrictive and uncomfortable. As nice as Craig's crowd were, Will yearned for some solitude, a shower, and his bed.

"Any chance you're ready to go home?" Will asked. "Sorry to be a bore, but I'm dead on my feet."

Before he had a chance to reply, Craig's best friend Kev flew over to the table and slammed a tray down with gusto, causing liquid to slosh from the tiny shot glasses.

"Shots! Shots! Shots!" He cried with drunken excitement and the rest of the group descended on the table, knocking back the vile alcohol.

Will eyed the remaining glass, feeling his stomach churn at the thought.

"Will?" Craig spotted his hesitation and handed him the glass. "C'mon! Shot!"

He laughed politely and shook his head, but Craig's arm stayed stubbornly outstretched. Reluctantly, Will took the glass and drained it grimacing at the bitter aftertaste. The table erupted into rowdy applause before the song changed and a chorus of whoops went up. Will felt himself being dragged in the direction of the dancefloor and he pasted a smile on his face, even as his heart sank at the thought of prolonging the night. After a sweaty hour of shaking his hips on the sticky dancefloor, Will slipped away from the crowd. Every bone in his body felt drained of life and he headed back to their table.

"Hey!"

Will felt a hand grab at him through the packed bodies and he braced himself for confrontation, immediately relaxing when he turned to find himself face-to-face with Raya. She pulled him into a tight hug and he temporarily forgot his tiredness, sweeping her off her feet to spin her around.

"Hey!" He exclaimed once he had set her back down.

"What are you doing in this neck of the woods?"

Raya held out the soaking jacket in her hands and he recoiled from the wet leather.

"Taking refuge. It's lashing down outside," she grimaced, dumping her belongings on the table, and flicking open the camera on her phone to check the damage to her make-up. "I think I'm going to call it a night and go home."

"Same," Will agreed. "Let me finish my drink and we'll get a cab."

"This weather makes me crave somewhere hot and sunny," she groaned.

"I feel that on so many levels," Will agreed. "I genuinely thought I was growing up and settling down. I was even thinking about trying to get a mortgage, but it's starting to feel like Groundhog Day. I just feel like taking off again."

"I love working together, but I've been looking at flights back to Oz," Raya admitted. "Fancy it?"

Her words kickstarted something inside him. With the thoughts of turquoise waves on golden shores, the tug of wanderlust he'd been trying to ignore resurfaced stronger than ever. The need to escape had always been inside him; leaving Hampton Dale at eighteen desperate for something that the sleepy, little village couldn't offer him. He had thought that the bright lights and bustling night life of Manchester were what he needed, but even then, living his best student life, he'd longed for something more. His mother's death had been the trigger for his first long-term trip. He had always figured that he'd settle down eventually, but the world was a big place. He'd fallen into a comfortable cycle of work, travel, repeat, and somehow his twenties had passed in a happy blur. The impressive debt he'd amassed and the niggle that he was getting too old to live out of a backpack had been the only reasons that he had decided to come home and have a go at building some semblance of a normal life. But the novelty was beginning to wear off.

"Sounds tempting," Will agreed. "How long are you thinking of going for?"

"Six weeks initially," she grinned, knowing that an extended holiday was always the start of months of globetrotting. "I just need to pay off one credit card, and then I'll look for flights. Head back via Japan."

"Oh nice," Will hadn't managed to fit Japan into his itinerary on any other trips. "I'd definitely be up for Japan."

Raya's eyes widened with excitement. "We could even start there. See the big cities, then maybe head to Shikoku?"

"Aargh!" Will jokingly covered his ears. "I'm so tempted right now."

"It's happening," she laughed, but then her expression turned serious. "Oh, crap, I really wanted to go this summer, but it's your dad's wedding, isn't it?"

"It's the beginning of June," Will replied.

Raya looked relieved. "Perfect timing. Have you spoke with him since?"

Will shook his head. "No. Rose has texted a couple of times. She's spoke with them and they're answering the landline now."

Will had told Raya about the alleged phone issues, and about how standoffish Linda had been. Raya had agreed that it sounded a bit off, especially when Will had mentioned his dad's plans to sell off part of the estate.

"Well, that's a positive," she said. "Did your brother look into the whole will thing?"

"Not sure," he shrugged. "I'm still no wiser as to what we get, what we don't get. It feels a bit morbid and callous to ask."

"But if your mum wanted you four to have it," Raya gave him a stern look. "It's not right that your dad's selling it off."

"I'll pluck up the nerve to ask Tim," Will promised. "Or more accurately to ask Rose to ask Tim for me. I'm sure Tim will know to the penny what we're due."

Before Raya could respond, Will caught sight of Craig weaving his way through the crowded bar towards them. "Raya, you remember Craig?"

"Nice to see you," Raya smiled up at him.

"And you," Craig nodded. "Do you want a drink?"

Raya waved a hand dismissively. "Thanks, but I think I'm about to head home?"

Craig eyed Will suspiciously and reached for his hand. "Why are you sat down? We're having fun."

"I'm just exhausted, sorry," Will replied. "Do you mind if I head off? I'll leave the door unlocked for you."

Craig covered Will's hand with his own. "You can't go! Dan's just got another round in. We're going to go to Kev's after last orders."

"Sounds good," Will answered diplomatically. "But I really am shattered. Do you mind if I call it a night?"

Craig's face fell. "Please?"

Will opened his mouth to object, but then he thought better of it. Craig had only just stopped sulking about him going to Hampton Dale without him, and that had been almost three weeks ago. He really didn't want to upset him; another weekend with an atmosphere would be unbearable. Raya frowned at the exchange and Will prayed that she wouldn't get involved, knowing how outspoken she could be.

Another couple of hours won't kill me if it makes him happy, Will told himself.

"Yeah, ok," he agreed reluctantly. "I'll see Raya to a

cab, and I'll be back."

He could feel his friend's eyes burning into the back of his head as she followed him to the door. Outside rain was pouring from the sky in sheets and brave revellers ducked in-and-out of doorways trying to avoid the downpour.

"If you're tired," she started the moment they drew to a halt huddled under the bar's canopy. "Just tell him you're going."

Will held back a sigh. He knew she wouldn't understand and would berate him for being a pushover.

"I'm not that tired," he lied. "Is that a free taxi? Jump in, quick before we drown. Text me when you're home!"

He could sense Raya was dying to say something as he hugged her goodbye, and he quickly shut the car door before she could. He flattened himself against the wall beneath the canopy to watch the car disappear into the night, and as he did, he felt a strong urge to jump into the next cab. He pictured himself swinging by Craig's apartment just long enough to grab his passport and a bag, and even though he knew it was just a wild fantasy, he could almost feel the weight of his problems float away.

Tim

On the other side of London, Tim darted from the station; his umbrella flapping uselessly in the gale. He surveyed the taxi queue feeling his irritation grow at the short line of commuters huddled against the wall of the building for shelter.

His direct reports, based all over the country, came to the city once a quarter for social events. The company paid for dinner, drinks and an overnight stay in a fancy hotel, and even though he lived locally he could have still taken advantage of the offer. The plan had been for Eleanor to accompany him, but she had bowed out at the last minute, anxious over Bea's temperature. Tim had tried to reason with her; they were leaving the kids with her mother, Bea was just teething, they would come home early, but Eleanor wasn't having any of it. It was a growing source of contention between them, although unspoken. Eleanor had been the one who had wanted children, he had always been quite honest that children never really figured in his life plan, but it had been important to her. It wasn't that he didn't love his children, he thought to himself as he reflected on the atmosphere between him and Eleanor after their slight disagreement, it was just he found them such an inconvenience. The change to the dynamic of their relationship hadn't been as marked when they had only had Hugo, but Bea's arrival had tipped their previously charmed life into a less desirable chaos. He'd been looking forward to spending some time with Eleanor this evening and he couldn't help but feel slighted that she'd put the children first *again.* The last few months in work had been stressful, plus he'd had the added inconvenience of the trip back to Hampton Dale and his sister calling him constantly about the most mundane matters. All he'd wanted was to enjoy a night out with good food and wine, and a bit of attention from his own wife. He couldn't see how that was unreasonable.

He arrived at the restaurant a little behind schedule and saw that most of his team were already seated.

"Who are we waiting for?" He asked as he looked around the table.

"Emma Boucher," Lisette, his head of operations in the South-East, informed him before her eyes flickered behind him. "Oh, speak of the devil."

Tim turned to follow Lisette's gaze feeling his pulse quicken at the sight of the newcomer. Emma Boucher was five-foot-eight-inches of tanned limbs, glossy caramel hair and the smile of an angel, and the last time Tim had seen her, she had left his head spinning following a very boozy Christmas party. He felt a rush of desire at just the memory of her brushing her full lips across his, tantalisingly slow before she'd disappeared into the evening.

"Emma!" Lisette rose to her feet kissing the woman's cheeks with gusto. "There's a space by Tim."

Tim stood up to greet her. "Emma, how are you?"

"I'm good," she replied. "It's been forever."

"It's good to see you again," he said politely, trying to ignore the way the heady scent of her perfume made him want to bury his face in her neck.

A slow smile spread across her lips as she sat down tearing her gaze from his to accept the proffered wine from Lisette. "I can't believe it's been three months since I was here."

"It was a great night," he said unable to resist probing to see whether she remembered her forwardness that night.

"So, you're alone tonight?" She raised her wine glass to

her full cherry-red mouth, and he knew in that moment that not only did she remember, but she was utterly unapologetic for any line she had crossed.

He caught the eyes of the rest of the team watching the interaction, and he quickly turned back to the table before Emma could draw him in any further. Tim did his best to pay equal attention to each of his employees throughout the meal but found himself slipping into quiet asides with the delectable woman over the course of the evening. They kept the conversation deliberately light, but it wasn't long before they'd looped back to that night.

"It was such a great party," Emma said in a teasing tone and he knew he wasn't imagining the flirtatious twinkle in her eyes. "Such a shame I'm not in London very often. It might have been interesting to follow a few things up from that night."

"Such as?" He held her gaze challengingly.

She slowly swept her hair to one side exposing the creamy skin of her shoulder, and he felt his breath catch in his throat at the thought of her naked. "I remember a very insightful conversation with you towards the end of the night."

He leaned forward keen for her to say more, but James the head of operations up in Scotland chose that moment to call across the table to them. "You two seem cosy! Care to share with the class?"

"Sorry James," she replied without skipping a beat. "Caught us talking shop again. Very naughty."

Tim held back a groan at the deliberate purr she added to the end of her sentence.

There wasn't a single thing about Emma that wasn't sexy. Why did she have to be so tempting?

Tim forced himself to give his undivided attention to the others for the rest of the evening, and it wasn't until they were all parting ways, tipsy and full of great food, that he got chance to speak to Emma again.

"It's been lovely to catch up with the team," she said looking up at him from beneath a sweep of dark lashes. "Are you staying at the hotel tonight?"

His heart sped up, and he berated himself for cancelling his reservation.

"I'm not," he replied regretfully.

"I'm sure everyone will be making use of the bar this evening," she said. "Care to join us?"

Tim turned to look at his team of Operation Managers, all slightly worse for wear from the free-flowing booze, and he knew that it would be wise to decline. It was all he could do to keep his hands off the stunning young woman, and he knew that a couple more drinks would lower his inhibitions and that wasn't a risk he was willing to take.

"Not tonight," he shook his head. "I'll leave you all to it."

The look of disappointment on her face almost had him changing his mind, but he resolutely turned away knowing it would be foolish to stay. He waited for his taxi alone, watching the enticing shape of her until she disappeared into a cab with the rest of the team, and alongside the relief that he felt that he hadn't crossed any line, he felt a tingle of excitement that he hadn't felt in a long time.

Rose

Rose was bone tired; the kind of exhaustion that starts in the morning when you peel your eyes open, that makes your body feel like concrete, and your soul feel weary no matter how many hours you'd led unconscious in bed the night before.

There was, however, an advantage to being bone-tired, Rose reasoned as she stared out of the grimy window of the bus. She no longer felt weepy and overwhelmed at every slight inconvenience or minor upset. She no longer cared.

The tipping point, she believed, had been the week after her visit home. Despite the mixed feelings from the day, she had enjoyed her lunch with Gareth, and she'd gone to sleep with her overactive mind playing out far-fetched scenarios where they met up again. A hellish week in work followed by her phone being cut off because her direct debit had bounced had brought her tumbling back to reality. She was angry at herself for her foolish daydreams, and there were a million worries circling her frazzled mind; guilt over her detached family, guilt that she'd let down her mother and that her father was being fleeced, worry about the boys at University, worry about meeting all her direct debits this month, worry about how she'd been messing up at work and an overwhelming loneliness as she realised with weary acceptance that she would never meet anyone who would love her. The thoughts spiralled through her head until she had finally fallen asleep in the early hours of the morning. She'd slept until her alarm, something she couldn't remember ever doing before, and she struggled to sit up in bed waiting for the sense of impending dread to return, but that morning, she found that it didn't come. The tiredness stayed with her and instead of fading away with her first shot of caffeine, it grew like a grey mist starting in her chest before working its way through her body and into every limb. She had glanced at the final demand that had been the reason for her panic last night and when the anxiety didn't return, she realised that she didn't care anymore. She felt distant as if it were happening to someone else.

Rose wondered if she should have felt some relief at the absence of her agonising anxiety. Maybe she should feel concerned that she just felt nothing. She was conscious that she *should* be feeling a certain way, but she just couldn't seem to summon up the energy to feel anything. Instead of dread when her new manager announced that she was flipping the new recruits onto outbound calls, she barely flinched.

"We were hired as Inbound Sales," Lena protested as the team were taken through a quick presentation on the difference.

The job that had they had applied for had been cross-selling loans and credit cards to XZ Finance customers who had called in to the Customer Service department for help. Rose had quickly learned that Customer Services would then resolve their query before bouncing the call over to Rose's team, usually without bothering to tell them why they were being transferred. After just weeks in the job, they were now being told to call existing XZ customers to try to increase the centre's sales.

"We're trying something new," the unsmiling manager replied curtly. "If you don't like it, you know where the door is."

Lena returned to her desk without a word but rolled her eyes at Rose in a show of defiance. They obediently logged into the system and within an hour, Rose was close to downing tools as she was sworn at and hung up on with every successful connection.

What is the point? She wondered as the manager prowled between their desks scowling at them if they dared voice their frustrations. *I should just leave before I'm fired.*

As the week went on, she began to grow more despondent as her colleagues began to make sales and the likelihood of quitting being taken out of her hands grew more and more likely.

"Hello, is it possible to speak with Mrs Palmer?" She began in a tone as upbeat and cheerful as she could muster when the line connected.

"Who is this?" Came the cool response.

"Hello, good morning to you," Rose parroted in the sing-song voice they were encouraged to use. "My name is Rose and I'm calling from XZ Finance. How are you today?"

"Fine," the woman's tone was guarded, but she hadn't hung up. Yet.

It was further than Rose had got all morning, so she pressed on.

"That's great. I'm calling as we've got a special introductory offer on credit cards. Can I ask who your current credit card provider is?"

"I don't have credit cards," the woman answered snootily, and Rose could sense her slipping away.

"Really? Wow, that's great to hear!" Rose exclaimed. "Have you ever had a credit card in the past?"

"I don't see..." The woman sounded angry now at the intrusive questioning and Rose couldn't blame her.

"The reason why I ask," Rose cut in quickly before the woman could hang up on her. "Is there's a lot of fraud going on at the moment, particularly online. Credit cards offer you and your money greater protection against this."

Rose hesitated and scanned her eyes across the script they had been given. She didn't usually make it to this point, and she was so surprised she had that she had lost her train of thought. A hand stretched from behind Rose to poke the script pinned in front of her. Rose looked up and met Lena's eyes, smiling appreciatively.

"Keep going!" Lena hissed through clenched teeth.

"Fraudsters are getting clever and it's scary how quickly they can get access to your details. For example, did you know more than 17 million people *in this country* were victims of cyber-crime last year?"

"Say 'isn't that scary'?" Lena hissed.

"Isn't that scary?" Rose parroted.

"Mmmm," the woman made a noncommittal noise.

"Could you imagine how devastating it would be to have your bank account drained?" Rose continued. "People have been left without money to pay their bills and to buy food. It's terrifying and emotionally stressful waiting for the bank to investigate. In many cases, the money is gone forever and there is no way of getting it back. Now let me tell you how a credit card works differently in this scenario..."

Lena nodded her head encouragingly and rolled her hands to signal Rose should keep talking. Rose tried to keep up the enthusiastic tone as she read out a paragraph about the consumer credit act to Mrs Palmer.

"Now say 'doesn't that sound great?'," Lena whispered.

"Doesn't that sound great?"

"I suppose..." Mrs Palmer still didn't sound impressed.

"Now, as well as *all* that protection and peace of mind, what if I told you I could offer you *zero* interest for the first three months on anything you spend?" Rose couldn't believe how far she'd got in the script. "As well as offering you a guaranteed way to protect your money, there's no charge at all for this card. How does that sound?"

"That's not bad."

"It's not, is it?" Lena mouthed theatrically. "Now what I'm going to do..."

Rose repeated Lena's words in a cheery tone.

"Is take some details to get this sent out to you."

Rose obediently chirped Lena's words at the customer.

"Oh no!" Mrs Palmer interrupted. "I don't want a credit card."

"You don't need to sign up to anything today," Rose read. "All we do today is conduct a quick approval check and I'll get all the information sent out to you. That way, you can read through the information yourself over a nice cup of tea. If there's anything you're not happy with, you can cancel this at *any* time for absolutely no charge at all. All I need to do is read this compliance information and I'll get the pack out to you."

"I don't want to take anything out," Mrs Palmer protested. "Can you just send me the information?"

"We do need to complete the quick check before we can send it out," Rose said apologetically. "But like I said, if you change your mind, it's quick, easy and free to cancel. There is no fee for this, Mrs Palmer, so there's nothing to worry about."

"Oh," Rose could tell the woman felt railroaded and she began to feel her resolve to sell to her slipping, but Lena was jabbing her finger at the sheet in front of her. Rose knew she that if she didn't make this sale her days at XZ were numbered and she *really* needed this job. She thought about the boiler that was just one more reset away from packing in, her overdraft, her credit cards, the boys' birthdays coming up. She needed this.

"So, what I'm going to do now," Rose took a deep breath and pushed on, ignoring the guilt she felt. "Is give you my details. Do you have a pen to hand? That way, if you have any questions, you can give me a call when you get your paperwork."

Lena's mouth broke into a wide smile and she rewarded Rose with a double thumbs-up. Rose pressed on through the legal jargon before clicking the submit button that would complete Mrs Palmer's application. Rose barely flinched as the search started; XZ Finance was the offshoot of a popular mainstream bank and their products were specifically designed for those with adverse credit histories, hence the extortionate interest rates.

They'd probably even give one to me, Rose thought wryly as she tied up the call.

"Yay!" Lena embraced her as she hung up the phone. "Well done, Rose! Now you've managed your first cold sale they'll start rolling in! The first is definitely the hardest."

"Do you ever feel bad?" She asked Lena later as they packed up their belongings to leave when the shift was finally over. "Selling to people who clearly don't want or understand what they're getting?"

"My father used to say, 'once among the crows, you do as they do'," she pulled a face. "At the moment, I need this job. It's just a stepping-stone to something better and then one day, when I'm in charge I'll make the way we do business better, but for now it's a case of needs must."

"That's a wise sentiment, but I still don't know," Rose tilted her head to one side regarding her pretty, younger friend. "It feels so wrong."

"I feel bad too," Lena admitted with sudden seriousness. "But what choice do we have? I'm skint, you're skint. As the saying goes 'Life is like a shit sandwich. The more bread you have the less shit you've got to eat'."

For the first time in weeks, Rose found herself laughing; a from-the-gut, belly laugh that made tears run down her face as she gasped for breath.

"Are you laughing?" Lena regarded her with concern. "Or crying?"

And Rose realised she really wasn't sure anymore.

Belle

Belle glanced up at the tiny strip window, the only natural source of light in the back room of the club. She could see the sky had lightened from an inky black to a dark grey and she rubbed her eyes wearily with the back of her hand. There were no phones allowed out in the club, and she could never get used to the frustration of trying to guess how much time had passed on the shift. She checked her makeup in the mirror, swiping away a smudge of eyeliner from beneath her lashes.

God, look at the state of me.

She grimaced at her reflection. In the harsh light of the manager's office, her striking green eyes looked dull and flat beneath heavy kohl liner and the tight, black dress looked cheap. Her shoulder-length red hair hung around her pale, bare shoulders in lacquered ringlets and she turned away, disgusted by what she saw. The muted lights of the club masked the ugly tackiness of both the décor and the costumes of the women who worked here. Seeing her image reflected in the looking glass reminded her of how far she'd fallen.

"Belle!" A brash blonde in a sequin G-string barrelled through the Staff-Only door. "Lucy's been over ten minutes in the private room and he's only paid for seven."

Belle nodded to acknowledge that she'd heard as she headed back out onto the floor. In the three months, she had been working as a hostess at Fantasies she'd quickly picked up the best way to keep the dancers in line and avoid any trouble. She glanced around the club as she entered, mentally clocking where everyone was and any new arrivals. Casey had followed her back out onto the floor and Belle quickly directed her towards a lone gentleman nursing an almost empty glass. She hurried over to one of the private rooms discreetly slipping through the curtain to signal to Lucy that her time was up. By this time of the night, some of the girls were wasted which is why it was Belle's job to keep everything running smoothly, enforce the club rules, and maximise the night's profits.

Her job was a solitary one, and she often found herself gazing enviously over at the dancers, chatting and flirting with the customers, or slipping off to the toilets discreetly in pairs to bitch about other dancers or in some cases, snort half their night's takings up their noses. Belle's job relied on her having her wits about her, so staying sober was a necessity. The first few shifts hadn't been so bad as she concentrated on picking up the job, but as soon as she had worked out a little routine for herself, the rot of mind-numbing repetitiveness set in and the biggest challenge in her shift was a tie between staying awake and staying sane. She thought about quitting maybe ten times a shift; when her eyes burned with fatigue and her mind screamed with boredom. Hard physical work she could cope with. Her body could grow accustomed to strenuous labour, but her mind craved stimulation and the monotony was torturous. She'd done all kinds of jobs since leaving home at sixteen; waitressing, bar work, retail before she'd started modelling. It had mainly been catalogue work, but she'd had a few national adverts to her name. She'd naively planned to keep modelling when she'd had the baby, but the irregular hours and travel just didn't work when you were a single mother with a support network of zero. Her last job had been on the make-up counter of a department store before she'd been sacked for taking too much time off due to childcare. As much as she hated her job at Fantasies, it was a necessity.

When you're going through hell, keep going.

It was the first week of the Easter holidays and for once, childcare wasn't going to be an issue. This thought, alongside the memory of the money she had tucked away for Toby's coveted Xbox kept her going until the club emptied of the last few stragglers. In the locker room, she stripped off the dress and heels replacing them with leggings, a hoodie, and trainers, scrubbing the heavy make-up from her face with a baby wipe. The chilly morning air hit her face, waking her a little, but it was only temporary, and she felt her eyes drooping again as she waited for her taxi to pull up. As much as working nights was a solution to her child-care issues, school holidays were tough. She usually managed to get maybe three hours during the day when Toby was off school, forcing herself to stay awake so he wasn't stuck on his own playing on the tablet. The taxi journey took just fifteen minutes at this time of day, but the vibrations of the car were hypnotic. As always, her mind was puzzling over a way out of the vicious circle of having no money and no childcare when her thoughts became fuzzy as her eyelids drooped shut.

Something heavy on her leg jerked her back into consciousness and her eyes flew open in surprise. The taxi had pulled to a stop in the layby of the carriageway in the short space of time that she'd drifted off and the beady-eyed driver had turned in his seat to face her. He pulled away the meaty hand from her leg, but his narrow, blue eyes were still fixed hungrily on her face.

"What the hell are you doing?" She yelled, yanking her leg away from him. "You pervert!"

"Calm down," disappointment shadowed the man's eyes, but he didn't look remotely concerned at her accusation. "I was just checking you hadn't overdosed."

Anger ripped through Belle's body giving her a boost of adrenaline. She knew from their surroundings that she was only a five-minute walk from home now, and she threw the car door open.

"You can go to hell if you think I'm paying you," she spat as she clambered out of the car.

"Oh, come on, love," he rolled his eyes but made no attempt to stop her, probably weighing up his lost fare against the odds of her calling the police.

She stormed off up the hard shoulder in the opposite direction, still furious, and he pulled off without a backward glance.

What a piece of trash, she fumed to herself as she marched up the road.

She hated feeling vulnerable and she suppressed the fear she'd felt, not allowing herself to acknowledge it, focussing instead on all the injustices that meant she had to put herself in situations like this time and time again. It was one more thing in the never-ending line of 'if only's' that churned through her mind daily. If only she had child-care. If only she had a good job. If only she could afford a car.

If only I could just go home.

She hadn't heard from anyone except Will since the Sunday that they'd all gone back to Bluebell Farm. She'd known deep down not to expect anything from them, but she'd hoped Rose at least would want to stay in touch. Somehow seeing them all had made her feel worse, reminding her of how broken and lonely she'd felt back when the doctors had told her mother that there was nothing further they could do. The boys and Rose started coming home on weekends, people from the village were constantly in and out of the house, stopping in to see Kathleen bearing home-cooked food for the freezer or flowers and well wishes, but nobody was there for her. She was the one who had sat beside her mum's bedside, brought her drinks and talked to her into the night, and she had been the one with a gaping hole in her life when her mother had passed away and everyone else had returned to their own busy lives. She closed her eyes temporarily against the sting of hurt and exhaustion.

As she approached the single carriageway that zipped past the estate, she could barely summon the energy to keep moving. She stopped to wait for a van to pass swaying violently in the rush of the slipstream. The blast of air made her eyes water and she blinked furiously, trying to clear her vision. She swiped the back of her hand across her face and glanced quickly left and then right, listening out for the tell-tale rumble of traffic around the hidden corner. Her whole body was aching with fatigue now and she moved her feet forward wearily.

Almost home.

The roar of an engine, a blur of metallic black and a warm, dusty blast of air hit her all at once. Everything was too fast for her blunted senses before a kick of adrenaline cleared the haze. A temporary heightened awareness took over, slowing down time and she was trapped, helplessly aware of the split-second before the car hit her. She heard the sickening crunch and saw in vivid high-definition the horror on the driver's face, before an excruciating pain exploded within her and everything went black.

Will

Will made the dash from the car park to the apartment as quickly as he could, but he was still soaked through when he reached the door. He unlocked the mailbox in the foyer and tucked the letters under his arm, taking the stairs two-at-a-time until he reached Craig's floor.

My floor, he corrected himself in his head.

He was still finding it strange to be living with someone as something other than flat-mates or a sub-let. He was so used to being alone with only his own needs to consider that the sudden responsibility of another person's feelings sometimes felt stifling. He sniffed the air as he opened the flat door, his mouth watering at the smell of Szechuan Chicken.

It was good to have someone else cooking though.

"Mmmmm," he called as he kicked off his shoes. "Something smells good."

He carried the mail through to the kitchen and was surprised to see Craig's sister and her fiancé sat at the table.

"Hi," Craig beamed at him. "I was beginning to think I'd have to put your dinner in the microwave."

Will flashed him a perplexed smile before moving to hug their guests in greeting. "What do we owe the pleasure, guys?"

"We're flying from Gatwick tomorrow ridiculously early," Kelly explained. "We were just going to get a taxi, but Craig said it would be cheaper to come up on the train today and sleep over."

"Where are you off?" Will feigned polite interest even as he felt his heart sink at yet another evening of socialising.

And where are they even going to sleep?

Kelly launched into an overly detailed account of their

trip to Barcelona, and Will smiled and nodded in all the right places as he waited politely for her to finish talking so he could excuse himself to take a shower. It wasn't that he minded Kelly and Dean, he reasoned when he was finally below the steamy jet of the power shower. He was just tired and had been looking forward to a quiet evening. He wished Craig had thought to give him some warning.

"How much does it cost to live here?" Kelly asked later when Craig had explained that they could take the bedroom and he and Will would crash on the sofa. The flat had a small second bedroom, but it was currently set up as a wardrobe and ironing room.

She choked on her drink in surprise when Craig told her. "That's crazy! You could get a massive house for that back home!"

"I know," Craig grimaced mopping up the wine she'd sprayed across the table. "That's London though. I could never afford to buy here."

"Have you thought any more about putting an offer in on that house in Mum's street?" Kelly asked.

"Not yet," Craig replied ignoring the confused look Will was throwing at him. "Will and I need to sit down and work out affordability and all first, see a mortgage advisor..."

"Uh," Will interrupted. "And discuss why we would buy a house there when both our jobs are in London!"

Craig laughed oblivious to Will's thinly veiled annoyance. "Oh, I know. I was thinking we could rent it out short term until we were ready to move. That's jumping the gun though, we have to have the dreaded money talk first."

Will stared at his boyfriend in disbelief, but if he noticed he masked it well. Kelly and Dean shifted awkwardly in their seats at the atmosphere making Will feel obliged to change the subject. The conversation would keep for when they didn't have an audience.

****

"What the hell, Will?" Raya looked aghast. "Why didn't you say anything?"

They were sat in the studio space they had rented for personal photoshoots, unboxing some props. He hated doing Hallmark-card type shoots, but edgy music and fashion shoots were few-and-far-between, and they both had bills to pay.

"I couldn't say anything in front of his sister," Will told her defensively.

"Well, you'll have to put him straight," Raya said decisively, hand on hip as she stared him down.

Will grimaced. "I will. I'll talk to him tonight."

Raya pulled a face. "We both know how rubbish you are at standing up for yourself."

Will rolled his eyes in response, but he had no comeback. They both knew she had a point. He knew he was a people-pleaser; he hated upsetting anyone.

"I'm going to have to say something," Will grimaced. "Even if I did want to get a mortgage and a three-bedroomed-house in Suburbia, no bank is going to give me that kind of money. Not with my credit history."

Raya's glare softened as she rested a hand on his shoulder. "If that's what you want, Will, I'm sure you'll figure out a way, but I can't help feeling that you're not happy."

She didn't say "with Craig", but she didn't have to. It hung there in the air between them, and Will sighed turning back to the box of props.

"Maybe it's not the worst idea," he said quietly. "Maybe Craig has got a point. We're throwing money away paying rent; we'll never be able to buy in London."

"Buying a property is a good idea," Raya agreed

carefully. "But with Craig? You've barely been together six months. Not to be rude, but it feels a little mid-life crisis-y."

"It's not a mid-life crisis. I'm thirty-five!"

Raya waved a hand dismissively. "A whatever-life-crisis. Whatever it was that made you feel like you had to put down roots, stick at a job, settle down with whoever."

"It's hardly a crisis, Raya," he defended himself. "Everyone has to grow up eventually. I can't live out of a backpack forever. Who the hell gets to my age without ever having their own place or a job for longer than six months? It's weird."

"Who cares what you do?" She exclaimed. "If six months saving for six months abroad makes you happy, that's awesome. If being married to the same person and working the same job for fifty years makes you happy, I'm happy for you. But forcing yourself into something because you feel it's expected of you, that sucks."

Her words echoed around his head, tangling with his already jumbled thoughts and feelings. He'd spent years chasing the next adventure, but the older he became, the more he couldn't shake the feeling of hollowness that followed him wherever he went. He'd thought it was his soul telling him that it was time to put down roots and he'd done just that, immersing himself into civilisation on a permanent basis. Job, check. Flat, check. Finance Agreements, check. Serious boyfriend, check.

That's what everyone else his age did, so why wouldn't that emptiness disappear?

Will shook his head to chase away the thoughts. "Right, let's park this for now and get today over with."

Raya forced a professional smile on her face, despite her heart aching for him. They'd been best friends since their paths had first crossed seven years earlier and Raya knew their connection was deeper than their shared profession and their love of travelling. After a long day of photographing babies and toddlers was over, she waved him away, offering to stay and lock up. She watched him getting into his car, the stress of the pending confrontation etched across his face. He might look like he had it all together; the looks, the job, the life, to the world outside, but to her, he just looked like a lost little boy.

Rose

A bang wrenched Rose from her sleep and she shot up in bed; wide awake, heart pounding. Hushed, slurred voices echoed in the hallway and she released her held breath at the familiar sounds. It was just the boys, home from their night out. She wriggled back beneath the duvet, but her pulse was still racing, and she lay awake, listening to their noise. A different voice, one she didn't know, floated up and she frowned.

Have they brought girls back?

She felt a stab of irritation at their lack of respect, and she pulled the cover over her head, hoping to drown out the noise, but her ears had tuned into their din and she could make out of almost every word. Someone fumbled with the switches in the hallway, flooding the landing with light, and exasperated she slipped out of bed to close the door. Rose reached for her phone almost crying out in frustration at the illuminated numbers on the display; she had to be up for work in a few hours. The boys *knew* she was working Saturday and it rankled her that they had no consideration. She had been so looking forward to them both being home for the full two weeks of the Easter holidays, yet somehow their presence had felt overwhelming. Working her long, anti-social shifts was bad enough without coming home to a messy house, an overflowing washing basket and empty cupboards.

She'd spent her whole life being their over-worked, under-appreciated mother, putting their wellbeing and happiness above all else in her life, at the cost of having a career of her own and probably at the cost of her marriage. Why would Phil have been happy with the slightly overweight frump at home when he had lithe, newly qualified colleagues in stiletto-heels fawning over him at work? Being on her own had given Rose the space she needed to take stock of her life and suddenly the sacrifices she'd happily made seemed less like choices and more like a gaping hole in her life that she would never get back. She knew neither Tom nor Jack had *asked* her to do any of this for them, but she couldn't help feeling resentful of the opportunities at their fingertips. Both boys were good students, and she was proud of them, but she couldn't help feeling she'd given up too much, been too much of a martyr. Somehow, she'd gone from wearing her 'middle-class stay-at-home Mum' badge with pride to feeling like a lonely, washed-up forty-year-old with no social life, no family and a job that she hated. She couldn't help feeling peeved that Tom and Jack were out almost every night, splashing money on booze, food, and clothes while she was struggling to make ends meet. Both boys had cars courtesy of their darling dad, and Rose couldn't ignore the pinch of resentment that Phil and Wife 2.0, the new, improved model, could afford to buy her children fancy gifts with their joint incomes. She hated feeling bitter that Tom and Jack sang their father's praises for the annual luxury gifts, but the sacrifices she made for them were expected and taken for granted.

She rolled onto her back and let out a deep sigh. She was sick and tired of everyone and everything, but above all, she was sick of the negative voice in her own head. Quietly in the darkness, she slid open her bedside drawer and fumbled for a blister pack hidden at the back. She popped one of the tiny white pills swallowing it dry. She tried not to take sleeping tablets, knowing they left her groggy the next day, but she couldn't bear her own thoughts any longer. She knew she had thirty minutes before it kicked in but knowing that an end to her mind's incessant, miserable monologue was in sight was enough of a comfort to be able to tolerate it.

Thirty minutes, she started the countdown in her head. *Right, let's try thinking about something else.*

She conjured up an image of Gareth in her head wondering if she'd ever feel confident enough to start a new relationship. Even in her fanciful daydreams, she knew that she wouldn't be able to get someone as handsome as Gareth, but any company as long as he was kind might be nice.

It would be nice to see Gareth again though, Rose thought to herself as her brain started to grow warm and hazy.

Even though the daytrip to Hampton Dale had been stressful, it had left her feeling homesick for the first time in years. When the boys were little, she had raised the subject of moving closer to her parents, but Phil hadn't been interested, and then when her mother had died it had seemed pointless. Now, there was no way she could afford it.

She hated herself for thinking it, but her thoughts wandered back to the talk of the will. As terrible as it was, the thought of someday having security from her share made her feel like there was something to hang on for. She couldn't help worrying about the conversation that Tim had had with their father, knowing that if all the land was sold off then all that would remain was a very basic house. After tax and splitting it four ways, she wouldn't even be able to pay off her mortgage. And that was if it didn't all go to their father's new wife. She pictured herself still working in a soul-destroying, dead-end job well into her late sixties and the thought was unbearable.

If it hadn't been for the sleeping pills, Rose thought she might have cried, but warm, seductive sleep was already beginning to wash over her, and she let it carry her away.

Tim

Monday morning was chaos. Tim usually felt sick to his stomach when he could sense a big announcement around the corner, but today he was buzzing with adrenaline. His strategy to streamline the operation drastically cutting costs had gone down well with the board, and he could sense that this win would be astronomical for his career.

"Are you ready for me?"

The scent of orange blossom and jasmine floated into his office and Tim felt an adolescent flutter in the pit of his stomach that had nothing to do with the meeting and everything to do with the attractive woman with the glossy caramel hair standing in the doorway, laptop clutched to her chest. At just the sound of her voice, he felt himself stand up a little straighter, puffing out his chest and broadening his shoulders.

"And I didn't think my day could get any better," he grinned confidently at her, inwardly thrilled when her full cherry-coloured lips turned up into a genuine smile. "It was a pleasant surprise to see you in my calendar today."

"I booked in some time with Georgia," she touched the arm of his suit jacket gently and, even in his preoccupied state, he felt the heady buzz that accompanies subtle flirtation. "So, it made sense to have my one-on-one with you in person while I'm here."

She raised one slim hand brushing a silky tendril of hair back over her shoulder and Tim's eyes moved to the creamy, exposed skin of her neck. He could feel her watching him; a knowing smile playing around the edges of her mouth.

"Are you staying overnight?" he asked.

"Not this time," she replied. "It's only a couple of hours

on the train so it didn't seem worth it."

He felt his stomach sink in disappointment. "Well, I'm happy to sign it off next time if you're seeing Georgia as part of your development plan."

Her eyes lit up. "I'll bear that in mind."

She fired up her laptop, and he reluctantly turned his attention to the business performance of the South-West region for the next hour. He could see the figures weren't great, but he found himself going easy on the woman where he would have given anyone else the grilling of their life.

Well, they'll all be outsourced sooner rather than later, he tried to justify his unique treatment of the woman.

"Thanks Tim," she beamed when the meeting was over. "I know it's not been the best quarter, but I'm confident that we'll be back stronger than ever in the next month. My team are working on a really promising trial to generate more revenue, but it's still too early to show much traction."

"Well, I look forward to hearing more about it," he replied. "And hopefully I'll see you again soon."

He watched her leave, his eyes hypnotised by the sway of her hips and found himself wishing very much that he would.

****

With the success of his day not even the germ-infested, sweaty carriage of the train home could dampen Tim's spirits as he headed home for the evening.

He'd been carefully weighing up the pros and cons of offshore operations for the past year, trialling a small, outsourced unit in India. The business was desperate to cut costs and he knew that his boss had expected excuses and resistance to job cuts and rollbacks, yet Tim had delivered a plan that gave over-and-above what was expected of him.

When he pulled this off, it would only be a matter of time before he stepped up to the next level. He was elated with how well he'd handled the pressure, every nerve buzzing with the heady thrill of success. He was under no illusion that the execution would be challenging, but the hard part, selling the strategy, had been achieved and he was more than confident that he could deliver.

This would elevate him to the next bracket financially. Another zero on the end of his salary, more shares, huge bonuses. He barely felt the biting April wind as he strode the short distance from the station to his house; his mind full of all the luxuries the next level would afford him. He pushed open the door to his home, still buzzing with excitement as he wandered through to the kitchen to share his news with Eleanor.

"Hey," she glanced over her shoulder to greet him. "Can you do me a favour and take a glass of water up to Hugo? I think he's got a sickness bug. He's not looking great, so I've put him in our bed to keep an eye on him."

"Our bed?" Tim frowned with annoyance.

She *knew* he didn't think children should sleep in their parents' bed and he didn't particularly fancy the thought of sharing his bed with a potentially-vomiting child, any more than he appreciated having orders thrown at him the moment he'd entered the house.

"Yes," she said in her gentle-but-firm tone that brooked no arguments. "I need to give Bea her bottle, unless you want to do it."

"I've just walked in," Tim felt his buzz start to sour.

Her lips turned up into a tight smile as she brushed past him to reach for a plastic tumbler from the cupboard.

"How was your day?" She asked as she flicked the cold water tap on to fill the cup.

Tim opened his mouth to speak, but before he could

answer there was a roar from the floor above them.

"Mummy!"

Eleanor had dropped the tumbler into the sink and bolted past him up the stairs before Tim had even had time to process the sound. He tilted his head, momentarily concerned, but the sound of retching made it clear that Hugo did indeed have a stomach bug and there was no life-threatening emergency. Left alone to his own devices, Tim pulled open the door of the warming oven and was appeased to see his dinner was made, and he set about portioning the sweet potato and lentil curry onto a plate alongside a homemade naan. He paused, wondering whether to make Eleanor's, but he could hear Hugo still heaving in the bathroom upstairs and he thought she might be some time. He opened a bottle of wine and sat down at the dining table with his meal-for-one. The curry was delicious, but he couldn't help thinking as he forked the meal into his mouth that this felt a little anticlimactic. He watched the wall clock tick away the minutes as he ate, and he was almost finished by the time his wife had returned. His first thought when she padded back into the kitchen was that she looked dreadful; her eyes puffy and bloodshot, and her hair up in a messy bun on her head.

"Is he ok?" Tim asked, before gesturing towards his plate. "I haven't put yours up yet as I didn't know how long you'd be."

Eleanor grimaced and waved a hand dismissively. "I couldn't eat anything after how sick Hugo's been. I'll take him up a water and get Bea to bed."

Tim watched her leave, plastic cup of water in one hand and baby bottle in the other, feeling a twinge of sympathy for her. He knew it wasn't her fault that he hadn't got the welcome that he craved, so he carried the bottle of wine and two glasses through to the sitting room to wait for her. His phone buzzed next to him with a message from Emma, and he hurriedly turned the ringer off feeling the first flicker of real guilt at the thoughts he had been having. Deep down, he knew Eleanor deserved better. He'd had his fair share of braying city girlfriends at university; interchangeable Sarah's and Rebecca's, but nobody in his personal life came close to Eleanor Mellish-Brown. To Tim, it was his marriage to Eleanor that had established that he'd finally made it to where he wanted to be; a respectable, card-carrying member of the upper echelons of society. He tried to remember this as he sipped his wine waiting for his wife to reappear; Emma's text unopened on the phone next to him. It was only when he had finished his second solitary glass that he called out to her. When no response came, he climbed the stairs in search of his wife, but the landing was dark with just the white glow of Hugo's night-light. Tim crept along the soft carpet peering through the open door of his bedroom.

A surge of disappointment followed by a prickle of irritation transformed his good spirits as his eyes settled on the sleeping body of his wife curled around their young son. Tim held back a sigh as he moved quietly into the room. Hugo was fast asleep; arms and legs splayed out like a starfish, sweaty curls stuck to his forehead, with his thumb tucked in his mouth. Tim scooped his pyjama-clad son up into his arms carrying the child into his own bed, before shaking his wife gently awake.

Groggy and disorientated, Eleanor peeled open her eyes.

"You feel asleep," he chastised her softly. "It's not quite half eight."

"Oh gosh," Eleanor forced herself into a sitting position, smoothing down her hair before she noticed their missing son. "Where's Hugo gone? I thought he was falling asleep too?"

"In his own bed," Tim told her firmly. "Leave him there. He's perfectly fine."

"He's been really sick," Eleanor protested as she rose to her feet.

Tim placed a warning hand on her shoulder. "He's better off being in his own bed. He'll sleep better and we'll hear him if he's unwell during the night. Now, come down and have some supper. You'll be no good to anybody in this state in work tomorrow."

Tim could tell from the way she pressed her lips into a thin line that she was cross with him as she tiptoed into their son's room, but after brushing Hugo's forehead with her fingertips she reluctantly followed Tim downstairs.

Once downstairs, Tim had assumed her attention would be back to him, but instead she began to tidy up the kitchen declining the proffered glass of wine.

"I'm exhausted," she announced once she had finished loading the dishwasher. "I'm going to bed."

Tim opened his mouth to convey his annoyance, but she had already left the room. Disgruntled and feeling neglected, he took his wine back into the sitting room. He picked up his phone idly, remembering Emma's message.

"Train delays = just got in! Wine required!" Emma's message read accompanied by a photo message of her slender hand holding a large glass of wine.

Tim had to double-take at the image. Despite the framing of the glass, there in the background was an unmistakeable slim, bronzed leg peaking from beneath a frothy mountain of bubbles. Tim studied the photo, feeling himself stir with desire. The wine glass was clearly the focus of the photograph, the background was blurry and out-of-focus, but his eyes were drawn back to Emma's naked limb and he couldn't stop himself picturing the full scene, no matter how hard he tried.

"We both deserve a celebratory glass or two," he settled on a safe response, batting the ball back into Emma's court.

As he hit send, he felt the addictive thrill of anticipation, and his stomach was in knots by the time her response came.

"Definitely. Drinks next time?"

Wow.

His earlier reservations had been well-and-truly snuffed out by the combination of Eleanor's lack of interest and Emma's boldness, and he was unable to resist sending back an eager acceptance.

Holly

Holly McAllister had been working on the Intensive Care Unit for four years and not a lot surprised her anymore. Her colleagues had tipped her off that the partner and child of the hit-and-run woman were sat with her and, with this in mind, she entered the room prepared for a barrage of questions. She'd learned, long ago, that she needed to detach part of herself from the tears and the emotion. She was far from heartless, but she had an important job to do, nursing the very sickest patients back to health or providing them with comfort and dignity in their final days. But no amount of experience could have toughened her enough for the scene that she worked into.

The hit-and-run mum, whose name was written in fresh, black marker pen on the chart above the bed, was heavily sedated. She looked peaceful; her face untouched by the four tons of metal that had smashed into her delicate frame, her eyes closed, long brown lashes resting against her fair skin. Tubes and wires snaked from various parts of her, but the medication being pumped into her kept her still and compliant. This wasn't the part of the scene that disturbed Holly, making her heart lurch in her chest as she struggled to keep her face neutral. It was the small boy, no older than eight or nine, stood at the head of the bed. In his left hand, he clutched at his mother's shoulder, the only part of her accessible through the delicate medical equipment, and his right hand covered his small face as if attempting to hide his anguish from the room. His skinny shoulders moved up and down with the force of his muffled sobs.

As upsetting as it was to see a child cry, Holly had seen children saying their final goodbyes to their parents before.

It touched her through the toughened mask of her professionalism, but the frightened child pulled at her heartstrings not for his heartache but for his loneliness. As the boy broke his heart, the partner of his mother sat in the cushioned chair against the window, legs stretched out. His body was angled away from the child, all his attention on the phone in his hand. Holly felt the hairs on the back of her neck rise in restrained anger at the man's lack of empathy for the child.

As if he could feel Holly's eyes on him, the man glanced up at her before looking away disinterestedly. A cheerful jingle trilled from the phone and Holly felt her blood heat up as she recognised the tune from a mindless game that she sometimes played to unwind.

"Are you alright?" She ignored the man moving to the little boy's side to place a hand lightly on his arm.

He lowered his hand, revealing red-rimmed teary eyes and a snotty nose. She handed him a tissue from the side of the bed and when he took it, clutching it in his hand not using it for the intended purpose, she took it back gently wiping his eyes and then his nose. She scrunched the tissue up and tossed it in the bin.

"What's your name?" She asked him in her firm, no-nonsense manner.

"Toby."

"My name is Holly," she told him. "I'm going to be looking after your mum. She's going to be a bit poorly for a while, but she's in the best place to get better and she'll be home when she's ready."

"Is she going to be ok?" His voice was small, and she could hear the desperation in his tone.

"She's going to be fine." Holly told him.

Her spleen was potentially ruptured, but she was a strong, healthy woman despite her small frame. The car that had hit her must have attempted to slow down as the impact had been moderate but not severe. Holly knew the road that the accident had happened on was notorious for reckless driving, but if she'd been hit at high-speed there was no doubt that the woman would be dead. She was young enough to have strong odds for making a full recovery, but it would take a while until she was on her feet fully. Holly was pretty confident that she'd make it, but the hard part would be recovery: avoiding overdoing it or infection. Holly felt her eyes move back to the deadbeat still playing on his phone. If that was all the support this poor woman had, Holly had real concerns for the woman and her child.

Tim

"Tim, I've got Eleanor on the line."

Tim's Personal Assistant stood in the doorway to his office, looking equal parts apologetic and uncomfortable.

I wish she'd learn to knock, he thought in annoyance as Emma slid discreetly to the left to put a few inches between them and restore the scene to a perfectly respectable meeting.

"I'm in the middle of a meeting," he tried to keep his tone even. He knew that the last thing he wanted to do was risk annoying Marie.

"She said it's urgent," Marie smiled apologetically. "I offered to take a message."

Grudgingly, Tim got to his feet glancing back at Emma wondering if the intrusion had unnerved her, but she settled back in the chair crossing one long, stockinged leg over the other with an air of unfazed confidence. She met his eyes and the corners of her lips curled up into a knowing smile. Even with Marie loitering behind him, he could feel the stir of desire at Emma's self-assuredness. Tim suspected that part of the attraction for her was the fact that he was married. It should have been a huge red flag, but for some reason it enhanced his craving for her.

"I'll be two minutes," Tim told her.

He pulled the door shut behind them accepting the phone from Marie without meeting her eyes.

"Everything ok?" He asked gruffly without preamble.

"It's your sister," there was a hint of panic to Eleanor's usually calm tone. "She's been in an accident. She's ok, but she's going to be in hospital a few weeks."

The fleeting concern Tim had felt was instantly replaced with irritation.

This is exactly why I don't take personal calls during the workday.

He cleared his throat ready to say just as much, but Eleanor began to speak again.

"She's down in surgery now," she explained. "The hospital has called around her next-of-kin to see if someone can take Toby."

"Toby?" Tim frowned in confusion.

"Her *son*," he heard exasperation slip into Eleanor's tone.

Tim had assumed Eleanor had been referring to Rose and he flinched as he thought of his red-haired, feisty youngest sister and her small, scrawny son.

"Can we talk about it later?" He asked, not seeing how it was any concern of theirs. "I've left a meeting for this."

"Tim, Belle's partner has left the boy at the hospital. He's sat at the nurses' station," Eleanor said with urgency. "Apparently he's got no father or grandparents that can take him. Rose and Will aren't answering their phones. If someone doesn't go and get him soon, they'll hand him over to social services."

Irritation spread through Tim's chest. He hadn't heard a peep from his family in years, yet now he was being expected to take calls in the middle of his working day about someone else's childcare problems.

"What are you expecting me to do?" Tim asked in frustration. "Do you expect us to take the child in?"

"Yes!" Eleanor exclaimed, ignoring his sarcasm. "Of course, I do. Ideally, Rose or Will could do it, but nobody can get hold of them. I'm assuming they're both in work. I would drive down there, but I've not met him before. You should be the one to go, plus you'll want to see your sister when she's out of surgery."

"Eleanor, I cannot just leave work," Tim argued. "Do

you have any idea..."

He trailed off, suddenly conscious of Marie's eyes on him. She had clearly heard the whole conversation, and he knew that she would be aware that he'd cancelled a meeting this afternoon in order to take an extended 'working lunch' with Emma. He felt his cheeks redden as he realised that if he didn't go, Marie might wonder why he'd abandoned his nephew and his ill sister to wine and dine one of his employees. And one that was spending far more time at Head Office than usual. It would only take Marie gossiping to one of the other PA's to have the whole office talking about it, and everyone knew that the directors got all the scandal from the assistants.

"You cannot abandon that child," Eleanor seized the space he left silent, her words forceful and strong. "I'll come with you. My mum is coming around to watch Hugo and Bea. I'll drive into London."

Tim's instinct was to argue with her, but deep down he knew it was useless.

"Don't drive in," he replied. "It'll be quicker if I get the train back to the house. I'll be there within the hour. Keep trying Rose and Will."

"I will," Eleanor's voice softened the moment he relented. "Don't you dare log back in. We need to be there as soon as possible."

Tim ended the call and turned to Marie.

"Hold my calls today," he told her in an attempt to regain some authority. "Family emergency."

Rose

The pixels on the screen danced blurrily, and Rose slid her glasses up on to her head rubbing at her aching eyes. She squinted at the pop-up box, but the words were just a jumble of shapes on the bright screen.

"Hello?" An irritated voice echoed in her ear snapping her back to attention.

"Hello, could I speak to Miss Griffiths please?" Rose chirruped in the sing-song voice that had become a habit.

"Who is this?"

"My name is Rose and I'm calling from XZ..."

Rose kept speaking even after she could see the connection had dropped, conscious of the sales manager hovering behind her.

"Another hang-up?"

It was too late; she'd been spotted. Her heart sank as she prepared herself for the patronising 'coaching' session that would follow. Adele the Sales Manager swished her shoulder-length hair over one shoulder perching her perky bottom on the edge of Rose's desk. Rose reluctantly raised her eyes to meet her glare.

"Keep going," she snapped. "I'll listen in to give you some pointers."

"Sorry," Rose bared her teeth into as close a smile as she could muster.

"Hello?" A man answered.

The slow, shaky enunciation made Rose's stomach drop as she recognised the tell-tale voice of an old person. She knew from experience that it was only the old, the lonely and the vulnerable that would succumb to their hard sales, and she felt a jolt of anger at the sight of Adele's miserable face reflected in her computer screen.

"Hello, is that Mr Landers?" Rose started hesitantly.

She struggled on through the sales pitch, the void inside her filling with shame as she knowingly manipulated Mr Landers into disclosing his personal details under the pretence of completing their security checks. The next fifteen minutes spent chatting with the clearly lonely man who willingly told her about his beloved, departed wife and his penchant for a flutter in the bookies had Rose hating herself for not standing up to the awful people who pushed sales on the most vulnerable of society. Her previous despondency was forgotten in the blaze of anger she felt at herself for needing this job so badly that she had abandoned all her morals and ethics.

The shame she felt caused the words to stick in her throat and she fumbled over easy hooks, desperate to let Mr Landers go before he ended up with a credit card that he had no desire for and would probably mismanage.

Does anyone really need a job this badly?

A stiletto-tipped nail reached over Rose and jabbed at the 'mute' button on the phone.

"You're losing him," Adele barked. "Stick to the script."

Rose swallowed nervously feeling disgusted with herself as she did as she was told. When the call was done, Rose looked up expectantly for the mortifying feedback, but the woman's ears were already pricking up at the sound of another sales agent struggling in the neighbouring row of desks. Overwhelmed and recognising the salty sting of tears of shame at the back of her eyes, Rose logged out and slipped away to the toilets. Once safely ensconced in the cubicle, she pulled out her phone desperate for a distraction, but her upset was temporarily pushed aside as she saw a string of missed calls. She couldn't remember the last time that she'd had so many, and her eyes scanned the notifications. An unknown number, her sister-in-law and

Tom. She jabbed at his number immediately.

"Hey," her panic subsided a little as soon as it became apparent that Tom was clearly alive, uninjured, and un-incarcerated, but she heard the sheepish tone in his voice. "Thanks for phoning me back."

"What's the matter?" She asked in a hushed voice. "I'm in work. Is it urgent?"

"Kind of," her son sounded hesitant. "I've just written my car off."

"What?" Rose felt the panic return like a lightning bolt. "Are you ok?"

"Yeah, yeah," he said hurriedly. "I'm fine. Took a turning too fast and the car's gone up an embankment."

She waited for him to continue knowing from his tone that there would be more.

"And down the other side into a field."

"Oh, Tom!"

"I know, I know," he cut in defensively. "Look, Mum, I need to get the car recovered, but I need to borrow some money."

"You'll have to call your insurance," she felt her irritation rising.

"But Mum!" He exclaimed sounding more like a petulant toddler than a twenty-one-year-old adult. "The car is on Dad's policy and he'll go mad if he finds out."

"Tom, I can't deal with this right now," she protested. "How much is recovery?"

"I don't know," he replied sulkily. "I've got your card details saved from that time you let me pay for my flights with your Mastercard. Can I just use it? I'll pay you back."

"No, Tom!" She exclaimed crossly. "You need to tell your insurance. You'll have to tell Dad anyway."

"Please," he sounded desperate. "I swear I'll pay you back."

"Tom, I've got to go," she said in a low voice as the door outside the cubicle opened. "Just call your dad and I'll speak to you later."

She made her way back to her desk, but a second wave of panic was already threatening to consume her as she started to worry that Tom was trapped on the side of the road somewhere, or the car might catch fire, or he might be arrested.

Oh, God! What if he's drunk?

No matter how unlikely it was she was stricken now, and she knew that she had to go to him. She glanced around nervously for Adele, spotting her hunched over one of the team. Rose tried to catch her eye, but the woman pointedly ignored her attempts to attract her attention.

"Hi," Rose took a deep breath feeling very much like a school child. "I'm really sorry to interrupt..."

"You'll have to wait," the woman barked turning her back to Rose.

The young man sat next to her grimaced shooting Rose a sympathetic look. She felt a burst of anger at Adele's rudeness, but it wasn't enough to propel her to cause a scene. She hovered uncertainly, torn between the need to go to her son versus the need for her pay cheque.

"Is everything ok?" Lena asked in concern as she appeared at Rose's side.

"My son has had a car accident," she told her. "He's ok, but I need to go and help him."

The rest of her colleagues turned to look at her, collectively voicing their sympathy and concerns, and the sudden din caught Adele's attention making her snap around to look at Rose.

"He's ok, is he?"

"Well, yes," Rose stuttered, the lack of empathy making her flinch. "But he needs to get the car recovered and..."

"How old is he?"

"Twenty-one, but..."

"And he's not injured?"

"No."

Rose was speechless at the woman's heartlessness. She had never felt so belittled and humiliated before, and she swallowed back the lump in her throat.

"I need to go," she said with as much dignity as she could muster. "Am I able to work the time back or take leave?"

Adele glared at her across the bank of desks, but she seemed to be weighing up how far she could push her authority before she crossed the line into tribunal territory. After a few seconds of heavy silence, she nodded. "You can work it back Saturday with the other team."

Rose wished that she could tell the woman where to stick her job but knowing that she would regret it when her direct debits bounced, she had no choice but to nod her head begrudgingly.

Will

It was still daylight when Will and Raya packed up their equipment and headed out of the rented studio space to go home after a long day of family photoshoots. They had been savvy enough to capitalise on the school Easter holidays in the absence of any exciting commercial work for the next few weeks, and while the day had been a financial success, they both had headaches from the forced smiles and constant cajoling of disobedient children into behaving for long enough to get the desired shot.

"It's nice to see daylight," Raya groaned blinking up at the sky dramatically. "Shall we have a drink to celebrate the end of the eternal winter?"

Will grinned as he flicked his phone off Flight Mode. "Usually I would say yes, but I promised Craig I'd be home at a reasonable time."

"Meh," Raya pulled a face, but before she could say anything further on the subject Will's phone began to ping incessantly. "You're popular!"

Will grimaced; he had started putting his phone on Flight Mode telling Craig that he had no signal in the studio. It was just a little white lie to save him being made to feel guilty for not responding to his boyfriend's constant daily updates but lying didn't come easily to Will leaving him feeling worse than Craig's passive aggressive sulks did. He expected to see the usual barrage of texts from him, so he was surprised to see that a number of messages and missed calls were from Tim's wife.

"It's my sister-in-law," Will told her frowning in confusion. "I'd better call her back. I'll call you later."

He was already dialling the number as he got into his own car, and Eleanor answered just as he was about to give up.

"Hi Will," she sounded harassed. "So sorry to have bombarded you with calls."

"Is everything ok?"

"Belle has been in an accident," Eleanor told him hurriedly. "She's injured, but she's ok."

"Oh, God!" Will exclaimed. "Are you with her? What happened?"

"She was hit by a car yesterday morning," she told him. "She was knocked unconscious and a passer-by found her. She's suffered some internal bleeding, some broken bones. I've only just found out this afternoon, but she's already had surgery and doing well in recovery."

"Thank God," Will released the breath he hadn't realised he was holding. "Can we see her?"

"Once she's out of recovery, so hopefully tomorrow," Eleanor assured him. "I'm with Toby at the moment," she added with careful enunciation. Will felt his heart sink at the implication that she couldn't speak freely, and that maybe his sister's injuries were worse than she was letting on. "Tim and I are just on our way back to ours, and Toby is going to have a sleepover with us, but shall I give you a call when we're home and all the children are settled?"

"Yes," he replied quickly. "Yes, please. Do any of you need anything? Does Belle or Toby? If you have a key, I can drive to hers?"

"Oh, yes please," Eleanor sounded relieved. "That would actually be so helpful as Toby will be here until his mum is well enough to leave hospital. We've got a key here, but I know it's awfully out of your way."

Will glanced at the time grimacing at the thought of fighting his way through traffic to pick the key up from his brother just to double back on himself to drive to Belle's. "How about I come and grab the key off you now?" He offered. "If Toby can manage tonight, I can stop by Belle's and pack some bits up and meet you at the hospital tomorrow afternoon?"

"If you really don't mind," Eleanor said gratefully. "I'll text you our address and we'll see you when you get here."

"Honestly," he replied, grateful that his sister-in-law had been on hand to pick their nephew up. "It's the least I can do."

*****

The following afternoon Will braced himself to enter the stark, soulless building, his stomach already turning in anticipation of the sharp, distinctive hospital smell that seemed to linger on his clothes and in his nostrils for days after. He wasn't sure when he had developed his intense discomfort around hospitals but armed with two bags of Belle and Toby's belongings, he had no choice but to press on. He'd stopped at the supermarket to buy a new charger for her phone and an array of snacks and sweets for both his sister and nephew. He wasn't even sure what phone she had or if it had even survived the impact, but her charger had been on the list that Eleanor had thoughtfully made and he couldn't bear to have to tell Belle that he hadn't been able to find it because her flat had been utterly ransacked.

His stomach churned again at the thought of the mess in her flat. The hallway had been untidy, but he hadn't thought twice about it until he'd caught a glimpse of the kitchen where cupboard doors were flung open, the contents clearly ransacked in a hurry. Worried that the flat had been burgled, he had crept through to the living room, the empty space where a flatscreen television had been marked by the rectangle of dust outlining its former place had made his heart leap into his mouth as his fears were confirmed. He'd backed out of the room hurriedly reaching for his phone when a woman had appeared at the doorway regarding him with suspicion. When he'd explained that he was Belle's brother and she was in hospital, the woman, who had introduced herself as Katie, had visibly softened telling him that she'd seen Belle's partner, or ex-partner as he clearly now was, loading his belongings into a car the previous evening. She had offered to help him clean up, but Will had been dubious about letting a stranger into the ransacked flat, instead picking through the mess himself to assemble two bags of clothes.

He followed the signs up the ward and was directed to his sister's bed. His chest ached with pity at the sight of her thin and pale against the sheets, tubes and wires criss-crossing her and a heavy cast on her left leg. Her eyes were shut, and he felt sick at the thought of how heartlessly she'd been treated, both by the driver who'd mown her down and driven off, and the boyfriend who'd abandoned her seven-year-old son for social services to collect before callously ransacking her flat. He stood beside the bed unsure whether to wake her when he heard a rustle behind him.

"Hey," Eleanor smiled warmly. Toby's hand was clutched tightly in hers. "Is she sleeping?"

"I think so," Will swallowed back the lump in his throat at the sight of his nephew's worried, innocent face.

Belle stirred in the bed opening her eyes slowly. For a second, she squinted at them in confusion, but her lips turned up into a smile at the sight of her son. She wriggled up onto the pillow, wincing with pain as she croaked. "Hey Toby."

"Hi Mummy," he let go of Eleanor's hand to bravely step to his mother's side. He glanced at her hand hesitantly and she nodded gently. "Do you feel better?"

"I do," she assured him. "I'm just a bit achy, but I'll be

back to normal soon. Did you have fun at Auntie Eleanor's?"

Toby launched into a blow-by-blow recount of his day with the confidence of an adored, only child who was used to a captivated audience, and Will was warmed to see Belle nodding her head in encouragement at his chatter.

"Tim's out in the waiting room," Eleanor told him quietly. "She's only allowed two visitors at one time. I'll go and wait with him, and you can bring Toby back out when visiting is over."

"Do you mind if I go and speak to him first?" Will asked quickly. "I'll just be a few minutes."

Tim was sat in the empty waiting room with an irritated look on his face and his phone in his hand.

"No bloody signal in this place," he said slipping it into his pocket as Will walked in.

"Hey," Will said ignoring his brother's lack of greeting. "Thanks again for getting here for Toby yesterday. I can't believe that her boyfriend just left him."

"Well, it was fortunate that Eleanor is off work with the children this week," Tim said shortly. "It doesn't seem likely the boyfriend is coming back to collect him."

"I've just come from their flat," Will replied gravely. "He's completely trashed it and it looks like he's taken anything of any value. I don't want to say anything to Belle and upset her, but I don't know whether I should phone the police."

"Bloody hell," Tim looked shocked. "Is it that bad?"

"I thought she'd been burgled," Will admitted. "But one of the neighbours saw him loading a car last night."

"You'll have to mention it to her," he grimaced. "She'll need a crime reference if she's going to claim on her house insurance."

Will doubted that she had any insurance, but he didn't say anything. He realised that his emotionless brother wasn't going to be any help to him in deciding whether to risk upsetting Belle further or to just leave it and try to clean up what he could before she was home.

"I've just spoke with one of the nurses and they say Belle will be in for at least the next week," Tim continued when Will didn't respond. "I was going to speak to you about having Toby until then."

"Me?" Will looked surprised. "Why can't he stay with you?"

"We're both working full time," Tim replied in a condescending tone. "Besides you live closer, and he'll want to visit his mum as often as possible."

"I can't take any time off work this week," he protested. "I'm self-employed, Tim, and I'm fully booked for the whole of the school holidays.

"You'll have to speak to Rose then," Tim replied irritably. "I know she's in Wales, but she could get him and take him back for a little holiday."

Will shook his head. "She can't. She said she's on probation in her new job and can't take any time off. Her next day off is Sunday and she said she'd come to visit Belle then."

Tim snarled in annoyance. "Typical."

"I can have Toby Sunday, and I can come and get him from yours in the week to bring him here for evening visiting if it's too much trouble." Will rubbed his hand across his jaw wearily already wondering how Craig would react to the disruption.

Just the thought of the return journey, battling through rush hour traffic after a full day's work, made Will feel exhausted, but the thought of Belle lying broken and vulnerable tore at his heart. He'd always thought of Belle as fiercely independent and strong. He had never thought that she needed any of them but seeing her like this made him realise that she wasn't as invincible as he had thought.

Belle

"Don't get up!"

Belle paused guiltily, one hand on the arm of the sofa for support as she hoisted herself up. Unable to hold the position for more than a split-second, she dropped back onto the seat heavily.

"I'm fine," she protested as Eleanor's mother breezed into the room snatching up the plate and mug that Belle had been planning on returning to the kitchen. "I can do it."

Rosemary sat down on the edge of the sofa eyeing her sternly. "I've no doubt that you can, Belle, but if you carry on overdoing it, you're going to end up straight back in hospital."

As if on cue, Belle felt a fresh wave of pain rip through her despite the copious amounts of medication she had taken.

"Sorry," she winced sheepishly. "I just feel so lazy and useless."

Rosemary's face softened as she moved closer to stretch a comforting arm around Belle's shoulder. "I know you might feel like that, but you're certainly neither of those things."

Belle allowed her head to rest for a moment against the woman's shoulder. Her brother's mother-in-law was possibly the warmest, most maternal person Belle had ever met, and she couldn't help wishing that she had someone like Rosemary in her life. She had finally been released from hospital after eight days under strict instructions to rest completely. It was agonising for Belle to be dependent on anyone, but her flat was on the third floor. There had been talk of Social Services providing help when the hospital realised she was a single mother and her siblings all lived too far away to be on hand, but she was loath to have them involved, fearing that they'd find any excuse to hang around after she was healed and stick their noses in. Her worst fear had always been losing Toby, closely followed by failing him in any way. The alternative, offered by a kindly Eleanor, was for Belle to stay with them temporarily. It was fine while Toby was off for the school holidays, but there were only a few days left and Belle still needed to figure out the logistics of getting him to school and back each day.

She had been so poorly that she had gratefully accepted Eleanor's offer to stay with them, and she'd been naively hoping, and desperately wishing, for a quick recovery so that she and Toby could be home by the start of term, but now she was out, a few more problems had cropped up that she needed to deal with. Eleanor and her mother were lovely; so much so that she couldn't understand how either of them tolerated her miserable brother. With a twelve-year age gap, she'd never had a lot to do with Tim, but she could see a striking resemblance to their father. She couldn't deny that she and her oldest sibling had both inherited their father's coppery-coloured hair and green eyes, but she'd always thought that any similarities were just skin deep. But just a few days in his presence had confirmed to her that Tim was as brusque and bad-tempered as Frank had been when she was growing up. He seemed to work all hours which Belle was almost grateful for as whenever he was around, he made her feel like her presence was a huge inconvenience. But Tim's surly attitude was the least of her worries.

The biggest issue was that her job with Fantasies was a zero-hour contract. When she'd finally been well enough to get in contact with her boss, she hadn't expected sympathy, but she'd at least anticipated a phone call. A curt email had informed her that she was entitled to a paltry Statutory Sick

Pay, and she had suspicions that she'd soon receive a follow-up to tell her that she was no longer needed. Will had had to break it to her that Ben had not only abandoned her child but had taken almost everything of any value that he could from the flat. Her expectations of Ben had been low to begin with, but the revelation that he had taken the hidden tin full of cash she'd been saving for Toby's birthday had broken her heart. She wished that she had the energy to be angry, but it was all too much effort. It had taken all of her strength to face tackling the endless forms to claim the benefits she would need to survive, and it felt horribly unfair that she could be waiting up to six weeks for her first payment. She'd tried calling to see if it could be fast-tracked before her monthly outgoings completely drained her current account, but nobody seemed able to help. The lease for the flat was up for renewal, and she knew there was no way she could afford to keep living there on her own. Her injured body and her groggy mind felt like they were working together to betray her. She had so much that she needed to sort out, but she didn't have the strength to deal with any of it. She had thought about mentioning it to Eleanor, but Belle couldn't bear to be thought of as a charity case. She was trying her hardest not to feel sorry for herself, grateful for Eleanor's warmth and the fact that she hadn't died in the hit-and-run, but she couldn't help feeling desperate and trapped.

"Do you want another cup of coffee?" Rosemary asked.

"Better not," she smiled self depreciatingly. "It takes me about an hour to get to the loo."

Rosemary laughed squeezing her shoulder gently before getting back to her feet. "Right, I promised I'd take the little ones out to the park and for a slice of cake. I'm sorry that we'll have to leave you here. Can I get you anything before we leave?"

"No thank you," Belle replied.

Rosemary was a hands-on grandmother and it seemed that she loved being around the children as much as they loved her. It made Belle feel sad that Toby didn't have any grandparents to dote on him like his little cousins. She reminded Belle a little of her own mother, and she thought that Kathleen would have been just as attached and involved if she'd had the chance. It stung that her father had never been interested, and even now that she was desperate, he'd be the last person that she turned to for help.

Once she'd waved off Toby and his cousins, she pulled out her phone to tackle the task she'd been dreading. Will was the only one she felt comfortable enough to ask for help, but the call went through to voicemail. Her stomach sunk at the thought of delaying the inevitable humiliating conversation. Being in Tim and Eleanor's beautiful house made her feel ashamed that she hadn't managed to make something of her life.

If it wasn't so depressing, Belle thought to herself as she stared blankly at the muted television screen, *it would be laughable that Tim of all people is the one moaning about Dad selling off the fields.*

She had overheard him on the telephone one evening snootily informing his father that if he did sell the fields then Tim would have to speak with a solicitor. The conversation was quite cordial on the whole; the threat was wedged in between Tim updating him about her accident and enquiring about the wedding. She felt a little like her brother had used her injuries to drop the warning in without creating a rift, but regardless, she was glad that one of the siblings was smart enough to make sure none of them were short-changed. While she'd been searching for cheaper flats online, she'd had a quick browse to see if she could figure out how much the farm was worth, and the results had caused her to inhale sharply in surprise.

It was an awful thing to think, so she tried to push it out of her mind, but she couldn't help thinking that if he died she'd finally have the money to free herself from the vicious circle she was trapped in.

Will

Will's phone buzzed in his pocket, but Craig's frown stopped him from reaching for it. They were sat in a stuffy office at Craig's bank, opposite a smartly dressed woman who was sweating uncomfortably trying to look like the lack of air-conditioning wasn't a problem.

"I'm awfully sorry," she tugged at the jaunty polyester scarf at her neck. "I might wedge the door open if you don't mind."

As she stood up, Will clocked the huge, healthy bump that was contributing to her internal thermostat and quickly got to his own feet to open the door for her.

"Thank you," she sighed dabbing at her brow. "I'm positively melting. So, you're looking to get a mortgage, is that right?"

Craig nodded enthusiastically.

"Have you seen anything you like?"

"Oh, we're just exploring options for now," Will protested quickly. "Obviously rent is so expensive that we're looking to see if there are better options."

"Oh, of course," she nodded turning back to Craig. "Craig, you bank with us, so I know your salary details, your expenditure, and so on. Do you have any loans or credit agreements with any other lenders?"

Craig shook his head confidently, and Will felt his heart sink as she turned to him.

"Did you bring some ID and your payslips?"

"I've got my passport," he said sliding it across the desk to her. "But, I'm self-employed so..."

"Oh, that's fine," she waved a hand dismissively. "I can work out an average if you've got some bank statements."

Craig had already demanded that he print them all out

ready to meet him on his lunchbreak, but Will's stomach was in knots at the thought of how annoyed Craig was going to be when he realised that he had downplayed his debts. He watched nervously as the woman scanned the documents before looking up at him, a flicker of sympathy flashing across her face.

"Uh, the business is quite new, is it?" She looked back down; her eyebrows knitted together seriously.

"Yes," he nodded.

"And do you have any other income at all?"

"No," he could feel Craig starting to fidget next to him.

"Ok," she went through a few more transactions, her expression growing bleaker with every entry she made on her computer. "Right, I'm just going to see if you pass our credit check."

Will was no banker, but he was pretty certain of the outcome before it came.

Back out on the street, Will apologised to Craig for the third time in as many minutes. He could tell that he was annoyed but trying not to show it.

"It's fine," Craig sighed. "At least we know how much I can borrow on my own now. I mean, it's not ideal and we wouldn't get anything decent around here, but back home, we could get a nice place for that. Once you've built up the business and your credit rating, you can always be added at a later date."

"Craig," Will felt awful but he couldn't keep going around in circles. "My job is here, and I don't know if I do want to move."

"It's such a waste paying rent though," Craig protested. "I've got a deposit saved up, and I should really be on the property ladder by now."

"If that's what you want to do," Will began hesitantly. "That's fine, but I can't agree to move to Bristol. I don't want to hold you back from buying though. You've got to do what's right for you."

"That's not what being in a couple is about, Will," he shook his head. "We have to make this decision together."

Will felt his heart sink. Raya was planning on leaving in a couple of months, and he could keep working easily enough on his own or even relocate like Craig wanted to, but in his heart, he didn't want to live five minutes down the road from Craig's mum, even though she was nice. He didn't even know if he wanted to stay in London.

"Don't worry about the money," Craig said gently when Will didn't answer. "I know it's a long way off, but one day you'll be back on your feet. Maybe you should start thinking about a normal nine-to-five. Photography isn't really a stable income."

Will tried to hide his surprise at Craig's comment, but before he could even begin to think of how to respond, his phone rang again.

"It's my sister," he told him grateful for a distraction. "Hey, Belle. Sorry I didn't call you back."

"Hey. I need a favour," she sounded nervous.

"Of course," Will replied quickly. "Is everything ok?"

"Yeah, well, no," she stuttered. "It's just being at Tim's is a little tricky. Toby is meant to be going back to school Monday, and I still can't walk further than from the sofa to the loo. Is there any chance you can help me or..."

"I thought Eleanor had a neighbour who travels that way who can take Toby?" Will asked.

"Yeah, yeah," Belle said hurriedly. "It's a short-term solution, and I'm very grateful of course, but we've still got to figure out how to get him back. I was thinking if Toby and I could stay with you, then after a week or so I could take him on the bus. I know it's a long bus trip, but I'll be sat down and..."

"But then won't you be back in your flat?" Will asked in confusion. He'd made the suggestion to Craig when she was in hospital, but he'd pointed out numerous reasons why it wouldn't work and they'd all agreed it made more sense for her to be at Tim's much larger, child-friendly house.

There was a long silence, before Belle cleared her throat.

"My contract is up at the end of the month," she admitted in a small voice. "I don't know when I'll be able to go back to work, and without Ben's income, I can't afford to stay there. I need to find somewhere else, but then that's going to mean I need a deposit and I can't keep being a burden on Tim, and I just thought..."

"Oh, Belle!" Will felt his heart expand in sympathy for his sister. "I'm so sorry. I didn't even think about all those things." He glanced at Craig who was frowning in concentration as he tried to pick up the gist from one side of the conversation. "I'll have to speak to Craig, but our place is so tiny, and I don't know..." He felt wretched letting her down, but he couldn't see how it could possibly work. "How long do you think it would be for?"

"Ummm, about six weeks," she admitted sheepishly. "Just until I get my first payment and hopefully get my deposit from the flat back."

"Is there anyway Tim could lend you the money?" Will was thinking on his feet now, desperately wishing he could help her. "I'm sure he would. Maybe you could find something ground floor too. That would be ideal."

Belle sighed heavily. "There's nothing I can afford. I've been checking online every day, and I've got my name down with all the estate agencies if anything comes up."

"Have you tried the council?"

She laughed bitterly. "Yeah, I've been on that list for the last three years. The only way I can become a priority is to become homeless and move Toby into a hostel or temporary B & B, and I really…"

"No, no!" Will interjected hurriedly. "You can't do that. Look, I can't promise anything, but I'll speak to Craig and have a think to see if there's anything we can come up with."

"Ok," her voice was hollow and dejected, and Will felt awful as he ended the call.

He recounted the conversation to Craig as they walked back to the car. He made all the right noises to convey his sympathy, and when Will finished with a sigh, he wrapped him in his arms.

"I wish we could help," Craig said earnestly. "But it just wouldn't work. You're barely home as it is, and it's not like you're any better off than her financially. Maybe try speaking to Tim's wife. She seems lovely and I really don't think they'd mind her staying longer or giving her a loan if they knew the extent of her situation."

He softened his words with a sympathetic smile, but it didn't lessen how useless Will felt at not being in a position to help his sister.

Rose

Rose watched the clock in the corner of her screen exhaling with relief as the end of the shift arrived. Exuberant whoops rang out from her colleagues that the weekend was finally here, and even though she had nothing more exciting to look forward to than a leisurely amble around the garden centre, their youthful excitement made her smile.

"Are you sure you don't want to come out?" Harry hung back from the group as she was putting on her jacket. Rose had developed a fondness for the polite, cheery young man who was the same age as her youngest son. "Just for a couple of drinks?"

"Thank you for thinking of me, but I really can't tonight," she politely declined. "I'm looking forward to hearing all the gossip on Monday."

She wished that she had a group of like-minded friends to make plans with, but sadly her few friends were always busy with their own family plans, and the rare invitations she received these days were either grossly expensive or clashed with her shifts. Since her trip back home, she'd resolved to make more of an effort to be sociable, but Tom's expensive accident had resulted in not only Phil's wrath but Rose having to go further into the red to stump up the five-hundred-pound insurance excess. Phil was apparently refusing to help to 'teach Tom a lesson', but Rose thought that his withdrawal of financial support to their son had more to do with his holiday to the Maldives with his new wife that she'd heard about when she bumped into a mutual friend at the supermarket. She rolled her eyes just thinking about pretentious Phil.

As she opened the door to her house with nothing

more to look forward to than a quiet few days in front of the television, her phone buzzed in her pocket. She withdrew it feeling a little flutter of excitement to see Gareth's name on the screen. They had exchanged numbers when he had helped her jump-start her car in case it cut out again on the way home, and she'd sent him a friendly text to thank him once she was home safe. He'd replied with a pleasant message, but it was worded in a way that made it impossible for her to respond without looking desperate to carry on the conversation. She might not have much dating experience, but she still had enough dignity left to know when someone wasn't interested in *that* way.

Even before she opened the message, she was already reminding herself to keep her expectations firmly on the floor where they belonged, but it was impossible to not feel a little hopeful.

"Hey, hope you're well," she read feeling her heart quicken at the length of the message. *That was promising.* "Random, but I'm in Cardiff tomorrow for a concert. If you're free, it would be nice to catch up before hand? I'll be there from three and have no plans until I meet my cousin at seven. Happy-face emoji."

Rose's fingers were already tapping a response when she stopped abruptly.

Don't be so keen, she warned herself, but she was already grinning at her phone. She forced herself to put the phone down and to distract herself, she put a pot of pasta on to boil. She wasn't really hungry, but she thought that the time it took to cook would be an appropriate gap between his invitation and her response. She composed a message that was just the right combination of enthusiastic and breezy, and spent the rest of the evening hastily applying a box dye and trimming her split ends with the kitchen scissors.

It's not a date, she had to remind herself for the twentieth time as she reapplied her lipstick on the bus into town. *Gareth is just an old school friend who happened to be at a loose end. Just because he's newly single does not mean he's interested in you.*

Nevertheless, Rose couldn't remember a time when she'd spent longer on her appearance. She had dug out her ancient diffuser to tame her usually frizzy mess into a bouncy chestnut mane framing her carefully made-up face. She'd spent an hour trying on different outfits before settling on her favourite black jeans that she hadn't been able to fit into for years, optimistically keeping them at the back of the wardrobe on the off-chance that she ever shifted that extra stone. She had been rotating the same trio of shapeless trousers for years; the elasticated waistbands stopping her from realising that she had unwittingly lost a good few inches around her hips since she'd been cooking-for-one. She'd paired the jeans with a silky purple top that she'd picked up in Primark on a whim, but never worn. Even she had to admit that she looked quite nice, feeling confident enough to add a rare slash of lipstick.

"Rose!" Gareth was waiting in the bar with a half-empty pint in front of him, looking cool and confident in a leather jacket over a band t-shirt with jeans, and he rose to greet her with a warm hug.

She felt herself tingle a little at the brush of his stubble against her cheek, and she tried to ignore how the woody scent of his aftershave made her feel. "Hi. It's so lovely to see you again. I hope you've not been waiting long."

He shook his head. "No, not at all. You're right on time. I'm staying in a hotel out of town, but I got a taxi in a little early as I had no idea if I'd be able to find the place or how long it would take to get in."

"Are you not staying with your cousin?" She asked.

"No, he lives in Swansea and he's working until five," he explained. "His girlfriend was meant to be coming with him, but they broke up so it's a last-minute thing. I'm a big Saving Mavis fan though so I couldn't pass up the opportunity." Rose frowned in confusion and he laughed. "I take it you're not really into late nineties Indie Rock?"

She smiled shaking her head. "No, sorry. Completely clueless."

"I'll bore you with all my very specific trivia," he joked. "But let me get you a drink to numb what's going to be a very boring conversation for you."

Rose laughed happily, secretly thrilled when Gareth waved away her attempt to pay for their drinks. They took their drinks to a table outside chatting and laughing as they sat people-watching on the busy strip of bars and restaurants. Gareth managed to talk her into sharing the biggest platter of halloumi fries, chicken wings and spicy wedges that she'd ever seen, and even though she felt a little self-conscious at first, they were both soon stuffing their faces giggling like a pair of kids as they dripped dipping sauce everywhere.

"Thank you so much for keeping me company," Gareth beamed after he'd received a text from his cousin to say he was on his way. "I've had so much fun. I almost don't want to go to the gig now."

"What's this sacrilege?" Rose joked pretending to be outraged. "You don't want to hear Lincolnshire's ninth most successful band of all time play their hit record that reached a dizzy number twenty-seven in the UK chart in nineteen-ninety-seven? Call yourself a fan!"

Gareth burst out laughing. "If I didn't know that you were jealous, I'd be very upset."

"Very jealous," she gave him a cheeky wink. Several

large glasses of wine coupled with how easy his company had been had melted away her nerves. "I'll be looking them up on YouTube the minute I'm home."

"You'd better," Gareth gave her a stern look. "There is going to be a test, young lady."

She got to her feet, wobbling a little and he reached out to steady her. "It's been lovely to see you."

"Are you going home now?" He asked. "I'll walk you to get a taxi."

"No need," she shook her head. "It's still early. I can get the bus just around the corner."

He insisted on walking with her, and they both laughed at how tipsy they felt as they wobbled over to the bus stop. The streets were a typical Saturday mixture of day-drinkers and shoppers, and Rose waved merrily as she noticed one of the youngsters from work on the other side of the road. As they drew to a halt at the bus stop, Rose suddenly felt a shift in the atmosphere between them. She wondered if she was imagining it, but Gareth seemed a little tongue-tied and shy as if they had come to the end of a date and he was trying to figure out how to kiss her. Her heart skipped a beat excitedly at just the thought, and she reminded her sozzled-brain that they were both forty-years-old and it was broad daylight on a busy street.

"You'd better go and meet your cousin," Rose smiled shyly. "My bus won't be long."

"Aargh, I don't want to," Gareth pulled a face and grinned sheepishly. "I feel like I'm about sixteen, Rose."

Her stomach fizzed with butterflies as they locked eyes and grinned foolishly at one another, the alcohol sloshing around their systems lowering any inhibitions. She held her breath waiting for him to make a move, but before either of them could pluck up the courage a red-faced woman pushing a double buggy drew to a halt besides them. The moment was broken, and Gareth looked down at his phone.

"My cousin is at the train station," he grimaced. "I'd better go."

Rose shuffled away from the newcomer to free up some space for a quick, fleeting hug from her old friend feeling a tug of frustration when he drew apart quickly.

"Have fun," she said as brightly as she could muster through her disappointment.

"Thanks Rose," she wasn't sure if she were imagining it, but she thought he looked as dismayed as she felt. "I'll text you."

She waved once before turning away, trying to ignore the sinking feeling in her stomach and focus on the positive day she'd had instead.

He's gorgeous and funny, she reminded herself sternly. *And way out of your league.*

"Rose!"

She turned in surprise to see that Gareth had retraced his steps. Rose hurried over to meet him, wondering if he'd picked up something of hers by accident or forgotten the way.

"Everything ok?" She asked when he didn't say anything immediately.

"Yeah," he nodded quickly before closing the space between them. "I just wanted to..."

He was only inches from her now, and she felt her cheeks flush at the closeness of his broad chest to her face. Her heart sped up, but she was terrified to look up, scared she was misreading the situation.

"Rose," he repeated her name until she looked up into his dark brown eyes.

Her heart hammered against her chest as he reached out for her, and she stepped forward closing the gap. She was so close to him that she could see her own reflection in his eyes, and she was surprised by how nervous he looked, but she forgot everything, completely melting when he leaned down to brush his lips against hers.

Tim

The sun was just starting to rise as Tim jogged down the stairs, still fastening the cuffs of his shirt. He was always the first awake in his house, but it was a narrow lead, and he was always cautious of the unpredictability of Bea's wake-up time. At this early hour, the last thing he wanted was to get into a conversation with Eleanor or the children, but he hadn't heard a peep out of anyone leaving him with a sense of relief as he took the last few steps and turned the corner into the kitchen. He startled as he walked straight into his dressing-gown clad sister.

"Bloody hell!" She jerked backwards in shock, and water splashed out of the tumbler in her hand all over him.

"Oh, for goodness sake!" Tim snapped irritably. "What are you doing skulking in the dark?"

"I was getting water to take some pain killers," she shot back fumbling for the light switch, and flooding the kitchen with light.

Tim winced at the sudden brightness, ignoring her feeble attempts to mop up the spillage despite the heavy, cumbersome cast on her leg, and brushing past her to retrieve his laptop and keys. His sister and her son had been here now for three weeks, and to his frustration, she was showing no signs of moving any time soon.

In the back of his mind, he was acutely aware that the distraction of two extra people under their roof had worked to his advantage as Eleanor hadn't said a word about the increased time he was spending out of the house. Tim had a feeling that the only suspicion she had was that he was avoiding his sister, and he pushed aside the familiar tug of guilt as he thought about the real reason that he hadn't been around. A cry from upstairs alerted him to Bea waking up and he hurriedly made his escape before the rest of the house were up, leaving his sister mopping the floor with a handful of kitchen towels.

It was only later in the day that he realised he couldn't find his personal mobile. He had shoved everything into his laptop bag in a rush when he had heard Bea wake up, and a jolt of worry shot through him as he pictured the phone lying abandoned on the kitchen worktop for anyone to pick up. He tried to not use work devices to speak to Emma, wanting no evidence of the line he had crossed, but he had no choice but to send her a quick, impersonal email warning her that he had left his personal phone at home. He figured she was savvy enough to be able to read between the lines.

He watched his inbox anxiously for a moment, before shaking off his fears and returning to work. As if on cue, her name flashed up on his work phone screen. He glanced at his calendar, torn between being late for his next meeting and speaking to her.

"Hello," his desire to hear the silky accent of Emma Boucher won.

"Just thought I'd call. Quicker than emailing. Is this a good time?"

"I've got a couple of minutes," he replied, smiling to himself as he pictured her sat at her desk in one of those tight dresses that clung to her curves.

"I just wanted to give you the heads up," she said without a trace of concern in her voice. "I sent you a message earlier. Nothing incriminating."

Despite her cool-as-a-cucumber delivery, he felt a sliver of dread in the pit of his stomach. While Emma was strictly professional in the workplace, she was the epitome of raw sexuality and to her, a nude photo was no big deal. Her definition and Eleanor's of "nothing incriminating" were likely to be two very different things.

He attempted a low chuckle, knowing that she would be annoyed if he became uptight about it. "What did it say?"

"Wouldn't you like to know?" She teased in a deliciously low whisper that made the hair on the back of his neck stand up.

"That's why I asked," he replied knowing she was deliberately trying to ruffle his feathers.

"Honestly," she replied reverting back to her no-nonsense, professional tone. "It was just checking the details for this evening. Are we still on?"

"We are still on," he confirmed, his stomach flooding with lust at the thought of her lithe, naked body.

It was all he could do to concentrate for the rest of the day, and he left the office earlier than usual, whistling and smiling making Marie look up suspiciously. He flashed her a charming grin as he headed off to the station for the short commute to Emma's hotel room. Despite Tim's roving eye, he'd never had a full-blown affair before. He'd had plenty of opportunities of course; he was tall and ruggedly handsome, with a high-flying job that had him working closely with plenty of young, keen, and eager women over the years. He'd given in to temptation and there'd been nights away with work where he'd been the tempter, but it was only ever a one-time thing and he had never wanted to get into the complicated, and potentially stressful, territory of an affair. Emma Boucher was a whole other story though. She was movie-star beautiful and deliciously self-assured. She was seven years his junior and unencumbered by the burden of a husband or children. Her free-spirited attitude was as sexy as her long, tanned limbs and deliciously curved body. After her risqué photo message, they'd exchanged increasingly flirty texts before she'd come back to London on the flimsiest excuse the following week where after-work drinks had ended up with him in her hotel room. From then on, he'd seen her on an almost-weekly basis, even making the long drive to her house twice to indulge in the type of passionate, adventurous sex that he had thought he'd left firmly behind in his twenties. Each time he had thought it would be the last, but Emma was enticingly addictive, and he couldn't bring himself to call time yet on their fling.

She answered the door in a skimpy silk wrap that had his breath catching in his throat. His eyes gravitated to the curve of her buttocks just visible beneath the robe as he followed her into the room. She moved deliberately slowly towards a bottle of wine bending provocatively to pour him a glass. He resisted reaching out to touch the smooth, firm flesh of her thighs, taking a seat on the edge of the bed instead to prolong the intense build up.

She sat down next to him tucking her long legs beneath her body, and treating him to a glimpse of high, firm breasts wrapped in something black and lacy. "How was your day?"

"Good," he replied. "How was yours?"

"Really good," she flashed him a devilish grin. "Oh, and guess what?"

He rose to his feet to remove his suit jacket, carefully laying it over the arm of the chair in the corner. He kept his eyes on her face as he removed his tie, loosening his shirt collar.

"What?" He asked after the deliberately long pause.

He sat back down, and she unfurled her long legs draping them across his lap. He ran an appreciative hand over the soft, smooth skin. She let out a tiny moan of pleasure that had all the blood in his body rushing to his groin.

"A role is coming up in Georgia's team," she told him her voice matter of fact even as she slipped closer towards him until her buttocks were almost in his lap.

"In Retail Change?" He tried to keep his focus on the conversation even as the urge to rip her clothes off almost overwhelmed him.

"That's right," she slid closer, the silk of her wrap slipping down one shoulder as she moved. "It would be a sideways move not the promotion I hoped for, but with the outsourcing likely, it makes sense to start thinking tactically."

She looked at him pointedly, but he remained quiet. He tried to avoid talking about work with her, knowing that he had already crossed a line that could get him in serious trouble.

"If the job appeals to you," he replied. "You should go for it."

She bent forward at the hips showcasing her flexibility to brush her lips across his slowly before breaking away to take a sip of her wine. "It would mean moving to London."

"If that's what you want," he took advantage of her slight movement to slip a hand inside her robe running his thumb over the hot lace encasing her body.

"The only downside," she continued calmly even as she squirmed against his touch. "Is how expensive property is here."

"Hmmm," he found the seam of the garment rubbing his thumb across it roughly making her squirm. "That's true. It's hard enough to buy in a nice area with two good salaries."

"You don't have a little bolt-hole somewhere I could rent from you, do you?" she shifted away eyeing him mischievously.

"I wish," he ran a finger lightly across the curve of her thigh back towards the spot he had been caressing.

"What would happen if you got divorced?" She mused

in a teasing tone.

"I'm sure I'll be fine," he responded dryly. He was ninety-percent sure that she was joking about him getting a divorce, but her comment rang alarm bells.

"You're leaving it late to think about these things," she continued. "One minute you're in a nice big house and the next thing you know, your wife has kicked you out and you're living in a studio in a commuter town. It happened to Dave White."

"Thank you for your concern," he felt a flicker of irritation that she would compare him to someone Dave's level. "I'm due a substantial inheritance from my father's estate, so once he pops his clogs, I'll be sure to purchase a batchelor pad."

"How very cheerful," she deadpanned as he gently removed her from his lap, refilling their glasses to hide his concern. "Well, as much as I'd like to drink to your father's good health, I may have my own agenda for hoping that inheritance comes in sooner rather than later."

He frowned at her in confusion. "And what agenda might that be?"

She looked at him for a moment in silence as if weighing up what to say, and her stillness unnerved him. She stood up, letting the robe fall to the floor. His jaw dropped as the delicate web of black lace covering her exquisite body erased all his concerns. She reached for his glass draining the red liquid in one mouthful and climbed onto his lap, the fragrance of her body making his head spin with desire. She ran her lips across his neck before catching the lobe of his ear between her teeth sending shivers of lust through his whole body.

"Because maybe I want you for myself."

Belle

Belle clumsily hobbled back to her makeshift bedroom in the ground floor study. Toby was upstairs in the spare room, and she hated that she couldn't even make it up the stairs to put him to bed or get him up in the morning. She had tried limping around the kitchen to help with the children's breakfast, but she was so slow that she ended up just getting in the way and making Eleanor late.

It was an awful feeling to be such a useless burden, but her sister-in-law handled it with grace; if she found Belle a nuisance, she never let it show. Belle was half-hoping the hospital would change her cast to a walking-boot, but half-hoping that they didn't. The moment she could manage the stairs would be the minute she had to leave the Joneses' beautiful home, and she still hadn't figured out where she was going to go.

She heard Eleanor descending the stairs closely followed by Hugo and Toby. The boys had become thick as thieves despite the age gap, and their little voices chattering away tugged at her heartstrings. She would love for them to continue their friendship after she moved out, but she knew that it was unlikely that she'd ever have a permanent relationship with her brother's family.

Still, she thought morosely as she tossed back a handful of painkillers before shuffling out to her son. *That's the least of my worries right now.*

"Don't forget Uncle Will is picking you up from Katie's today," she reminded him. "So, make sure your shoes aren't muddy before you get in his car."

"Any plans for today?" Eleanor asked as Belle waved Toby off with Eleanor's kindly neighbour who had been dropping him to the school's breakfast club on her own way to work.

"Still flat-hunting," Belle gave her sister-in-law a wry smile. "I promise I'll be out of your hair at some point. I just need to speak to my landlord about getting my deposit back, get this thing off my leg and I'll be gone."

"Don't be silly," she replied hefting Bea up onto her hip. "It's more important that you find the right place for you and Toby. I know Hugo will miss him when you two go."

"We'll miss you too, Hugo," Belle affectionately ruffled his hair. "I really do appreciate you all."

"That's what family are for," Eleanor dropped a kiss on to her head as she passed leaving Belle flushing with pleasure at the sweet gesture.

Exhausted from her fitful sleep, she crawled back into bed for an hour before forcing herself to get up to tackle the stressful task of chasing down her landlord. After being promised a call back by the letting agent, she limped into the kitchen to make herself a sandwich when she noticed Tim's phone light up on the counter next to her. She glanced at it, her eyes narrowing in disbelief as she scanned the line of text in the notification.

No! She stared at the text in shock. *Tim might be a crap brother, but he wouldn't cheat on Eleanor, surely?*

Belle might be a lot of things by her own admission, but naïve had never been one. She'd had enough experience with liars and cheaters to know the signs, and the more she stewed over the content of the message, the more his long working hours and weekend plans seemed suspicious. He was barely ever in the house, and when he was, he was snappy and irritable. She had seen enough married men who were just like him, in their expensive suits throwing their surplus cash around in Fantasies.

Poor Eleanor, she thought as she pushed the phone away in disgust. *She deserves better.*

It wasn't her business she reminded herself as she aggressively packed away the ingredients, no longer hungry.

For all I know Eleanor could be well aware of Tim's antics, she tried to convince herself but somehow, she didn't think it was the kind of thing Eleanor would put up with. *It's not like she's reliant on him financially; she must earn good money of her own. No, she wouldn't have it.*

If it were one of her friends' boyfriend, she wouldn't hesitate to confront them. But Tim was her brother, and she was staying in his house. She was still fretting over what to do when the letting agency called back; the short exchange immediately pushing Tim's philandering to the back of her mind. She had just hung up when Will pulled up onto the drive to drop Toby home from school.

"What's happened?" He asked seeing the expression on her face.

"The bloody landlord did a property check ready for me to hand the keys in Friday," she groaned. "He's withholding over half of it because he's found a burn in the carpet that Ben did by accident."

"He should pay for that, surely!" Will knew how much she needed the deposit back for a new place.

"That's not the worst part," she grimaced. "Because we were both on the agreement. He reckons he'd give us half of the remaining amount each, but he wants both keys back first, and guess who I can't get hold of?"

"Oh, that's a nightmare!" Will looked genuinely gutted for her. "Surely Ben will give it back to get his money?"

"With the burn in the carpet and the landlord claiming it needs a deep clean, it's only going to be five-hundred-pounds," she looked devastated. "He might hand the key in for that incentive, but it was all my money in the first place! I used the deposit I had back from my old flat, and not a penny of it was Ben's, but there's nothing I can do to get it back."

"That's so expensive," he winced, wondering how anybody could afford to pay a deposit, moving fees and the first month rent while they were out of work. "What are you going to do?"

"No idea," she sighed despondently.

"You'll have to ask Tim," he grimaced. "I'm so sorry I can't help."

"I really don't want to ask him," she replied. "I'm here rent-free, eating their food; they've even bought Toby loads of presents for his birthday. Plus, how would I ever afford to pay them back? I won't be able to work for ages, and now I've got no childcare. It's hopeless."

Will wrapped an arm around his sister hugging her tightly as he racked his brain for a solution.

"London is so expensive," he empathised. "Even Craig is thinking about moving because he could get so much more for his money elsewhere."

"It's not even a nice place to live," she said glumly. "Unless you're loaded like Tim."

"Have you thought about moving out of London?" Will suggested as an idea came to him. "You'd need much less deposit, rent would be cheaper, and you'd still get the same benefits until you're back in work."

"Where would I go though?" The thought had crossed her mind, but she was terrified of being stuck in the middle of nowhere with absolutely no network. Even her scrappy little patchwork of estranged siblings and friends had been invaluable after her accident.

"Well, you still talk to some of your school friends back home," he said. "And even though he's useless, Dad is still there."

"I doubt he'd be any help," she replied sullenly, but her heart skipped a beat as she realised the suggestion appealed to her. "Although, I do think it's a better place to bring up Toby."

"Oh, definitely," Will felt a glimmer of hope that they may be getting somewhere. All he wanted to do was help his sister, but without money it seemed there was nothing that he could really offer. "Hey, maybe Dad would be able to lend you money!"

"I doubt it," she pulled a face. "He's hardly rolling in it."

The seed of the idea had been planted though, and Will tapped the keys in his hand against his leg in contemplation.

"Why are you looking like that?" Belle regarded him suspiciously, but Will could read her well enough to see there was a glimmer of hope in her expression.

"Look," he began tentatively. "It's just an idea, but what if Dad would agree to sell the fields and let us all take a share." He thought of his own crippling debt. "Even split five ways that would be enough until you're back on your feet."

She felt a flicker of excitement, but just as quickly she reminded herself to not get her hopes up. "Do you really think he would? Did anyone even find out if we had any right to anything after he gets married?"

"I don't know, but there's no harm in asking," Will said trying to remain positive. "And there's no harm in having a look at how much it would cost if you moved. You've already said that there's nothing close to Toby's school that's affordable, and he'll probably have to move again anyway."

She was trying her best to ignore the quickening of her pulse at Will's suggestion. It *did* make sense; she was still in touch with a few of her old friends who lived close to the village, and some of them had children too. In the village, he'd be able to ride his bike out on the street, call for his mates and go to the park without her trailing behind him terrified he'd be run over or worse. Even as a teenager, the worst she'd ever seen in the village had been drunken behaviour and the occasional bus shelter graffitied.

Even if Dad doesn't want anything to do with us.

The thought still stung, but it was impossible to not get excited after a quick search online that left both her and Will speechless at the difference. She could get twice the space and a garden for the money she was paying here. Even if nobody would lend her the money, if she was really thrifty and stayed here for another few weeks, she could probably manage to scrape together a deposit.

"Look," Will said wisely. "As soon as you've had your cast changed, let's go down there. I'll ask Dad for you, and maybe we can get the lay of the land, look at a few places..."

"Yeah," she nodded her head feeling more bolstered than before. "That's a good plan, Will. Thank you."

She tried to keep her hopes from rocketing, but thoughts of a place of her own, green spaces and a proper family for Toby were already taking over her head. She would have to swallow her pride to ask Tim if she could stay a bit longer, but now that the seed had been planted, she could barely contain her excitement.

Will

"Is it weird," Will turned down the volume on the stereo as they zipped past the sign proclaiming that they had arrived at Hampton Dale. "That I always feel like I'm about fifteen when I come back here?"

They'd been driving in silence for the last part of the journey, both lost in their own thoughts. Belle had been feeling exactly the same, and she was relieved that it wasn't just her.

"And me," she admitted. "It's funny because I couldn't wait to get out of here, and I never thought I'd want to come back."

Will took his eyes off the road to look at her over his sunglasses. "Do you still feel that it's what you want to do? Or are you going to see how Dad is first?"

"I've got zero expectations of Dad," she pulled a face, but he noticed how she had started fidgeting with the end of her plait as she spoke, a nervous habit that she'd had as a little girl. "He's never done anything for any of us. I'm amazed he even remembered that he had kids to invite to his wedding. I left the village *because* of him, not because I didn't like it there."

He swallowed back his discomfort forcing himself to ask her the question that had been on his mind for a while. "What was he like after Mum died?"

Belle rolled her eyes. "Exactly the same; hardly around, moody, and irritable when he was there. No change really, but I'd always had Mum to balance his coldness, and the atmosphere was unbearable without her."

"He wasn't always like that though, was he?" Will frowned. It was hard to remember what was real and what was just nostalgia after so long. "He was alright with you all before Mum..."

"No," Belle turned to shake her head at him. "Absolutely not. He was always that bad. He did nothing for us unless Mum made him or there was something in it for him."

Will pressed his lips together thoughtfully but said nothing.

"What are you thinking?" She pressed him.

He shook his head. "Nothing."

"No," she insisted. "Go on."

Will was silent for a moment. He was too self-conscious to admit what he'd always thought about his relationship with his father, but it felt like he'd been keeping too much in lately. His sister was refreshingly honest; she was hot-headed and always said what she was thinking. Will wished he could be more like her instead of repressing everything, scared to upset anyone.

"I always thought," he took a deep breath deciding to take the plunge. "That Dad was always off with me because I was gay."

He waited for Belle to laugh or dismiss the concern that had festered at the back of his mind since he was a boy. It was part of the reason he'd never come back, and part of the reason that he found being around Frank Jones so hard. His sister surprised him when she didn't reject his belief immediately.

"I don't know," she admitted. "I honestly couldn't tell you if the old man is an outdated bigot. I don't get him, Will, at all. He's the most closed person, emotionally, I've ever met." She flashed him a grin. "And I've dated in London."

Will laughed, grateful for her attempt to lighten the heaviness at the mention of their father. She flipped down the sun-visor fussing with a tiny smudge of eyeliner in the corner of her eye as she continued. "I would like to think that he doesn't think like that," she said seriously. "He's the kind of person who would say something if he did, don't you think?"

"I don't know," Will admitted, but what she was saying did ring true. Growing up, Frank had had an opinion about every one of their neighbours, and they'd all heard his grumpy outbursts on numerous occasions. "I guess."

"Look," Belle shut the visor glancing over her shoulder to check Toby was still occupied beneath his headphones. "He's a lot of things, but I don't think he's that vile." She frowned as if considering her words. "No, I don't think he's ever even thought about it, because that would mean having an opinion about any of us. Which he clearly never has."

"Maybe." He fell quiet as he contemplated Belle's logic. He had always felt that the non-existent relationship was down to his father's prejudice, but even though her reasoning seemed plausible, it was too tragic to cheer Will up at all.

He steered the car off the High Street, driving in silence past the pub until they reached the gates of Bluebell Farm. Today the gate was wide open, and Will slowed the car taking care to avoid the potholes in the long drive.

"The car's not there," Will pointed out. "Maybe they're out."

"I told him we were stopping by," Belle sounded annoyed, but even despite the awkward walking-boot on her foot that had finally replaced the cast she was the first out of the car. "Well, I spoke to Linda. He 'wasn't available'."

Toby hopped out of the car scampering ahead of them around the side of the house. Even though he'd only been here once before on their brief visit, he had talked about the lambs and the fields constantly since. Belle had admitted to Will that it had made her feel guilty that he rarely got to go on daytrips, let alone holidays. They followed him through to the back of the house, but nobody answered when they knocked.

"Typical!" She exclaimed in annoyance, but when she pushed the door handle sharply it flew open. Belle leaned over the threshold to call into the house. "Hello? Dad? Linda? It's Belle."

"Shall we go in?" Will asked her when there was no response. He had had to psych himself up to come here today, and only then because he knew how hard it would be for his sister to swallow her pride to ask their father for help. He could see in the clench of her jaw that she was furious that he wasn't here. Even worse though, he knew her pride was wounded. They had an appointment to see a house in the next village, and Belle had even been speaking to a school friend about a potential job. All she needed was some money for a deposit and to tide her over, and they had both really hoped that their father, despite all his faults, would come through for her.

She shrugged as if she didn't care, but he could see the hurt glistening in her eyes, and it gave him the courage to brush past her into the house. He stepped into the kitchen, calling out and drew to a halt as he peered around the corner into the sitting room that had been Tim's bedroom. His father was fast asleep, sat up in the armchair with his chin slumped against his chest. Will could hear his quiet snores, and he felt his heart soften at the sight of the vulnerable, old man who seemed a million miles away from the father they'd grown up with. They drew to a halt looking at each other uncertainly.

"Hi Grandad!" Toby skipped into the room oblivious to their indecision. "Hey, is Frank asleep?"

Will didn't miss Belle flinch at her son's greeting, but

before she could react further, their father stirred in his armchair opening his eyes. He stared at them with a look of bewilderment, and Will felt a jolt of panic that their own father didn't recognise them.

"Hi Dad," he tried to sound calm even as he remembered how disorientated his father had seemed for the first few minutes of their last visit. "We told Linda we were coming."

Frank blinked twice blankly at them before he seemed to even notice they were in front of him. The cloud seemed to lift as he rubbed a hand across his eyes. "Oh, have you been here long?"

"No, we just got here," Will felt a glimmer of relief. "I think Linda's gone out, but the door was open."

"Oh, has she?" He still seemed a little confused.

"So, how are you, Dad?" Belle asked in a faux-bright tone. "Have you got much left to do for the wedding?"

He shook his head. "No, Linda is taking care of all that."

An awkward silence descended over the room, before Toby, full of excitement at the day trip, burst out. "You were sleeping when we came in!"

Frank barely glanced at him, and for a horrible second Will thought he was going to ignore the little boy.

"That's old age for you," he said finally.

"You're not that old," Will reminded him. Even though his dad seemed coherent now, he was only seventy; Will was pretty sure he shouldn't be so decrepit. "Is everything ok? Have you been ill?"

Frank shook his head. "No, I'm fine. Anyway, what do I owe this pleasure?" He looked at them pointedly as if to emphasise that he remembered. "Twice in a year."

"I did tell Linda we were coming," Belle replied coolly, before slipping back into a more cheerful tone. "I'm thinking of moving back down here. I'm going to view a house over by Nelson's Garage."

"Moving?" He sounded surprised. "Down here?"

"Yes," she tried to sound breezy, but Will could see hear the edge to her tone. "It's cheaper down here than London, and a nicer place to bring up kids."

"Oh," his face was back to an impassive mask. "Well, that'll be nice."

"Any more news on selling the fields?" Will asked trying to sound conversational.

"Not got around to looking into it yet," Frank replied curtly.

Will flinched at his steely tone but pressed on. "I bet Mr Howells would snap them up. What do you think they'd go for?"

Frank eyed him suspiciously before replying. "About two hundred, Linda thinks."

"Two hundred?" Will repeated. "That's not bad for just the bottom fields. And it's not like you'd ever suddenly want to use them."

"Dad, do you think if you sold them that maybe we could get some of our share?" Belle spoke up quickly, her desperation overriding her reluctance to ask.

"Oh, this is nice," Linda's voice from the doorway made them all look up in surprise. Will felt his cheeks flame in mortification at how this must look. "I did wonder why you were coming down again so close to the wedding."

Will looked away guiltily, but Belle met her eyes boldly.

"Hi Linda," he pasted a friendly smile onto his face. "We're actually on our way to view a house that Belle's interested in."

The woman curved her lips into a cool smile that didn't reach her eyes.

"Have you got much left to organise for the wedding?" He asked when she didn't respond.

"No," she replied bluntly. "Are you staying long?"

Even Frank wasn't immune to her impatient tone, and Will saw him frown at her.

"We can't stay," Belle got to her feet before he could answer. "Our appointment is in half hour." She reached for Toby's hand but didn't take her eyes off Linda once. "Hopefully, we'll be seeing a lot more of you both."

He expected his sister to be livid, but the moment she laid eyes on the house she was viewing, she perked back up. Toby had barrelled around the garden squealing with excitement, and for Belle that had sold it to her. She was careful to manage his expectations, Will noticed, but he could see she was brimming with enthusiasm of her own.

"What are you going to do about money though?" He asked levelly when Toby had finally fallen asleep in the back of the car. "Are you going to ask Tim?"

"Probably not," she admitted. "I've been living rent-free in his house, and he's already lent me three-hundred quid for Toby's birthday present. That's going to take me forever to pay back as it is."

"So, what are you going to do?" Will hoped she wasn't going to ask him again. He was trying his best to build the business, and save money, but he was practically living off Craig as it was.

"The house is available from 1st July," she said calmly. "I just need to put the deposit down to secure it, and then I'll get another month's payment for the first month's rent. If I can get a job as soon as I get down here, I should be fine."

Will frowned. "But you'll have to live somewhere until then."

She shrugged. "I can't go anywhere until I can manage the stairs."

"I thought you were more mobile with that thing on,"

he was trying to be diplomatic, but even he hadn't missed Tim's passive-aggressive comments about her moving out despite only speaking to him a couple of times since Belle had been there.

"Well, I'm not," she replied defensively. "I'm sure Eleanor won't mind. Worst case scenario, we'll have to go into a hostel temporarily or crash on Katie's sofa."

"You can't do that," he cut in quickly.

"I might have to," she eyed him pointedly. "I'm not losing out on that house, Will. It's perfect. I'll do whatever I need to make sure it works."

He rearranged his expression into what he hoped was a supportive smile, but hours later he was still worrying. He had no doubt that his strong-willed sister would do whatever it took to make her plans come to fruition, but that would mean almost another two months at Tim's and he had a feeling that it wouldn't go down well.

I'm going to have to speak to Dad, he resolved as he waved his sister and his nephew off. *We could all do with the money, and it would solve all Belle's problems.*

Rose

Rose grimaced as yet another phone was slammed down on her. She should have grown used to it by now, but with every passing shift she was only growing more and more disheartened. She'd been at XZ Finance for three months now; optimistically hoping that the initial struggles would become easier as time went on, but every day felt like a steeper climb than the shift before. A quarter of the team that she'd started with had quit already, and in the past month Rose had taken a leaf out of their books firing out applications left, right and centre, knowing that it was a case of when, not if, she was either fired or had a complete breakdown from the relentless role. Not one application had resulted in even an interview yet, and she felt her hopefulness slip further away as she opened yet another 'thank you but no thank you' email on her lunch break.

"Everything ok?" Lena asked as Rose let out a gloomy sigh. "Tough morning, huh?"

"Pretty rubbish," she agreed. It was only marginally reassuring that hardly anyone had made a sale during the shift so far. "I don't know how long I can keep doing this."

"Think of the money, Rose," Lena gave her a sympathetic smile. "Any word from that hunk of yours?"

Rose had felt like a teenager confiding in her new friend about Gareth, their kiss, and the following flirtation. Today though, even that was a sore subject, and she shrugged woefully.

"We text most days," she admitted. "But between the distance and our shifts, I can't honestly see it going anywhere."

It had been almost three weeks since the kiss, and as surprisingly keen as he'd seemed to pursue something between them, the only weekend neither of them had been working Gareth had had plans with his children. She couldn't help but be realistic that his interest would start to wane. She was already mentally preparing herself to not grow too attached to his attention.

"It is what it is," she continued quickly, not wanting to put a downer on an already miserable day. "I found a nice dress for my dad's wedding though."

She pulled up the photo on her phone passing it to her friend. They fell into an easy conversation about dresses, weddings and hair that was far more cheerful than missed sales targets and long shifts until it was time to log back into their systems ready for a long afternoon of bombarding people with their sales patter.

Adele seemed more stressed and bad-tempered than usual, and Rose's heart sank when she was told to log off and directed into the meeting room, suspecting she was about to receive a dressing-down for her performance. She felt a flicker of panic at the thought of the pay cheque from this job being pulled before she had something else to go to.

"So, you probably know that your sales have been abysmal since you joined."

Rose flinched at the harsh opening. The door was still open, and her colleagues were within earshot. Admittedly, she wasn't a top seller and she suspected that she never would be, but she was only a few sales off the department average. She felt a rare flash of anger at being singled out in such a humiliating manner. "I think abysmal is a bit strong."

As the sales manager's eyes widened with surprise, Rose realised she'd been seen as an easy target to be made an example of. Adele recovered quickly though tossing her head haughtily. "I disagree. It's below average, and it's dragging my team down. I'm happy to accept your notice with immediate effect, or we'll go straight into a disciplinary after this. What would you rather?"

Rose's jaw dropped incredulously. "You can't do that!"

She saw uncertainty flicker across Adele's eyes, but the woman held her ground. "I think you'll find I can. What's it going to be?"

Rose's stomach knotted in fear as she frantically weighed up her options. There was no way she could just hand her notice in. With the added expense of Tom's accident last month, she was even further behind on paying her bills. Without a full month's pay, she would go from barely treading water to completely drowning, and she felt sick at the thought. She looked at the hateful woman desperately trying to figure out what to do for the best. She could sense her colleagues' eyes on her, and she glanced in their direction, too scared to be proud any longer. They were all watching in horrified fascination, and Rose had a sinking feeling that she was being sacrificed to scare them into working harder.

"If I hand my notice in," she said quietly with as much dignity as she could muster. "Do I get paid until the end of the month?"

"No," Adele shook her head scornfully. "You'll get paid for what you've worked minus any leave owed. You will be leaving with immediate effect."

"It's a week notice though," she argued. "If I hand my notice in, I work until next week, so I get paid up until then."

"That would be at my discretion," she hit back confidently. "It's either leave now or disciplinary."

Rose was almost certain that Adele must be breaking some kind of law with her heavy-handed tactics, but she had no concrete knowledge of what she was or wasn't entitled to. She could feel her hands beginning to tremble with adrenaline, and she balled them tightly into fists at her sides. "Can I think about this? It's a lot to take in."

"No," she seemed to thrive on Rose's upset. "It's one or the other. Otherwise I'll be pulling the notice option off the table, and that's your reference gone."

Rose stared at her, stunned into silence. She could feel her face heating up, no longer caring about the humiliation of the audience. She was livid that she was being forced into a corner by the obnoxious bully.

How dare she?

"Disciplinary," she replied coolly. "Can I get a copy of the policy first please?"

"It's online," surprise flickered fleetingly across the woman's face. "I'll wait here."

Rose was shaking with nerves as she returned to her desk. She could feel all eyes on her as she fumbled with the keyboard.

"Are you ok?" Lena had moved quietly to her side, and Rose looked up at her grateful for her show of support.

"I'm fine," she lied. "Don't put yourself in the firing line. She's watching."

On cue, Adele barked at Lena to get back to work. Rose nodded hurriedly to her, not wanting to get her friend into trouble. "Honestly, I'll be fine."

She had never had reason to access the company's internal homepage before, and it took Rose a few attempts to find the correct section. She could sense all eyes on her, and after a few minutes of going around in a maze of incorrect links, Adele walked up behind her to stare unnervingly over her shoulder. Rose moved the mouse ready to click into the policy when the banner on the homepage transitioned to the next image making Rose doubletake.

Head of Customer Operations discusses how we're leading the way for Digital Banking.

It can't be… Rose clicked on the link to take a closer look at the thumbnail image.

"What are you doing?" the woman snapped irritably behind her. "Can you hurry up please?"

Rose barely heard her in her surprise as she recognised the headshot of her smartly dressed older brother next to the article. She scanned the text, but it was just waffle about webchat and online banking; it meant nothing to her.

Would this be leverage? She wondered feeling like a miracle had dropped into her lap. Desperation at the thought of her mounting bills spurred her on.

"Oh, look," Rose glanced up at Adele feeling a rush of hatred for the cruel woman. "It's my brother."

Adele frowned stepping forward to take a closer look; a beetroot flush replacing her smug expression. Rose couldn't be sure if it was the name-drop or the company policy that stopped Adele sending her packing that very same day, but after a terse conversation the woman had no choice than to adjourn the meeting, issuing her with an invitation to a final hearing the following week.

"You didn't say your brother worked for XZ!" Lena said in surprise as they walked out together at the end of the shift.

"I didn't know he did," she admitted. "I knew he worked for a big bank, but I didn't even make the connection."

"He must be pretty high up," Lena said in a low voice as they reached the bus stop preparing to part ways. "Do you think he can help you?"

Rose shrugged, torn between her pride and her desperate need to hang on to the job for as long as possible. "I hope so."

Lena pulled her in for a quick hug. "Right, good luck. Let me know how you get on."

She managed to get hold of Tim on her third attempt that evening, and she felt her stomach knot with nerves when he finally answered.

"Everything alright?" He asked curtly.

"Hi," she ignored his lack of manners and ploughed on. "It's nothing to do with Dad. This is a work question."

"A work question?" He sounded confused.

"I work for XZ Finance," she launched straight into a summary of her disciplinary. "They can't do that, surely?"

"You work for the sales team?" He sounded incredulous. "Why are you working for them?"

"Because I needed a job, Tim," she replied defensively. "They're horrid, but I need the money until I find something else. Can you help me?"

"No," Tim responded abruptly. "I can't go getting involved in things like that. Take it up with HR or your union rep or something. Bloody hell, Rose, of all the things to phone me about. First Will and now you."

Rose's heart sank at his cold response. She should have known better than to think high-flying Tim would dirty his hands to help her, but she had at least hoped for a little empathy.

"What did Will want?" She asked, just for something to say. Hurt and dejected, all she wanted to do was to hang up on her brother, but she knew that it wasn't fair to blame him for her bad luck.

"To talk about the fields that Dad wants to sell," he told her. "He wants me to see where we stand when Dad gets remarried. He's got it into his head that we could persuade Dad to pay us a chunk when he sells the fields, like an early inheritance."

Rose felt a flicker of interest at the thought of a cash sum. "That's not a bad idea. Has anyone asked him what his intentions are? Or checked that our interests are protected?"

"I've not had time," Tim snapped. "I don't see why everything has to fall on me. You're all capable of finding these things out."

His tone barely resonated with Rose as her head began to spin with optimistic calculations. "How would we find out? Would we have access to Mum's will? Or we would have to check with Dad what he's going to do. I mean, it's not a bad idea selling the fields if he wants to, and it would certainly solve my work problem. It would help Belle and..."

"I don't know," he cut her off abruptly. "Now, I really do have to go."

Rose gaped as the line disconnected. She sank down onto her sofa, feeling furious at her selfish brother and humiliated at her own dire situation.

Tim

Heavy footsteps and loud voices followed by a crash and a burst of laughter pierced Tim's deep slumber, and he sprang awake already annoyed before he'd even opened his eyes. He struggled to sit up in bed, the mild ache of a hangover already playing at his temples, bristling with indignation at the sound of his five-year-old son yelling out to his older cousin.

This has gone too far, he thought irritably. He slid his pyjama-clad legs from the bed stomping towards the landing, ready to put a stop to their noisy, early-morning game.

"Ready or not!" Hugo bellowed, his volume belying his diminutive stature. "Here I come!"

"What is this din?" Tim opened the door abruptly. Hugo, who had been hurtling across the landing with glee, came to a hasty halt.

"We're playing hide and seek," the small boy looked up at his father, his eyes wide with panic at the stern tone.

"What's the matter?" To Tim's annoyance, he heard his sister call up the stairs, and he looked over the bannister to see her face frowning up at him.

"This noise is the matter," he replied. "Hugo, get in your bedroom. Toby! You, too! You can both sit quietly in there until you can learn to behave."

Toby peeked out from behind the bathroom door where he'd been hiding. "We were only playing."

"You were like a herd of elephants," Tim replied bluntly. "Bedrooms now!"

"Woah, hang on!" Belle called up the stairs. "That's a bit of an overreaction, Tim. They're just playing."

"It's not even nine o'clock on a Sunday morning!" Tim

snapped back. "Where's Eleanor?"

"She's gone to the gym," Belle told him. "Boys, come down here so Tim can sleep."

"No, boys. In your bedrooms, separately."

"Tim! Stop being dramatic." Belle snapped. "They can play downstairs with me and Bea. Just go back to bed."

He stared at his sister, teeming with rage at her insolence. Her wide green eyes glared back at him, unphased and challenging, making his blood heat up with fury. The two little boys' eyes darted between him, Belle and each other as they weighed up who to obey. Their uncertainty over who was in charge tipped Tim's temper over the edge.

"Hugo! Bed!" He bellowed, and the boy scampered into his room letting out a whimper of fear.

"Toby, downstairs," Belle's voice was calm, and her self-control was like a red flag to Tim's anger.

Enough is enough, Tim raged as he threw on some clothes. *I won't be spoken to like this in my own home.*

The week of recovery had turned into six long and exhausting weeks of his free-loading sister and her son living in his house. Every week she came up with another excuse to lengthen her stay, but this was the final straw.

Eleanor might be a mug, he growled to himself as he stormed down the stairs prepared to give her her long-overdue marching orders. *But I certainly am not.*

His sister was sat on the floor of the living room; her leg encased by the walking boot stretched out in front of her, Tim's daughter at her side. Her red curls were loose around her shoulders, obscuring her face as she passed puzzle pieces to a chuckling Bea. He paused at the scene, seeing the likeness of his mother in her profile. For just a fleeting moment, he was reminded of how serene his mother had been, like an anchor in a choppy sea.

Not that Belle is anything like our mother, he reminded himself of his sister's spiky, challenging temperament, casting the tug of nostalgia aside. His mind turned to Eleanor, who *did* have the sweet demeanour of Kathleen, but with that thought came a flash of unwelcome guilt.

"We need to have a word," he forced himself to focus on the matter at hand. "Toby, can you watch Bea while I speak to your mother?"

The little boy tore his eyes away from the television, but instead of consenting immediately, he glanced at his mother for approval. Tim watched as Belle's jaw tightened, but she nodded at her son before awkwardly clambering to her feet. She followed him wordlessly to the kitchen stopping in the doorway.

"I don't appreciate the way you just spoke to me," he said through gritted teeth. "You've been here too long. You need to leave."

He watched as her eyes, a mirror image of his, blazed with temper.

"Eleanor said it was fine," she said coolly. "I'm sorry that the boys woke you up, but there's no need to overreact."

"It's been six weeks," Tim snapped. "It's not an overreaction. You need to find somewhere else by the end of the week."

"I'm moving in July!" She exclaimed defensively. "I know it's not ideal, but Eleanor said..."

"Well, now I'm saying!" He burst angrily. "We're not a hotel; you can't stay here any longer."

Her pretty features twisted into an ugly scowl. "You sound just like Frank," she spat bitterly. "And you've got just as much compassion as him."

Tim rolled his eyes contemptuously. "Oh, grow up, Belle. You're thirty-years-old. Don't you think it's time you got your life together?"

"I'm trying," she hit back venomously. "I haven't got the luxury of a wealthy wife taking care of everything while I swan in and out with my bit-on-the-side."

Her accusation was unexpected, and he jerked backwards with shock at her words before he managed to catch himself, swiftly rearranging his expression into one of incredulous disgust.

"What?" He regarded her with contempt. "Now you're just being ridiculous."

Her nostrils flared, a tell that showed him how far gone she was in her temper, but she glanced around to check that the children were out of earshot before she spoke.

"You might treat Eleanor like she's stupid," her voice was a low growl. "But she's certainly not. It's only a matter of time before she finds out about your little friend Emma. She deserves better than you, Tim."

The mention of Emma's name filled his chest with icy fear, and he was struck by the realisation that he'd underestimated his sister.

"You're wrong," he snapped back, but he could tell from the twist of her mouth that she didn't believe him. "Don't you ever try to blackmail me. I want you out of this house."

"Get Dad to cut us in on the fields then," she said without missing a beat. "I need the money. The only one who doesn't is you, but maybe a divorce will be an incentive for you."

"Are you threatening me?" He squeezed his fists to his side fighting the urge to physically throw her out onto the street.

Belle tossed her head haughtily, a glint of satisfaction in her eyes at the reaction from him. "Not at all," she replied coolly. "I wouldn't do that to Eleanor. I would never tear apart a family, or intentionally upset anyone."

Her boldness unnerved him. He never backed down from his decisions, but he felt an uncharacteristic stab of doubt. It wasn't just her threats that had him on the brink of a U-turn, he realised as he stared at her as if seeing her properly for the first time. He had always thought of his brother and sisters as weak. That was if he thought of them at all, but the fire in Belle's eyes was like looking in a mirror, and despite his anger he felt a begrudging respect for her.

"Look," he scowled. "I know Eleanor likes having you and Toby around, but surely it would be easier if you stayed with Will until you move."

"I won't stay where I'm not wanted," she crossed her arms across her chest defiantly, but he saw the shadow of hurt in her eyes.

With nothing more to say, she turned away from him. Even though he felt that she had had the upper hand in the fight, there was a dejected slump to her shoulders and he realised with a spark of satisfaction that she wouldn't risk hurting Eleanor for revenge.

Belle

"Thanks for helping me," Belle said to her brother as he heaved the final black bags into the car.

Will swiped a hand across his perspiring brow exhausted from carting her belongings down the stairs from her friend's flat. "That's ok," he grimaced. "Sorry that I couldn't fit any more in."

Belle shrugged trying not to think about all the clothes and kitchenware she'd had to give away due to her hasty move. She knew it was just stuff, but the thought of having to buy new pots, pans, plates, and bedding from an already-tight budget was another worry to add to her ever-growing list.

"That's ok," she tried her best to look upbeat. "I couldn't expect Katie to keep any more of my stuff anyway. She's already done enough." She shot him a grateful smile. "And you have too."

He grimaced. "I wish I could do more, Belle, I really do."

It had stung her when Will had told her that she and Toby couldn't move in after the showdown with Tim, but she could see that her brother was genuinely remorseful. Even in her preoccupation about her own situation, she knew he was having his own problems, and her heart went out to him.

"How's everything?" She asked sympathetically as he started the engine carefully reversing out of the parking bay. "Are you two ok now?"

Belle had a feeling that her call to Will asking if she could stay for a few weeks had been the catalyst for his own relationship problems. He'd gone away, promising to check with Craig and get back to her, but the same day had called her back ruefully explaining that they'd had an argument, and he was going to be crashing at his friend Raya's for a few days. Will had been adamant that it was completely unrelated, but she wasn't convinced.

"Yeah," Will tried to look upbeat, but Belle could see straight through him, and she tilted her head questioningly until he continued. "It's tough. I really like Craig, but he's at the stage in his life where he wants to buy a house, settle down and I just don't know if that's what I want."

"You're back home now though, so I thought you guys had come to a compromise?"

Will wrinkled his nose. "I don't know. We love each other, but we're just going around in circles. It's more of a truce at the moment until it comes up again."

Belle frowned disapprovingly. "Will, you still haven't told him that you want to go to Japan, have you?"

He flushed guiltily. "No, but then I don't even know if I will go."

"Why?" She'd seen her brother's eyes light up with excitement when he'd recounted the possibility of the trip, whereas she'd only seen his eyes glaze over when Craig talked about mortgages and relocating to Bristol. "It's clear that's what you want, Will."

"It's stupid though," he sighed heavily. "Craig is right- I do need to grow up. I could do ok if I keep up the business on my own when Raya takes off. The family photoshoots are pretty lucrative, and I can set up in Bristol just as easily. Within two years, Craig says I should be able to come onto the mortgage with him so we could get a bigger place or even a rental property. Or this time in two years, I could be living out of a backpack in exactly the same position."

"I'm sorry," she shook her head dubiously. "But just because that's what Craig wants, doesn't mean it's right for you. Will, I know you want to go to Japan and then wherever the wind takes you. Can you honestly say that photographing babies for the rest of your life is what you want to do?"

He shook his head. "I know, I know. It's just so hard to hurt Craig. I feel so guilty."

"You need to make a decision," she warned him. "The longer you drag this out, the worse you're going to hurt him. And you cannot give up all your dreams to make him happy."

"I'll talk to him," he promised. "I just need to decide what to do for the best. I'd really miss him if we broke up, but it's not fair to expect him to wait for me to be done gallivanting around the world."

Will eased the car to a stop outside their brother's house, and helped Belle carry the bags to the garage where she was storing her meagre belongings until her move. Tim had reluctantly agreed to extending her deadline after Will's rocky relationship had put paid to her back-up plan. They had come to an uneasy truce, but Belle was finding it tough; overwhelmed with guilt that she knew about Tim's other woman. Her brother had even spent a few nights away from home, citing the flimsiest excuses to an oblivious Eleanor, and Belle cringed with shame at being complicit in his double life. She had a horrible feeling that the secret was rising closer to the surface with every day that passed; as selfish as she felt thinking it, she just hoped she wasn't still there when it all came to a head.

"Are you staying down the night before the wedding?" Will asked conversationally as they sat in Eleanor's kitchen drinking tea.

"We were going to drive down in the morning," Eleanor said. "Are you all going down the night before?"

Will nodded. "Rose is staying down Friday night in a B & B. Craig and I thought it would be a nice idea rather than rushing down. We can help with setting up the gazebo on

Friday. Belle, are you still going down on the Thursday?"

Belle nodded. She was staying with an old school friend, and she had a job interview lined up on the Friday. It was half-term for the schools, so it was a nice opportunity for him to get to meet some kids from the area.

"Tim didn't say," Eleanor looked mildly annoyed. He was conveniently out all day as he'd been gifted corporate tickets to a football match, although Belle didn't buy his story. "That's actually a great idea. What hotel are you staying at?"

"The Red Lion," Will told her before hurriedly adding. "It's not a hotel as much as a few rooms over a pub. There's a nice Spa hotel a few miles out though."

Eleanor's eyes lit up. "Oh, really? That sounds nice. To be honest, it's been forever since we had a night away. It would definitely make more sense than driving down and back."

Will pulled up the hotel on Eleanor's phone. Belle balked at the cost per night for a family suite, feeling a flicker of envy as Eleanor tapped her card details in for two nights without batting an eyelid. She and Toby were making do with a Megabus there that she'd paid for in advance to get the best deal and staying on a friend's sofa while they were in the village.

"Do you want me to order anything for Toby to wear?" Eleanor asked her later when Will was gone, and Belle felt herself flush with humiliation.

She hated feeling like a charity case, and she knew Eleanor was just being thoughtful, but Belle had seen the price tags on Hugo and Bea's little outfits. She'd never be able to afford to pay her back, even if she did get the new job. Plus, it was inevitable that when it all came out that Tim was playing away, Eleanor would want nothing more to do with his family, Belle included.

"No, thank you," she said gratefully. "But thanks for offering."

"Well, if you change your mind," Eleanor replied looking like she wanted to push it but choosing not to. "Don't worry about paying me back. That's what family are for."

Belle felt a lump rise in her throat, grateful for the distraction when Bea took that moment to knock over a beaker of water. She hurried to fetch the paper towels as quickly as the plastic case on her foot would allow her to.

"It's just a bit of water," Eleanor reassured Bea who was on the verge of tears. "Don't worry, sweetheart."

She's such a great mother, Belle thought as she watched her sister-in-law comfort the toddler. *And she was the one who offered us a place to stay, not Tim. God knows what would have happened to me and Toby without her.*

A flame of anger hotter than anything Belle had felt before sparked up in her chest as she thought of Tim out with his fancy woman while Eleanor had no idea. It took her spiralling back to the long months when her mother had been unwell, and Frank had breezed in and out of the house, coming and going as he pleased, leaving everything to Belle even though she was just a child herself.

He's just like Dad, she thought angrily. *They're exactly the same.*

She thought of the meagre balance of her bank account, and the house where she and her mother had been happy, and she thought of Tim and Frank, so alike and selfish, both blocking her from being able to stand on her own two feet and provide for her son with dignity; a blaze of pure fury coursed through her.

I'm not going to let them win, she vowed heatedly. She didn't know how, but she was determined that she would gain the upper hand sooner rather than later.

The Day Before the Wedding

Tim

Tim flinched as his phone buzzed again in the pocket of the door, loud and intrusive even over the chattering of the children buckled into their seats behind him. He kept his eyes fixed firmly on the road ahead, but he could feel Eleanor's eyes dart to him when it buzzed for the fourth time in succession.

"Do you need to get that?" She asked, and he thought there was an uncharacteristic edge to her tone.

You're being paranoid, he scolded himself.

The stress of juggling two lives paired with the strain of his siblings' constant neediness was clearly getting to him. Emma had been livid that he was staying in a hotel with his own wife for two nights, and the force of her jealousy had unnerved him. He had genuinely believed they had both been up for a no-strings-attached fling, but her behaviour was starting to concern him.

He shook his head pressing his foot down hard on the accelerator. The sooner this wedding palaver was over and done with, the sooner he could focus on sorting out his own mess before it came back to haunt him.

Rose

Rose tossed the dress carelessly onto the back seat of Jack's car, not caring if it creased. She'd spent hours searching for the right dress, hoping that she might see Gareth after the wedding and wanting to look her best, but since she'd been unceremoniously sacked from XZ Finance, she had called time on her flirtation with him. The sense of failure had hit her hard. Another rejection would tip her over the edge, so she had nipped the blossoming romance in the bud in a polite-but-curt text message citing the distance as too much.

She knew that she had done the right thing. It was too humiliating to have to admit to him that she'd been sacked. There was no way that Gareth, so handsome with a good job, would want to date someone who had no money and no prospects.

Rose had already paid for two nights in a cheap B & B weeks before the wedding, otherwise she thought she would have cried off with an imaginary illness, and she was dreading the two days ahead of her. The last trip to Bluebell Farm, when she took meeting Gareth out of the equation, had highlighted how cut off she really was from her family.

Let's just get this over with.

This trip would probably be the last time she saw her family together, and as she started up the engine, she felt lower than ever.

Will

Will glanced at the message on his phone, feeling his heart speed up at Raya's message telling him that she had booked her flights.

"Who's that?" Craig asked looking up from the road ahead.

"It's just Raya," he answered, and before he could force himself to broach the conversation that he'd been avoiding he heard himself add hurriedly. "Work stuff."

Craig made a non-committal noise before going back to humming along to the radio, and Will's stomach knotted with guilt. After his conversation with his younger sister, he'd come to the realisation that he needed to be honest with Craig. He'd tried to raise the subject of travel several times, but each time he'd swiftly backed off and he was angry with himself for his cowardice.

As soon as the wedding is over, he told himself sternly.

Belle

Belle's interview had gone fantastically, and she was buzzing with excitement as she walked the short distance from the shop to the park where her friend was waiting for her with Toby and her own daughter.

"How'd it go?" Stephanie called out as she approached.

"Nailed it," Belle sighed happily. "They pretty much said that it was mine if I want it."

"Yay!" Her friend threw her arms around her excitedly. "I'm so happy for you. It's going to be so good to have you back!"

"Thank you so much for letting me stay," she said as Stephanie dropped her off to the B & B later that day to meet her sister. "And for lending me all these dresses. You really are the best!"

Belle had been planning on staying with her friend for the whole weekend, but Rose had called her out of the blue to ask her if she wanted to go halves on a hotel room. It was only forty pounds, but she was watching her pennies, so her initial reaction had been to decline until Rose had told her that she had lost her job. With a little coaxing, her sister had admitted that she was struggling, emotionally and financially. Knowing how that felt, Belle hadn't had the heart to say no.

She had zero desire to attend the wedding. Linda couldn't have made it any clearer that she had no intention of playing happy families, and after the last few months tiptoeing on eggshells around Tim, Belle was in no rush to be made to feel unwelcome ever again. But in the back of her mind, she couldn't shake the hope that Frank might still want to do the right thing and cut them into the profit from the sale of the fields. She'd been wrestling with worries about the will since they'd received the invitation, but as time ticked on it seemed more and more likely that she would be left out in the cold when the time came.

But the more Toby and I are around, she thought with fierce determination, *hopefully the less chance that he'll decide to cut us out completely after the wedding.*

Tim

"Are we not all going to help your dad set up?" Eleanor asked in surprise when Tim suggested that she take the children off to the hotel's indoor swimming pool for an hour.

Tim shook his head briskly. "No, the children will get in the way and it makes sense for at least one of us to enjoy the facilities. I'll go on my own."

She looked disappointed, but now that he'd mentioned the pool in front of the children there was no way she could insist without a mutiny on her hands from an excited-looking Hugo. He felt a flicker of guilt at the expression on her face, but the weight of his phone in his pocket reminded him of the increasing urgency of Emma's messages. He needed privacy to resolve the issue.

He tried calling her on the drive over to Bluebell Farm, but there was no response. It was typical that she called him back as he was stood holding up a pole in the middle of the field waiting for his brother to secure it in place.

"Can someone grab this?" He called to his sisters who had just arrived. "I need to take this call."

By the time Belle had ambled over with the heavy boot on her foot, the call had rung off. He passed the pole to her wordlessly, feeling her eyes on the back of his head as he redialled.

His face reddened with discomfort as a hot-headed Emma launched into a barrage of weepy accusations as soon as the line connected. He heard himself uttering assurances that he had no intention of keeping, desperate to placate her to buy himself a few days reprieve while he figured out the best way to break off their arrangement. He hadn't reckoned on her irrational reaction to the mention of his weekend plans, assuming the feelings she had mentioned were just pillow-talk.

He didn't want to lose Eleanor, he realised with sickening clarity. He loved her, and the life they had. He had only wanted the illicit thrill of an affair with the wild, adventurous Emma. He had made no promises to her, presuming that she understood that their time together was just a fling, albeit an addictive one. Her teary emotional outburst had him terrified that he had bitten off more than he could chew.

"Everything alright?"

Tim had stopped to make his call in the semi-privacy of the lane between the house and the field, and Frank had emerged from the garden gate looking sprightlier than he had at their previous visit. He hadn't heard his father approach, and he hurriedly shoved his phone back into his pocket.

"Yes, fine," he said quickly.

His father looked better today, Tim thought to himself regarding his father in the cloudless daylight.

There's plenty of life in the old man yet, he thought. *We must have just caught him on an off day.*

"Thanks for coming to help get everything set up," Frank said awkwardly. "Linda and I appreciate the help."

"That's ok," Tim said already turning back towards his siblings setting up in the field opposite the house. It was the one remaining parcel of land that Frank hadn't leased out to the neighbouring farmer, and Tim remembered his brother and sisters' comments about asking for a cut. His head quickly ran the calculations. Compared to his in-law's fortune, even *with* the fields Bluebell Farm was a comparative pittance, but between Emma's increasing demands and his gnawing paranoia since Belle had somehow cottoned on to his secret, Tim suddenly felt a flicker of fear at the thought of losing his portion of the estate, and he turned back to his father sharply. "Can I ask what your intentions are when you're married? I vaguely remember that you and Mum had mirror wills, but I imagine you'll be looking to make an amendment to provide for Linda."

Frank's eyes flickered away from Tim's shiftily. "Of course," he responded tightly. "I haven't got around to speaking to my solicitor yet, but I imagine I will in the next few weeks. I need to get the ball rolling with the fields anyway..."

He trailed off staring over at the gazebo, and in that moment, Tim knew intuitively that his father had every intention of cutting them out completely. A spark of indignation ignited in the pit of his stomach, and he opened his mouth to press him on the matter when Will appeared at the gate to the field.

"It's up, Dad," Will stated proudly. "I was just coming to get you."

The relief was evident on Frank's face as he sauntered away after his younger son, leaving Tim stood in the lane alone. His legs felt like stone, and instead of following after them, he turned in a slow circle looking around at the rolling green of Bluebell Farm. The land had been in his mother's family for decades, and his eyes travelled back to the farmhouse settling on the cheap double-glazing that Linda's nephew had installed after his last visit home. He blazed with fury at the thought of that wretched woman taking what was rightfully his. At the back of his mind, he remembered all the times that his siblings had tried to raise the subject with him. He flushed with humiliated regret remembering that he had cut them off; too preoccupied with his own life to have time to consider their warnings.

No, he pushed away any accountability fiercely turning

the blame back onto the three of them, *they should have been the ones to raise it with Frank. Why should I be the one to go chasing after solicitors?*

He stood at the gate watching his father and his brother stroll across the field towards his sisters. He felt his hackles rise at the sight of Belle. He had noticed that her limp seemed to have magically disappeared now that she was back in Hampton Dale, and he felt a secondary swell of anger rise up deep from the pit of his stomach so strong that it threatened to burst from him in a mighty roar. But instead, with practised deliberation, he pressed it back until he could feel the vibrations of his rage settle into his core. Nothing good would come out of him losing his temper with them all, he knew.

No, he would have one shot to convince his father, and he knew that he would have to play his hand carefully. And then he would never have to set eyes on any of them again.

Rose

Rose stretched up on to tiptoes to tie the bunting to the corner of the gazebo, but she couldn't quite reach. She stepped back to look around for someone to help. Belle and Toby were tossing a ball back and forth, and her brothers had disappeared.

She spotted Craig's head over the hedge and waited, idly watching as Toby threw the ball wide and Belle nimbly threw herself up into the air to catch it. Rose grimaced as she watched the heavy boot take off thinking her sister had forgotten about her injury, but Belle barely flinched when she landed. Rose's phone buzzed from the back pocket of her jeans. She fished it out, her heart skipping a beat at Gareth's name flashing up on the screen.

Just ignore it, she told herself, but willpower had never been her strength.

"Hello," she answered cautiously.

"Hey," Gareth sounded endearingly nervous making her stomach flutter with hope. "I hope you don't mind me calling. I heard you're in town."

When she had made the decision to end things with Gareth, it had been entirely out of self-preservation, but she couldn't switch off the magnetic pull she felt towards him.

"I am," she confirmed quietly. "How are you?"

"I'm ok," he replied. "I was just wondering if you had time to get a coffee?"

She hesitated, and he added quickly. "Just as friends if that's all you want, Rose."

It's not what I want, she thought glumly. Even though there had only been one kiss, they had spoken enough for Rose to know that she really liked him. *Just friends,* her heart was already trying to trick her into accepting, *it would be rude to say no. You're in town, where's the harm?*

"That would be nice," she heard herself reply guardedly. "I'm staying at The Red Lion if you fancy a proper drink later."

"I'm working this evening," his voice brightened instantaneously at her response. "Any chance you can meet me at the café on the High Street in half hour? Or I can pick you up?"

Despite her own reservations, she found herself smiling as she made her excuses to her brothers and sister to drive into the village to meet him. Gareth was already waiting for her in the little coffee shop, with two lattes and a blueberry muffin on the table. His face lit up when she pushed the door open, and she felt her resolve weaken when he wrapped her in a friendly hug.

"I didn't know whether to call you," he admitted sheepishly. "I remembered it was the wedding, but I bumped into my sister Steph earlier with your sister."

"I'm glad you did," she admitted unable to resist his infectiously warm smile. "I didn't realise that her friend was your sister though."

"That's Hampton Dale," he joked before turning serious. "Look, Rose, I totally respect everything you said about the distance thing, and I totally get it..."

He paused, and she found herself holding her breath, suddenly wanting him to talk her around more than anything. A big part of her was thinking that she'd been too hasty, cutting her nose off to spite her face. She couldn't bring herself to speak, but she met his eyes across the table feeling the invisible sparks fly between them.

"But I really like you," he finished nervously. "And I'd still like to be friends if nothing else."

The last of her resolution crumbled when he tentatively covered her hand with his own, and she felt a burst of butterflies from the pit of her stomach.

"I like you too," she admitted. "It's just I've had a lot going on, I've just lost my job, I'm skint." She laughed hollowly. "I'm not much of a catch right now and you deserve better. I'm not the best company, and I've got quite a lot of figuring stuff out to do."

"Oh, Rose!" Sympathy clouded his eyes. "I'm so sorry to hear that, but I do understand what you mean. I was made redundant just after my separation, and it totally knocked my confidence. It's only after I got into the police that I really started to feel like myself again. I promise that we can do this completely on your terms, it's just…" He trailed off smiling shyly at her.

"It's just?" She couldn't help smiling back at him.

"It's just you're the first person I've really wanted to date," he admitted. "But if you'd rather just be friends, that's totally fine too."

She felt her heart skip a beat with excitement, but she reminded herself to be cautious. "Things are just a little tough at the moment, but I think I'd like that. Maybe when I'm a little more fun to be around."

"You are fun," he insisted. "But I totally understand what you mean."

They chatted easily until they realised the café owner was closing up around them, and they both laughed at how quickly they'd lost track of time absorbed in one other's company.

"Have you got plans with your family now?" Gareth asked as they stood outside on the pavement.

Rose shook her head. "Not really."

"I'm working a night shift, but you're welcome to come back to mine for some food if you want," he said before quickly adding. "Just as friends, of course."

Rose felt her pulse quicken "I'd love too."

Will

Will could sense Craig growing impatient as Linda marched across the field to dump another armload of decorative hearts fashioned from twigs and twine onto the trestle tables, and he pasted a cheery smile on his face.

"Is there much more?" He asked his step-mother-to-be as brightly as he could muster.

"If you've got somewhere to be…" she sniffed haughtily.

He could feel Craig shooting him an imploring look, but he shook his head hurriedly. "We can help for a bit longer, can't we, Craig?"

Linda turned on her heel flouncing away without a response, and Will shot his boyfriend an apologetic look. "We won't be much longer. I'll finish putting these up, and then we can head back to the pub."

Will's phone pinged from the table where he'd left it, but before he could descend the stepladder Craig had picked it up. He felt a flicker of irritation at the invasion of his privacy, followed by a sharp stab of panic that it could be an incriminating travel text from Raya.

"It's from your sister," he said. "She's met up with a friend and wants to know if we can drop Belle and Toby back to the B & B."

Will reached for the phone to reply before tucking the phone into the safety of his pocket.

"I didn't realise she was still here," Craig said, and Will could hear the thinly veiled annoyance in his tone.

"I think her foot was hurting," he replied defensively. "Her and Toby were going to help Dad in the house."

When Craig didn't respond, he braced himself to ignore his boyfriend's strop, but after a minute he felt too guilty and slipped an arm around his shoulders. "Sorry that we've been roped into this. I really do appreciate you helping my dad out though."

"That's ok," Craig sighed visibly softening. "To be honest, it's been nice to see where you grew up and meet your family properly. You're always so closed off about them. I always wondered what the mystery was."

"I don't mean to be," Will admitted. "And there's no mystery. We just all kind of drifted apart. This has been nice though."

"Well, it's solved the mystery for me," Craig raised an eyebrow throwing his arms wide to gesture to the fields around them. "I can see why you've been so reluctant to get excited about a three-bedroom-semi in Suburbia when you've been sat on this gold mine."

"What?" He shook his head frowning in confusion. "It's not that at all. And it's hardly sitting on a gold mine, Craig. I'm as skint as I've always been."

"Only short term though," Craig retorted triumphantly. "God, if my mum was leaving me all this, I'd be living like a playboy and jet-setting around the world too."

"No, that's not how it is," Will stared at his boyfriend in disbelief. "I'll get, like, some of it in twenty years or whatever. If Dad doesn't leave it all to Linda now."

He grimaced at the thought, but he had already come to terms with the fact that there was little that they could do about it. Tim had shot down all his attempts to discuss the will, and Belle hadn't got anywhere with her plans to ask their father for a cut of the sale of the fields. Will couldn't help feeling gutted at the unfairness of it all, but money wasn't everything. Like Raya always said you can't miss what you never had.

"You get a quarter of it, or a fifth of it," Craig pressed the issue making Will turn away in annoyance. "Which is more than enough to buy a massive house or even a few smaller ones. Invest in property and spend half the year travelling the world on the income. Will, you've got it made."

"No, Craig," Will said when it was clear that he wasn't taking the hint. "I don't know what I get, and it doesn't matter. It's years away."

Craig raised an eyebrow. "Still, it makes me understand, so that's a good thing. I really thought that your doubts were because you didn't want to settle down with me."

"Really?" Will felt his guilty conscience resurface through his annoyance, and he knew that he couldn't put the conversation off any longer. "Do you really think that I want to live like a gap-year student while I wait for my dad to pop his clogs so I can move into the family manor?" He realised how harsh he sounded, and quickly added to soften the blow. "Craig, I love you, I really do, but I just don't want to settle down and live a nine-to-five life." He felt Craig stiffen next to him, but he pressed on knowing it was long overdue. "If I did, it would be with you. I know it's immature to want to be travelling all the time and not putting down roots, but I can't help how I feel. I've always had wanderlust, but I thought I'd grow out of it. I guess it's just part of who I am."

He braced himself for an onslaught from his boyfriend, but Craig was still looking surprisingly upbeat.

"Exactly!" Craig exclaimed. "And you having all this means you can do both! You can have a base at home and afford to live your dreams. We can do it together."

Will narrowed his eyes in confusion. "Craig, you're not listening to what I'm saying. I'm not waiting for a cheque to come in. It'll probably never happen. I want to go travel the world, because it's part of who I am."

"Maybe," he shrugged unruffled. "But I totally get it and I understand now that you can do both."

Will regarded his boyfriend in disbelief that he was that pig-headed that he still couldn't hear what he was trying to tell him. He took a deep breath before dropping the bombshell that he had been dreading.

"I've been thinking about going to Japan this summer," he forced himself to press on. "Raya has already booked flights and I was still trying to decide what to do for the best."

"This summer?" It was Craig's turn to frown. "But that's so soon."

"Yeah," Will looked down at the ground guiltily. "But it doesn't have to stop your plans to find a job and somewhere closer to your family, and it's up to you, but if you still wanted us to be together…"

"Of course, I want us to be together," Craig cut in quickly. "But this summer is a bit soon."

"I know," he replied sheepishly. "But it's a trip I've always wanted to do."

"It's a lot to take in," his face fell. "Maybe next year would be better? You might be in a better position, and then we could both go."

Will felt his heart sink, but before he could say anything else Linda reappeared with a box of fairy-lights.

"I think your sister is ready to go," she reported curtly. "I can take over from here."

"Oh, ok," Will replied flustered by her dismissiveness. "If you're sure…"

Will had been pleased when his father had asked them if they wanted to lend a hand; it had been the most time that they had all spent together in years. Linda, however, hadn't seemed happy at all about the impromptu family reunion, leaving Will feeling uncomfortable around the spiky woman. He glanced at Craig for his reaction, but he had already started to walk ahead towards the house making Will's heart sink as he realised that the dreaded conversation would have to be postponed yet again.

Belle

Belle felt a sharp pain shoot through her ankle, and she winced cursing her foolishness. Worried that she may have somehow made her injury worse, she wandered back to the house with Toby in search of somewhere to rest. Frank was unloading boxes from the car, and he stopped what he was doing to invite them to join him in the kitchen. He offered them a drink, and as stilted and as forced it felt to be around him, she felt a glimmer of hope that this could be the start of some semblance of a relationship.

"Can I make a tea?" She asked her father more as a test than a desire for a hot drink.

"Go ahead." Frank said loitering awkwardly by the door.

She still felt like a cuckoo in his nest, bustling around a kitchen that had once been her and her mother's domain. It was like a not-quite-right Deja-Vu; opening the familiar cupboards to items that were all in the wrong place.

It's been sixteen years, she told herself sharply as she felt the threat of tears stinging the back of her eyes. You can't expect time to have stood still here. Grow up, Belle.

But it hurt to think of Frank getting on with his life with no thought for his children spread out like strangers around the country, or the world in Will's case. All she had ever wanted, even before Toby had come along, was for there to be a safety hole she could bolt to if needed, for there to be safe arms to run home to and for there to be someone who would always welcome her back. She wanted roots, but Bluebell Farm just felt like an abandoned nest.

She was careful not to get her own hopes up, but she felt like her father seemed to be showing a fleeting interest in getting to know Toby. Despite her reservations about her father's ability to be a good parent, she wanted, more than anything, for Toby to have at least one grandparent in his life for his sake. It terrified her how helpless she had been after the accident, and her mind flickered to the times she had had to rely on Ben; she never wanted to be in that situation again.

He might not have been the greatest father, she thought to herself as she poured boiling water into two mugs, but he's better than nothing.

"The field looks lovely for tomorrow," she said as she took a seat opposite him. "The weather is on your side."

He nodded. "Thanks for the help. It's been nice to have you all down."

"It's been nice to be here," she could hear the stiffness in his tone, and she wondered at a man who found emotions so difficult being with someone as loving and warm as her mother. "Hopefully, Toby and I will see more of you soon."

He nodded again but didn't say anything. Annoyance clouded her optimism as they fell into an awkward silence. He took a sip of the tea, and grimaced getting to his feet to spoon sugar into his mug.

"Sorry," she rolled her eyes at his back. "You should have said you wanted sugar. You never used to take it."

He surprised her by turning back with an apologetic smile. "I shouldn't really. Meant to be watching my diet, but everything tastes bland these days."

"Is everything ok with you?" She had spotted a pill dispenser on the counter, and it hadn't gone unnoticed how infirm he had seemed at the start of their last visit. "What are you on medication for?"

"Oh, nothing," he waved his hand dismissively. "It's just vitamins, and aspirin to keep old age at bay."

She frowned uncertainly; the seven-day box prepped

with two pills for every day looked like a serious affair. Through her detachment, she felt a glimmer of concern for her father.

"Honestly," he caught sight of her cynical face. "I'm fine- just old and tired."

"But you take them every day?" She asked dubiously.

He shrugged. "Not every day. I pulled my back the other month," he reached for the pill box flicking open the lid that read 'Friday'. He took out a small nondescript white pill passing it to her. "It's just aspirin. Here, your leg is hurting isn't it?"

She was surprised that he had noticed her slight limp, feeling a lump form in her throat at the unexpected fatherly concern. She tucked the pill under her thumb wanting to say more, but unsure where to start.

Don't be so pathetically happy, she warned herself.

"Oh!" An irritated voice at the back door interrupted them. "Frank, I thought you were meant to be helping with all this."

Belle watched as her father's eyes narrowed in annoyance at the sight of his pouting wife-to-be in the doorway. "I'm just having a cup of tea with Belle. She needed a sit down with her leg."

"Probably all that running around on the field you've just done," Linda said disapprovingly. "Maybe you should go home and rest it."

Belle flinched at the coldness in her tone; she'd gone out of her way to be civil to the woman since she'd arrived, but she was beginning to wonder why she'd bothered. She glanced at her father, but the moment Linda had appeared he had hastily drained his mug and returned it to the sink either pretending not to notice her rudeness or not caring. She clambered to her feet as gracefully as she could to place the mug next to her father's, not bothering to wash it like she usually would wherever she was visiting.

Linda has made it perfectly clear that we're not wanted, she thought angrily.

"Come on, Toby!" She called unable to look at her father through her upset. "We're going."

Tim

"Done already?"

Tim looked up surprised to see Craig storming past him towards the house with Will trailing behind him. It had only taken the best part of two hours to get the gazebo and decorations up, but he had spent the majority of the time fielding Emma's accusations out of earshot of his family.

"Linda is going to take over." Will pulled a face, and Tim read between the lines that their labour was no longer required.

"Right," Tim dug his keys out of his pocket as his brother drew to a halt next to him.

They stood side by side in the garden awkwardly for a moment; reluctant to be the first to announce their departure.

"Is Dad-?" Will started to Tim.

"Is he back in the-?" Tim asked him at the same time.

They both laughed uneasily, and Tim gestured for his brother to go, but before he could say anything further Belle appeared from the back door of the house with a face like thunder.

"Oh, good," she brightened slightly to see Will. "Are you all done? Are we ready to go?"

"Uh, yeah," Will looked between his sister and the house. "Linda said she doesn't need any more help. Unless Dad..."

He could feel Belle's anger and Will's awkwardness at the situation rolling from them in waves, and Tim felt a sharp pang of annoyance at his father.

What an absolute joke, he fumed silently. *He's dragged us all the way down here for this shamble of a wedding. Yet, he's got no interest in any of us. We might as well all be bloody strangers.*

"He's in the kitchen with Linda," Belle jerked her head towards the house. "I'll wait by the car if you want to say 'bye."

She flounced off without a backwards glance, and even Tim in his preoccupation couldn't miss that something, or more likely someone, had rankled her. He raised an inquisitive eyebrow at his brother, but Will shrugged and sighed heavily.

"God knows what they've said now," he said in a low voice as the brothers headed to the house to say their goodbyes. "I'm beginning to regret coming down here."

Tim chuckled mirthlessly in agreement. "You and I both."

As they approached the kitchen, they could hear a low, heated exchange between Frank and Linda, and Will diplomatically called out to warn them of their presence.

"We're just checking to see if anything else needs doing?" Tim said as they loitered on the doorstep.

"No, I don't think so," Frank replied quickly before looking to Linda for confirmation.

The sour-faced woman nodded her head, but rudely refused to look up at her future stepsons.

"Right, well," Will looked decidedly

uncomfortable at the lack of a warm welcome. "We're going to head back to The Red Lion then if you don't need anything else. You're welcome to join us if you've got time for a drink?"

There was another long silence from the house, and Tim felt his irritation soar further at the blatant disrespect.

"We'll take that as a no then," Tim said with annoyance. "Right, see you both tomorrow then."

"See you tomorrow," Frank replied flatly, offering no apology for his lack of response to Will.

From the corner of his eye, Tim saw his brother's cheeks flush at the dismissal, and he felt a sliver of sympathy for his younger brother. Out of the three of them, Tim thought that he probably had the most time for Will. He didn't seem as chaotic and as needy as the others, and even thought they were clearly both living completely different lifestyles, Tim thought that his brother at least seemed like he was doing alright for himself, with a nice car, a partner, and his own business.

"I don't know why we've bloody bothered," he remarked to ease Will's embarrassment at their father's lack of manners.

"No, I don't either," Will agreed before shaking off his upset. "Are you heading back to Eleanor and the kids now? You're both welcome to join us at the pub." He wrinkled his nose. "Although to be honest, if I had the spa facilities at my disposal, I'd be making the most of them."

Tim considered his brother's invitation. It certainly wouldn't be his first choice of how to spend the day, but he was acutely conscious of Emma's erratic phone calls and texts. Restricted to the suite in the hotel, it would be impossible to check his phone or respond to her next outburst. There would be safety in numbers, and the distraction of Belle, Will, Toby and Rose, when she deigned to come back from wherever she had gone, might be useful. As if on cue his phone buzzed in his pocket, and he pulled it out. Tim hastily cancelled the call and gestured for Will to go ahead; his mind already on the dilemma of calming down another angry tirade from Emma.

"No, I'd better get back," he told his brother distractedly. "We might pop over later, maybe. I'll let you know."

His father's rudeness forgotten, Tim quickly slipped into his car and reconnected the phone to the Bluetooth before driving away. He'd had the foresight to disconnect the phone before they had set out on the journey; the last thing he needed was to accidentally answer a call and have Emma's voice booming out to his family. He drove a mile or so before he forced himself to call her back.

"Emma," he said coolly when she answered. "I'm in the middle of trying to help my father set up for the-"

She cut him off with two words in a clipped, calm tone that was at odds with her frantic manner of only an hour ago. "I'm pregnant."

His stomach flipped heavily.

"What? How?" He felt his mouth moving, but words came out of their own accord.

She laughed bitterly, the sound filling the car. "How? Really Tim?"

He was too consumed with panic to react. "Are you sure?"

"I've literally got the test in my hand," she said, the hint of glee in her voice making him feel sick to his stomach.

"They can be wrong," he felt his chest tighten and unable to concentrate on the road anymore, he pulled the car to a stop in a layby.

"I'm late for my period," she countered. "My hormones are all over the place."

Tim grimaced. He couldn't argue with the last point after the last few days.

"I did pick up a test just in case, but after our conversation I thought I should just find out," she crowed. "I was going to wait until you were home, but this changes everything."

He felt a wave of nausea rise inside him. This could not be happening.

"Tim?" She said his name sharply and he realised he hadn't responded.

"This is a lot to take in," he managed to reply. "And like I said, it could still be wrong."

"I don't think so," she said, but there was a hard edge to her tone. "You'll have to tell your wife."

"Well, it's still early days," he stuttered. "And if you are, well, there are always options, so we needn't be hasty."

"We needn't be hasty?" She bellowed furiously. "Seriously? I've just told you that I'm carrying your child, and you're telling me 'there are always options'? Are you kidding me, Tim?"

His temples beaded with sweat. His mind already racing to search for an outcome where his whole world didn't come crashing down around him.

Oh God, this was awful.

"It's a shock," he said quickly just wanting her to stop shouting so he could think clearly. "I don't know what to say."

"Well, it changes everything," she said, and he detected a smugness to her tone.

"Look," he swiped his hand across his forehead. "Can we talk about this in person?"

"Now?" She sounded hopeful.

"I can't," he shot back. "You know it's my dad's wedding."

"Not until tomorrow," she hit back. "You could drive down now."

He knew that she didn't seriously expect him to do this. She just wanted to pick a further argument.

"I can't," he said firmly. "And I think we both need a few days to digest this. Plus, you'll want to do another test just in case."

"I *know* I am," she replied tetchily. "I had a feeling, and the test has confirmed it. There's so much to think about. Where are we going to live? What am I going to do if the centre does get moved abroad? What will this mean for your job when work find out about us?"

"Emma!" He boomed needing her to stop talking. Everything she was saying was already flying through his head, but it was all too much to take in at once. "There's plenty of time to discuss this, and a few days will give us both space to think about what's for the best."

"Where are you?" She asked sulkily.

"I'm still helping my dad," he lied not wanting her to know that he was heading back to his wife and children, knowing this would anger her further. "We're going to spend the rest of the day with him, so I've got to go now."

After a few more empty assurances to her, he was able to end the call and utterly exhausted from the exchange, he slumped against the steering wheel. All thoughts of his father and his anger at the will had flown from his mind at Emma's revelation, but as he sat in his car blindly trying to figure a way out of the mess, feeling desperate and trapped, his thoughts turned back to the estate. Maybe there was a way he could convince Emma to keep her mouth shut.

Rose

She couldn't remember a time when she had so much fun, and as Gareth cleared away after their fish and chip tea, her stomach muscles ached from laughing. He was working a night shift, and as much as she would have loved a proper drink, she declined his offer of wine conscious that she would have to drive her car back to The Red Lion.

After all, she had joked, *I don't want to risk being over the limit and you having to arrest me on the way home.*

He finished tidying away, and came back to join her on the sofa, this time sliding a little closer and angling his body towards her. His knee brushed hers, but instead of moving away she discreetly wriggled closer.

He's bloody gorgeous, she thought to herself as she drank in his handsome features.

"So, could you ever see yourself coming back to the village?" He picked up the conversation from where they'd left it.

"I've not thought about it for years," she admitted even as a tingle of excitement flashed through her at the thought of maybe one day moving back here for him. "But it has been nice being back, and now that my sister is coming home, it would be nice."

His mouth broke into a wide grin, and his enthusiasm was infectious making her smile back.

"You've got a lovely smile," he told her making her whole stomach erupt in a flutter of happiness.

"Thank you," she felt her cheeks flush and she lowered her eyes coyly. "So have you."

There was a heavy pause, and she could feel the atmosphere shift from one of fun flirtation to something electrically charged and serious. When she dared to look up, his eyes were still on her face and his hand reached forward for hers. There was just the smallest gap to bridge between them, but he crossed it with determined confidence, and she lifted her face to meet his lips. All her worries seemed to fizzle away as he kissed her softly. The solid warmth of his arms pulling her close was enough to make her melt, and she kissed him back with a passion that she didn't know she possessed.

Soon, their hands began to wander of their own accord, and they pulled apart breathless and half-wild with their desire for one another.

"Is it awfully forward?" He whispered against her neck making her skin tingle. "If I ask if you want to come upstairs?"

Rose had a list of body hang-ups that she was pretty sure would be as tall as her if laid out end to end, but even stone-cold sober her yearning for him outweighed her worries of flabby bits, and mismatched underwear. She offered up a prayer of thanks that her hairy bits had all been seen to as part of her wedding day prep as she nodded in confirmation that she would very much like to follow him upstairs.

Any inhibitions that remained were pushed to one side the moment that he wrapped her in his arms and lowered her gently onto the bed. Gareth trailed soft kisses across the delicate flesh of her throat; slow and tantalizingly sensual until her whole body was quivering with desire. She was pleased to see that he was carrying a little extra padding, just the same as her, as clothing was stripped away between breathless kisses. He grinned at her sheepishly in the dimming light of the afternoon, and she felt her stomach somersault slowly with something more than just lust for this handsome, charming man. She had no expectations of fireworks, but as their kisses grew deeper and they slipped between the sheets to explore one another's bodies, she felt an almost-animalistic pleasure rip through her.

Afterwards, he held her with a tenderness that made her heart ache, and they lay together talking and laughing with none of the awkwardness that she might have expected.

"I wish I didn't have to go to work," he groaned pulling her back to him.

Phil had been the last man that she had been with. And there had only been one boyfriend before that. But she felt remarkably comfortable being with Gareth, and just for a moment, she allowed herself to close her eyes and picture spending every day like this.

"So," he said a little later when he had begrudgingly accepted that he needed to get ready for work. "Do you think you'll be able to spare me a few hours of your company this weekend?"

Her heart fluttered at his hopeful smile, and she had to press her lips together to stop the happiness that she felt inside bursting out of her.

"I think I'd like that," she replied.

Her whole body was still tingling with pleasure as he kissed her goodbye.

Maybe it could be the start of something special, she thought savoring the renewed lightness in her soul. She tried to cling onto the feeling, but as Gareth grew smaller in the rearview mirror, the doubts had already begun to creep in.

Just don't get your hopes up, a little voice in her head warned her.

Already the flames of warmth had started to wane as the logistics rushed back to her. Nothing had changed in her situation. She was still broke, and jobless. Gareth was still miles away.

It isn't fair, she thought as she squinted through the windscreen at the rapidly darkening sky. The moon was visible, but the sky was still too light for it to be any more than a pale shadow in the sky. Something twinkled on the horizon, and although she knew that it was likely an aircraft of some kind, she pressed a silent wish upon it.

A fresh start. That was all she needed. *A lottery win. Debts wiped. A blank slate. Just something.*

She felt the last flame of the afternoon's pleasure flicker away, and the coldness of her loneliness crept back into her bones.

Will

"Are you ready to go up?"

Will had had low expectations for the weekend to begin with, but he had still dared to hope for some semblance of quality time with his family. Instead his sister had been staring glumly into the dregs of half a pint of lager for the previous hour while Craig huffed and puffed about everything from the limited menu at the pub to the lack of nightlife in rural Gloucestershire.

"Not yet," Will shot Craig a loaded look of annoyance at his lack of tact, but Belle seemed oblivious.

As much as he had enjoyed the earlier months of their relationship, he had to admit that the last few weeks had been a chore, and he wished that he had had the guts to insist on attending the wedding alone. At the time though, he'd thought that he would be the awkward third wheel, assuming that his brother and sisters would all have partners and their children with them. He was acutely aware that the time he had with any of them was fleeting, and he wished that Tim and Rose had cared enough to want to spend the evening together even if it was blatantly obvious from this afternoon that Frank didn't.

Belle had barely said more than a few words since they'd left the house, and Will had a feeling that she'd have been more likely to open up without Craig's constant griping. They had grown close recently with Belle beginning to let her guard down and confide in him, but she seemed reluctant to share whatever it was that was on her mind.

"Mum," Toby came rushing back over to the table through the patio doors where he'd been playing outside with some other children. "Can I get an ice cream?"

She looked up from her phone at her son, but Will saw

the way her eyes darted to the paper menu on the table first.

"You've just had dinner," she told him.

"You made me have a kid's portion," he reproached her in a scornful tone that would have made Will laugh under any other circumstances. "I'm still hungry."

"Ice cream isn't real food." Belle responded quickly. "I've got biscuits upstairs in the room. You can have some before bed."

"Oh, Mum!" He started to protest, but she shot him a warning look and he closed his mouth.

"Aw, get him an ice cream." Craig tried to make a joke, but Belle barely raised a smile.

"I think I'm going to head up in a bit," she ignored the comment, addressing her brother instead. "Sorry, I'm rubbish company today. I'm really tired."

"Yeah, no worries," Will tried to catch her eye, but she avoided his questioning gaze. "It'll probably be a long, old day tomorrow."

His pointed tone did the trick though, and she lifted her head to offer him a small smile.

"God, won't it just?" She picked up her glass to drain the remainder of her drink and sighed. "I can't believe we've come all this way for this."

"No, nor me," he grimaced. "I wasn't expecting them to roll out the red carpets, but I am starting to wonder why they even bothered inviting us."

"Perhaps we should blow off the wedding," she joked with a wry smile. "They've got a really nice new big Tesco that I wouldn't mind checking out."

They both grinned, but before Will could press his sister any further on the matter she clambered to her feet.

"Right, I'll see you both in the morning," she said after she'd managed to coerce Toby to leave the play area.

"What's up with her?" Craig asked the moment they were out of earshot.

"She's just had a tough day," Will replied sharply unable to hide his irritation at his lack of sensitivity. "It probably didn't help that you were moaning that you wanted to go all afternoon. How would you have liked it if I was nagging you if we were meant to be spending time with your family?"

Craig pulled a face at Will's tone. "Well, actually, that's exactly what you're like. You were all quiet and moody when Kelly and Dean stayed over ours, and you couldn't wait to leave when we went out with Kev and all the other week."

He flushed guiltily, knowing Craig had a point. "Sorry, I didn't mean to be. And anyway, that was because I was knackered both times. Plus, she's on her own, Craig. I didn't want her to feel like she had to leave."

Craig shrugged, but Will didn't miss the slight eye roll.

"I think I'm going to go to bed as well." Will said when he didn't respond.

"It's not even half eight," Craig scoffed. "Let's have another drink."

"You were dying to go a minute ago."

"No, I wasn't."

Was he actually for real? Will stared at him in irritated exasperation.

"Fine," Craig conceded. "Let's go up and watch a film on my iPad. That's if the Wi-Fi even works."

He bit back a sharp retort, deciding a film where neither of them would have to speak and risk upsetting each other was probably the safest bet.

"Are you even watching this?" Just half an hour into the movie, Craig turned to look at Will who was idly thumbing through his phone.

"Yeah," he replied unconvincingly.

Raya had sent him a link she'd found for a great itinerary for Shikoku, and he hastily locked his screen to turn his attention back to the horror film playing on the small screen.

"You've been off all day," Craig remarked after a moment of silence. "Anyone would think we were going to a funeral, not a wedding."

"Sorry that we're not the Von Trapps like your family," Will snapped back. "But it's not all raindrops on roses."

"We're hardly the Von Trapps," he laughed taking no offence. "That's more like your family than mine. I can imagine your dad blowing a whistle and you all running back like sheepdogs."

"What's that meant to mean?" Will flinched at the implication even though he knew he had started it.

"He's hardly the sunniest guy, is he?" He replied in a flippant tone that set Will's nerves on edge. "And your brother and sisters are all a bit standoffish."

"It's complicated," he snapped back defensively. "Everyone has got their own stuff going on, and no, he wasn't the warmest father in the world, but he's still my dad."

"Is it the will then?" Craig eyed him thinking back to their earlier conversation. "Is that why everyone is sulking? Because you're worried that you'll have to share it with Melania or whatever her name is."

"It's not the money," Will protested, ignoring his attempted quip. If anything, he knew he should be grateful that the penny had finally seemed to have dropped after Craig's tactless earlier excitement about the size of the estate, but he was so done with the amount of space it was all taking up inside his head. "It's the principle. Bluebell Farm was in my mother's family for a century, and it's all we have left of Mum."

"Well, you'd have to sell it one day," Craig shrugged. "And it's not like you ever go there. Although, when we live in Bristol we can probably get back here more."

"It's not about that," Will retorted in a flash of temper. "And I've told you, I'm not sure what I'm going to do. I told you I'm thinking about Japan."

"Oh, God," Craig groaned dramatically. "Not this again."

"Yes!" Will burst in exasperation. "This! Again! I'm trying to be honest about what I want, Craig, and I'm sorry it's not what you want, but that's all there is to it."

"I'm just saying," he shot back. "That it wouldn't kill you to wait for your holiday like normal bloody people do, instead of swanning off like a gap-year kid with no responsibilities."

Will felt his blood beginning to simmer, and weeks of frustrated anger rose like a bubble from the pit of his stomach. He saw the shadow of doubt cross Craig's face, and he knew that even he was aware that he'd pushed him too far. Will could feel all the words, and thoughts, and arguments that he had repressed fighting to surface, but even in his temper, he was wary of saying something that he could never take back.

Instead, he choked back the emotion snatching up his jacket and phone. "I need some air."

He stormed from the room, and down the steps out into the car park battling back the need to scream and shout in utter frustration at the way that he felt. Because deep down, he knew that Craig's overbearingness was just the tip of the iceberg. He knew that it wasn't fair to lay the blame at his feet. He knew that it wasn't a coincidence that he'd developed an overwhelming urge to flee at the same time Frank's invitation had landed at his lap.

It's not just Craig. He allowed the voice in his head to admit it aloud, and with the admission came a rush of hatred and hurt that he had buried so deeply that he had no idea that it had been lurking there all these years.

It was all Frank's fault. Maybe if he'd bothered being even a half decent father, we'd have all been closer, and we would have had this conversation months ago. I wouldn't be taking off around the globe the moment that the going got tough, and Belle wouldn't be forced to count her pennies to clobber together a pub meal for her child.

The force of his confession startled him, but it felt good, it felt liberating, to admit it. Will paced the carpark unable to keep still with the adrenaline.

I should have said something, his anger began to turn inwards now at himself for not wanting to rock the boat, and he wondered if he had left it too late.

Belle

A tiny sliver of light shone into the room from the hallway, but it might as well have been a stadium-size floodlight to Belle's sensitive eyes. The room that had seemed spacious and comfortable when she'd arrived this afternoon felt cramped and tiny; the walls pressing in around her. She screwed her eyes shut as if it would help her to drown out the muffled noises that managed to slip through the gap beneath the door, but it was no good. Footsteps echoed in the corridor, just another guest leaving their room, but they may as well have been kicking a football against the paper-thin walls as the fine hairs at the back of her neck rose in irritation.

Belle sighed heavily, rolling onto her back to stare up into the darkness at the ceiling in exasperation. Toby snuffled in his sleep besides her, and she placed a hand gently on his pyjama-clad arm, needing the comfort of his warm, slumbering presence. She could hear her sister's gentle snores, and she envied her ability to fall asleep so quickly. Rose had walked through the door barely an hour ago, and Belle who had been idly thumbing through her phone while Toby slept had perked up a little at the promise of company. It had all been downhill after the initial excitement of landing a new job, and she was over the worst of her sulk and ready to talk it out with someone. But Rose had showered and gone straight to sleep quicker than Belle had ever seen a sober adult pass out in her life, leaving her lonely and full of her own wretched thoughts.

She had attempted to lie down to follow them both into sleep, but after ten minutes it became clear to her that her mind just couldn't shut off. All the little threads of annoyances and upsets seemed to have tangled together in an overwhelming knotty jumble, and as much as she knew that she had to work through her feelings, she had no idea where to even begin.

It started and it ended with Frank.

She knew that much, and she wriggled carefully up into a sitting position to begin the arduous task of facing her demons. Belle knew that she had a fresh start within her grasp, and while she had hoped that her dad would help her, she wasn't naïve enough have to put all her eggs in that unreliable basket.

It doesn't matter, she tried to reassure herself cross-legged in the darkness of the hotel room.

But it did matter. If it didn't, it wouldn't hurt so much. It hurt to feel like an unwanted visitor in the one place that held all her memories of her mother. It hurt to feel like she wasn't welcome, and to know that she never would be. There were people that you connected instantly with, and there were people that grew on you, but Belle felt it in her gut that there was going to be no magical late bond between her and Frank. And certainly not now Linda was on the scene.

No, Frank had made his choice. And we will never be it.

She was sick of the feeling of anger coiled in the pit of her belly. No matter how many times she tried to look on the bright side, count her blessings, it was always there. She had thought that forgiveness was the key to ridding herself of the horrible sensation, but it was proving harder than she imagined to be the bigger person when he was just so unwilling or unable to be anything other than cold and distant. If it weren't for how excited Toby was, she knew that she wouldn't bother going to the wedding tomorrow.

Just the thought of spending a full day watching Linda and Frank swan around her mother's home made the anger heat up and sizzle within her, and it crossed her mind to wonder how she would deal with being so close to them when she moved back to the village. Panic bubbled up in her veins, and she fought to push it away quickly.

I'll deal with it, her jaw clenched tightly in defiance. You haven't come this far to just come this far.

Returning to Hampton Dale where she had a job, a lovely house, and some good friends would be perfect for Toby. She wasn't about to let her feelings for her father ruin it for them.

She had so much she needed to get off her chest, and she had a horrible feeling that the will would be the last straw once the palaver of the wedding was over. She was done with tiptoeing around Frank now. He held the power, disrupting their lives when he summoned them back here, snatching their safe place and their mother's legacy from them.

I'm not going to wait for the last kick in the teeth, she decided.

The decision made her feel stronger, and she got to her feet needing to do something with the sudden burst of restlessness. Her eyes, now adapted to the darkness, moved to the door and then back to her sleeping son.

He won't wake up. And if he does, Rose is here just a few feet away.

The Wedding Day

Rose

Rose felt a wave of nausea pierce through the dull fog of her mind. On shaky legs, she rushed to the bathroom to kneel over the porcelain toilet bowl and retched violently until all that was left was acidic bile that burned her throat.

"Rose?" She heard her sister call out, and her heart sank at the thought of relaying the news.

Rose washed her face and her hands, buying herself a few moments to compose herself. Even through her own shock, she was conscious of her nephew, just a child, in the room.

"Is everything ok?" Belle was sat up on the end of the bed. "Who was on the phone?"

Rose glanced at the still outline of Toby in the bed to check that he was still asleep before she drew a deep breath. "It was Father Harris from the church. Linda went back to the farm this morning and she found Dad. Belle, he's dead."

She watched numbly as the colour drained from her sister's face. Belle stared back at her, confusion swirling in her clear green eyes. "What? There must be a mistake?"

Rose felt a secondary wave of nausea rise inside her. "He didn't have much information." She looked at her sister helplessly. "Should I phone Linda or...?"

"Oh my God, Rose!" Belle's hands flew to her face in despair.

Rose crossed the room to her sister's side wrapping an arm around her just as the first few tears slid from Belle's eyes. "I'd better call the boys."

With shaky fingers, she dialled Will's number first, and his flat voice told her that he'd received the same news. After a short exchange, she hung up.

"He had the same call but doesn't know any more. He's going to try Tim now, and Linda. Although…"

She trailed off wondering at the horror Linda must have felt to find her fiancé dead on their wedding morning. A wave of sadness overwhelmed her, and she felt Belle's arms tighten around her as the tears began to fall.

Will

"I'm so sorry."

Craig looked devastated, but Will barely heard him through the echo of blood rushing in his ears. He looked up at Craig's lips moving without hearing him properly, and a wave of anger, startling in its ferocity, rose from the pit of his stomach at his boyfriend.

"I'm going to go and see my sisters," he said coolly, throwing on the clothes that he'd worn the day before.

"I'll come with you," Craig said hurriedly getting to his feet.

"Don't bother," Will replied coldly.

Craig had been reaching for a t-shirt, and he jerked back like he'd been punched at Will's uncharacteristic tone.

"Please, Will. If this is about last night, I didn't mean it like that. You know it was just hypothetical. I was just trying to get my point across to you."

"Well, you got what you wanted," as soon as the words were out of his mouth, he regretted them. He shook his head to clear a path through his anger when he saw how hurt Craig looked. Will thought of the one-way flight that he'd booked in the heat of the moment knowing that when Craig found out, they would be well and truly over. In the fresh light of the news about his father, Will realised that none of it mattered.

"Look," he rubbed a hand across his eyes with a sigh. "I didn't mean it. I'm just shocked and I need to find out what's happened."

"I can come with you," Craig looked hopeful.

"No, I just want to be on my own."

Will shut the door gently behind him knowing deep down that, for him, the relationship was over, yet he was too floored to care. He knocked on the door to his sisters' room, and Belle pulled the door open gesturing for him to come in.

"Be careful what you say," she whispered glancing over to Toby who was sat up in bed now, rubbing the sleep from his eyes. "Rose is on the phone to Eleanor."

"Has anyone spoke to Linda?"

Belle shook her head. "Not yet. I can't believe it, Will."

"Nor me," he blinked away the tears that pricked at the back of his eyes.

Rose emerged from the bathroom where she'd gone to make the call in privacy, and she folded Will into her arms on sight. "Oh, Will! It's terrible."

Toby called out to his mother curious as to the huddle of adults around the bathroom door, and they sprang apart quickly.

"Any update?" Belle asked in a hushed whisper.

"Let's go down to breakfast," Rose said wisely. "Eleanor said Tim is going to drive down to the farm. She says you can drop Toby to their hotel, and she can watch him if you need?"

Belle looked uncertain. "I'll have to tell him. I just want to find out what's happened first in case he's got any questions."

"Tim should know more once he's got hold of Linda."

"I can't believe it," Will said. "He seemed fine yesterday. In fact, he seemed better than he was the last few times we saw him."

"I thought the same," Belle agreed. "He didn't seem so old, did he?"

Will heard the anguish in his sister's voice; his heart expanding with empathy for her.

"Do you and Toby want to get dressed and meet us downstairs at breakfast?" Rose had already slipped on some clothes quickly, and Belle nodded in agreement.

"Is Craig not coming?" Rose asked as she and Will walked down the stairs to the pub below.

"We had an argument last night," Will admitted sheepishly. "I just need a bit of space from him."

Before Rose could respond, she caught a glimpse of a police car pull into the gravel car park outside. She pointed it out to her brother. "Do you think they've come to speak to us?"

"I don't know," Will felt his heart quicken as they rushed down the last few steps to watch as two uniformed officers appeared at the main door of the pub.

Belle

Belle could barely bring herself to meet Toby's eyes for fear that he would see her sadness. She was struck by just how devastated she felt. Her defences were already scrambling to rebuild the barriers that she'd allowed to fall over the last few months, but it was too late. Her heart felt like it had been shattered.

You need to tell him, she warned herself stonily. Before he overhears something.

She took a deep breath, steeling herself to look into his big, innocent eyes. Her heart almost burst with the love she felt for her child, and her eyes filled with tears in anticipation.

"What's the matter, Mum?" He asked, his little voice full of concern.

"It's sad news, I'm afraid, Toby," she managed to keep her voice calm even as her chest burned with the pain. "Your grandad Frank, my dad, has passed away in the night."

Toby wrinkled his brow. "Is that, like, the same as dead?"

She swallowed as she nodded watching Toby's face fall, wishing desperately that she could go back in time to throw the invitation away, and protect themselves from this hurt.

"That's a shame," he said surprising her with his frankness. "I'm sorry we didn't get to know him, Mum. You must be very sad."

She didn't trust herself to speak instead wrapping her son in her arms and holding him tightly to her chest. She tilted her head so her silent tears ran onto the arm of her hooded jacket not wanting him to know that she was crying.

"Are you ok?" She asked when she felt able to speak.

He wriggled free suddenly, forcing her to quickly swipe her eyes dry.

"I'm a bit sad," he looked up for her to see the shiny tears in his own eyes. "But we'll be ok, Mum. You've got me."

"That's right," she fought back a second wave of tears. "Hey, shall we go and get some breakfast?"

Toby nodded hopping off the bed to reach for her hand. "Come on, Mum."

As they walked in silence down the stairs, Belle was surprised to see two police officers in the foyer talking to her siblings. The four adults turned to watch her approach, their eyes taking in the small child apprehensively.

"That's my sister Belle," Will told the police officer hurriedly. "You can speak to her now if you like. I can take her son in for breakfast."

The young male police officer looked relieved. "That would be really helpful, thank you."

Belle waited for Toby to be out of earshot before she turned to the police nervously.

"What's happened?"

She had no idea if this was standard protocol, but the visit felt ominous and official. The older of the pair stepped forward to introduce herself.

"We're very sorry to hear about your father," she said. "I've explained to your brother and sister that due to the nature of the incident we do need to ensure we conduct an investigation, and we had some questions we needed to ask each of you."

Belle glanced at Rose, who looked as shocked as she felt. "What exactly happened?"

"Your father was found by his partner at around seven o'clock this morning," the officer replied gravely. "It's too early to confirm the cause of death, but there was no sign of forced entry, but there are injuries consistent with a fall."

She felt a wave of nausea rise inside her and her mind flickered to the memory of Rose vomiting noisily in the bathroom that morning.

"Were you aware of any medical conditions?" The officer asked when she couldn't bring herself to reply.

"No, nothing," Belle told them, looking at her sister for verification. "We don't live locally, and we weren't here regularly. I think Linda would know more than we do."

She saw the younger officer grimace, just a tightening of his jaw that was gone as quickly as it appeared, but the gesture alarmed her, and she looked between the two expectantly.

"Linda confirmed that there were no serious underlying health conditions," the older of the two said slowly. "But she also said that there'd been several discussions with your father over the course of the last few months about the will."

Belle flinched at the implication. "What's that got to do with anything?"

The officer looked uncomfortable as she met Belle's eyes. "Like I said, we do need to ensure we investigate fully, which means we do need to ask you all some questions."

Tim

Tim shifted in the uncomfortable plastic seat in the waiting area of the police station, feeling irritated to be kept waiting.

"Mr Jones?" A kind-eyed older woman appeared in the doorway. "If you'd like to come through."

As he rose from the seat, a message from Emma pinged onto the screen of the phone in his hand. He dismissed the notification, his chest tightening with stress that had nothing to do with his father's death.

"He was seventy," Tim said with a small shrug when the detective leading the interview offered her condolences. "These things happen, I guess. I'm not really sure what more I can add."

She looked uncomfortable. "His partner Linda mentioned there had been a few conversations regarding the will and until we can ascertain the cause of death, we do need to conduct a full investigation."

"What's that supposed to mean?" Tim asked sharply looking up at the woman in surprise. "That she thinks we had some hand in this? That's utterly absurd! How could we?"

"I understand this must be upsetting," the woman replied calmly. "But as you can appreciate, we do need to ensure we look into any concerns raised. Are you able to confirm your whereabouts last night?"

"Do I need a solicitor?" Tim asked haughtily with no trace of alarm in his tone.

"It's completely up to you," the woman replied before launching into an explanation of voluntary interviews and rights.

"It won't be necessary," Tim cut her off abruptly. "I

arrived at my father's property about three o'clock yesterday afternoon. I was there for a couple of hours, and then I returned to Cedar Vale Hotel and Spa where I remained with my wife and children until I came here." He glared at the woman when he was finished before adding. "I don't see why all this is necessary. Linda would have known if one of us came to the house."

"She spent the night away from Bluebell Farm," she replied matter-of-factly. "She found your father on her return this morning."

Tim fell silent as he tried to process the scene her words conjured up.

"God," he said finally. "That must have been awful for her."

She nodded her head and for a moment, the room fell into a respectful silence before she continued.

"What we usually do is cross check any alibis, just so that we don't have to disturb you again unnecessarily. But, just for the record are you able to advise of the discussions regarding the will at all?"

"There's nothing to discuss," he replied calmly despite the heat rising beneath his skin at the thought of them speaking to Eleanor. "There was some talk by my father of selling the land around the house to the neighbouring farm to raise money for home improvements. Nothing more than that really."

The woman noted this down on the pad besides her. "So, who exactly is set to inherit on your father's death?"

"Originally it would have been my siblings and I," Tim sat up straighter in his chair not liking where this was going. "I imagine he would have made some provision for Linda, but it wasn't anything that we talked about."

"There must have been some discussion?" The detective set down her pen to eye him sceptically. "It must be worth a fair whack."

"The only discussion was over selling the land," he responded. "I advised him it would devalue the property, and that there were more sensible ways to finance any refurbishments. That's about as far as the conversation went."

"What about your brother and sisters?" She asked. "I find it hard to believe that nobody would have any concerns about what would happen to their interest after he remarried."

"You'd have to ask them." Tim replied in a brusque tone to match her own.

"And can I ask about your financial situation?"

The question made Tim stiffen in annoyance.

"My situation is good, thank you," he responded snootily. "I'm a Head of Operations at a major bank, my wife is a Dental Surgeon and a partner of her own practice."

"And your siblings?"

"You'd have to ask them," he repeated. "The only comment I can make is my youngest sister Belle was in quite a bad accident recently which meant she lost her job. She and her son have been staying with my family while she recovers, however she's on the mend and is actually moving back to this area in the next month."

The detective nodded her head. "Well, thank you for taking the time to stop by and answer our questions. Is there a number we can take for your wife just to confirm your whereabouts? Just for the record, of course."

Tim felt his stomach lurch a little at the mention of Eleanor, but he nodded. "Of course."

Will

"Will!"

His heart was already hammering against his ribs at the thought of the impending conflict, but he had two choices; keep walking or get this over with. He felt his hands curl into fists at his side as he turned to face Craig.

"You just left me in the hotel room!"

Will had been bracing himself for an emotional onslaught, but his mouth dropped open in shock at the self-centredness of Craig's opening words. He stared at him for a moment in utter disbelief.

"You know my father has died, right?" Even as he spoke, his tone dripping with disgust, hearing the words aloud were enough to make his chest ache.

Craig recoiled as if he'd been hit. "Oh, God, I'm so sorry. I didn't mean it like that…"

Will looked at him properly, taking in the red-rimmed, puffy eyes. He looks terrible, he thought, a sliver of pity slipping through his own upset.

"Will, please can we just talk?" In a flash Craig had changed tack from the aggressor to the victim. He reached out a hand tentatively touching Will's shoulder. "I saw the police wanted to talk to you all. What did they say?"

"They're not sure what happened just yet," he replied flatly. "Linda found him this morning. We think he might have fallen."

"Oh, God, that's awful."

"Yeah," Will looked down at the ground, unable to deal with the pain in Craig's eyes as well as his own.

"Where are the others?"

"Rose has gone to clear her head, and the police wanted to speak to Belle so she's just text me to say she's going back down the police station."

"They want to speak to Belle?"

Will looked up sharply at Craig's tone. Revulsion rose from the pit of his stomach as he noted the sparkle in Craig's eyes, somewhere between scandalised and thirsty for gossip as if they were talking about some soap opera or office drama.

"Routine." Will responded as coolly as he could muster before turning away.

He seemed oblivious to Will's tone. "What are they saying suspicious or unexplained or…"

"What the hell, Craig!" He burst out in anger. "This is my family you're talking about!"

"I wasn't saying anyone had done anything! I just meant with the will changing and all, they might think…"

Anger flared up inside Will's chest, and he turned away knowing that if he didn't, he would regret the next words that came out of his mouth.

"Come on, Will," he felt Craig behind him, but he kept his eyes fixed firmly ahead. "I mean, you and Belle both went out late at night; you need to be realistic about what they're going to think. I can speak to the police if they want and vouch that you were back here."

He spun around to look at Craig in confusion.

"Belle went out last night?" The words were out before he could stop them.

"Just after you." There was no malice in Craig's voice, only concern which somehow felt worse.

Will turned back to the pub, but the building swam fuzzily before his eyes, and for a horrible moment he thought he was going to pass out. He took a deep breath and released it slowly, focussing his eyes on the swinging sign above the door until his vision cleared.

"I don't know what you're trying to say," Will

responded finally. "But my father has died, Craig. I can't do this right now. Maybe you should just go home."

Although he spoke in a cool, measured tone, Will could feel the bewilderment mixing with his upset already to form a heady cocktail of emotion.

"Will, please," Craig reached out for him, but Will pulled away from his grasp.

"Craig, I just don't have the energy to do this right now. I need to be with my family, and everything we talked about yesterday still stands. I'm going to Japan, and I'm sorry that it's not what you want."

"I can't just leave you now," Craig protested. "And this changes everything."

A bolt of anger burst through Will as he stared at Craig in disbelief. "Just go home, Craig! It changes nothing. All you've done is put pressure on me to do what you want to do. If you had any respect for me, you'd just go home and leave me alone!"

Craig's jaw dropped open, but Will brushed past him not waiting for his response.

"But how will you get home?"

"Craig, I can make my own way," he sighed heavily as the adrenaline begin to drain away leaving him exhausted.

"Does this mean we're over?"

The pleading tone made Will stop to look back at him. I don't have the energy for this, he realised as he saw the hurt on Craig's face. I'll never be able to give him what he wants.

"I think it's for the best," Will replied with a heavy heart.

As Craig stiffened, Will paused anticipating the same never-ending argument that there could be no winner to, but instead Craig nodded coldly.

"I'll just get my things."

Will exhaled in relief as Craig retraced his steps to the hotel room, but the sense of respite was fleeting as his head turned back to the accusations that he had made. An uneasy dread settled into Will's chest alongside the suspicion that it wouldn't be the last he heard from him.

Rose

Rose didn't hear the footsteps until they were right behind her, and her heart leapt into her throat in the split-second before her brain registered his face. Her panic faded away, and the smile she gave him was genuine as she stood up to dust the grass from her jeans.

"Hey," she allowed Gareth to fold her into an embrace resting her head against his chest, savouring the feeling of safety in his arms. "How did you find me?"

"Your sister said you might be here," he pressed a gentle kiss to the top of her head before they stepped apart and he passed her the takeaway cup he was carrying.

"Thank you," she pressed the cup to her lips to inhale the rich coffee aroma. "This is where we came to scatter our mum's ashes."

"It's beautiful up here," he said softly taking her free hand. "You can see the whole of Bluebell Farm."

Rose nodded, glad that he understood.

"I'm so sorry about your dad," he said.

The news of Frank's death had clearly swept like wildfire through the village, but even through her sadness Rose felt pleasantly surprised that he had made the effort to seek her out.

"It's horrible," she sighed. "I feel so sorry for Linda, but she doesn't want to speak to any of us."

As Gareth regarded her quietly, she noticed for the first time the apprehension in his deep brown eyes, and she wondered if he was regretting what had happened between them last night. She'd had no choice but to admit to the police in the foyer this morning that she'd been with him until just before nine o'clock when he'd left for his night shift. It crossed her mind that he must feel embarrassed at having his personal life offered up to his colleagues, particularly the way she looked this morning red-eyed and unkempt.

It must have been humiliating for him, her heart lurched at the realisation. *And now he feels too sorry for me to tell me it was a mistake.*

"Look," he started tentatively. "There's a reason that I came to find you."

"About last night," she cut in, mortification making the words come out in a tangle. "I had a lovely time, but there's no pressure for a relationship. Everything is even more complicated, and I'll be even worse company than I was before if that's possible."

She attempted a self-depreciating laugh, but it came out as little more than a strangled yelp. She saw sympathy flash across his face which hurt more than any rejection.

"Rose, I had an amazing time," he told her earnestly. "That's not what I came here to say though."

He puffed up his cheeks and exhaled like it was taking considerable effort to summon up the courage to continue, and icy fear coiled around her ribs as she waited for him to finish.

"The police wanted to speak to your sister again, Rose," he grimaced. "About her whereabouts. They'll probably want to speak to you too if you've left anything out of your statement," he looked away from her as if urging her to not confirm or deny anything to him. "I'm sure it'll all be fine, but Belle has gone back down the station. Toby is with my sister. I can't really talk about this to you because it's a live investigation."

"Oh God," she clasped her hand to her mouth, feeling a jolt of panic in the pit of her stomach. "I'd better go and find out what's going on."

Gareth nodded grimly, but she noticed that he looked

relieved when she didn't press him further. He waited for her to get into her car before leaning down to push a strand of hair back from her face. Her jangled nerves made her pull away sharply from his touch before she caught herself mid-reaction. Clumsily she took his extended fingers in her hand and managed a half-hearted squeeze that she hoped conveyed her gratitude to him for being so kind.

"Just let me know how you get on or if you need anything," he said, his voice thick with concern. "I've explained to my sergeant that we've been dating, so I won't be involved in the investigation at all, but I'm sure it'll all be resolved pretty quickly and I'm here for you if you want to talk about your dad."

She nodded unable to trust her voice through the riot of emotions racing through her, and as much as she craved the solid comfort of him she was glad when he closed the door and stepped away from her car. With trembling fingers, she started the engine, her mind already turning to her sister and the police investigation. But before she turned the corner out of sight, she glanced into the mirror to watch him growing smaller and her heart ached with disappointment at yet another almost.

Tim

Tim drove towards the police station for the second time that day. Eleanor had been asked to provide a statement to corroborate his whereabouts, and he felt sick to his stomach as they drove through the village to the manned station in the nearby town.

"I've never given a statement before," she licked her lips anxiously as he drove. "What will they ask?"

"Just our whereabouts in the last twenty-four hours," he replied exasperated at her nerves. "It's just procedure. Nothing to be worried about."

"What did you say to them?"

"I told them where I was," he responded. "We got to the hotel about two-thirty, checked in. I went to my dad's for about a couple of hours, came back and we were at the hotel until this morning when they phoned. Honestly, Eleanor, don't worry so much."

"But what if they ask if you left the room?" She looked at him uncertainly. "You were gone for a good two hours last night."

"I was in the hotel bar," he stated with irritation. "You know that."

"Did you say that?" She shot back with uncharacteristic impatience.

"I just said I was at the hotel," he replied with ease as if it hadn't been eating at him all day. "That covers it. There's no need to go into detail. We're hardly suspects."

Eleanor pressed her lips together in a thin line, but Tim pretended he didn't notice her apprehension. He pulled into the car park wishing that she'd listened to him and left the children at home with her mother.

Although, he thought of his whereabouts over the last

twenty-four hours, *that would have made it harder to get anything done.*

While he waited for Eleanor, he took the children over to the small enclosed park across the road. She returned forty minutes later looking anxious and stressed out.

"You were ages!" He exclaimed, already fed up with the children's constant demands. "Did they keep you waiting too?"

She shook her head. "No, but they were pretty thorough, Tim. They asked a lot of questions."

He frowned in annoyance. "I've half a mind to put a complaint in when all this is done. We've lost our father today; they should be leaving us alone to grieve."

Eleanor retrieved a whining Bea from the swing setting her down on the ground. "Should we stay tonight or just go home?"

Tim had been hoping she would be the one to propose going back to London, and he perked up at the suggestion. "There's nothing more we can do here," he said as though the thought had only just occurred to him. "It'll be better for the children if we go home. They're very unsettled."

"You should probably make sure the police don't need anything further first," she said as they crossed the road back to the car. "And check in on Will and your sisters."

As he was buckling Bea back into her seat, a squad car pulled up. He squinted in disbelief as his youngest sister emerged from the back.

"Belle!" He called hastily clicking the straps to secure the infant before rushing over to the car. "Is everything ok?"

She looked pale, but she nodded. "Yeah, they just had some more questions that they wanted to ask me."

Tim looked over at the officer for confirmation, and the young woman who'd been driving nodded. "Miss Hudson is just helping us with some further enquiries."

"So, you're not in trouble?" He looked at his wayward sister doubtfully.

"No, of course not," she replied scornfully. "Are you all coming to The Red Lion for food? I'll see you back there."

"No," Tim shook his head. "We're going to head back to London. The children are unsettled and there's nothing more we can do here."

The officer that was escorting Belle glanced back at him questioningly, and he eyed her with irritation. "Is everything ok?"

She nodded, before walking away, and his sister rolled her eyes at the officer's back before following her into the police station. "I'll call you later, Tim."

"Ok," he nodded slowly. "But if you think you need a solicitor..."

She shook her head. "No, of course not!"

He turned back to his car, feeling baffled and irritated by the whole process when he heard his name being called.

"Is everything ok?" He asked to the more senior-looking officer who had appeared in the doorway. "I take it you have everything you need from my wife and I?"

"Actually, Mr Jones," the officer replied with an apologetic smile. "We do need to go over your whereabouts with you."

"I've been through this," he felt his temper rising. "I really do need to be getting back. I've got small children with me, and this has been a very difficult day."

"I'm sorry, Mr Jones, but I am asking that you cooperate on a voluntary basis to avoid unnecessary delays in the investigation."

There was something in her tone that broached no arguments, and Tim felt a flicker of dread beneath his irritation.

"Of course," he said as calmly as he could muster. "I'll

just let my wife know to go ahead back to the hotel without me."

Bloody Eleanor, he thought as he waved her off through gritted teeth. *She must have given every last detail and then some.*

Belle

The interview room didn't look anything like Belle had expected when she slipped into the stuffy, windowless room. It looked more like the soulless, budget office of an inner-city headteacher whereas she had been expecting something a little more like the interview rooms from American cop shows with one-way glass and bars covering the peephole in the door. The friendly officer who had driven her down to the station had disappeared, and two more serious-looking detectives took seats opposite Belle. She looked up to meet their eyes with a polite smile, feeling a flash of panic in her chest that was stronger than the jittery nerves she'd felt in the back of the police car.

You've done nothing wrong, she reminded herself even as her pulse quickened.

"Thank you for coming down, Ms Hudson," the older of the two started after a brief introduction. "We appreciate that this is a difficult day for you and that you've already spoken with one of our officers this morning at The Red Lion."

Belle nodded but remained silent.

"Could you just talk us through your whereabouts in the last twenty-four hours?"

"Yes sure," she moistened her lips with the tip of her tongue, instantly regretting the unconscious movement. She'd watched enough detective films to know she should be aware of her body language. *Was that meant to be a sign of guilt? Or nerves? Or were nerves a sign of guilt?* "So, I stayed with my friend Steph Thursday night. I had a job interview in the morning. Steph dropped me to meet my sister at the B & B about three-ish and then we went to our dad's house. I was there until about five or six with my

251

brothers and my brother Will's partner. We went back for food, and then went up to our rooms."

"Back to The Red Lion?"

"Yes."

"You arrived back there about six?"

"Around then," Belle shrugged hoping she looked casual. "I didn't really pay much attention to the time."

The woman glanced down at her notes. "You were sharing a room with your sister Rose Connors and your son?"

"That's right."

"And you both said neither of you left the room until the following morning at around eight?"

Belle shook her head. "No, I didn't say that. The police this morning only asked if we'd left the pub."

"So, you left the room. Was that together?"

"No," she shook her head. "My sister came back about nine-ish and went straight to sleep. I left them both sleeping to go outside for a cigarette."

"What time would you say that was?"

"I don't know," Belle shrugged. "After ten."

"And who were you with?"

"Myself."

"Did you see or speak to either of your brothers?"

"No."

"And did you leave the pub grounds while you were smoking your cigarette?"

"I sat on the grass bank behind the pub," she replied as calmly as she could muster. "I don't know if that's technically the pub grounds, but I could see the pub from where I was sitting so I would class that as not leaving."

"How long were you outside?"

She felt her heart sink. "Maybe an hour. I don't really know."

"An hour," the woman pressed her lips together in a thin line as she shuffled her papers. "Can I ask how your relationship with your father was?"

Belle shrugged. "We weren't close."

"But you had agreed to go to his wedding?" The woman pressed on. "And you had been down to the area three times in the past few months?"

"Yes," Belle nodded.

"Prior to learning about your father's engagement, when was the last time you had been back to visit him?"

She swallowed nervously. "I think maybe ten years before. Maybe longer."

"And you had recently lost your job after an accident, is that correct?"

"It is," Belle agreed before straightening in her chair. "Can I ask why this is relevant?"

"We're just looking to determine the facts," the woman replied. "You spent time with your father and his fiancée yesterday at Bluebell Farm. How would you say that visit went?"

"It was fine," she responded cautiously. She could feel the change in the detective's tone; the unspoken accusations hanging in the air between them. "My brother helped them set up the gazebo for the wedding. I couldn't really help because of my leg."

"You'd recently raised the subject of the sale of some land to your father," the woman continued. "And the will."

"He raised it," she shrugged. "He said he was going to sell the fields."

"Did you speak to him about how his marriage may change the will?"

"No."

"I understand the farm was passed to your mother from her parents, and then to your father on her death," the woman moistened the tip of her finger to leaf through her notes. "At the time she made her will, it was on her understanding that on his death it would pass completely to her children."

"I don't really know much about wills, and I was fourteen when she died," Belle replied struggling to keep her tone level. "But that sounds about right."

"So, did you believe that on his marriage your inheritance would reduce or disappear altogether?"

"I don't know," Belle let her eyes rest just over the woman's shoulder. "I didn't like to ask."

"You said that you were outside for maybe an hour?" The detective swiftly changed tack surprising her. "Long enough to walk to Bluebell Farm and back?"

"No!" The abrupt change of subject made her exclaim before she could stop to think about her reaction. She felt a flush creep up her cheeks at her outburst, and she quickly added. "I can't walk that far," she gestured to her foot.

"Really?" She turned back to her notes. "Do you wear that walking boot at all times?"

Belle winced inwardly, but she sat up straighter, conscious of not physically shrinking away from the onslaught of questions. "Most of the time."

"Have you worn it constantly since you were in Hampton Dale?"

"No," she admitted. "I put it back on when I came back to The Red Lion to meet my sister."

"And you kept it on since then? Including at your dad's?"

"Yes."

"But you weren't wearing it before your brothers and sister came to town," the detective stated coolly. "You didn't wear it to your job interview."

"No," she agreed. "I didn't want my new employers to

think I wouldn't be fit and well for my start date."

"Is that the only reason?"

Her mouth felt too full of saliva, and even though she didn't want to she couldn't fight the reflex to swallow. "Yes."

"And your sister didn't actually know that you left the hotel room last night?" The detective continued. "You don't have anyone who can confirm how long you actually were outside for?"

"I was about an hour," she replied. "I'm sure the pub has CCTV or something."

"It does. You and your brother left your rooms within ten minutes of each other. You return separately."

"Will?" Belle looked surprised. "I didn't see him."

"He had access to a car," the detective told her. "If you were sat behind the pub, you would have seen him drive past you."

"Well, I didn't see him," she shot back quicker than she intended. "I didn't know Will went outside. If I had seen him, I would have remembered."

"Did you go to your father's house last night?"

Belle flinched at the directness of the detective's question before she shook her head. "No."

She'd felt nervous at being asked to attend the station for some follow-up questions, but Belle had assumed that it was just standard procedure. But, as the detectives circled around her statement repeating and rephrasing questions as though she were on trial, Belle felt herself growing truly frightened.

Will

Will watched from a distance as Craig's car turned out onto the lane, and disappeared from sight. He waited to feel something; relief, sorrow, anything really, but he just felt numb.

Dad should be getting married today, he thought morosely still unable to get his head around the fact that he was gone. His chest tightened painfully at the thought of never seeing him again, and he almost wished that he hadn't come back here; chasing a family and a connection just to have it ripped away.

He pulled out his phone to check the time sighing when he saw the missed calls from his sister. The temptation to ignore them was huge. He could easily disappear back into the big, wide world leaving the burden of emotional ties behind for good. The phone rang again, Rose's name flashing up on the screen, as the thought crossed his mind. Guilt forced him to answer, knowing that his sisters were as alone in the world as he was; he couldn't just abandon them now.

"Hey," he could hear the stressed edge to her voice. "Belle and Tim are both at the police station, being asked some more questions. Do you know what's going on?"

"No idea. Belle did say they had called her and had offered to pick her up from her friend's, but she didn't seem worried," he said to his sister. "Where are you?"

"I just drove down to the station," she replied. "Gareth told me the police had collected Belle, so I came straight down to make sure everything is ok. I'm sat outside, but I just saw Eleanor and she said Tim has been asked back down too."

"I'd come down," Will offered. "But Craig has gone

256

back to London with the car."

"Can I come and get you?" She sounded worried. "I could do with the company."

He didn't bother going back to the hotel room, instead waiting outside for his sister to appear. Not even the sight of his forty-year-old motherly sister in the boy-racer car made him smile though, and he realised how worried he really was.

"Do you think this is normal procedure?" She asked nervously as they whizzed through the village. "Gareth couldn't really say much with it being a live investigation, but he seemed a bit concerned."

"No idea," Will replied his mind still on Craig's words. "What actually happened? Craig said he saw her leave the hotel room last night. Do you think it was about that?"

"She didn't leave the room," Rose took her eyes off the road to look at him in confusion. "Not after I got back."

"Craig said he saw her," Will admitted.

"If she did," Rose chewed her lip nervously. "It was when I was asleep. She didn't say anything and that leaves a hole in my statement as I said we were in from nine-ish."

"You would have heard her though," Will frowned. "What time did you get back?"

"About nine, nine thirty," she replied. "But I pretty much went straight to bed, and I was out like a light."

"I wonder why the police want to speak to them, and not to us," Will wondered aloud trying to ignore the fingers of panic beginning to creep up inside him.

"I just don't know," his sister's hands tightened around the steering wheel and he saw her knuckles were white with the ferocity of her grip. "Nobody is saying anything other than he had..."

She trailed off unable to finish her sentence, but Will could guess what she was thinking. The only information they had been given was that Frank had been found dead in the hallway of Bluebell Farm. There were no signs of forced entry, and the provisional thoughts had been that he had suffered from a fatal heart attack before he had gone to bed. The reports of a head injury were consistent with a fall.

"He looked fine yesterday, didn't he?" Will said quickly unable to deal with the grisly scene his imagination was painting.

He heard his sister take a deep breath as if to compose herself before she managed to reply. "Yeah, I thought that too. Belle said he was on a lot of medication though."

"He was seventy," Will reasoned feeling mildly appeased by this. "I guess it could have been the stress of the wedding."

Rose clamped her lips together, but she nodded.

"I didn't know Linda wasn't staying the night," he continued just to fill the silence that felt too loud. "If I'd known maybe me and Tim could have stayed with him. I didn't even think to ask if he wanted us to make more of a fuss. Like a stag do, or something."

"He was seventy," she replied scornfully. "And we were all here, weren't we? Although, God knows why he invited us. Belle said he practically chased you out yesterday once the gazebo was up."

"He was alright with us," Will replied, not wanting to speak ill of the dead. "Linda couldn't wait to see the back of us though, yet again. I'm surprised she even invited us to begin with. She's shown no interest in getting to know any of us."

"Did anyone," her voice caught in her throat and she had to start again. "Did anyone speak to him properly about the will?"

"I don't know," Will tried to hide his surprise at the question. "Belle and I talked about it, but it wasn't something either of us felt comfortable bringing up. Tim was meant to be looking into it, but nothing ever came of it."

"Nothing ever does with him," she remarked wryly. "I wonder why they've asked to speak to those two, and not us? Do you think they'll want to speak to us again next?"

"No idea. I imagine so," as he spoke, it crossed Will's mind that they might have to stick around in the village a little longer and he felt a rush of desire to flee this suffocating place.

"Why Belle though?" Rose frowned. "She was with me all night. Aside from what Craig said, and we don't know for certain if that's even true. He could have been mistaken."

"I left the room too," he grimaced. "I did tell the police that I'd been out of the room, but they didn't seem concerned."

"Did you?" She took her eyes off the road to glance at him. "In the night?"

"Yeah, not for long," he replied defensively.

"I didn't mean anything like that."

"I know, I know, sorry." Will immediately regretted his tone. "Me and Craig had a massive row."

"I'm sorry," she took a hand from the wheel to squeeze his arm. "I did wonder where he was this morning."

"We've been having some problems lately because he wants to settle down and I want to go travelling again. He upset me yesterday going on about how much the farm was worth and just being generally insensitive." He pulled a face. "Bad timing really, and I think I took all my upset out on him this morning."

"Craig wouldn't have just made it up, would he? Belle going out at night, I mean."

"I don't think so," Will grimaced. "But honestly, I have no idea. Poor Belle though; she's had such a tough time lately. She was up-and-down with Dad. Like, she said she didn't care, but I could tell she was hurt by the way he was after Mum died, and no matter what she says, I know she wanted them to have a relationship."

"He didn't upset her at all yesterday?" Rose looked increasingly anxious. "She seemed quiet when I got back."

"She wouldn't have done anything," Will reiterated firmly with more conviction than he felt. "Although, it was the hardest on her, I think, being stuck home with him after Mum died. I can't stop regretting not being there for her. And then she had Toby, all on her own."

"I know," Rose had been thinking the same since she'd been back in touch with her siblings. "I was so wrapped up in my own life, I didn't even think of how she must have felt. I should have known that Dad wouldn't have been the easiest to live with for a teenage girl."

"She was really short with him the few times we visited," Will admitted. "You could see she was hopeful that he'd take to Toby, but he was so closed off and Linda didn't help. Even yesterday, you could tell she didn't want us around."

"Do you think Linda might have upset her?" Rose had thought her sister's luck had been changing, but who knew what else could have been going on in her private life.

"She didn't say anything," he replied, not wanting to share how quiet she had been out of loyalty to his younger sister. He turned to Rose resignedly. "Should we speak to Tim? See what he thinks?"

"No way." Rose looked horrified. "I know there'll be a good explanation for Belle going out if she did, but if she did go to Dad's for a showdown, it will look terrible. What would happen to Toby if she were arrested? We can't trust Tim. He doesn't give a damn about any of us."

Will flinched at the venom in her voice. He knew that

Rose had been sacked by the bank that Tim was high up in, but he had thought the issue had been resolved. Clearly Rose was still harbouring some hard feelings.

She's right though, he thought to himself. *It would look really bad on Belle and I know that she's innocent.*

"You're right," he nodded reluctantly. "Let's just keep this between us."

Tim

Tim felt sick to his stomach as he left the interview room, but he tried to mask his discomfort and instead shook the detectives' hands firmly thanking them for their time. He walked back through reception, already reaching for his phone to call a taxi. He knew he should call Eleanor, but he needed some space to clear his head.

"Tim!"

His stress levels soared at the sight of his brother and sister in the waiting room. He was mentally exhausted, and their high-maintenance emotions in the wake of their father's death were the last thing he felt like dealing with right now.

"Are you giving your statements?" He asked them, still bristling with humiliation at having to disclose his personal circumstances to prove his alibi. "Belle went in earlier."

"No, we're just waiting for her and to see if the police need anything more from us."

He registered the concern in their eyes before dismissing it, desperate to get away from this place. "Right, well…"

"How are you feeling?" Rose mistook his awkwardness for emotion. To his horror, she clambered to her feet to wrap him in a hug.

He felt a tug of guilt at her warmth remembering how desperate she'd been for his help, and how abrupt he'd been when he had turned her away.

"It's a shock, isn't it?" He fumbled for something to say to mask his unease. "I mean, he seemed like he'd aged a lot, but he looked fine. And the day before his wedding…" He trailed off and shook his head as if in disbelief. "Tragic. They haven't determined whether there was any underlying illness and I know they have to eliminate anything untoward first, but still. Very upsetting."

Will and Rose exchanged glances at his impassive monologue, making Tim flush with annoyance at the gesture.

"I really do need to get back," he turned away from them impatiently. "I'll let you know when there's any news."

He could feel their eyes on him as he left the station, but he was already turning his attention back to the very real problem at hand; a new batch of messages had come through while he was speaking to the police. He sighed as he made the phone call he'd been dreading.

"Hello?" she sounded out-of-breath like she'd rushed for the phone, and while the husky voice usually did strange things to him, he felt nothing but irritation.

"Hello Emma," he cleared his throat. "Are you alright to talk?"

"Where have you been?" She sounded annoyed even through her breathlessness. "You haven't replied to my messages. I know that it's your father's wedding, but..."

"My father died last night," he cut in feeling a flare of anger at her neediness.

"What?" Emma sounded shocked. "How? What happened?"

"He was found dead with a head injury," he replied emotionlessly. "Possibly a heart attack or a stroke that caused him to fall. We won't know until the coroner's report."

"Oh, wow," she was remarkably fit, and her breathing had returned to normal. "I'm so sorry, Tim. That's so sad."

He gritted his teeth, not wanting to continue but knowing he'd have to. "Listen, Emma, I'm sorry to have to do this, but there have been some slight complications."

Her tone instantly hardened. "Go on."

"His fiancée has raised some concerns to the police, all nonsense of course, that there may have been foul play," he swallowed back his discomfort. "I think it's just been a shock to her and terrible timing, but to assist with eliminating anything untoward, we have all had to provide alibis for last night."

"That'll be easy for you," Emma replied her frosty tone back. "You were with your wife in a hotel."

He ignored her attempt to start an argument. "I was, of course, speaking with you for over an hour last night, and so I've had to let the police know."

There was a heavy silence, and Tim could picture the cogs turning in her head as she carefully assessed what he was saying.

"Emma," he continued when she didn't respond immediately. "They will be contacting you to check the details."

"Did you tell them everything?" She suddenly sounded nervous. "About what we were talking about?"

"I didn't go into detail," he replied uncomfortably. "But I had to mention that we'd been having a, uh, relationship as such."

"Is it in your statement?" She asked.

"Yes." He had tried to find a way to omit these details, but the police were relentless, pressing him until he had no choice but to confess.

"Does Eleanor know?" He hoped he was imagining it, but he thought he could hear a hint of satisfaction in her tone.

"Not yet," he felt the nausea return at just the thought. "My father has just passed away, Emma. There's a lot going on at the moment..."

"But you're going to tell her?" Emma pressed him.

Tim thought back to the way Eleanor had been acting over the past few days, and he had a sneaking suspicion that she had already grown wise to the fact that something was going on. He had been adamant that he was going to draw an end to the affair, but that had been before Emma's revelation had complicated things.

"Now really isn't the best time," he said cautiously. "Can we talk about this another time? My dad has just died, Emma."

"It'll all come out," she warned him stiffly. "You're just delaying the inevitable. Don't you think it would be better coming from you?"

They were going around in circles, just like they had last night. Tim cursed himself for getting in over his head with Emma. He had been so arrogant to think that he could have his cake and eat it, and now he was left to clear up this colossal mess.

"It's complicated right now," he sighed heavily. "Can we just talk about this another time?"

"But you expect me to tell the police my private life?" Tim flinched at the anger in her voice.

"It's the police," he tried to reason with her. "Telling the truth isn't really an option with them."

She gave a short, bitter laugh. "Whatever, Tim. If I hear the call, I'll tell the truth of course." He could hear the threat in her words, and he prayed that she wouldn't purposely be awkward to spite him. "I've got to go. Talk to you later."

He felt his heart sink as she ended the call and he was left staring at the blank screen, wondering whether to send her a message to try to make amends.

She isn't stupid, he reasoned. *She's just upset.*

He swiftly deleted the call record, and the thread of messages before he headed back to the hotel.

You just need to hold your nerve until this mess has all been cleared up, he told himself firmly, but somehow he knew that it would take more than a stiff upper lip to come out of this unscathed. It would take a miracle.

Rose

Rose watched as her brother paced the car park, phone pressed to his ear. She had come outside for some air but watching him striding aimlessly from one side of the pavement to the other, she felt her unease return. Everything felt so surreal like their lives were spiralling out of control.

Yesterday had been perfect, and she sighed as she thought of the lovely evening she'd had with Gareth. A warm tingle ran through her as she remembered how amazing it had been after so long being on her own. She hadn't expected things to move so fast, but it had been wildly liberating and exciting to make love to him. She had felt like a teenager, like she had had the whole world at her feet, instead of an exhausted divorcee that had past her prime.

Your dad is dead, she reminded herself guiltily, forcing her thoughts back to the present.

"Are you ok?"

She turned towards the sound of Will's voice, hoping that her face wouldn't betray her worries.

"Just getting some air," she replied. "Tim seems stressed out."

Will glanced over his shoulder to check who was within earshot.

"Is it me?" He asked quietly. "Or does this feel a little more serious than a routine investigation?"

Rose sighed heavily. "I was just thinking the same. Do you have any idea what is up with Tim? I thought he'd be cut-and-dry as he was with Eleanor the whole time."

"It certainly doesn't look that way," Will replied. "I don't know what to think. Neither of them would have done anything though, and they'd have told us if they went back to the house for any reason."

She pressed her lips together in a tight line as she considered the facts.

"How did Dad seem yesterday?" Rose felt another twinge of guilt. "I feel so bad that I didn't really stick around to help with everything."

"Honestly?" Will sighed dropping down to sit on the curb, and she sank down next to him. "He seemed really good compared to the last times we were down. Remember how he was when we all came down together?"

Rose nodded sadly. "He seemed to have aged so much. I feel so guilty that I didn't come down more."

"I felt bad too," Will admitted. "I haven't been to see him for years. But it wasn't just one-sided, was it? He never made the effort with us. In fact, I was shocked we were even invited to the wedding."

"I can see why Linda might feel suspicious of us all," she grimaced. "It does look terrible that we all show up and now this has happened."

"He was the one who asked us though," Will reminded her. "It's not like we've all turned up and demanded to see his will."

"Well, if they think that's the motivation then Tim is safe. It's not like he needs the money," Rose tried not to let the pang of envy creep into her voice, but she could hear it there.

"I didn't think he did either," Will gestured to their brother still pacing like a caged tiger. He lowered his voice again to look at Rose. "Belle thinks he's been having an affair."

Rose looked aghast. "No! He wouldn't, would he? Eleanor is so lovely."

"I know," Will pulled a face. "I wish Belle hadn't said

anything, but she was livid with him and they'd had words over it apparently when Tim tried to kick her out. She wanted to stay at mine, but Craig was really against it because the flat is so small. I think Tim backed down when Belle brought up this woman he's been seeing."

Rose was shocked to her core that Tim would do something like that. She couldn't deny that he had fallen in her estimation when he had refused to help her, but she had never thought that he would be capable of cheating on Eleanor.

"I can't believe he would do something like that," she shook her head slowly. "Belle should have said something though if it's true, Will, not use it as leverage. Poor Eleanor."

Will frowned as he considered his sister's words. "I don't know, Rose. I feel terrible for Eleanor, of course, but you've got to appreciate how backed into a corner Belle was. She had no job, no home, and she needed to rustle up the money to move. She's got Toby to think of, and nobody to support her. I couldn't even help her."

She flushed with guilt at her brother's words. She, too, had done things that she didn't agree with morally at XZ Finance, because she'd been desperate for the money. They both fell quiet as they watched Tim finish his conversation, and stuff his phone back into his pocket. She had never seen him look so agitated.

"He was the one who said he'd look into the will. Maybe he did speak to Dad or the solicitors, and that's why they want to speak to him," Rose chewed her lip nervously before turning to look at her younger brother. "Without the fields, what do you think the house is worth?"

"In the current state? Probably not much more than a normal three or four bedroomed house in the village. As an estate though, Craig reckoned around one-and-a-half million."

Before she could reply, the heavy station door opened behind them. They both turned expectantly towards the noise expecting to see Belle, but the detective from earlier was stood in the doorway.

"Oh, brilliant," the woman looked pleased to see them. "I was wondering if you were still here. Is it Will? Are we able to just check a few more things with you, please?"

Will nodded politely, but as Rose watched her brother walk back into the station, she felt an uneasy dread settle over her chest.

Belle

Belle crossed her legs before uncrossing them again. The plastic chair she had been sat in for the last half-an-hour was stiff and uncomfortable, and she could feel her back slicken with sweat beneath her cotton t-shirt. The more questions the detective asked her, the more her discomfort grew. She couldn't help but squirm nervously even though she knew it was making her look suspicious.

The room wasn't even that warm, she tried to reason with her traitorous nervous system. *Just a little stuffy and claustrophobic.* The team that had been circling around her statement with increasing pressure were both dressed in full-sleeved shirts and trousers. Neither of them looked remotely uncomfortable, yet her skin felt clammy and hot in short sleeves.

"I think that's everything," the lead detective finally finished up, and Belle let out a sigh of relief before she could stop herself. "Thank you for your time."

They had nothing on her, she tried to reason with herself, but sitting in that chair, everything had felt so intense. No matter how hard she had tried to remain calm, she couldn't help her mind running away with her. She wasn't sure why she felt so worried; maybe it was the hard-learned knowledge that life wasn't just and fair. It was like she almost expected something bad to happen. She rose from the chair discreetly wiping her clammy palm on her jeans before she accepted the outstretched handshake.

Rose and Tim were outside the station, and at first, she felt a stab of annoyance at the sight of them. She had purposely left the B & B that morning to go to her friend's, needing some space from her family to digest the shock of everything that had happened. She had nothing against

271

Rose; it was just sometimes she could sense her sister felt a bit awkward around her, and it served to remind her that they barely knew each other. Tim on the other hand, she could barely look at without feeling a flare of anger rise inside her. He'd categorically denied any affair during their showdown, but once it was in her head, all the signs were strikingly clear; the late nights, the weekend plans, the phone that never left his side. She felt ashamed of herself for keeping it from Eleanor. If she didn't desperately need the short-term stability for Toby, she'd have wiped the floor with him. Instead they just gave each other a wide berth, but Belle knew there was only so long Tim could keep his dirty, little secret hidden for.

"Was everything ok?" Rose asked anxiously as soon as Belle emerged from the station.

Belle nodded. "Yeah, fine. Any news?"

Rose shook her head. "Nothing yet. I don't really know how long these things take."

"What's he doing?" She gestured towards Tim who was squinting against the sunlight at his phone screen.

"Looking for a taxi to take him back to his hotel," Rose replied. "I did offer him a lift, but Will is just answering a few questions inside, and he can't wait until he's done."

Belle snorted contemptuously calling over to him. "In a rush, Tim?"

He looked over, and she felt a childish glint of satisfaction at his expression. All day she had felt overwhelmed and tearful, but the annoyance on Tim's face gave her a tiny rush of satisfaction.

"How did it go?" He asked.

She shrugged petulantly. "They don't think I killed my own father if that's what you're asking."

"Belle!" Rose's jaw dropped open with shock, but Tim just rolled his eyes in irritation.

"Of course, that's not what I'm asking," he retorted sharply. "Have some sensitivity, for crying out loud."

"Well, that's why they're interrogating us all!" She felt her temper finally snap. "This isn't normal procedure, surely! They don't harass the family of an old guy who's popped his clogs. They clearly think one of us has done it."

"I'm sure they don't think that." Rose tried to sound soothing, but Belle could hear the stress in her tone. "It's just ticking boxes until they can tell what happened."

Belle turned to scowl at her sister. "It's either an accident or it's not, and the only one who can tell us what happened is conveniently dead right now."

"Belle," Tim shot her a warning look as Will appeared in the doorway with a police officer at his side. "That's enough."

Rose hurried over to Will, leaving them alone for a moment. Belle glared at him, wondering how someone could look so much like her yet be so hateful and arrogant.

"It's true," she argued back, but this time dropping her voice, conscious of the police officer within earshot. "All it would take was for one person to link any of us to that house, and we could be arrested. We've all got a motive."

"We've hardly got a motive," Tim scoffed, but Belle caught the slightest twitch of his jaw, and she knew he was worried. *Stop it now,* a little voice in her head warned her. *Before you go too far.*

When she didn't reply immediately, he eyed her with disdain and turned back to Will and Rose. The dismissive gesture sent a fresh bolt of fury coursing through her.

None of this is fair, she raged internally. Everything had been lined up perfectly. *All I had to do was get through the next few weeks and now it's all ruined. I'm back to having nobody.*

"Belle, are you ok?" Will was the only one that noticed

her whole body was physically trembling, and he rushed to her side.

She could already feel hot, spiky tears flooding her eyes. She swiped at them furiously, but she was helpless to stop the rush of emotion.

"Yeah," she manged to choke out, still defiantly angry through her upset. "I'm great. Everything is great."

"Oh, Belle," Rose tucked a motherly arm around her, and Belle had to fight the urge to pull away. She didn't want their comfort. All she wanted was for all this to be a horrible dream.

"Everything will be ok," Will said hollowly, but she could hear in his voice that he felt as wretched as she did.

"Did they say any more?" Tim asked him. "I don't see why we have to keep going over the same grounds. It's not like any of us were hanging around outside the house. You were all together, and I was with Eleanor. It's ludicrous that they're treating us this way."

"It's Linda!" Belle spat through her upset. "She's made out like we're only here for the money. He invited us! He brought up the will, now they're all looking at us like we're vultures."

"I drove past the house." Will suddenly burst out in barely more than a whisper. "I didn't go in, but what if something else comes out and they don't believe me?"

His words were enough of a shock to rip Belle from her misery as she spun around to face him with disbelief. "Oh, Will, they won't! Everybody knows you would never..."

Will's face was deathly pale, but he shrugged bravely. "It feels like a witch hunt now."

"Why did you go past the house?" Tim asked in a low voice, suddenly looking uncomfortable. "Was Craig with you? That's an alibi."

Will shook his head. "No, it was just me. And it was

around the time that they think..."

"That doesn't mean anything," Tim insisted, and for once Belle was glad that he was there. "If they had any suspicion, they'd arrest you."

"No," Belle corrected him quietly. "They need more than suspicion. They need evidence."

"I was the only one near the house," Will responded hollowly.

"I was out of the B & B," Belle offered. "I don't even have an alibi."

"Is that why they brought you back in?" Tim asked.

"Yeah," she nodded. "I didn't go to the house, but they kept asking if I had. By the end, I felt like utter shit."

Tim sighed heavily. "Yeah, they do make you feel a little flustered."

"I'm not going to lie," Belle reached for Will's arm. "We could both be screwed. Imagine if Linda says she saw one of us there. That's all it could take; someone else's word against ours."

"It's not just you," Tim admitted quietly. "I wasn't with Eleanor around that time either."

Rose looked at him in confusion. "Where were you?"

"I was just talking to a colleague on the phone," he replied defensively.

Belle met his eyes until he looked away uneasily.

"But they can vouch for that," Rose reassured him quickly. "Gosh, it's only my word that I was in the room on my own. They'll probably want to see me again."

"No, there's CCTV that shows anybody who enters or leaves the pub," Will tried to reassure her.

Belle frowned at his comment, unsure why his words rang a bell in her frazzled mind, but before she could remember what it was, they had reached Rose's car.

"I can drop you all back to wherever you need to be if

you're all in a rush," Rose said clicking the fob to unlock the doors. "But it would be nice if we could get lunch and maybe pay our own respects to Dad amongst all this."

Belle looked over at Tim, certain that he would decline, but she was surprised when he nodded.

"Yes," he agreed, and she thought that she heard a quiver of emotion in his voice. "I think he'd like that."

Will

As Will filed into the pub behind his brother and sisters, he tried to push his worries to the back of his mind. The day had felt like an awful nightmare, and his head was spinning trying to process it all. He could see from the faces around him that they all were feeling the same.

"What are we going to do?" Rose asked anxiously. She didn't need to elaborate for any of them to know she was talking about the suspicion that had landed on them.

"There's not a lot we can do," Tim snapped.

"Nothing we can do," Belle proclaimed at the same time.

They glanced at each other uncomfortably before everyone fell silent again.

Even through his despair, he was struck by the similarities between his brother and younger sister. On the face of it, they were worlds apart, yet they were so alike to look at, and shared the same body language and facial expressions.

"Can we just talk about something else for a bit?" Will suggested when Rose's face fell.

She was the only one who had nothing to worry about, but Will wouldn't put it past Belle or Tim to not lose their temper and snap at her. The last thing he needed right now was for everyone to fall out.

"I saw Christian Lennon yesterday in the little Tesco," Will offered the first meaningless snippet that came to his head. "Can you remember him?"

"That's a blast from the past. Remember when he pushed you off the tyre swing down the river and Rose chased him all the way back to the woods?" Tim surprised him by replying with an amused smile.

"Everyone was terrified of Rose," Will grinned back at his brother, keen to move the subject to lighter matters if only for a brief reprieve. "Remember when you broke your arm falling out of a tree getting my football back?"

"And we were in A & E for about eight hours," Rose groaned. "We were all moaning about how bored we were."

"Mum had to stay overnight, and we were waiting ages for Dad to pick us up," Will frowned. "I can't remember him ever coming."

"He couldn't take time off from work apparently," as the eldest, Tim remembered it clearly.

"Poor Mum," Rose voiced all their thoughts, and the laughter that had been on their lips died away.

"I feel like we should try to say something nice," Belle spoke up bravely. "But all my memories are just me and Mum. By the time I was old enough to play out, most of you had your own lives, and Dad was just never around."

"That's true," Will admitted sadly. "I don't even know what to say or to feel, and I feel so terrible for thinking like this. Even though he was our dad, I kind of feel that I've got no right to feel sad because I never really knew him, and he didn't know me."

"I feel the same," Belle admitted. "But I feel angry too. I tried to make an effort when Mum was ill, and then I tried reaching out when Toby was born, but he didn't want to know. I'm angry at myself for thinking that the invitation was his way of making amends, when in reality he probably only invited us to make up the numbers. And now we're all in this mess."

Rose grimaced. "He loved us in his own way."

"No offence, Rose," Belle shot back. "But it might be different for you and Tim, but Will and I hadn't seen him for years. He wasn't interested in our lives."

"I don't think it was different for us," Tim interjected,

surprising them all by coming to Rose's defence. "We were probably in a position where it was easier for us to pay a visit every now and again over the years, but that was more out of duty. We can't claim to have a deep bond with him anymore than the rest of you."

Will considered their words feeling a sharp tug of sadness at how hopeless it all felt. He'd spent the best part of his life travelling the globe; the excitement of the next adventure had been enough to chase away the quiet ache for a place he could always call home. The call had grown louder over the years until he had thought that the only answer was to put down roots himself. Yet when Craig had offered him all those things, the security and the predictability of the same home to go back to every night for the rest of his life, he had realised deep down that it wasn't what he wanted. It hit him, with startling clarity, that what he had been yearning for wasn't a big house with a partner and a regular job, but for the childhood home that had ceased to be a reassuring refuge when his mother had died. He missed Kathleen with every fibre of him but sitting amongst his siblings, he recognised how much he had craved the collective sense of belonging that had died with their mother. She had been their anchor, and without her they had been cast adrift. The hardest part, he thought as he regarded his siblings, had been knowing that Frank could have been the tie that they needed, but he had chosen to turn his back on the role.

"He wasn't a bad guy," Will sighed heavily, suddenly overcome with sorrow. "And I think that makes it harder, because at least then we could be angry. He was who he was, but it's not our fault."

Belle flashed him a look, and he knew then that she, at least, had needed to hear that.

"He's right," Rose swallowed back the lump in her

throat. "It's not our fault, but I get what you mean, Will. Even as an adult with kids of my own, the expectation for a parent to care about you never goes away. When I was going through my divorce, I wanted Dad to ask me how I was and show that he cared, but he just wasn't like that. It's ok to feel angry and resentful, at the same time as being sad that he's gone."

"I am angry," Belle admitted. "I'm furious that he dragged me back into his life, and I'm furious that I was stupid enough to think that he gave a damn about us."

"I'm glad that it made us all get in touch though," Rose reached out to cover Belle's hand with her own. "I was so wrapped up in my own life that I didn't think how hard it must have been for you when Mum died, and all I can think about, now that my boys are older, is how sad it would have made her for us to have ended up as almost strangers."

Will felt tears sting his eyes at his sister's words. "I agree, Rose. Despite the circumstances, it has been lovely to get to know you all again."

Belle's phone buzzed on the table interrupting them, and she glanced down at it. "Steph's going to drop Toby back. I'll go and wait outside."

Tim drained the rest of his drink before rising to his feet. "I think I'm going to make a move too."

Will felt his heart sink a little with disappointment. Even though he hadn't expected his detached, uncaring brother to morph back into the childhood friend and protector that he had been, it would have been nice to spend a few hours together before they all went their separate ways.

Or got arrested, his mind skipped anxiously back to the ongoing investigation.

"Well, let us know if you get any update," Will said numbly.

He exchanged a weary smile with Rose as the two remaining siblings watched the others leave the pub. As the eldest, Tim had always been the one that they looked up to, and Will couldn't help comparing his lack of emotion for the rest of the family to their father's. Despite his own troubles, he'd been hoping that they could strengthen their bonds but maybe Tim, and Belle to some extent, were too much like Frank for them to ever be the family that Will so badly craved.

Tim

Tim tried to ignore the strange sensation that bloomed in his chest as he walked away from his brother and sister.

You don't have time to be sentimental, he reminded himself sternly.

In the space of twenty-four hours, his whole world had started to fall apart. He had enough to think about without getting caught up in nostalgia and emotions. There was a very real chance that his affair was going to come to light, and the imminent threat had made him realise how badly he didn't want to lose Eleanor.

He let out an audible groan as he thought of the power that Emma now held. She was his only alibi, and while he knew she would cooperate and that there'd be phone records to back him up, he hated the power that she could now wield over him. And that was before he even began to figure out what to do about the pregnancy.

"Are you going back to the hotel?" Belle asked as she walked to the smoking area around the corner of the pub, hopping up onto a low wall to wait for her son in the sunshine. She pulled a packet of cigarettes from her bag and lit one up.

Tim stepped away from the stream of smoke, fanning his hand in front of his face to convey his irritation. "Yes, I just texted Eleanor. We're going to head back home."

"What if the police want to speak to you?" She asked, shielding her eyes from the sun with her free hand to look at him. "And what about when they release Dad's body for us to say goodbye to him?"

"I doubt the police will want to speak to me again," he shrugged with more confidence than he felt. "It's just the formality of checking my alibi. Once this is all cleared up, I'm sure Linda will be in touch regarding the funeral."

"Am I ok to collect my things tomorrow?" Belle asked unexpectedly.

"Oh," he felt a jolt of relief that she was moving on. He had assumed that she was staying until she moved to Hampton Dale at the end of June. "I didn't realise you were going."

"I wasn't going to," she countered. "But with everything, it's just going to be too awkward to stay."

"With everything?" He frowned at her.

"I'm assuming that Emma is your alibi," Belle replied scathingly. "And after everything Eleanor has done for me, I can't add to the stress she's going to be going through by being in the house."

He flinched at hearing Emma's name from his sister's mouth. "It's not like that."

Belle took a deep drag on her cigarette. "I'm not stupid, Tim, and neither is she. How long were you talking to her? I'm guessing you must have been gone a while for the police to be so interested."

"Does it matter?" He shook his head in annoyance. "It's just a routine enquiry to eliminate us all. She's a colleague, and we were discussing work."

"On a Friday night while you were away with your wife?" Belle scoffed. "Please, Tim, have some respect."

"Nothing is going to come out," Tim replied through gritted teeth. "Because I've done nothing wrong. However, I do think it's for the best that you find somewhere else to stay."

Belle turned her back to him as she extinguished the cigarette. "Do you have any idea how guilty I feel knowing about this?" She tossed her head haughtily. "I hate liars, Tim, and I hate that I'm keeping this from her. She deserves better."

"You're making something from nothing," he followed her as she started to walk away, surprising himself at how badly he wanted to justify himself to his sister. "It's nothing like that."

"It's going to come out," she spun around to face him, anger flashing in her green eyes. "You need to tell her, Tim!"

"Tell her what?"

Tim's blood turned to ice at the sound of Eleanor's voice behind him. In the split-second before he tore his gaze away from his sister's, he thought he saw the horror he felt mirrored back in Belle's eyes.

"Eleanor," he forced his voice to remain calm even as his pulse quickened in panic. *This is it*, he realised surprised at the force of the guilt he felt. "I didn't see you there."

"What's going on?" She ignored his comment, her eyes darting between Tim and Belle.

Tim glanced over her shoulder at Hugo waving cheerfully from the back of the car, and a secondary wave of regret rocked him.

"Rose!" Belle burst out unexpectedly. "We were talking about Rose. Tim was in a position where he could have helped her keep her job, but he's refusing to get involved."

Tim turned to look at his sister, startled that she would defend him. Belle narrowed her eyes at him, and he could only nod, speechless by her actions.

"Well?" Belle glared at him. "Don't you think that it's worth sticking your neck out for your own sister?"

Tim fell into character, shrugging dismissively. "Can we talk about it another time?"

"No," Belle shot back, and he saw a spark of enjoyment at his discomfort flash across her face. "You should have helped her when she came to you. She should at least get paid for the full month. I personally think she should drag them to a tribunal."

"What happened?" Any suspicion on Eleanor's face was replaced by concern.

"It's a long story," Tim reassured his wife before turning back to Belle. "Look, you're right. I'll look into it as soon as I'm back in the office and find out what happened. To be honest, the centre is going offshore at some point regardless, but I should have made time to help her out."

Belle nodded satisfied before turning back to her sister-in-law. "Tim says you're going back to London already. We've just ordered lunch if you and the kids want to eat first? Toby is on his way now."

Eleanor looked at him doubtfully, expecting him to dismiss the invitation in his impatience to get home, but he nodded, suddenly wanting to enjoy the time he had with his family before the inevitable fallout.

"Sure, why not," she agreed when Tim seemed willing. "I'll get the kids."

The moment she was out of earshot, Tim turned back to Belle.

"Why did you do that?" He asked in confusion. If anything, he would have thought his sister would have enjoyed him getting his comeuppance.

"Look, I'm not happy with what you've been doing, but at the end of the day, you're still my brother and, deep down, I think you know you've messed up," Belle sighed. "Without her, Tim, you'll end up like Dad; lonely and old, with kids that don't know you."

He felt the familiar destructive anger of self-defence bubble to the surface at her hurtful words, but he recognised the truth in what she was saying.

"I'm in over my head," he admitted pushing away his instinct to deny fault and to lash-out. He realised now that his temper was just a distraction from the uncomfortable feeling of shame pressing down on his chest. "I don't know if I can put this right."

Belle shrugged. "That's on you, Tim. I still think you're going to have to tell her, but you're my brother and even if I think you're wrong, I'll be here for you."

He trailed after his sister and his family, trying his best to push the thoughts from his head. Her comparison of him to their father had pierced the tough shell of his conscience, making him see how desperately he wanted to change the path that he was on.

Belle

She stepped away from the table to withdraw the last cigarette, tossing the empty packet into the bin. The evening was still warm, but there was a breeze in the air, and the beer garden was beginning to empty as drinkers headed home or to the cosiness inside. The Red Lion sat on the outskirts of Hampton Dale. The pub faced the main road, but the garden had clear views of the hillside. Belle watched as the sun dipped low behind the green slopes; the only trace of the summer's day the rose-gold streaks it left behind. She lit up the cigarette, feeling an immediate prickle of guilt as Toby swooped back to the table from the climbing frame to take a sip of his drink, and shot her a disapproving look.

"Mum!" He scolded her sternly. "I thought you didn't do that anymore."

"Sorry," she said, meaning it. "This is my last one, I promise, and then no more."

Belle knew that she had never been physically addicted, always able to kick the habit for months or even years at a time. It was more of a psychological crutch, but one that she'd needed to handle her nerves at coming back to the village for the wedding. She waited until Toby had turned back to the play area, Hugo trailing behind him, and she inhaled deeply.

"We're going to make a move," Eleanor said when she returned to the table. "Hugo is going to be furious, but they'll both be getting grumpy if they're out much longer. I'm glad we didn't check out or it would have been a long night."

"Thank you for staying so long," Belle held her arms out to embrace her sister-in-law. She was glad Eleanor and

Tim had ended up spending the afternoon with them. It had been a surreal day, but Eleanor's maternal presence seemed to draw them all closer together.

"Are you sure you'll be ok to get back tomorrow?" Eleanor asked. "We can always fit Toby in if you need?"

"It's fine, thank you," Belle shook her head. "I might stick around a little longer with my friend."

"What about you, Will?"

"Honestly, I'll be fine."

Will squeezed Eleanor's outstretched hands, and Belle glanced up at her brother with a sympathetic smile. The plan had been for her and Toby to get a lift home from Craig, but the break-up had left them high and dry.

In the grand scheme of things, a few nights on a sofa and having to catch a few buses home are the least of our worries, she reminded herself silently.

"Right, well if either of you need a place to stay..." Eleanor trailed off uncertainly.

Tim awkwardly hugged them goodbye with none of the warmth of his wife.

"It's been good to see you," he said to Belle. "Just let me know if you need me to drop anything off to you, or maybe give me a call if you need to stop by."

He might be an arse, she thought as she waved until the car was out of sight, *but at least he's trying.*

"I'm going to head off in a bit," Rose said sheepishly.

"Are you seeing that guy?" Will smiled with what felt like the first genuine grin of the day. "Good for you, Rose."

"His family are lovely," Belle vouched. "After Mum died, Bev and Alun were amazing to me. It's been so good to spend time with them again."

"No, I just meant I was going to go home," Rose smiled self-consciously. "They do seem like a lovely family. She must be a close friend to you."

"She is," Belle agreed. "She used to come up and stay with me in London before we had kids. The whole family are one of the main reasons that I wanted to come back. Bev's already offered to help with school runs and the holidays until I get myself sorted. It'll be nice for Toby to have that stability that we've never had." Belle noticed the guilt flash across Will's face, and she reached out for his hand quickly. "Sorry, that's not a dig at you both. It's no-one's fault."

"It's still crap, though," he grimaced.

Rose tried to look optimistic. "Well, as horrible as this has all been, I hope that we can use it as a fresh start and try to see each other more regularly, or stay in touch in your case, Will, if you're heading back overseas."

"I agree," Will nodded. "Although I'm starting to worry that I won't be able to go anywhere unless they find out what happened with Dad."

"I'm sure it'll all be tied up within a few days and we can all try to move on." Rose offered, a hint of worry in her voice. "I did send Linda a message, but she hasn't responded. I think I'll try again once this is all sorted; the last thing we want are any bad feelings around the funeral."

"I'm trying to be reasonable," Will said flatly. "Because I know it must have been horrible for her to find him, but for her to say that we could have done something..." He shook his head in disbelief. "I don't know if I want to see her at all. I feel really angry, and if I'm honest, scared that I'm being accused of the most awful thing."

Belle nodded her head in agreement. "I feel the same. I didn't like her anyway; she was so rude."

She looked at Rose as she spoke, and while her sister smile sympathetically, there was a flicker of concern in her eyes. Belle hadn't been able to shake the feeling that her sister had been a little off with her. There hadn't been anything tangible in what she'd said or done; just a niggle that was playing on Belle's mind.

I'm fed up with us all tiptoeing around each other, she thought suddenly. *If we just said how felt in the first place, maybe we'd have never got to this point.*

"Rose, is everything ok?" She asked. "I can't help feeling you've been a bit quiet with me."

Belle caught Rose's eyes flick questioningly to Will. Her stomach flipped uneasily that her suspicion had not only been right, but her brother was in on whatever the issue was.

They've been talking about me, she realised as hurt flooded her chest.

"If this is about the walking boot," she snapped angrily as her instinct for self-preservation kicked in. "Then yes, I did only wear it to stay on at Tim's. I should have been honest, but you have no idea how desperate I was for somewhere to stay, and neither of you came running to help me. But if you think that means I could have walked to the farm, murdered our Dad, and gone to bed like an absolute psychopath then you can both go to hell!"

Will's eyes widened with panic as he reached out for her. "Hang on a minute! Nobody thinks you did anything. Belle, I drove past the farm late at night. That looks much worse."

"Belle, I would never think that of you!" Rose protested. "I was just worried that Dad had upset you yesterday. I just didn't want you to think you couldn't talk about anything because of what happened."

"I'm fine," she shrugged, but she felt herself soften as she turned to acknowledge Will. "I know how you feel. I would be lying if I said I'm not worried that Linda is going to make something up..."

"If only we could prove we weren't there." Will grimaced.

"Oh!" His comment opened a locked memory that she'd forgotten about. "There was a security camera at the side of the house. Linda shouted at Toby when we first went down for hitting it with a ball. That will prove that we were never there."

She saw the relief on her brother's face, and if she hadn't already been certain of it, his expression would have been enough to convince her that he was innocent.

Rose

It was almost dark by the time she pulled the car to a stop outside her house. She blinked once, almost startled to see that a navy-blue night sky had rolled in around her as she had driven the sixty-plus miles on autopilot. A heavy fatigue hung from her shoulders, and she barely had the energy to unfurl her tired body from the car to make the short walk into the house. Rose took only her handbag; too tired to face carting in her weekend bag. She locked the door behind her, grateful for once for the emptiness of the house, and without bothering to potter she walked straight up the stairs to climb into the bed.

She waited for the familiar worries to come creeping out of wherever it was that they hid during the daytime, but her mind was empty and still, and she closed her eyes to let sleep take her. The irony wasn't lost on her even as she was washed away into unconsciousness. She had spent the last five years fighting to grasp sleep, relying on alcohol, or medication, or sometimes both; the most mundane troubles built up by her mind until they were huge and unconquerable. Yet now with the loss of her father, the worries about her siblings, no job, Gareth, the list went on, she found that her mind had simply shut off under the pressure of it all.

The room was flooded with daylight when she finally woke, and she lay still for a moment feeling only a slight ache in the centre of her chest as she remembered everything. With no job to wake up for, she stayed in bed until the pressure of her bladder could be ignored no longer. Methodically, Rose fetched her bag from the car, made a cup of tea and carried it back up to the bathroom to shower, but it wasn't until the lukewarm water hit her that she felt the full force of the emotions return more powerful than ever. Hot, salty tears mingled in with the water as she finally gave into aching sadness.

It was all such a mess, she thought bitterly as she tried to work through all her thoughts one at a time. But there were too many threads to her despondency, and she couldn't manage to see one to the end before the next upset came to her and it was all too big and powerful for her to even know where to start. Unable to cope with the thoughts alone, she dug out a bottle from beneath the sink to add a slug of gin to her now tepid mug of tea. She gulped it down, ignoring the nasty taste, and then immediately disgusted with herself she scrubbed the cup in the sink, drying it and putting it away like that would undo her actions. She opened her overnight bag throwing her clothes hurriedly into the washing machine, even the dry-clean-only dress that had gone unworn. She switched the machine on, realising as the cycle kicked in that the tags were still in the dress and that she could have got her money back, and with the realisation that she had just thrown seventy-pounds that she could ill afford down the drain, she pulled the bottle back out from where she had hidden it. This time though she poured it into a glass.

"I've just lost my father," she said aloud as if the house was judging her.

Rose rummaged through the cupboards for a mixer, but the shelves were despondently bare, so she slugged it back neat. The biting taste and the instantaneous heat that flooded through her centre eclipsed any shame, and she felt the cloak of fatigue on her shoulders lighten a little. She retrieved her phone from the depth of her bag holding down the power button until it sprang back to life. She glanced at the screen as it buzzed with a steady influx of messages and notifications, and as tempted as she was to turn it back off and pour another drink, she knew that she'd have to reply eventually. Rose boiled the kettle again, making a more respectable breakfast drink *sans alcohol* this time. It crossed her mind to pour away the rest of the gin, but she decided that that would be dramatic and unnecessary.

I don't have a problem, she smiled wryly at her own thoughts.

She turned her attention back to the messages, working through them methodically. Lena had sent a friendly text enquiring about the weekend, and Rose bit her lip wondering how to reply without coming across like a complete fun sponge, as her sons would say.

Wedding cancelled. Dad died. Police think my brother or sister might have done it. Shagged Gareth though. Smiley face.

She chuckled to herself at the absurdity at the same time that her eyes clouded with tears. Her laughter caught in her throat and she collapsed into noisy sobs at the kitchen table, until she was red-faced and breathless feeling utterly wretched. When she was spent, she turned back to the phone determined to respond to the lovely, kind Lena who had been a consistent comfort to her over the past few months. She didn't deserve to be left in the lurch, but Rose didn't want to drag her down into the ugly, pathetic mess of her life. She typed and then back-spaced several times before she settled on a safe "Will call you in the week. Let me know when you're free". She moved on to the messages that she had received from Will and Belle, sending them both generic placeholder responses much like the one she had sent Lena.

How ironic that she had spent the last few years desperate to forge some meaningful relationships, and now she was too completely wiped out to connect with anyone.

She wondered at what curse had been cast over her for her life to be such a shamble. Everything she had wanted had seemed within reach, but it had all come at either a horrible price or been snatched away. She could hardly bear to look at the messages from Gareth. After years of a loveless marriage with Phil where sex was transactional and any self-esteem she had started with had been torn to shreds, she had never dreamed that she could be on the receiving end of a good man's attentions. Rose had never dared to hope that she could meet someone so lovely, and handsome, and respectful.

"Hope you had a safe journey home. Let me know when you're home safe x."

She tried to ignore the fuzzy warm tingle that shot through her misery, reminding herself that it was not just foolish, but pathetic to even think that she could allow herself to fall in love with this man.

It was probably just sex to him. Just a rebound. she reminded herself even though it hadn't felt like that was all he wanted. He was bound to lose interest now that her family tragedy had been broadcast around the village and surrounding areas. And in his job, it would be doubly embarrassing for him. No matter how easy she was, no man of Gareth's standing was going to risk public humiliation by standing by a jobless, fat forty-year-old's side while her family's collective reputations were dragged through the mud. Rose still had no idea what would happen with the will; whether it had been changed already, whether anything was due to them, or whether the uncertainty around Frank's death would end in lengthy court battles. She knew that she couldn't afford the distraction of emotions clouding her judgement. Even in the teeny, tiny probability that she would inherit enough to eliminate her money worries, it would be a long way off and she had a stack of crushing debts, no job and the boys to consider. It had been hard enough to juggle before she had had grief to add to the mountain.

What could I even offer him? She grimaced as she deleted the message without responding.

His name disappeared from the screen, and immediately she was struck by regret.

I can't just ignore him like that, she thought as panic ballooned in her chest. *He's still a police officer. He might think it's a sign of guilt, or I'm hiding something…*

She stared at her phone, feeling less like a grown woman and more like a clueless teenager. For a moment, she wished she was sat in the oppressive office of XZ Finance; Lena would have known what to do for the best.

Maybe I'll just be friendly, but not too keen. She tapped her finger against the table. *Then if everything works out ok, I haven't cut off my nose to spite my face.*

She tried to force her mind to imagine the best-case scenario; one where the will paid out, she had no money worries, a relationship with her siblings, and Gareth fell madly in love with her. It wouldn't change anything, or bring her dad back though, she thought as she slumped against the chair.

Still, it was the sensible thing to do to keep her options open. If only to afford her little bursts of escapism in her head. She typed and retyped until she felt the message sounded natural, and not borderline unhinged like she actually felt.

"Sorry, my battery died and I was so tired last night I fell asleep without checking my messages. Thank you for being so kind."

She was placed her phone down, unsure whether to turn it off when it began to ring facedown on the table besides her making her startle. Rose turned it over, already tormented whether to answer or let it go to voicemail when she saw her brother's name flashing up on the screen, and she was so relieved that it wasn't Gareth that she answered it without considering whether she wanted to speak to him right now.

"Hi Tim."

"Hi," Tim sounded more uptight than usual. "Belle has just been on the phone to me. What's this about CCTV?"

Rose's heart sank. She had pushed the conversation with Belle immediately out of her mind, more concerned with packing up and getting out of Hampton Dale.

"Oh, she did mention that she thought that there might be some security cameras," she replied. "But I don't remember there being any. I think it was one of those cheap fake jobs to be honest, or the police would have noticed. There's no way Linda wouldn't have brought it up..."

"There was a camera," he cut her off. "I took it down. The day before the wedding."

"Why would you do that?" Rose felt her blood run cold at the implication.

"Linda asked me to," Tim sniffed haughtily. "Why else would I? We had the ladders out for the gazebo, and she asked me to take it down while I was there. It was hanging by a thread, and she said it didn't work anyway."

"Oh!" Rose heartrate slowed a little. "Well, that's fair enough."

"Don't you think that looks bad though?" He pressed her with an urgency that alarmed her. "What if it did work, and now she's got some footage of me taking it down?"

"Why would she do that?"

"Has anyone mentioned it to the police yet?" Tim asked, ignoring her question.

His tone made her stomach knot a little, but she tried to sound calm when she answered. "Ummm, I'm not sure.

Belle mentioned it to me, but I completely forgot about it."

"Well, Linda would have known there were none," Tim sounded mildly placated. He cleared his throat noisily and when he spoke again, he seemed back to normal. "Well, if you hear anything let me know."

"Ok," she was about to ask him when they could expect an update on the cause of death, but he had hung up without even saying goodbye and she was left speaking to herself.

Tim

Panic tightened around his chest leaving him breathless and feeling utterly out of control as he struggled to calm the chaos of this thoughts. He should have felt relieved after speaking to Rose, but the missing security camera was just another complication to add to the long list of worries.

Why is this happening to me?

Never in his life had he felt so powerless and for a moment, he embraced the physical pain, wondering numbly if a heart attack would be a pleasant alternative to facing up to the fallout. No matter how he tried to spin the situation, he just couldn't picture an outcome where he came out on top. Defeated, he sank down onto a park bench, head in his hands. They had checked out of the hotel as soon as the children woke up, and he had promised himself that he would speak to Eleanor once they were home but he just couldn't seem to find the words. He had left the house on the pretence of going for a run, unable to bear the tension in the air. His phone felt heavy in his pocket, and he took it out wincing at the string of messages from Emma.

His mind flickered to the meeting scheduled for the end of the week, and he felt the second wave of panic lock its steel jaws around his chest. The outcome was pre-determined, and he knew that there was no way he could back out without rousing suspicions, but he needed to do something.

Think! He implored himself desperately, but his head was too jumbled. He just couldn't summon the strength to untangle one problem at a time.

His phone buzzed as another phone call from Emma flashed up on screen. Tim knew that he couldn't afford to anger her, but even in his desperation there was still a part of him too arrogant to allow her to force his hand. He sent the call to his voicemail, and within seconds a short, angry text message came through.

She's a liability, the rational, risk-adverse side of his brain reminded him.

He knew that she had to be dealt with as a priority. She was the one at the centre of each strand of the chaos; if he could just get her under control then everything else would follow. He straightened up on the park bench to read the chain of increasingly furious messages, trying to ignore the flare of anger he felt at her thinly veiled threats. Her phone call to him the evening before his father's death had been the catalyst for the mess he was in, but he knew that he had only himself to blame.

Belle bringing up the security camera had added to his worries. Without that being thrown into the confusion, he knew that one phone call to Emma would have cemented his alibi. Even knowing how volatile Emma could be, he knew she would have handled the conversation. There was no chance that he could cut ties with her completely when he needed her to remain on side until this was all over. The only way to keep Emma sweet would mean losing Eleanor for good, and the thought tore at his heart in a way that his father's death could never. There was no outcome that didn't result in him losing something that mattered to him. For the first time, he envied his siblings for their uncomplicated lives as well as the bonds they'd forged over the last few months. It had crossed his mind to speak to them, to share the burden of the whole mess that he was in, and not just the part that Belle knew about. But to do that he'd have to trust them.

It's bad enough that Emma has got all this control, he thought as he reluctantly dialled her number to face up to the inevitable outburst. *The last thing I need is to pour my heart out to them and end up getting myself in a bigger mess.*

Belle

"I don't know how you can get any sleep in here," Stephanie said as she watched Belle carefully folding away the blankets from her makeshift bed on the sofa.

Belle stretched her aching back as she smiled at her friend. "Honestly, it's fine," she lied. She had barely managed more than an hour at a time the past few nights, but she was grateful for a place to stay until she tied up all her loose ends. *And anyway,* she thought as she gratefully accepted the proffered cup of tea, *I don't think I'd be able to sleep in a king-size bed in a five-star hotel with everything on my mind right now.*

"I'm so glad that you're staying," her friend said. "I didn't know whether you'd change your mind with everything that happened."

"Me too, to be honest. But even with my dad..." Belle trailed off, her voice catching with emotion. She cleared her throat before she trusted her voice to continue. "Even with everything, it still feels like the right thing to do."

She held back from saying that she felt strangely closer to her family when she was there, knowing that it made no sense. Her family were further away than ever, and her father's sudden death had opened a whole new can of emotions for her to contend with.

"We love you, Belle," Stephanie leaned down to hug her and Belle let herself melt into her friend for a moment before pulling away cautious of not allowing herself to get tearful when there was still so much to do.

The school at Hampton Dale had a place for Toby, so she had arranged to stay with Steph until her new house was ready. She had no reason to go back to London, so Will had collected her belongings from Eleanor's garage. It was left unspoken that he'd have to return for the funeral, but after that she had no idea when or even if she'd see her siblings again. She pushed the thoughts away, unwilling to add another layer to her sadness, but she couldn't quite shake the heavy feeling in her heart even as she strolled along the high street later that day with Toby and Steph's daughter Harley skipping along beside her.

It wasn't the first time that things had felt like they were finally going right for her just to come crashing back down, she reminded herself determined to find a positive in the mess. She smiled at the sound of Toby's excitable chatter as she glanced back to check that the children were in sight. Back in London, she'd have been clutching his hand terrified of the never-ending traffic or the dubious characters lurking on corners. Here, they were always within a stone's throw of green spaces, and *everyone* knew everyone.

"Annabelle!" As if on cue, Brenda Howells stepped out from the hair salon almost ploughing Belle to the ground with her ample bosom. "Oh, sweetheart!"

She hadn't set eyes on the neighbouring farmers for sixteen years, but in Hampton Dale time meant nothing, and she felt herself swept into the woman's arms.

"I'm so sorry about your dad," Brenda clucked when she finally released her, taking a step back to regard Belle sympathetically. "But look at you! All grown up. Oh, your mother would have been ever so proud of you."

It was such a cliché, and under any other circumstances Belle would have had to force herself not to roll her eyes, but she had fond memories of Brenda turning up at the house with heavy, warm pots laden with casseroles when her mother was poorly and she was aghast to feel her eyelids prickle with spiky tears.

"Do they know what happened?" Brenda continued

not waiting for a response. "Terrible, terrible tragedy."

"We're waiting for the coroner's report," she replied politely.

Brenda made another clucking noise of sympathy. "Awfully sad. Are you staying at the house with Linda? If I'd known I would have stopped by."

"No, I'm staying with Alun and Bev's daughter Steph," Belle tried not to flinch at the thought of being back in the house where Frank had died. It hadn't even crossed her mind that Linda would be there, but of course she would. After all, it had been her home for the past six months.

"How's Linda?" Brenda lowered her voice conspiratorially. "I was just saying to the girls," she nodded her head back towards the salon. "That I wondered what would happen now with the place."

"We're not sure," Belle glanced over her shoulder partly out of habit to check on the children who had their faces pressed up against a shop window and partly to break Branda's steely gaze. "I, uh, need to speak to Dad's solicitor at some point, but it's all very fresh still."

"Of course," Brenda nodded her head solemnly.

Belle was preparing to seize the opportunity of the brief lull in the conversation to make her escape when Brenda's eyes flickered to a spot behind her, and she saw the woman's whole body stiffen. She glanced behind her curious as to what could have unnerved the unflappable farmer when her eyes settled on the bottle blonde stalking towards them and her blood turned to ice.

"Linda," Belle felt her pulse quicken at the grim expression on her almost-stepmother's face. Frank's familiar saloon car was idling at the curb, and Linda was crossing the pavement towards Belle with purposeful strides. It was clear from the narrowed eyes and puckered mouth that she hadn't pulled over to exchange pleasantries.

"I'd heard you were still here," Linda spat through gritted teeth. "But I didn't believe that you would have the gall."

Belle felt her cheeks flame red with humiliated indignation, but she struggled to remain civil.

"Linda, we've tried to speak to you," it wasn't exactly a lie- Belle knew that Rose had at least. "We're so, so sorry. We can't even imagine how horrible that must have been..."

"Don't you dare!" She roared with a force that made Belle and Brenda jump. "The police might be slow to act, but I know that it was you. You came back and you killed him!"

The accusation hit Belle like a blow to the chest, and she gasped physically winded by the attack. Her eyes danced of their own accord to her son, and his pale, pinched face was enough to snap her back from the shock.

"Linda, please," she forced her tone to remain calm, but she heard it quiver giving away her nerves. "I know this is a shock but if you think for a minute..."

"Oh, no!" Linda almost bellowed, still running on pure adrenaline. "I don't *think* anything. I know, and there's proof. When you're in prison, believe me I will contest that will for Frank. He didn't want any of you ungrateful, money-grabbing murderers..."

"Linda! That is enough!" Belle had almost forgotten Brenda's presence, and it was with mortified gratitude that she watched the strapping older woman seize Linda's scrawny arm and begin to pull her away.

"Linda, I..." Belle opened her mouth to say something, but she had no words, and seeing Brenda's sharp nod at her, she took Toby and Harley's hands as calmly as she could muster and walked away.

"Mum! Mum!"

Belle was halfway back down the high street when she

finally heard Toby calling up to her, and she guiltily shook off her own alarm to answer him.

"Why did she say you would go to prison, Mum?" She saw the terror in his eyes, and she felt a flare of anger rip through her upset at the encounter.

"She's off her head, Tobes," Belle reassured him. "She's a horrible lady, and she's making things up."

"Why would she say that though?" He persisted. "Because Grandad Frank died?"

"No, Toby." Belle cut him off. "She's had a shock and she's saying silly things. She needs to go to the doctor."

"Is she going to die too?" Toby's eyes widened further, and Belle felt the gravity of the situation pressing down on her shoulders threatening to floor her completely.

"No, Toby..."

"You're not going to go to prison though, Mum?" The rising desperation in his voice clawed at her heart.

"No," she said in her firmest tone. "Now, let's stop being silly and get a cake from the baker's, shall we?"

She pushed open the door to the shop, ushering the children in ahead of her, but as she stood in the queue, she had to push her hands deep into her pockets when she realised how much they were trembling. It had been three days since she had been sat in the stiff, plastic chair at the police station, and even then, she had managed to master her fears, reassuring herself that it was just protocol. With every passing day that there had been no follow up from the investigation, she had felt her anxieties ease to allow her grief to come to the forefront of her mind. But the accusation, violent and angry, had brought all her worst fears flooding back.

Will

His stomach knotted with nerves as he swiped his clammy palms across the back of his jeans, wishing he didn't have to do this. The Coroner's report had come back, and instead of dispelling any concerns it had added more uncertainty around his father's death.

"Do you want me to come?"

Raya looked up at him, her eyes wide with concern, but he shook his head exhaustedly.

"No, it's fine," he said trying to sound brave. "I feel bad enough leaving you in the lurch with this job." He smiled wryly gesturing around her tiny flat at the mountain of his sister's belongings next to his own meagre pile. "And for putting all this on you."

She had been sat on the edge of her sofa with an assortment of lenses spread out around her preparing for a shoot, but she pushed them to the side and got to her feet.

"You'd do it for me," she reminded him gently. "That's what friends are for, right. Come on. I'll help you load the car."

Neither of them spoke as they carted Belle and Toby's bags back and forth until Will's car was piled high, and resignedly he slipped into the car turning on the engine. Raya stood on the pavement, and despite the bright smile on her face he could see the worry in her eyes. They had skirted around his fears, latching onto any distractions instead of talking about it, but he could feel her concern rolling from her, hot and suffocating.

"What if they think it was me?" The words burst from him in a momentary lapse of control that he regretted as soon as they were out of his mouth.

Anguish spread across her face, and he wanted to claw

his words back; wanted to go back to pretending that it was all alright.

"Ignore me," he tried to laugh before she had a chance to speak, knowing that he couldn't handle the conversation. "It's the stress of it all."

She nodded her head once, but she didn't look convinced. "It'll be fine. They're just being thorough. Phone me when you get there."

He forced himself to pull his eyes away from his best friend, turning up the car radio to silence the nagging voice that wondered if he'd ever make it to Japan like they'd planned. The miles of road passed by unnoticed as his mind replayed the events of the weekend scrutinising everything that had happened.

It looked awful. He couldn't deny that. No matter how much he tried to reason with himself, he couldn't deny that emotions had been running high for all of them. The only one who hadn't shown the slightest hint of being stressed and on edge had been Frank. They had all thought about the will in the months, and certainly the days, leading up to the wedding, but none of them had raised it properly.

How could we? Will thought through the torment of the what-ifs. He felt the familiar flicker of anger that Frank had put them in this position, but he pushed away any thoughts of the injustice of Linda receiving their mother's land. He hadn't been able to bring himself to think about it before Frank had died, and he certainly didn't want that in his head now.

Would there have been a different outcome if they'd just talked about it like adults?

He shook his head hard. No, of course not. He couldn't go down that route. That would be like admitting Linda was right with her accusations.

She was a horrible person, he acknowledged sticking to

the safer ground that he could manage. Kathleen would have been devastated that Frank was doing this to his children. She would have been heartbroken that he had barely seen any of them in the past few years, and Will knew she wouldn't have blamed them.

Tim had confirmed that the will had remained unchanged, but Will couldn't find any comfort in that. Not now, not until this was all settled, the investigation was over, and Frank had been laid to rest. The will was the centre of it; all Linda's accusations and the police's concerns rested on a piece of paper. It felt horrible, and cheap, and sordid.

For him, it had never been about money. He had no idea whether the will had changed or remained the same until afterwards. He had to admit though that he had had suspicions about Frank's intentions, so he couldn't help but wonder how his brother and sisters had felt about it.

If only we had been closer, he thought as helpless desperation spread through his chest. *If only we were the kind of family to sit down and talk about it properly.*

But they weren't, and he knew that it was unlikely that they would ever be that family again. Everyone was too wrapped up in their own problems, and Will knew that he couldn't blame them. He hadn't been there for any of them, swanning off the moment he was old enough to. His life a series of exotic landscapes and sunsets. How could he possibly know for sure what they were capable of, what would have triggered them to snap.

Belle, for all her gentleness with Toby, had a streak as fiery as her copper-coloured hair. She had been at rock bottom; left for dead on the side of the road, robbed by her boyfriend while she lay unconscious in the hospital, sacked and broke, made to feel like a burden by the family that should have been there for her. His chest ached with pain for his sister. They had all let her down badly, leaving a fourteen-year-old to grieve alone with their uncaring father. No matter how well she seemed on the face of it, Will knew that there were years of bad feeling buried beneath her bravado.

She had the most reason to snap, he knew even though the thought made him feel physically sick knowing that she had the most to lose. For her, and for Toby. He wasn't a religious man, but he had prayed silently that she hadn't gone to Bluebell Farm that night.

He turned his attention to his brother, knowing that he was the only one who had a temper to match Belle's. Despite Tim's life appearing perfect on the surface, it was clear he was a man on the edge. His high-pressured job, and his affair; it was all threatening to cave in around him.

Could Tim have snapped?

Will felt certain that he was capable of hurting someone, but their father? He shook his head, not wanting to let the scene take shape in his imagination. It was too grisly to comprehend.

He forced his thoughts to Rose, and he was glad that his motherly, mild-mannered sister didn't appear to be in the frame. He had caught just the briefest glimpse into her life over the past few months, and it had completely changed how he had viewed her. He had always pictured her as calm and collected, a Mother Earth type; much more grown-up than him, with her teacher husband and her family. But he knew now that he had no idea of who she was, and he had just pasted his own memories of his mother over the image he held of Rose. She wasn't Kathleen, that was abundantly clear to Will now. It was clear that Rose hadn't had the textbook, perfect, small-town life that he'd imagined. There was something desperately lonely about his big sister, and the knowledge gnawed at him uncomfortably.

He knew that he needed to stop dwelling on them. There was nothing that he could do, but he still felt guilt lying heavy on his chest knowing that he would be leaving the country the moment he had the chance.

Rose

"Is everything ok?"

Rose gazed down at the phone in her hand with a heavy heart. She had started the week with such good intentions, but every day she had managed to convince herself that she was too busy to reply to Gareth, or any of her siblings. It was surprisingly easy to be productive when you were avoiding someone; her house had never looked so clean and tidy, and the notebook on the kitchen table was full of jobs she had applied for.

I'll reply to him later, she promised herself, trying to ignore the ache of regret as she left Gareth's message unread.

She slipped on the smart navy jacket that she reserved for best and spritzed herself with the dregs of her perfume bottle. At some point during the night, she had woken up with a sudden surge of energy and it had felt like the perfect time to give the kitchen cupboards a thorough clean. While she was elbow-deep in soapy water surrounded by tinned goods and miscellaneous household objects accumulated over the years, she had decided that she needed to be more pro-active in her job hunt. She would head into town to visit the numerous recruitment agencies and see what she could find. No matter how sad she felt about her father's death, she knew that she had to remain practical when she had bills to pay and no income. The downside of her motivated job hunting had been that she'd been forced to turn her phone back on. As well as messages from Gareth, she had missed calls from Will and Belle. She knew from Will's message that the coroner's report had come back, and he was being asked to attend another interview. Belle had had a particularly horrible run in with Linda in the village, and as much as Rose's heart went out to them both, she had to remain practical.

It's all well and good wanting to swan back and forth to Hampton Dale to be there for them, she reminded herself as she methodically packed her handbag, *but I need to get a job.*

She knew that her brother and sister hadn't hurt their father. She had been worried that they may have gone to Bluebell Farm to have it out with him the night before the wedding, but her only worry about that was that they would be in some way falsely implicated. She had received no news on any security camera footage, so she knew she could safely assume that there was none. It was just bad timing that they had both left the B & B at the same time.

They'll both be fine, she reassured herself firmly as she set out to the bus stop. There was absolutely no reason for her to go the village. At least, not until the funeral.

She swallowed at the thought of that hurdle ahead of her, knowing that at some point she would have to face up to her grief. Aside from her emotional breakdown when she'd returned to the safety of her home, she had managed to keep the lid on that particular box, knowing that she could ill afford to be swept any further into misery. Not if she wanted to keep a roof over her head for the sake of Tom and Jack.

At the back of her mind, she dared to imagine that a day would come when the investigation was over, and the estate was settled where she would be free of the shackles of worrying about her bills. Maybe then, however far down the line that was, she would be able to consider selling up, paying off her debts, and maybe even picking up where she'd left off with Gareth. She smiled wryly to herself at the thought as she boarded the bus and took a seat towards the back, but immediately she felt guilt wash over her at daring to have such optimistic thoughts in the wake of her father's death.

Tim

The walls of the stuffy office felt like they were closing in on him as he tugged weakly at the collar of his shirt. The day that he had been dreading had finally arrived, and the meeting had been concluded. The draft communication was sat in his inbox, but he couldn't bring himself to send it. The emails and phone calls had started pouring in, and he turned away from his desk feeling suffocated by the onslaught.

It's done, Tim told himself. *The worst part is over.*

He had somehow managed to keep Emma at bay with false promises and long, complex answers to her short, angry demands that answered nothing but spun her around in the circles. If Tim had learned anything in his life, it was that people would hear what they wanted to.

It's her own fault for being so unrealistic. She knew that it would have to be her sites that closed, he tried to reason with himself as her name flashed up on the screen of his phone for the tenth time since the meeting. *I did nothing to make her think otherwise.*

It wasn't even a lie, he tried to justify to himself, that the decision was out of his hands. With the numbers in black and white, there was no way his boss and the rest of the team would accept any other site being the first to close. The Cardiff office was a tiny sales site for their low-credit affinity brand XZ Finance, and the Bristol office housed several hundred staff for their main brand's customer service team. It was the logical site to move first, but until it was in black and white, Emma seemed to be struggling to understand that it was inevitable.

He knew that he was far from out of the woods yet; everything he had done so far had been a stall to make it to the trigger point of today's meeting. Now that he had made it, his plan was to give Emma some space to cool down. She had already spoke with the police over the phone to corroborate his statement, and they had seemed satisfied that he was speaking to her for the entire time that he was not with Eleanor inside the hotel room.

The Coroner had found no medical reason for Frank to drop down dead, but the head injury was consistent with a fall. If it wasn't for Linda muddying the water, then Tim was confident that the case would be stamped accidental and they would all be allowed to move on. The lack of a solid alibi for Will and Belle seemed to be dragging the investigation on unnecessarily, and it niggled at the back of his mind that they might inadvertently drag him back into their mess somehow. The last thing he needed was to have to go back over his statement. It was all there in black-and-white, and he dreaded Eleanor finding out that way.

His temples prickled with sweat as Emma's name flashed up again on his personal phone. Part of him was tempted to cave and to answer her call, but he held firm watching until it rang off. No, he needed to wait this out. He'd already decided that he'd give her space to cool down; the last thing he wanted to do was tip her over the edge with an off-cuff comment or a scathing tone. If he simply did nothing, she would calm down eventually. She would see that it wasn't the end of the world, and that there had been nothing further he could do. Once she was in a more reasonable frame of mind then he could talk her properly. In the meantime, though, she wouldn't risk sullying her own name just to drag him down. She had threatened him out of sheer desperation, he realised as the week progressed, but she hadn't gone through with any of her threats. She hadn't gone to his boss, or called his wife, and she hadn't phoned the police and told them he'd offered her money like she'd hysterically screamed at him that she was going to do. He'd managed to talk her down, but he was still acutely aware that, even if she didn't know it, she held all the power right now.

A soft rap at the door interrupted his troubled thoughts, and he looked up to see Marie's face, pinched with worry, peering through the glass at him.

"You're not answering your phone," she said as if that explained the interruption.

Tim glanced back down at the screen in confusion as she slipped into the office gently closing the door behind her.

"Your work phone," she corrected him.

He reached for it, seeing for the first time the missed calls from his boss. Marie grimaced, but held out a hand to stop him redialling.

"He's just called my line," she told him apologetically, as if it were her fault for answering it. "He wants to see you upstairs immediately."

Tim felt his blood run cold with panic. In all the years he had worked for MG Bank, his boss had never gone through his assistant. Nothing was ever that urgent.

"Did he, uh, say what this is about?" It took all Tim's willpower to try to recover his composure, but when he looked up at Marie, he saw a flicker of sympathy in her eyes.

The Personal Assistants knew everything that was going on in the office before it happened, he knew that. He wondered if the workplace grapevine had been working overtime, or if she had worked out that something had been going on with Emma.

Marie swallowed nervously, but she shook her head. "Sorry, Tim. He didn't say."

"Ok," he rose to his feet resignedly. "Hold my meetings

this afternoon please."

*****

The journey home was horrendous. The packed, delayed train was stiflingly hot, and Tim's head was throbbing from the events of the day. All he wanted to do was to get home to clear his head, but that would mean having to act natural in front of Eleanor, and how could he do that with everything going on in his mind.

Emma had gone to his boss and told him they'd been having an affair. He still couldn't believe that she'd actually done it. Fortunately, he'd managed to downplay it, and while he knew that there'd be repercussions for his indiscretion, there would need to be more evidence of wrongdoing to sack him outright. He knew that if it got out, it would scupper any realistic shot at a promotion, but if he managed to ride it out as a one-off blunder then he might be ok.

In a way, he thought as he squeezed through sweaty passengers as the train pulled into his station, *if it was going to come out at all, then today was perfect.* It had thrown doubt on Emma's motivations for her to choose the day her site closures were officially announced. If anything, she should have been briefing and preparing her staff for the next part of the process, not deciding that now was the perfect moment to reveal that she'd slept with her boss. It just made her look vengeful, which had actually stood him in good light.

As he approached his home, he braced himself. He didn't seriously think for a minute that she would have somehow got hold of Eleanor as well as his boss. For a start, Emma had no idea of where they lived or her telephone number, she didn't know what his wife did for a living and Eleanor wasn't active on social media at all. But even so, he still felt a pang of worry as he approached the front door.

When this is all over, he promised himself, *I'll make amends with Eleanor. I'll make more of an effort in the relationship and make sure this doesn't happen again.*

He slipped his key into the lock calling out to announce his arrival as he pushed the door open. There was a shuffle from the kitchen, and his wife appeared in the doorway.

"Tim," she said calmly, but the stony expression on her face belied her quiet tone. "There are some police here to see you."

His chest constricted tightly, and he ceased slipping his feet from his shoes, instantly rooted to the spot. A uniformed officer appeared at her shoulder, and Tim hurried to recover his composure for now the third time in a day.

"Is everything alright?" He managed to find his voice.

"We're here on behalf of our colleagues at the Gloucestershire Police Force. We have a few questions in relation to your father's death," the officer replied. "Would you mind accompanying us to the station?"

Tim looked from the officer to Eleanor, frantically trying to read how serious this was. All prior conversations had been him voluntarily 'popping' into the station or over the phone. The fact that they were here, at his house, waiting for him to get home from work was a bad sign.

Emma, his mind was yelling. *It must be something Emma has said for them to be here.*

Eleanor held his gaze for a moment, and he flinched at the hardness in her eyes. Through his panic at the investigation, he realised with startling clarity that she knew.

It's over, he thought even as he nodded dumbly to the police officer. *It's over.*

Belle

"Mum!"

Toby's roar from Stephanie's front garden jolted Belle out of her daydream. She had been sat at the kitchen table writing a list of everything she would need for Toby's new school and the new house. She dropped her pen with a clatter onto the table, already on her feet at the sound of her son's call. He and Harley had been playing in the quiet cul-de-sac with some of the neighbouring children, but Belle had insisted on leaving the front door open, unused to her son playing out of her eyeline.

Worried that he had hurt himself, she rushed to the doorway, but her heart leapt into her mouth at the sight of the uniformed police officers at the front gate. On her friend's advice, she had called the police about Linda's confrontation, and they had advised they would make a note of it. They had told her that they would be in touch with some more questions, but there had been no urgency in the young officer's tone. She had been expecting a phone call, knowing that Will had received one, but somehow them turning up at the house felt horribly serious.

"Hi," she hoped that the panic that she was feeling wasn't evident on her face. "Is everything ok?"

They were the same officers that had picked her up the day Frank's body had been found, but that had been different. They hadn't turned up unannounced. They had proactively offered to collect her when she'd explained that she could walk to the station, but she might be some time. It had felt friendly and accommodating then; the kindly local constabulary supporting the bereaved family.

She scanned their faces for some sign of whether she should be worried, and her stomach knotted with apprehension when the younger of the officers refused to meet her eyes.

"There have been some developments," the older woman stated. "Are you able to accompany us down to the station to answer some more questions?"

"Developments?" She looked between the officers nervously. "What do you mean?"

The woman's face remained impassive, but Belle didn't miss the way she shifted her weight from one foot to the other. "It would really be better if we go over it at the station."

Her chest tightened in fear at the frankness of her tone. "I'm just waiting for my friend to get back. Can I come down later?"

She caught the involuntary grimace of the younger officer from the corner of her eye.

"We really do need to see you now," the woman replied calmly before turning her attention to Toby who had darted to Belle's side. "Is there someone to watch your son?"

Belle felt her blood turn to ice as she looked down at the frightened eyes of her son. She reached for his hand to squeeze it in what she hoped was a reassuring gesture. She was about to tell the police officers that she was watching Toby and Harley, and that she'd have to make her own way down when Stephanie's car came into view pulling to a stop outside the house.

"Hey!" She could see her friend was masking the alarm she felt with a bright smile. "All ok?"

"I just need to go and answer some more questions," Belle met her friend's eyes, silently imploring her to remain calm for Toby's sake. "Is Toby ok to stay with you?"

"Yeah, of course," Stephanie moved past the officers to stand by her side, and Belle felt a flicker of gratitude through her fear at her friend's presence. "I can drop you down if you like."

"There's no need for that," the officer cut in quickly. "We can take you."

There was something ominous in the urgency, and if Toby hadn't been at her side, she would have felt brave enough to ask if she was being arrested. She met her friend's eyes hoping to see some reassurance, but she looked as apprehensive as Belle felt.

"Right," Belle bent to drop a kiss on Toby's head, straightening up with more confidence than she felt. "Be good for Auntie Steph. I won't be long."

She couldn't bear to look back at her son as she followed the police officers to the car, knowing that if she saw any fear in his little face it would be her undoing. She buckled herself into the backseat, fighting back the growing waves of panic as she did.

There is no way they can arrest you, she reminded herself as she forced herself to concentrate on keeping her breathing regular. Her chest felt tight like there wasn't enough air in her lungs, but she was terrified that the officers would hear her ragged breathing and see it as a sign of guilt.

At the station, she was led into the same room as she'd sat in previously. She had been through this all before, she reminded herself. She knew what to expect.

It's going to be fine.

And then a serious-faced detective began the interrogation, repeating the same questions that she'd already answered until he suddenly changed tack.

"Whose idea was it to remove the security camera?"

The question caught her off guard, and she gaped at him open-mouthed.

"Huh?"

"The security camera that your brother Tim removed the day before the wedding," the detective prompted.

"Oh," she nodded temporarily relieved. "That. I asked if anything had come of that, but apparently Linda asked for it to be taken down. Something about it not working." She looked at the detective guardedly. "It's a shame as it would have proved that we weren't there."

"Linda said that it hadn't worked for years," the detective stated. "But there was no way that anyone who didn't live at the house would know that. Hence her concerns that the removal indicates premeditation."

"What?" She felt her heart quicken at the sharp turn in the interview. "What's that supposed to mean?"

"Ms Lambe categorically denies that she asked for this to be removed," his words made her blood run cold. "Your brother has confessed to removing the camera."

"What's that got to do with me?" She asked with more bravado than she felt. "Why would Tim even do that? I've already had to speak to the police about Linda threatening me on the High Street yesterday. Maybe she's the one who should be in here."

"At the moment," the detective replied with deliberate exasperation. "It appears to be her word against his over who sanctioned the removal."

Relief inflated beneath her panic, but then he spoke again.

"What we do have though is an independent witness who saw a female matching your description drive into Bluebell Farm Friday night."

"I haven't got a car for a start," Belle's words were defiant, but her body tensed defensively.

"You have a full driving license," the detective responded confidently. "And access to a car."

"Well, whoever it was," she replied. "It wasn't me."

"Ms Hudson," the detective leaned forward on the table between them with a steely glint in his eyes that unnerved her more than his interrogation. "We have someone who is willing to testify that they saw you. We also have a strong case for premeditation in that you told your brother to remove the security camera. We're well aware of the tensions between yourself and your father over not only the will, but over your dislike of his wife-to-be. We can do this the easy way, and you can let us know what actually happened, your side of the story and all. Or we can do this the hard way."

Her heart skidded to a stop in her chest in horror.

"I didn't go to my dad's house," she managed to choke out the words.

"You won't object to being recorded to be ruled out in a video identification parade then."

Rose

The weather had turned a little in the last week. A prematurely warm May that had teased of a great June ahead had given way to dull grey skies, and as she drove through the village a light smattering of rain coated her windscreen. She turned into the country lanes, following winding, quiet roads aimlessly. She slowed as she approached Bluebell Farm and although she hadn't been planning to go there, she turned off the road pulling the car to a stop at the top of the access lane.

She wasn't brave enough to go onto the property, but she sat and stared at it for a while; a wave of sadness sweeping over her that, regardless of the outcome, the house would go to a new family. She wondered what her mother would have made of it all. Tears pricked at Rose's eyes at the realisation that Frank's death had slashed the final anchor to their childhood. Will had called her here, and even in her own state she couldn't ignore his heartfelt plea, but when it was over and all this mess ironed out, she imagined that the other three would vanish from her life as if the past few months had never happened. She imagined her mother's disappointment as tears misted her view of the farm.

Families were meant to be like trees, with branches growing in different directions but roots remaining as one.

The last few months she'd started to feel like that was true; the invisible connection to one another showing for the first time in years as they all came back together with shared goals; checking in on their father and then helping Belle. Rose hadn't realised how badly she'd needed to feel that link until now, nor how badly she wanted to hold onto it. She wiped the tears roughly from her face with the back of her hand and forced herself to start the car. She had come here for a reason, and with a heavy heart she turned the car in the direction of The Red Lion where her sister was waiting for her.

Her blood had turned to ice when she'd finally returned Will's call. She hadn't expected this. Not Belle. She had barely been able to speak to her brother as he relayed the news with panicked urgency.

"I'm on my way," she had replied feeling the emotions of the past week finally break free from where she had locked them away, piling distraction after distraction on top of them to keep them submerged.

And then she had ended the call, and a strangled cry had burst from her lips, a horrifying half-yelp, half-howl like a trapped animal in the final throes of death. But then she had felt strangely calm.

She knew what she had to do to put an end to this awful mess, and with a renewed sense of purpose, she had tidied up her dishes from that morning, disposed of anything in the fridge that wouldn't keep, and using her last twenty pounds to fill up the car, she had set off for Hampton Dale with nothing more than her handbag and the clothes on her back. She had one destination in mind, but first she needed to speak to her siblings and explain. She owed them that much.

She spotted Belle straight away in the pub garden sheltered from the light rain beneath the canopy. Her copper-coloured hair hung long and loose around her shoulders, but even from across the car park, Rose could see the shadows of worry and exhaustion around her eyes.

"Where are the others?" Rose looked around unable to meet her sister's eyes.

"Will has had to go to answer some more questions," Belle puffed up her cheeks and exhaled heavily. She ran her hands through her hair close to the scalp, scrunching and knotting her hair with her fingers in frustration. "Oh, Rose, it's such a mess. They think we did it." Her voice rose desperately. "Did he tell you everything?"

Rose swallowed, and then unable to trust her voice she nodded.

"Tim thinks they're going to try for premeditation. We haven't been charged yet, which Tim says shows they've got no solid proof," she continued. "But there's some technical issue with the video identity parade apparently. They took Tim in for questioning in London yesterday, grilling him over his statement, over the money he offered Emma, over the camera, talking about perverting the course of justice. That's why they've got Will back in. Trying to find inconsistencies in his story. They think we were all in on it. He says they're just trying to scare us. Well, it's working, Rose. I'm fucking terrified."

Rose flinched at the violence in her sister's words. "Oh, Belle, I…"

She tried to speak, but the words were thick, and they stuck at the back of her throat choking her. She tried again.

"Belle, it's ok," she said. "I'm going to put this right. I'm so sorry for putting you through this."

Belle's lips had already parted to start speaking again, but Rose's words silenced her, and her wide, green eyes narrowed.

"Rose." The softness of her name on her sister's lips belied the confusion in Belle's eyes, and then like a switch had been flicked, Rose saw the realisation hit her sister.

Countless times she had wondered how she would feel when the game was up, but not once had she even dared to imagine the utter relief that rushed through her. Her blood that had flowed sluggish and heavy like tar through her body for the past week poured warm and fast through her veins like her heart was finally beating again. The guilt had felt like drowning; spiralling, swirling, lungs burning, unable to see which way was up in the darkness.

"I did it," she said wanting there to be absolutely no doubt. And then the world felt calm, like she was floating.

It's over. It's over. The words echoed in Rose's head as she sank down onto a bench, suddenly exhausted not just from the guilt, or the deceit or pretence, but from the never-ending battle to just keep going.

I'll go to prison, her throat suddenly felt itchy and dry as she realised that she wouldn't be able to get a drink there, and she turned towards the door to the pub wondering whether to have one for the road before she went to meet her fate.

Aside from her sudden desire for a drink, she felt fine. Relieved. Lighter. Glad that Belle, and Will, and even Tim would be off the hook. She knew even through the confusion and blankness of her mind during the past week that she would never have let it get this far if she'd thought that they would be implicated. Even Tim. She had just panicked; the utter horror at what had happened had paralysed her leaving her unable to make a decision. She thought that if the police had taken her in, like they had to the others then she would have crumbled and told them everything. But in some unbelievable twist of fate, they had never called her in for questioning.

She felt calm now, and she raised her head to meet her sister's gaze resigned to see horror and disgust in her eyes.

"Can you tell me what happened?" Rose felt Belle's hand move to her arm, and she was surprised at the gentleness of her sister's tone.

She must think I've lost it, Rose thought, but she opened her mouth to speak knowing that her sister deserved the truth.

"I spent the afternoon with Gareth," she began feeling the words come of their own accord. "Do you know that I've never dated anyone since Phil left me?" She laughed bitterly at her own confession. "It's embarrassingly pitiful. And it got me thinking how Phil was very much like Dad.

I'd never really thought about the similarities, but they were. He ran me down, didn't help with the house, or the kids. Just like Dad did to Mum. I accepted it from Phil, and I knew deep down that I was a doormat. By the time he left me, I was a shell of a woman. I still am. My own sons have no respect for me; it's not their fault though. How can they when I've got no respect for myself? I'm in so much debt, Belle. I was the top of my classes in school, and now I can't even keep an entry-level call centre job. And I had never connected the way Phil treated me with the way I felt so worthless. And then I met Gareth, and it was wonderful, and I felt like I was someone. For the first time in twenty years, I felt like..." She trailed off as her eyes misted with tears knowing that her actions had put paid to any chance of a relationship with Gareth, but even that couldn't extinguish the warmth in her belly knowing that someone good and kind could desire her. "And as I drove back here afterwards, I thought about Mum, and I thought how I would feel if I died and Phil gave everything to some woman he barely knew and not to the boys. How angry I would be if Tom or Jack desperately needed money, just like we did, and that Phil could help, and he chose someone else over them. How cold, and callous! I was overcome with anger, Belle. I'm not fiery like you or Tim, I find it hard to stand up for myself, but then I thought about how we had all let you down. We should have been there for you. We all knew that Dad would be useless when Mum was ill, and then when she died. I'm ashamed to say that I did know. I can pretend all I like that the thought never crossed my mind, but it did.

The boys were still small, and Phil just made it so difficult for me to get here. The easy option was doing what he wanted, and I'm so ashamed to say that's what I did."

The memory of the anger that she'd felt came back to her, flaring through her veins just a shadow of the fury that she'd felt at Frank, and at Phil, and at herself for being so weak. The force of her epiphany had flattened her foot on the accelerator propelling her to Bluebell Farm to finally speak up. Even in her blind rage, she hadn't believed for one moment that she could change Frank's attitude towards them. But she was determined that she was about to stand up for herself, and the memory of her mother.

"I felt really angry," she continued feeling the recollection of the emotion fade away and leaving her startlingly calm. "I knew that I had to say my piece to Dad. It wasn't even about the money. I'm not naïve enough to think he wouldn't cut us all out, but I was sick of pussy-footing around it and pretending that it was ok that he had clicked his fingers and summoned us all here after years of not giving a crap about us. When I first got the invitation, I thought this could be the beginning of a new relationship, but the cynical part of me thinks he was enjoying rubbing our faces in it. I *had* to say something.

And as I was approaching the turning to the farm, I saw Linda's car. She mustn't have seen me. I can't think of any other reason otherwise why she wouldn't have told the police. I was almost disappointed that she wouldn't be there as I had wanted to give her a piece of my mind too. But then, I figured that she was just a stranger. This was between me and Dad. I knocked on the front door, and he answered it, but he didn't invite me in. And that made me even angrier. This had been my home! This was Granny and Grandpa's house. Not his. What right did he have to make their flesh-and-blood stand out in the darkness like a stranger? Who the hell did he think he was?"

Another bolt of anger struck out from the centre of her chest, just like it had that night. Words were exchanged. She didn't remember them all. It was a furious blur of words and feelings spilling out into the darkness, marring the peace of the evening.

"We argued," she said simply unable to recall the exact details. "It felt like it happened so quickly, but I think I couldn't have been there for more than a few minutes."

She pictured his eyes hardening when he realised that placid, obedient Rose was daring to speak out against him, and she heard his cruel laugh in her ears as he had stepped backwards into the hallway and pushed the heavy oak door towards her face. Shutting her out. The gesture, so cold, so dismissive, had taken her anger to another level. She could hear the blood rushing in her ears. So, so angry. She could feel it in her veins, in her nose, in her mouth. The fury was no longer just an emotion; it completely overwhelmed her.

"He tried to shut the door on me." It all came back to her. Her mind must have blocked it out, knowing that seeing it again, reliving it, would be her undoing and she felt the memory coil like a vine around her lungs, crushing the air from them. She gasped for breath, unable to continue, and then Belle's arms were around her, her hair tangled around her face and the coconut scent of her sister filled her nose and mouth bringing her back to the present.

"It's ok, it's ok," her sister murmured into her ear, her arms cradling her back and forth softly.

Somewhere in the warm embrace of her sister, Rose found the strength to finish. "If I had knocked the back door, it wouldn't have happened, but the front door was so heavy. He pushed it closed, and I pushed it back as hard as I could. It must have knocked him off his feet. There was a thud and a scuffle, and then the door swung back. I could see his slippers. I knew he was on the floor, but I didn't think..."

She gulped as sobs began to rack her body.

"Rose," Belle's gentle voice was there again, centring her and keeping her from losing herself in the agony of the memory. She closed her eyes and allowed herself to be held, somehow feeling her mother's comforting arms were around her through her spirited sister. "What happened next?"

"The door had swung back, so it was almost shut, but not quite," she managed to speak between breathless sobs. "I pulled it closed, I think. And then I got in the car and drove back to the room. I don't remember the drive back. I don't remember how I got back, but then I showered, and I must have taken a sleeping tablet. I knew that there was no going back for our relationship, but I didn't have the energy to just drive home. But, then they phoned and said he was dead." Rose pulled herself free to look at her with beseeching eyes. "I didn't know he was seriously hurt, or I would never have left him like that."

Belle's eyes were bright with shiny tears, and she released Rose; her hands reaching up to worry at her hair again.

"I expected to be arrested," she continued. "I thought Linda must have seen me, but she couldn't have. If they'd asked me, I would have told them."

Her sister began to cry, and Rose felt the space between them widen. She knew that it was inevitable that they would be disgusted with her. She forced herself to her feet, straightening the strap of her handbag that was still hanging limply on her shoulder.

"I'll go straight to the station," she said gently. "I'm so sorry, Belle. Tell the others that I'm sorry, and that I love you all."

Belle's knees were pulled up onto the bench, her face hidden behind them, her shoulders shaking as she muffled her sobs against the denim of her jeans, and Rose's heart ached as she turned away from her.

She had to accept that she would never see them again. She doubted she would get any visitors in prison, but that was ok. She was used to being alone. Hopefully, the will would still stand, and Belle would at least get something, but she knew that that was out of her control now. It was funny, but she had barely thought about how her arrest would impact Tom and Jack, she realised regretfully. But she thought that after the initial shock that they would be ok. They had Phil and his wife to go home to at holidays until they started their own families, and anyway, they both had their own lives now. They didn't need her anymore.

"Wait!"

As she reached the car, a cry from behind her wrenched her from her thoughts, and she turned to see her sister rushing towards her, copper hair flying behind her in the breeze.

Rose stopped, watching Belle's face anxiously, daring to hope for some final warmth before she made the journey to confess.

"Just wait." Belle drew to a halt in front of her, and Rose could see a steely glint behind the red, puffiness of her sister's teary eyes. "I need to think."

"Belle, I…" Rose began tentatively, but Belle held a finger up to silence her.

"No," she said firmly. "Just wait a second. It was a horrible accident, Rose, and I know that you didn't mean for it to happen."

"No," Rose nodded in agreement. "I would never…"

"But it's happened now," she said determinedly. "And we can't change it. But nobody else knows."

"They think you…"

"They *think*!" Belle exclaimed, and Rose saw a glimmer of hope in her sister's eyes. "That's all they can do is think. I wasn't anywhere near the house. Their identity parade won't prove shit, because I wasn't there. And now I know Will wasn't, and Tim wasn't, and for whatever reason, they think you being back here at nine or whenever completely eliminates you. So, if they never speak to you, they'll never know."

"But…"

"Listen," Belle cut her off. "You will go to prison for this, Rose."

"I know," she nodded solemnly. She had accepted her fate.

"But it's not your fault," she grasped her sister's shoulders. "Rose, I know that you wouldn't hurt a fly intentionally."

"No, of course not. But I can't…"

"I don't know if Linda will try to contest the will," Belle continued. "But if you're found guilty of his death then she might have grounds to."

Rose looked at her sister in disbelief, not daring to believe what she thought her sister was suggesting.

"Just go home for now," she urged her. "Try to put it out of your mind. If they bring any charges against me, or the boys, although I can't see how they possibly can. He fell, he hit his head. None of us were at the house. But if it comes to it, then you can speak up. But let's just see what happens."

"Belle, I can't do that." Rose's heart ached at the bravery of her sister. "It's my fault. I have to…"

"Do it for me then," she lifted her hand to Rose's chin tilting her sister's face to meet her eyes. "I want that money, Rose. But more than that, I want Mum's estate to go where she wanted it to go. She wouldn't have blamed you, and neither do I. You were standing up for yourself, and for Mum's memory. All I'm asking is for you to wait this out. I've never asked anything of you, have I?"

"No," Rose felt her voice quiver with emotion. "No, you haven't."

"Well, now I am," she said fiercely. "Can you do this for me?"

Rose thought about all the times she had let herself and her sister down, and she found herself nodding.

Will

The journey had become almost second nature, and he smiled to himself as he passed the welcome sign that was obscured by the abundance of planters bursting with blooms. It seemed forever ago that he'd felt sick to his stomach with nerves at the sight of that sign. Over a year had passed since Will had received that invitation, and despite everything he was glad he hadn't thrown it in the bin.

"This is becoming a habit," Will joked as he pulled up to The Red Lion to greet his sisters who were waiting for him outside.

He opened his arms wide to envelope them both, noticing with satisfaction that Rose seemed healthier than when he had seen her last. She had seemed so broken and withdrawn in the wake of Frank's death. She hadn't been able to bring herself to view the body with the rest of them, and for a while it had seemed like she wasn't going to make the funeral either.

"Leave her be," Belle had warned, *fiercely protective, when both he and Tim had tried to convince her to come. "Everyone deals with grief differently."*

In a way, Will thought Rose might have had the right idea. He had seen bodies before, including his own mother. Nothing had been more difficult than saying goodbye to her but seeing her had at least given him some semblance of closure. But the memory of his father in the casket had haunted him for months afterwards. For a while he had wondered whether it was a delayed reaction to the shocking circumstances, or the aftermath from the turmoil of the horrible investigation. In the week that followed Frank's death, Will had experienced pure terror for the first time in his life. Even thinking about it now was enough to make his pulse quicken. But the gruelling interviews had ceased as abruptly as they had begun, and then the body was released, the funeral organised and somehow life had gone on for them all.

But the image of Frank had stayed with him for a while. *He looked so small and old. And so dead.*

He'd been a formidable man. Cold. Distant. Will could feel bitterness lurking in the hidden corners of himself, and he had hated himself for a while for being unable to shake it off. He had taken off to Japan for the summer, but it had followed him there until Raya had forced him to confront it. Saying it aloud, for Will, had been the key to beginning to heal. He was angry at Frank for not being the parent that they had deserved. Fear at the threat of wrongful imprisonment had made way for a simmering anger at his father for putting them in that position. But he couldn't reconcile that image of Frank so dead and pitiful to the father that had never been there for him.

"Is Tim not here yet?" He asked.

Will had only flown back into the country yesterday, but he had been in regular contact with Belle, and made an effort to call Rose at least every few weeks whether he had anything to say or not, but he had only spoken with his brother a handful of times. He knew from Belle though that Tim had promised to come down to scatter Frank's ashes.

"Yeah, he came down last night," Belle replied. "He's got the kids this weekend, so they're all staying over mine."

Will tried to hide his surprise. "At yours? I didn't realise you'd have a houseful! I'll see if I can get a room in the pub."

"No, you won't!" She protested with a mock stern expression. "Rose is going to stay too. It'll be such a laugh. You want to see all the food and drink I've got."

He turned to look at his older sister, half-believing that Belle was having him on. Of all the people to agree to a family pyjama party, he would never have put pompous Tim at the top of the list. Rose smiled at his incredulous expression, before nodding in confirmation.

"Belle is the head of the family now," she joked. "What she says goes."

"Well, I'm sure all those years sleeping in noisy hostels will have given me enough practise to get by for one night," he joked.

Belle swatted him playfully before gesturing towards the pub entrance. "Come on then. We'll grab a quick drink while we wait for Tim. He's just nipped to the big Tesco as he forgot to pack clothes for the baby."

"He's got *all* of them?" Will's jaw dropped in shock. "Even the baby?"

"You should see him, Will. He looks so harassed trying to deal with the three of them," Belle chuckled with delight, before adding seriously. "It's been such an eye-opener for him being a single dad, especially with two baby Mamas who don't particularly like him, but I honestly couldn't be prouder of him. He's really trying, isn't he, Rose?"

Rose smiled again. "He is. He phoned me last time he had them to ask me how to make rice krispie cakes."

For a moment, Will and Belle stared at their sister in disbelief before looking at each other and bursting into laughter.

"He's from another planet, isn't he!" Belle was still laughing at the thought of him up to his elbows in melted chocolate and cereal when he finally made it to the pub looking flustered but in good spirits with a gaggle of children in tow.

"Oh, look at her!" Rose, who Will had thought seemed quiet and withdrawn, seemed to come alive when she saw the baby in her car seat. "Oh, Tim, she's beautiful."

Not wanting to leave Hugo and Bea out, Rose quickly turned to make a fuss of them too. "And look at you two! You've grown so much!"

Will watched his sister fuss over the children, and Tim enjoying the respite sank into the chair next to him.

"It's good to see you," Tim greeted him surprising Will by pulling him in for a manly, one-armed hug. "How's globe-trotting? I was having a scroll through your pictures yesterday. It looks like you're having the time of your life."

"I saw you'd joined the world of social media," he teased his brother. "You'll be using google next to find the recipe for rice krispie cakes."

Belle snorted from across the table, and even Rose looked up from where she was animatedly chatting to Bea to laugh.

"Rose told you then?" Tim grinned good-naturedly. "God, I was in a right old state! It's taking some getting used to, this parenting lark."

Tim had lost everything in the months following Frank's death. Eleanor had kicked him out when she'd found out about Emma's pregnancy, and while he hadn't been sacked from work for his inappropriate relationship, they had announced a restructure shortly afterwards and he hadn't been surprised when he was made redundant. They had all expected him to become bitter and resentful in the aftermath, but he had astonished them taking his shared custody of Hugo and Bea, and then little Millie when Emma had given birth a few months ago, very seriously.

"You're doing a great job," Rose told him affectionately as she sat back in her chair with Bea already clambering onto her lap. "I must admit, I'm surprised at how well you've taken to it. If someone had told me last year that you'd have been baking with the kids at nine o'clock on a

Sunday morning, I would have laughed in their face."

Tim chuckled, but Will saw his brother's face flush slightly with pleasure at the compliment.

"Where are you heading to next?" He asked Will once their sisters had turned their attention back to the children.

"We're thinking Australia again," Will told him surprised at his brother's interest.

"Amazing," Tim nodded appreciatively before turning serious. "Just don't go blowing all that money, mind. If you want any advice on investing, I've a friend who can help you. Although, you can't go wrong with property."

"That's what I'm doing." Belle chimed in from across the table. "I'm going to have one big holiday, treat myself to a car and then the rest is going on bricks and mortar."

"I haven't really thought about it yet." Will admitted.

The will, when it was finally read after months of paperwork and complications that Will didn't even pretend to understand, had felt like a double-edged sword. He hadn't expected Bluebell Farm to sell so quickly, and he could hardly bear to look at his bank balance when the money finally came through just weeks before. It felt something akin to what he imagined survivor's guilt might feel like; knowing that if Frank hadn't keeled over the night before his wedding, it was very unlikely that they would have ever seen a penny of it.

"How can you not think about it?" Belle rolled her eyes playfully at Tim gesturing to Rose and Will. "How are these pair even related to us?"

Will smiled at her joke, but there was a touch of sadness to his expression that Rose noticed.

"Are you ok?" She nudged him quietly.

He nodded, trying to shift the sombre mood, but seeing the concern in her eyes he found himself opening up. "I just feel a bit guilty about having it, to be honest."

He expected her to dismiss his confession, but she nodded in agreement. "No, I know exactly what you mean. I do, too."

"It was Mum's money." Belle, as always didn't miss a thing, and she looked up sharply to interrupt. "She would have been devastated if the wedding had gone ahead and that witch got her mitts on it."

"I know," he sighed heavily. "I can't help how I feel."

He looked up at his younger sister for her response, but her eyes were fixed on Rose. He frowned as he watched a silent exchange between them, but before he could try to interpret the emotions each sister was conveying to the other, Rose had looked away and he couldn't be sure that he hadn't imagined it.

"You're right, Belle," she agreed in a more upbeat tone. "I totally get what Will means though. I'm not going to do anything exciting though; just pay off the mortgage and my debt, put some aside for deposits for houses for the boys." She paused as if unsure whether to go on before admitting sheepishly. "I've been thinking of going back to uni."

"Oh my God, Rose!" Belle practically shrieked with excitement startling the baby and making everyone around the table hold their breath for a moment in fear that she was about to wake up howling. Thankfully, she just emitted a funny, little squeak followed by a deep sigh, and then seemed to go straight back to sleep. Belle grimaced at Tim apologetically, dropping her voice to a whisper. "I'm so sorry!"

"It's fine," Tim laughed. "If she can sleep though Hugo and Bea's arguing, she can sleep through anything." He turned to Rose with interest. "That's great news. What are you thinking of studying?"

"I'm not sure yet," she said. "I was thinking of maybe accountancy. Believe it or not, I used to be pretty good with numbers."

"You'll be wonderful at whatever you do," Tim told her, and this time it was Rose that flushed with pride.

Any anxiety that he had been feeling about this trip melted away as Will watched his brother and sisters hustle the children out of the pub to begin the trek up to the top of Bluebell hill. He had never expected to see them come together like this, and he felt a warm, fuzzy sensation spread through his chest.

"Hey," Belle noticed him trailing behind the group. "What's that smile for?"

"I was just thinking," he admitted. "That Mum would be pleased to see us all like this. To see us looking out for each other, and her grandkids playing together."

"I think she would," she agreed. "All I've ever wanted was to make her proud."

"She would be," Rose had been walking alongside Tim with Bea holding both their hands and Millie in an overly-complicated sling strapped to Tim's chest that had taken all four of them to figure out how to operate, but she slowed to allow Will and Belle to catch up. "She *will* be. We're all proud of you, Belle. I would have been lost without you this last year."

"And I would have been useless if you hadn't terrified me into thinking I was going to end up with kids that hated me," Tim said with an air of humility that Will hadn't been expecting.

"I didn't say that!" Belle protested before laughing when she saw that he was grinning. "Well, ok, I might have said something along those lines."

"On more than one occasion may I add!" He shot back with a chuckle. "I think your actual words were that I'd end up like Frank. With kids like strangers, and just some gold-digger for company who was counting down the days 'til I popped my clogs. Hard words to swallow, but do you know what? I bloody needed them. I was an arrogant pig, and despite the challenges," a shadow of regret crossed his face and Will would have bet money on it that he was thinking about losing Eleanor. The shadow passed and he offered a crooked grin to his sister. "I'm glad you had the guts to say it."

"I was very emotional at the time," Belle cut in quickly with an apologetic shrug when she saw the look of horror on Rose's face. "But I'm glad I said it now if it worked."

"It worked," Tim laughed. "I never thought I had it in me to be a good parent. I just accepted that I sucked at it and left it to Eleanor. Turns out I'm alright with a bit of effort."

"You're better than alright," Rose smiled affectionately at him. "Like Belle said, I think Mum would be proud of you all."

They drew to a stop as they reached the clearing at the top of the hill, looking down at Bluebell Farm nestled in the crook of the winding lane with the village spread out beneath them.

"Should we say something?" Will gently withdrew the urn of ashes from the bag that Belle had carefully packed it in.

When Linda had learned that she had been left nothing in the will, she had redirected the Funeral Directors to contact Belle to make the arrangements. She had left the house and the village shortly afterwards, and they had heard from Brenda Howells that she had taken up with a gentleman in Ross-on-Wye that she had met through an online dating site. Will had grimaced at the time, realising that he had assumed that Frank had met her in the village not trawling for women on the internet. It had made him feel sad that father had had four children who would have been happy to spend time with him if he'd only shown a fleeting interest.

It just seemed like a very sad end to a very sad man.

The ashes had been sat on a shelf in Belle's cupboard for a year before she had called a family reunion to scatter them. With a no knowledge of what he would have wanted and the one person who might have known too busy planning her winter wedding to a retired barrister named Cyril, they had collectively decided to scatter his ashes in the same spot as their mother.

"Can you say something?" Belle asked suddenly looking quite tearful. "I don't really know what to say."

Will looked to Tim and then Rose, hoping that one of them might have something fitting and heartfelt prepared, but Tim shrugged, and Rose had stepped away from the huddle of adults to keep an eye on the children.

"Rose?" Will removed the lid carefully and waited for her to join them, but Belle shook her head.

"She's alright where she is, Will," she told him quietly but firmly.

He caught his sisters exchange a silent look and figured that Rose must have something going on. She had been the one to take the lead when Kathleen had died, and the words that she had spoken came back to Will.

She had written a moving tribute to their mother, finishing with a quote that she had attributed to Albert Einstein.

"Our death is not an end if we can live on in our children and the younger generation. For they are us, our bodies are only wilted leaves on the tree of life."

It didn't feel right though for Frank, Will realised as his throat grew dry and scratchy. He was just a shadow in all Will's happy childhood memories; barely there, ill-tempered, and distant. He racked his mind for something poignant, or warm to say, but there was nothing he could think of that wasn't an empty cliché. He felt the silence stretch out amongst them, intuitively knowing that they were all struggling to find the words to say for a man who had been a father only in name to them. There were no funny, touching anecdotes to relay, or fond remembrances. He hadn't ever even shared any memories of his own childhood with them, and Will realised he knew nothing about Frank's upbringing. Essentially, Frank had been little more than a stranger to them.

In the months leading up to his death and the immediate aftermath, Will had realised that it wasn't just him who had been impacted by Frank's indifference. But what he did know was that no good would ever come out of holding onto the hurt.

"I'm sorry that we didn't seem to be compatible in this life, Dad," he said finally, and as the words came, he felt the heavy ache of his heart lighten. "We had a wonderful life here with Mum and each other, and I wish that I could reel off memories of you taking us to school, or playing with us, teaching us to ride bikes or dressed up as Father Christmas. Anything really would be good to say right now."

His voice cracked, and he felt his brother step to his side and then there was a solid steadying hand on his arm.

"I don't know why it was so hard for you," he continued strengthened by his brother's presence. "But I'm sorry that it was, because you've missed out on four pretty great kids and some adorable grandchildren. I'm glad that we got to spend even the smallest amount of time with you though, Dad, before you passed, and I have to thank you for bringing us back together again.

For a while, I thought there was something wrong with me for you to not want a relationship with me, and then when I realised that it was just who you were, I wondered if maybe I had your bad blood. Maybe that's why I was thirty-five and incapable of settling down like everyone else around me, but looking at the family that you gave me, I know that there's no such thing as bad blood. Some people are meant to be parents, but some people just aren't that good at it. That's not our fault; it's just your loss.

We loved you in our own way, Dad, and I'm sure you loved us in your own way. So, I hope you've found your peace now, and the little boy in me wishes desperately that you're looking down on us with love."

With trembling fingers, he attempted to open the lid to the urn unsuccessfully before Rose's gentle fingers took it from his hands.

"Thank you, Will," she said tears streaming down her own cheeks. "I think we all needed to hear that."

Belle slipped an arm around him from the other side, resting her own misty eyes against his shoulder, and Tim stepped forward to join the huddle, albeit carefully with a sleeping baby strapped to his chest.

"It's a shame he never had a brother or sisters like you," Tim smiled fondly. "Or things might have been a little different. But you're right, Will, and while I'm sure he loved us in his own way, there's no point us dwelling on what could have been. He gave us each other, and for that, I'll always remember him by."

Will took a deep breath, and stepping free from the comfort of their pack, he took the urn back from his sister. With tears sliding down his face, he stepped forward to release the ashes to the light summer breeze. The gritty fragments swirled in the gentle wind for just a moment, and then Frank was gone.

The End

About The Author

Bad Blood is the seventh novel by Lily Hayden. She is also the author of Project Terra under the name S.J Woods.

For more information, new releases and news, follow Hayden Woods Creative on social media or visit www.haydenwoodscreative.com

Also by Lily Hayden

Butterflies
Lucy has had enough of being unappreciated at work and at home. Ready to quit her job and her marriage, she soon loses hope that there's anything better out there for her.
A modern tale of a woman trying to have it all.
"Gripping, entertaining and hilarious"
"A modern love story"
"Twists and turns that I didn't see coming"

The Village Online
Oak Village are online and opinionated. The local social media group was meant to connect the residents, but it's not long before the whole village is dragged into a nasty dispute that ends in a murder.
"A very modern murder mystery"
"Classic whodunnit"
"The plot twists were unexpected. I couldn't wait to find out who the killer was."

Summer Down South
Three college grads have the world at their feet. Three sizzling summer romances in one story. Sexy and Sizzling- everything is hotter down South.
"Chick Lit at its best"
"Perfect summer read"
"...absolute page turner"

New Rules
Kate knows how to get what she wants, while Ellie is barely holding it together. When the two women are thrown together on their workplace mentoring scheme, they soon discover that success comes at a cost. It might be time for some new rules.

"...some wonderful life advice and one of the most uplifting endings I have read lately."
Lucy Mitchell, Author of Instructions for Falling in Love Again
"This was a great story and I was hooked from the start." Kelly T's Space
"New Rules definitely hits the spot from start to finish."
Stacy is Reading

Coming Back to You
From the moment that Emma met Ryan, she knew he was the one for her. A bittersweet romance about first love and second chances.

"A definite five star read for me only deserving of a lot more." Book Lover 87
"Strong friendships and serendipity characterise this heartwarming story." Jane Hunt Writer
"I adored this heartbreaking story." Abbi Reads

Cassie Cancels Christmas- A Festive Novella
After a string of Christmas catastrophes, Cassie is cancelling Christmas much to the horror of her festive-loving family.
A fun, festive countdown through the most ~~stressful~~ wonderful time of the year
"A sweet read to make you remember what Christmas is actually about."
"... heart-warming, funny, bit of a tear jerker and thoroughly lovely!"

Project Terra- SJ Woods
Dane Alexander a young soldier from the isolated state of Apatia is part of a secret military operation, but when he uncovers some grisly state secrets, he has no choice but to flee into the wilderness. In a world of Artificial Intelligence, can his instincts keep him alive?
"Interesting and Captivating"
"...will make you hold your breath"
"...thrilling and exciting..."

Printed in Dunstable, United Kingdom